Anything You Do Say

Gillian McAllister has been writing for as long as she can remember. She graduated with an English degree and lives in Birmingham, where she now works as a lawyer. Her debut novel *Everything but the Truth* was a *Sunday Times* top ten best-seller. You can find her on Twitter @gillianmauthor.

Anything You Do Say

GILLIAN McALLISTER

PENGUIN BOOKS

PENGUIN BOOKS

UK | USA | Canada | Ireland | Australia
India | New Zealand | South Africa

Penguin Books is part of the Penguin Random House group of companies
whose addresses can be found at global.penguinrandomhouse.com.

First published in Great Britain in Penguin Books 2018

002

Text copyright © Gillian McAllister, 2018

The moral right of the author has been asserted

Set in 12.5/14.75 pt Garamond MT Std
Typeset by Jouve (UK), Milton Keynes
Printed in Great Britain by Clays Ltd, Elcograf S.p.A.

A CIP catalogue record for this book is available from the British Library

ISBN: 978–1–405–94170–9

www.greenpenguin.co.uk

Penguin Random House is committed to a
sustainable future for our business, our readers
and our planet. This book is made from Forest
Stewardship Council® certified paper.

To Suzanne, my sister and a doctor. Here's to all the texts that begin: *What if . . .* and your responses: *It's quite complicated, but . . .*

I

It starts with a selfie. He is a random; we are not even sure of his name. We are always meeting them whenever we go out. Laura says it's because I look friendly. I think it's because I am always daydreaming, making up lives for people as I stare at them, and they think I'm inviting them over to chat.

In the frame of his phone screen – camera facing forward, to us – his teeth are white and slightly crooked, his nose hooked.

Laura leans over to press the button on the phone. Her long, slender arm is captured at the edge of the display. It's covered in bangles and bits of thread and a homemade bracelet. She's a hippy at heart.

She takes the photo, and now we are frozen on his screen. I wonder if he'll keep it, that photograph of us that now belongs to him.

'No filter,' he says to us.

'What?' Laura says.

She doesn't use Instagram. She feels no need to check into places or share her moments with anybody. She is nowhere on the Internet, and I'm sure her life is better for it.

We break apart from our tableau at the bar but he stays standing next to me. He rocks up and down on the balls of his feet. He's all in black, except his red trainers.

I turn to Laura. She's had her hair cut. It's a pixie, again:

messed up, the fringe sitting in her eyes. She looks androgynous, slightly goofy. I could never pull off that haircut. People would mistake me for a child. She never wears any make-up, but doesn't need to, with straight, white teeth, naturally peach cheeks and dark lashes. Her eyes crinkle at the corners even when she is not smiling. What she wants more than anything is to be an artist – she creates hyperreal paintings that look like photographs – and she doesn't want to live her life like other people. She's obsessed with it. She will sometimes say things like, 'What's the correlation between wearing a suit and doing a good job?' or, 'Why do you need a house in the suburbs and a mortgage like everybody else?'

I would never say such things.

'Great shoes,' she says now, dipping her head down underneath the bar.

They're new. Cream silk, with ribbons that tie at my ankles. Laura favours flats, the sides of her feet dry and hard from never wearing shoes at home. They live on a barge, Laura and Jonty. They moor it wherever they like. I sometimes want to do the same, bored of our tiny basement flat, but Reuben tells me I'd hate it; that I am a fantasist.

'Thanks,' I say. I bought them on a credit card, at almost midnight, the other night. I'd forgotten until they had arrived, experiencing a familiar sense of wonderment, and then recognition, as I tore into the parcel.

'Are they Reuben-approved?' Laura says.

Reuben is one of the only people she consistently misreads. She converts his shyness into something else. Disapproval, maybe. She might be right. He had raised his eyebrows as I unpacked the shoes, but said nothing.

I shrug now. 'What's his is ours,' I say, though I'm embarrassed by the notion. Reuben works far harder than I do. Everybody does.

Laura's bony shoulders are out, even though it's December. Her top is simple, a plain white vest that's too big for her. It's the kind of material that doesn't need pressing. I don't iron anything. If I ever try to, our iron deposits a brown sticky substance everywhere, and so I have given up. In my head, I call it my *Joanna-ness*: situations in which I fail where most others succeed.

'Looks like you've got a friend for life,' she says.

I turn. The man is still standing next to me. I can feel the entire length of his leg against mine as he shifts his weight, trying to get the bartender's attention.

'Two more for these ladies?' he says.

We say yes to the drinks, and maybe we shouldn't. We are becoming giggly. They arrive, placed on black napkins which dampen with condensation from the glasses. Laura sidles slowly away along the bar.

I follow, but so does he.

'Your work or mine?' Laura says, her head bent towards me so that he can't hear.

This is how our long chats begin. We once joked we should have an agenda, and now we kind of do: work, relationships, family. Then everything else. Whatever comes up.

I let out a sigh, but it does nothing to dispel the knots that have appeared as soon as she mentions work. 'I did a sudoku puzzle on my lunch break that was more stimulating than my entire day yesterday.'

I started work on the mobile library bus because I loved it so much as a child. I loved choosing a fat, new stack of books to read that week. I loved the nooks and crannies and finding my brother hiding in the thriller section. But, after six years in the job, that isn't enough any more.

'Mmm.' She sucks in her bottom lip, looking thoughtfully across the bar.

We hate our jobs in completely different ways. I have no idea what I would like to do. Laura knows exactly what she wants to do, and can't do it.

'You need a Thing. I need *not* to have a Thing,' she says.

'Yep. That's about it.' Nobody else could say something like that to me, except maybe Reuben. 'I'm one-dimensional,' I say to her.

'You're too smart for your own good,' she says back.

'No. I'm the thick Murphy.'

My brother, Wilf, went to Cambridge, and now owns a whole host of London properties, and none of us can ever forget it.

'You're a very bright *Joanna*,' she says. 'Oliva or Murphy.' Oliva. Reuben's surname.

I look down at my drink, stirring it with the black straw whose end I've chewed. Reuben says I should just forget it. Stop torturing myself. Nobody truly has a Thing.

'Er,' Laura says, looking at a spot just above my head, as though she's seen a spider on the wall.

I turn, and the man is leaning over me, a protective arm right behind my shoulders. Now I know he's there, I can feel every molecule of him. His arm lands across my back like a heavy rucksack, and I wince. I try to shrug it off, but he claps it down on me. It's weighty, unpleasant. My body is against his, unwittingly, and his armpit is warm and sweaty against my shoulder. He smells beery, of

4

that sweet alcoholic scent usually reserved for the morning after the night before. A kick of mint behind that. I see that he's chewing gum.

'Haven't even introduced myself,' he says, interrupting my thoughts. 'I'm Sadiq.' His dark eyes appraise us. He holds a hand out to me, then to Laura.

She ignores it, but I take it, not wanting to offend. He passes me a business card, in his hand, as swiftly and smoothly as a spy. Sadiq Ul-Haq. I don't know what to do with it, so I tuck it into my purse, barely reading it.

'Thanks. I don't have one,' I say back.

'Thanks for the selfie, but we're good now,' Laura interrupts. 'Just catching up. Alone.'

Even this does not put him off. 'Baby, don't be cold,' Sadiq says.

I can't help but look sideways at him. I can't place his lilting accent.

'We're not cold. We want to speak to each other, not you,' Laura says.

It's typical of her. All through university, people would underestimate her. She was softly spoken, small-boned, would sit, almost huddled, with her arms folded right across her middle, so people thought she was meek. But she wasn't, not at all.

She wordlessly picks up her drink and we walk across the makeshift dance floor, squeezing against bodies that jolt unpredictably. The only place available is right next to the speaker, which is pumping out a dance hit I would have loved five years ago. It's thrumming in my ear, the bass reverberating in my sternum. Opposite me, I can see a couple standing close to each other. The woman has an

Afro, a slim waist exposed between a black top and trousers. His hand is on the wall behind her. He's talking softly in her ear. I wonder what their evenings look like. I bet they listen to indie music on the radio while cooking from scratch. Or maybe they paint together, every Sunday: a weekend ritual. Abstract art. It would get all over their clothes, their walls, but they wouldn't care.

She catches me looking, and for the millionth time in my life, I am pleased that nobody can read my mind. She draws a hand up to her hair, embarrassed. I look away, but not before noticing that her nails are painted a jewel-toned plum; glossy and perfectly even. Ah. She is one of those. A Proper Person, I call them in my head. Proper People have well-fitting clothes and neat hair and glowing skin. You can break it all down into its component parts, but the thing is – they just look . . . groomed. They are doing something right. Something intangible. I wonder if they've all been told, like some rite of passage, and I haven't.

'What?' Laura says, following my gaze.

'Oh, look,' I say, as the couple embrace again.

'Oh to be young and in love,' she says.

I look curiously at her. I realize that I no longer see Jonty kiss her. Their relationship seems pally, somehow; more about teamwork than romance. No doubt she thinks the same of Reuben and me. Reuben seems reserved, remote, dismissive. Until the door closes behind us, that is.

'He was a weird one,' Laura shouts, pointing with her drink over to the bar. 'Sadiq.'

'I know.'

'Pushy.'

'Oh, he'll leave us alone now.'

6

Laura raises her eyebrows but says nothing. 'Jonty is acting strangely,' she says after a moment.

I look up in surprise. 'Really?'

'He said he didn't like my latest project. He's never said that. He's never cared.'

'No?'

She rakes her fringe back. It snarls, sticking up slightly before drifting down. She puffs air into her cheeks.

Lovely Jonty; he's been sacked from every office job he's ever had because of lateness. He often forgets he's going on holiday and has to be ushered to the airport in surprise. Posh and affable and a bit hopeless: what *he* wants more than anything is a quiet life, a G&T in his hand. I like to consider what everybody I meet truly wants. I started doing it when I was a teenager, and I haven't been able to stop.

'What's going on with him?' I say, frowning.

He has been temping, recently, painting perfume bottles with glitter for the Christmas season. He says it's quite meditative.

'I have no idea. Do you?'

I am often asked for advice about people. Nothing else, of course. Nothing highbrow. I am never asked for my opinion on medicine or law or planning permission or transfer deadline day or the war in Syria. Just people, and the things they do.

'What's he saying to you?'

'Nothing. Just – talking about the future more, maybe.' She shrugs.

She doesn't want to discuss it any further, I can see.

'How's that master's?' she adds.

'What master's?' I ask absent-mindedly.

'The cultural theory one.'

I frown. It does ring a bell. 'Oh, still pending,' I say vaguely.

I am forever applying for master's courses and grants and pitching articles to the *Guardian* and thinking maybe I would like to be a coffee-shop owner. *Maybe I will farm cocoa beans in South America?* I will WhatsApp Laura. *You burn too easily, though*, she will send back. *Maybe wheat in England instead?* And even though it's endless, my career pondering, and must be tedious, she takes each and every whim as seriously as the first.

'Good luck,' she says with a smile. She looks like she's going to add something else, but then her gaze drifts to just behind me, and she never starts her sentence. Or rather, she starts a different one. 'Okay, leaving time,' she says.

I look behind me, and there's Sadiq. I shrug, irritated, and move away a few feet, but he follows, an arm reaching out.

'Leave us alone,' Laura says.

'You don't want to be talking to me like that,' he says.

My head turns, and the song stops, leaving a beat before a new one starts, during which time I can hear blood pulsing in my ears.

And suddenly, it's not funny any more. A frisson of fear moves through me. Images pop into my mind. Images of women followed down alleyways, coaxed into passenger seats, dismembered in car boots.

I move further away from him, towards the wall, away from Laura. I think of the couple I saw earlier, and how happy they looked, and I wish Reuben were here. He wouldn't say anything; he wouldn't have to. He has a presence like that. People seem to behave for him, like naughty children.

Sadiq follows me, blocking me in. Behind him, Laura's eyes are narrowing so they are almost entirely closed. And now he is squaring up to me, right in front of me. I walk away from him, dodging around him, but he grabs me, pulls me back, and grinds into the back of me, his hands either side of my hips – either side of my bum – like we are in a sex scene.

I stand completely still for a second or two. Shock, is it? Whatever it is, it's two seconds during which I can not only feel his hands, his breath on the back of my neck, but his erection, too. Hard against the back of my thigh. I can't help but imagine how it looks. The thought intrudes in my mind like an unwanted Internet pop-up, and I wince. I haven't felt another man's penis in over seven years. Until now. What would Reuben say? He'd call him a fucking dickhead, that's what he'd say. The thought comforts me.

I move slowly away from him, smiling awkwardly because I don't know what else to do, the shock of being touched against my will like jumping off a pier and into the sea. I can still feel him. The warmth and hardness of him. My teeth start chattering. I don't say anything. I should, but I don't. I just want to be gone.

Laura is taking the drink out of my hand and trying to find a surface to put it on. In the end, she places it on top of the speaker – she can only just reach – and she grabs my coat, and my arm, and we turn to leave.

He grabs for me again. A catlike swipe. He catches just

9

my finger, as I'm leaving. I try to pull it away from him, but he's stronger than me. I could shout, but what would I say? A man grabbing a woman's hand in a bar hardly feels like a crime, though maybe it is. Instead, I am complicit, almost holding his hand. Nobody knows it is against my will. Nobody knows what's going on in my head. His hand is momentarily like a manacle around mine.

He squeezes hard, enclosing my hand in the whole of his palm. He releases, and squeezes again; a kind of sexual threat. And then he lets go of me entirely.

Outside, the winter air puffing out of my mouth like chalk dust, I can still feel his body against mine. I am imagining it, but my thigh feels wet. I reach a hand down to check. It isn't.

Laura hands me my coat. 'Jesus,' she says. 'I've not had to leave a bar because of a nutter for a while. Are we twenty again?'

She's making light of it, and I'm thankful for that. I can still feel him between my legs; that pressure, the feeling of fullness. Was that a sexual assault? I guess it was. But maybe I am somehow to blame. I shudder, wrapping my coat around me to try and keep the rain out.

'You alright?' Laura asks.

I nod, not lifting my head again, looking at my cream-ribboned shoes. I don't want to discuss it. Like the congestion zone charge I ignored until it was too late, and we had to pay double, and Reuben got cross, I sweep it away into a back room in my mind.

'Yeah,' I say. 'I'm grand. It's not a Friday night without a nutter.'

'Okay,' she says, still looking warily at me. 'I had a bad feeling about tonight.'

It's a very *Laura* thing to say, and it's another reason she and Reuben don't get on: her mysticism, his vehement logic.

She tugs at a scarf that's wrapped around the handle of her bag and puts it on. Over the road, two restaurants have their Christmas lights out; champagne-coloured fairy lights are wound around potted trees.

'So that's Little Venice,' I say.

We like to explore the hidden parts of London. We always go somewhere new. Our rent is too high to endlessly go to the same places: it feels like we are making our money back, somehow.

'Maybe we won't do it again,' she says.

I check my watch. It's too late to go on anywhere else. I'm enticed by the thought of Reuben at home in our living room. He'll be wearing soft clothes. He'll have the lights dimmed. The television on low. A glass of red on the arm of the sofa, the stem held between his elegant fingers. He likes wine; will even drink it alone. I drink Ribena when I am alone.

'Which way you going?' Laura says to me. She points with a thumb behind her.

'Warwick Avenue,' I say. 'That's the easiest.' I see a dark figure dart behind her, in the awning of the bar we've just left, but it disappears before I can get a proper look. Maybe it's the couple, moving as one, off home, I think. I look over my shoulder again anyway, just to check. There's nothing.

Laura smells of cologne as she reaches to hug me. She's

wearing a maxi skirt and biker boots. 'WhatsApp me when you're back,' she says.

I nod. WhatsApp is our medium. Tens of messages a day. Newspaper articles. Tiny snapshots of her art. Beers consumed in the middle of the day with Jonty. Screenshots of funny memes. Selfies from me, bored at work. We love it.

I set off towards the canal, crossing the bridge. It's wrought iron, blue. It reminds me of the playground at school. My fingers trail over the bars. It's ghostly out here. There's nobody around. The rain gets slightly heavier and a wind chills me.

That's when I hear it. Them. The footsteps. Surely I'm imagining it? I stop. But no. There they are. A heavy tread.

I could turn around. Go back to the bar. But is the bar safe?

What do you do, I find myself thinking, when you think somebody is following you down a deserted strip of canal? When you could become a statistic, a news piece, a tragedy?

Nothing. That's the answer. You carry on. You hope.

I never thought something like this would happen to me. I suppose that's what makes me behave as though I'm in a film: I have no idea what else to do. I stop, for a moment, testing him, and his footsteps stop too.

I start again, this time faster, and I hear him begin too. My imagination fires up like a sprinter off the starting blocks and soon I can't tell what's real. Is he right behind me – I can't look – and about to reach for me? The pounding of his footsteps is consistent, slapping against the wet concrete, but I can't tell any more than that.

I will call somebody, I decide.

I turn left down a side alley I would never usually go down. Just to see what he does. I walk past white houses with balconies. Millionaires' houses. The occasional bay window is lit up, little orange squares in the night, tasteful Christmas trees glowing amber like fireflies. I would usually peer in, invent lives for them, backstories, but not tonight.

He has followed me. Five more steps. His footfalls thunder along behind me. I can't look over my shoulder. I am frozen.

I start to plan. I could call Laura. Could she get over here quickly? No. I break into a little run. These stupid shoes.

I could knock on a door. But . . . am I definitely being followed? They'd think me mad. It is strange how much I think of people's opinions, their perceptions of me, right now, just like I did in the bar when I didn't cry out when he grabbed my hand. I want these people, these strangers, this collective unconscious, to like me.

I turn right, off the side street, back to a main road and cross it. I get out my phone, ready to dial. 999? No, it seems too extreme. I call Reuben instead. He takes an age to answer, which is not uncommon – he hates the telephone, unless it's me calling – but then his deep *hello* echoes through me.

'You alright?' he says.

I can picture him now. It's a comfort. He'll be reclining against the sofa. His hair will look auburn, not ginger, in our dimly lit living room. He will be frowning, his eyes a dark, foresty green.

'Reuben,' I say.

13

'What?' he says. He will be sitting forward now.

'I'm being followed,' I say in a low voice. I don't know why I don't shout it out.

His eyebrows will draw together. 'By who?'

'This bloke. From the bar.'

'Where?'

'Can you just – stay with me? Walk me to the tube – virtually?' I say.

'Of course,' he murmurs.

'Okay,' I say.

'Okay,' he echoes, but his voice is crackly.

I pull the phone away from my ear and look at it, the light from it illuminating the clouds of my hot breath. *Shit*. No signal.

There's a set of stairs in front of me, leading down to a bridge. I dart into the corner where the stairs begin, to see if he follows. I put one foot on the first step, frozen, not able to look behind me.

And now he is behind me, too. And now, it's not my imagination. I know. He is right behind me. His body ready to hold on to my hips again. To push himself into me, against my will.

I see his red trainer. Oh God. He is here. I am too scared to turn around and look at him properly. I cannot do it.

'Hello?' I say desperately into the phone.

Reuben crackles back, and then . . . the three beeps. *Call failed*.

I start to sprint down the stairs, and I'm a few steps down them when it happens, as I knew it would. His gloved hand behind me. It lands on the railings like a bird of prey. The gloves are exactly the sort he would wear, I find myself thinking. Designer. Sporty. He looked lithe.

I hear an intake of breath, and know he is about to speak, to threaten me. Perhaps his mouth is right next to my ear, his body poised to grab mine, to thrust again, and so I reach my hand out to grab the railings. They're cold and wet; they soak my gloves.

And then I am acting before I know it.

He comes down by my right-hand side, ready to over-take me on the wide stairs. I turn. His hood's up, but I can tell it's him from his gait. I am remembering his body against mine again, and imagining yet more horrors – his sweet breath in my mouth, his penis up against my under-wear, against my jeans, a full, damp, painful wetness – I bring my hand down on his, briefly, hard. He lets out a surprised cry. And with my right – my dominant hand – I push his body, firmly, squarely, the hardest I've ever pushed anything in my life. I release his hand as he falls – I'm surprised he falls; he's at least six feet – and he tumbles like a stuntman down the concrete stairs to the towpath. He stops there, on his stomach, at a strange angle. I am breathing hard, and I stand, watching him, astonished. That I have done this. That I am safe. That he is lying there, not moving, and I am here, almost at the top.

I start to feel a weird, panicky hotness. I reach to undo my coat, wanting to feel the sharp winter air on my sweat-covered chest. My glove is sopping wet as it touches my skin. My forehead is slick with moisture, from perspir-ation or the fine mist descending from the sky around me, I don't know. My bowels want to open, and right in the pit

15

of my stomach I feel a hornet's nest of fear beginning to buzz. Oh God. What have I done?

One minute ago I was scared for my life, and now I am scared for his.

My mind scans over the time in the bar. Feckless Joanna. I should have ignored him, told him to piss off, like Laura did. I never do the correct thing. I end up in messes. I avoid things and then they get much worse.

I close my eyes. Oh, please let me go back to Before. Before we met Sadiq. Before we left. Before he followed me. Before I pushed him.

But we can't. I can't. And now . . . it is After.

I look down at Sadiq. His left arm is underneath him, twisted strangely. He's fallen only seven steps, but they're concrete, and wet. His right arm must have reached out in front of him. It's landed just to the side of his face. He hasn't moved at all.

I should go to help him. Call an ambulance. Confess.

Or I should run away, in case he's about to get up again. Sprint home. Pretend I never did it. Go back to Before, even though I know I can't.

The street lights are too bright, refracted a hundred times in each drop of misty rain. I can see moisture on the concrete steps like thousands of beads of sweat. I can feel the cold air seeping into my coat. Sadiq is lying still but breathing in and out, in and out, and I look down at him and then around me, and think.

I could run, or I could stay and call him an ambulance.

Now it is decision time.

2

Reveal

I stand and stare at Sadiq. I could walk away. Avoid, like I've done for my entire life.

I turn around, my back to him, and take three steps away. And then I stop, looking over my shoulder, sure that he will have risen up behind me like a villain in a fable. But he hasn't. He's still there. Still lying down. Still not moving.

Fat raindrops are striking my nose and leaving a trail of smaller ones as though they've been split apart.

I am still looking over my shoulder as I think it: I could leave. Little Venice is deserted. I check, up and down the length of the canal. Nobody.

And that's when the sweating gets worse. I puff out my cheeks and raise my eyes heavenwards and try to think, but all I'm doing is panicking. It's as though all of the world's dread and fear and madness have been set free inside my abdomen. My mind is racing but saying nothing, my hands are flexing and making fists – alternating clenched and open, like starfish – and my legs are wobbling.

I look down at Sadiq. Are those headphones? One earbud has fallen out of his ear, the cord white against the concrete like a worm.

I wonder what Reuben would do. Perhaps I can call him back, and ask him. No. I am certain of what he would say. He always does the right thing. His favourite poem is 'If'. His favourite TV show is *The West Wing*. He is a social worker for an Islamic charity. My mind throws up these headline points in support of its application to make me leave, now, and never tell him, and it won't stop. Reuben stacks chairs up at the end of the working day, even though it is the cleaners' job. He was adopted, thirty-two years ago, and has never once held a grudge. I scraped another car's door once – so lightly as to be almost imperceptible – and reached to rub at the scratch with a tissue, and Reuben was on his feet and writing a detailed note, leaving our numbers, before I could even protest. He chooses, again and again, *the right thing* – even though it is hardly ever the easy thing.

For God's sake, ring 999, he would say, panicked, astonished I was even asking the question.

Perhaps this moment will forever change how he looks at me; that I even have to ask. He will – finally – see me as I truly am: flawed, selfish, pathetic.

No. I can't be like that.

I venture down two steps. I can hear something. A voice. I stop again, sombre for a moment, saying a mournful goodbye to my life as I know it. Am I sure? If I call now, there'll be a procedure. An ambulance, dispatched immediately. I'll be in a system. Not Joanna any more, but . . . somebody else. A number.

It's been over a minute. Maybe two. One hundred and twenty seconds of staring.

Where is that noise coming from? I am sure it is a

woman's voice. I creep two steps closer, and realize: the headphones.

And even though I have decided what to do, I am procrastinating. Trying to put off the moment when I have to make the phone call, even though I know that makes things harder, not easier. I've been procrastinating my entire life, and I'm not stopping now.

One more minute passes.

I don't know what spurs me into action. Perhaps I needed those three minutes to come to terms with how things will be; to move into the After. Perhaps it was to make sure he wasn't about to reach for me, grab me. I don't know, but I pull out my phone, standing almost at the bottom of the stairs, and dial 999. I have never dialled these numbers in my life, though it feels as though I have, from BBC dramas and books and films.

It doesn't ring. There's a strange noise, then an operator answers immediately. I step gingerly down the remaining stairs as I hear a Scottish voice, as if I can only get close to him now I have her protection.

'What's your emergency?' the woman says.

'I . . . there's a man who's been injured,' I say.

As I stop, above his body, I can hear the noise again. It *is* a voice. *Take a deep breath in for five counts*, it is saying. Some sort of hypnotherapy. Meditation, maybe.

'Okay, my love, how badly injured is he?' she says.

'I . . . don't know.'

'Alright – what's your name?'

'Joanna Oliva,' I say, though I wonder after uttering it whether I should have used a false one.

'Okay, Joanna. We're going to send a first responder,'

she says. Her tone is neutral. She doesn't provide reassurance. She doesn't explain what a first responder is.

I wonder what her hopes and dreams are. Maybe she had an emergency, once, and now she wants to help others. I close my eyes, imagining I am somewhere else, and on the phone to a friend. Perhaps I am by the sea, on holiday, and calling a friend because I am bored. Or maybe I am idly calling Reuben on the way home to him. He always takes my calls on the way home, and we chat, often right up until I get to our door.

I give her the address. Well, an address of sorts. 'One of the side bridges. The centre of Little Venice. The canal.' I can hear her typing.

'And now I'd like you to assess the man, is that going to be alright?' she lilts.

I wonder if she was hired because of the soothing quality of her voice. Maybe she does television adverts in her spare time. I cannot stop the thoughts. It strikes me as strange that I am still me; still overly imaginative, even when thrown into these most extraordinary of circumstances.

I lean down and tentatively touch his shoulder, his black jacket. It's softer than I thought it would be; fleecy. He's in tight black trousers, almost leggings. I was sure that he was in jeans, in the bar. But there are the red trainers. Just the same.

'He's face down,' I say. 'On some concrete – he fell . . . he fell down some steps. Seven,' I add uselessly, because my guilt has made me count them.

'Okay, and is he breathing? I don't want you to move his neck. Okay? Okay, Joanna?'

Her tone frightens me. Everything frightens me. It's

like the world's been filtered, black, and I can feel the hot, sweaty nausea again. I say nothing.

'Okay?'

'Yes,' I say. There's a man lying injured beneath my fingertips and I did it. I can hardly dare think about it. It's like looking at the sun.

I can't turn him over. I can't do it.

The voice from the headphones is still speaking – about imagining a beach scene, waves rolling in and out – and I listen to that instead.

'Can you look, listen and feel for whether he's breathing? Do you know his name?' She enunciates these words like a primary school teacher.

Look, *listen* and *feel*. I do not know what these words mean. I look over my shoulder, at the illuminated street, slick with rain, and along the canal, to the bridges stacking behind us, almost all aligning, tessellating, like my vision has gone blurred.

Look.

Listen.

Feel.

I stare at him, face down on the pavement.

I run my fingers underneath his shoulder and crouch to look at him. 'Oh, oh,' I say to her, involuntarily. His face is sopping. At first I think it's blood, when my fingers touch the wetness, but it's cold and thin-feeling.

And then I realize. My eyes see it as they adjust to the dark. It grows in front of me: a puddle at the bottom of the steps. Caused by a tree a few feet away, its roots pulling up the pavement, cracking it, making it uneven, creating great craters.

One of which is filled with water.

He's totally submerged, in dark water, on the dark ground.

'He's face down, in a puddle,' I say.

Surely she will help? She is on my side; she must be. She is a good person, working in the 999 call centre.

'Roll him on to his side, quick as you can, out of the water,' she says. 'Does he have a head or neck injury?'

'I . . . I don't know. I pushed him. And he fell, down the stairs,' I say.

Nobody can blame anybody for being honest. Nobody can prosecute for an innocent mistake.

'Quick as you can,' she repeats.

I roll him over. His black hood is still drawn partially over his face. The rest is in shadow.

'Now I need you to check he's breathing. Look, listen and feel, remember? Can you repeat that back?'

'Look, listen and feel,' I say woodenly.

'Look for his chest rising. Listen with your ear at his airways. Feel for his breath.'

I stare at his chest. I lean my head down. I can hear everything, suddenly. The roar of distant traffic. The trickle of water into the canal. The sound of the raindrops splattering on the concrete. But nothing from him.

I take my glove off and rest my hand against his nose. There is no breath against my fingers. Nothing tickling them at all. It is still, unnatural, like looking at somebody with a vital detail missing, like eyelashes or fingernails. The contents of my handbag scatter over the ground as I lean over him. Lipsticks I never wear because they make me self-conscious roll all over the place.

'He's not breathing,' I say. Panic rushes in again.

'Is he definitely not?' she says. 'Put your cheek to his mouth. I want you to tell me whether you can feel his breath against your face.'

I wince, but do it anyway.

There's nothing against my cheek. No movement. No warmth. No rustling of the strands of my hair by a breath. Nothing.

'He's definitely not breathing,' I say.

Her voice is crisp, patient, sympathetic. 'We're going to do five rescue breaths first,' she says. 'Because he's been drowning.'

Drowning.

'Okay.'

'Open his mouth. Lay him on his back. Tilt his chin back. Being careful of his neck. Chin lifted high, alright, Joanna? Tilt his head back. Are you ready?'

I move him on to flatter ground, and as I do so, his hood falls away and I see his face.

It's not Sadiq.

His eyes are widely spaced, but that's where the similarities end. His features are delicate. There's no heavy brow. He's got hollows underneath his cheekbones. It's not Sadiq. It's not Sadiq. It's not Sadiq.

'I . . .' I don't say any more, though maybe I should. 'Shit. I'm – I'll do it now,' I say.

But inside, my thoughts are rushing like water through a burst pipe. *It's not him. It's not him.* I have pushed – I have injured – a stranger. This man wasn't harassing me. He didn't follow me. I look at his trainers again. They're the same. The same stupid trainers.

But of course: he was out running. Trainers. Head-phones. All black. How could I have made such a catastrophic error? How could I not have checked?

The voice keeps coming out of the headphones, getting louder and quieter as I move.

I could hang up the phone. I could run away. Get a flight somewhere before I'm stopped. Would I be stopped? All of my knowledge has come from the television. I can't remember the last time I cracked open a newspaper. I know nothing about the real world, I think bitterly. Reuben would know what to do. He is a Proper Person who knows about global politics and can point to Iran on a map and knows what sautéing is. But of course, Reuben would never be in this situation. Good Reuben.

My body feels strange. My eyes are dry and heavy. The world shifts as I look at it, like I'm in a kaleidoscope. Perhaps I am drunk. I have had four drinks. I lean over and breathe into his mouth. It's strangely intimate. My lips have only touched Reuben's, for seven years.

Five breaths. Nothing happens.

She tells me to start chest compressions. There are *no signs of life*, she says.

I lean down and lace my fingers as she tells me to, the phone on speaker on a step. His chest yields under the pressure, surprisingly so, and I compress a few inches easily.

It happens suddenly, after five chest compressions. He reacts to me, his lips tightening. He sucks in a breath, his slim chest expanding and his body jerking as though the ground's moved beneath him.

'He's . . . something's happening,' I shout.

And then he's coughing. Hacking, productive coughs.

24

I look away, not wanting to be privy to these moments. Maybe he'll open his eyes. Maybe he'll stand and walk away, disgruntled and inconvenienced, but fine, like we are motorists who've damaged each other's bumpers. Maybe. Maybe. I close my eyes and wish for it.

'He's coughing,' I say tonelessly. I can't tell her I got the wrong man. I can't tell her anything.

'Okay, good. The ambulance is nearly with you,' she says.

Sadiq – no, not-Sadiq – is still lying there. His eyes closed. Chest rising steadily.

'Can you put him in the recovery position?' she says.

Another surge of fear rushes through me like the tide's coming in, and I try to ignore it, biting my lip. It is no longer fear of Sadiq. It is fear for what will happen to me now.

'Okay,' I say. 'Okay.' I heave him over.

There is no sign he's conscious. His eyelids don't flutter like Reuben's do just before he wakes on Sunday mornings – the only morning of the whole week that we always spend together; the one where he is not with his charges or helping his MP or leading protests. This man's arms don't hold their own weight like Reuben's do when he rolls over and beckons to me, wanting to hold me, even in his sleep. Instead, they flop on to the ground like they're weighed down unnaturally, curling like an ape's.

And then, when he's in the recovery position, one knee bent up as the woman tells me to, I see the ambulance. The lights are flashing in the glass-fronted shop windows along the street above us. I see the ambulance's blue light

3

Conceal

The world closes to just me and Sadiq, lying there, motion-less, face down.

And then the panic comes. Panic in such a pure form it could be an injection.

Sweat breaks out over my body. The street light is too bright. I pinch at my coat, at the neckline, trying to get some air. Within seconds, I'm drenched in sweat that feels like needles as it evaporates off my skin.

I stand, doing nothing except feeling the feelings – dread like spilt black ink in the bottom of my stomach, panic like bricks sitting on my chest, guilt like a shrinking feeling in my lower abdomen – and staring at Sadiq.

It's been one minute. Two. I'm looking down, along the canal. There's nobody here. Nobody except me and him. I feel myself rise up above the scene. I can see myself: a woman, thumbnail in the corner of her mouth, chewing on it, looking down at a man who's lying face down on the ground; a dark canal, opaque with frost, illuminated in yellow patches by the street lights. Beyond us, a moon. Beyond that, space.

The sweating's getting worse. I can't . . . I can't do it. I don't have the human reserves I need to stay. To help him. To make that phone call.

I turn and look at him again. Perhaps he fell. Maybe I am mistaken. Maybe it's not as important as it feels right now. Maybe I have misread it somehow. He was pursuing me. He was a pervert, a sexual predator – and he fell. Yes, that's what happened.

For a moment, my body longs for Reuben, the way it sometimes does, unexpectedly, while I'm shutting the skylight at work, or boiling the kettle when he's away. That strong, silent soul of his. The way he always stands closer to me than he does to anyone else. That he lets only me in. That he takes great pleasure in sexting me from across the room at parties, and watching me blush. Nobody would believe what he's like, privately, even if I told them.

Oh, Reuben. Where are you now? Why didn't you come tonight? Can you help me? I think of him on the sofa at home, alone, and wish.

Sadiq is still motionless. I can't do it. Not without Reuben. Not alone. It's better if I just . . . it's better if I leave.

Someone will find him soon. It's London. They'll think him drunk or disorderly. Clumsy. He'll be okay.

I stagger backwards, two steps, and then I do what I do best: I avoid it. I turn around and walk away.

I take one step across the bridge to Warwick Avenue. That's all it takes. One step, and then I'm off. Another step follows. And then another, as sure as the sun will rise tomorrow.

My heels – those lovely shoes I put on so optimistically just hours previously – make hollow thumping sounds on the bridge. Two minutes ago they were followed by Sadiq. Now I'm alone. And so is he.

*

I pause twice, but I don't turn around. As I approach the brightly lit entrance to the tube, though, I am crossing the Rubicon. It's the point of no return, the Rubicon. Is that right? Didn't Reuben refer to it once, laughing just a little, in his understated way, when I didn't know the reference? Not patronizingly. Just ... him. I had looked it up privately, when he had left the room. I had spelt it with a *k* in the middle, and not a *c*.

And now I'm inside the tube station.

This is it, forever, I tell myself. Always acting. Nobody can ever know. Perhaps if I spend enough time with the lie, in both the telling of it and my own thoughts, I can become it. Like a chameleon, taking on the colours of things next to it. I try not to run, not to draw attention to myself, but I'm hurrying, my walking becoming running, until I remind myself to slow down again.

A man selling crisps and cans of Coke and slowly dying flowers ignores me, staring down at his phone.

I'm safe. Sadiq's gone now, I tell myself. Far behind me. My breathing slows as I look straight ahead. At the fluorescent lights and the posters for musicals, the billboards for books I'd usually be wanting to read. I descend underground, and the air takes on that synthetic, hot, dusty quality. My heartbeat is slowing down now. I close my eyes and picture him lying there, but I push the image away, looking instead at the platform as I arrive on it.

A woman is already standing there. She's alone. She's wearing faded grey skinny jeans, beige boots, a pink coat. Her clothes are neat, her hair absolutely, perfectly straight at this, the end of the day. I imagine she has 'offline weekends' and reads post-modern literature.

Why not her? I think to myself. Why me? How come it's always me?

I look up at the sign. *1 min*, it says. And then I see it's to Harrow, and I cross the platform to the other side.

This platform's empty, though I can still hear the echo of the woman's boots across the way.

I can feel my brain trying to figure it out, to package everything away into little boxes, but I don't let it. The selfie from the bar, it says. That's evidence. That woman with the pink coat: she'll say I looked distressed.

Instead of listening to these thoughts, I turn my head and look at one of the posters. *She's watching you*, an advert for a psychological thriller reads. A pair of eyes, brown like mine, look out, until they are obscured by the stopping tube.

A call from Reuben lights up my phone as I emerge from the underground. *Shit.* I didn't even let him know I was okay.

I don't answer it. When he rings off, I can see he's left two voicemails and a text. An unprecedented amount of contact from my often non-communicative husband. I stand outside the tube at Hammersmith, listening to them.

'Hi. Only me. You alright?'

'Hi, me again . . . just getting a bit worried now.'

'Jo – call me?'

I could call him now, and tell him.

But I know what he would do. I have known – and loved – him for seven years, and so I am certain of what he would say.

He would hand me in. I know he would. And I can't . . . I can't. I can't go back tonight. I can't be marched to the police tonight, and back to that man lying on the pavement. Back to that sweaty, claustrophobic panic. I'll tell him tomorrow. When nothing good could come of handing me in. Sadiq will be fine. He will get up, and he will be fine.

It is familiar – comforting – to me, to procrastinate. I've been doing it my whole life. Preparing for nothing. I will start the essay when I've made a cup of tea. When I've read the *Guardian*. I will cancel that direct debit next month. Definitely before the next payment. Definitely.

Nobody follows me. Nobody says anything to me on the way home. I pass a few people near the Hammersmith flyover and none of them looks at me. The universe has changed, for me, but nobody knows. The molecules of the air are the same. The rain is the same. But somewhere, a man lies on a slab of concrete because of me. It feels far away, now I'm nearly home, a tube ride away from it all. As though it's theoretical, an abstract concept. As though, if I can just turn it around, and look at it differently, it might *be* different.

I send Reuben a text. *Almost home, all fine :)* x

I guess that is why I start running. Because I'm away from the scene, and don't have to act normally any more. And because I keep seeing Sadiq's face in the bar, imagining him behind me, chasing me. Imagining the police. A manhunt.

I trip on an uneven paving slab, and I can't stop myself. I hit the ground, and skid along it, my wrist mangled, trapped underneath me.

I sit for a second in the road, tempted to cry like a child, but get up. I check my hands. Only a slight graze. My left hand throbs, but I ignore it.

I keep running and now can almost see our basement flat. My parents and Wilf think we are stupid, that we should shell out for a two-up two-down in Kent and commute in, but we like it. We like to be in London, we say, like it is a friend we don't want to move too far from.

I descend the stairs to our door – there are only five steps – and I wonder if I will always think of this when I am walking down them; if I will always remember this night. But I shake the thought away. Reuben opens the door before I have to rifle through my messy bag for my key – he knows these things about me, and he is always trying to help.

'Hi, alright?' he says, and I see that I have worried him.

He pauses for a second, framed in the light from the narrow hallway, his eyes taking me in. I must look wild.

I pat my hair down, trying to appear normal. 'Yeah – sorry,' I say.

He turns and ambles into the kitchen where he opens our large silver fridge, waving a pint of milk at me.

I shake my head. 'I want wine,' I say.

'Oh, oh no,' he says, setting the milk down and coming straight over to me.

I almost wince as he takes my hands, but manage not to.

Reuben is tall and lanky. His hair is ginger and his beard – currently at stubble length, though it varies – is a darker auburn. His skin burns easily and is freckled. His hips are slim. His face is more lined, these days, at thirty-two, though there are no grey hairs on his head. But I know we must be getting older because the people I mistake him for are older. A red-headed man in the street I'll think for a moment is him – he will have Reuben's light gait, his gracefulness, his grumpy way of looking at people – won't be. And, on closer inspection, the man will be about forty, and I'll be surprised that I might have mixed them up at all. He doesn't like pointless chatting and his worst quality is that he's so blunt he is often rude. His hopes are to live in a better world, I suppose.

He is my most favourite person in the entire world.

I think often, recently, of the babies we will have. They will have his beautiful, bright red locks, his pale eyelashes, his green eyes. People on the street will smile at me and my ginger family.

'What happened?' he murmurs into my hair. 'The man from the bar?'

I nod, once, against his chest.

'Awful.' He says, rubbing his hands up and down my back.

I swallow stomach acid that's sloshing around my mouth and turn my head to the side to look around the kitchen. As I thought it would be, it's immaculate. I can see the soil in our many plants – it was one of my recent fads, to set up a kitchen garden – is wet. He's watered them. He's washed up, too. He'll no doubt have done some work, watched a film. He is calm, organized. I piss away my evenings, spent shambolically on BuzzFeed and looking up old school friends and thinking I ought to pre-heat the oven but don't want to move, and then it is eleven o'clock at night and I haven't eaten.

'Have a good night?' I manage to say, though every few seconds the wave of sweating begins again and I can almost feel my pupils dilate and my hands shake.

'Sure,' he says, looking down at me briefly.

'What did you do?'

'Load of box-ticking,' he says. 'Form-filling for my client.'

Reuben is one of those people with too many jobs. He's a social worker, for an Islamic charity. He is starting to assist his MP at her surgery, especially where gang culture is concerned. He's a social work expert, occasionally appears in court and tells lawyers what social workers should have done; whether they did the right things. He doesn't sleep much and there is forever *something* on his horizon. He is fastidiously organized, writing up case notes late at night and filing them immediately. He never seems to wane in his enthusiasm. He can never not be bothered. He never puts things off.

He releases me, and a peculiar sensation comes over me, as though these are my final moments in this world: a world of these First World problems. Writing up case notes and tidying the kitchen. I'm wrong, of course, I tell myself. Everything's the same. I've avoided changing my world by avoiding making that call. I step back towards Reuben, riding on a wave of relief, and he immediately raises his arm, as he always does. I step underneath it, and it seamlessly falls around my shoulders.

'Be alright,' he says to me. It's one of his phrases. 'You'll be alright,' got shortened; a couple's language we often speak.

I nod, tears in my eyes, which he wipes away.

His hand slides down my back. Even my coat is damp with sweat, but he doesn't say anything. He never would.

He pours me a glass of red and I sip it in my right hand,

my left hanging limply. It's becoming stiff and feels strange. I'll enjoy tonight, our wine together. I'll try to dispel the shakes, the dread. And then tomorrow – tomorrow I will face it.

Reuben goes to sit down in the living room. It's in the same room as our kitchen.

I look out of the window. Our neighbour is outside. She's one hundred and two years old. Her seventy-year-old daughter comes to visit her, bringing her teenage dogs. Everyone is old in that flat, Reuben and I joke. Edith's face appears beyond our plants, and I make out her features before raising my hand in a wave. An alibi, I think uselessly to myself. I'm glad she's a night owl.

Reuben comes into the kitchen again and picks up a piece of paper from the kitchen counter, his body just brushing mine.

I'm remembering again. The feel of Sadiq's body against my gloved hands. The way he tumbled so easily, like a domino, falling after the gentlest of flicks.

'Edith behaving herself?' Reuben says to me, throwing me a look.

I once told him I pretended Edith was a robot; that nobody could be that old. That she was a government experiment. He laughed so hard his face went bright red, and he said, 'Never change, Jojo.'

'Yes,' I say woodenly.

And then I'm remembering before that. The feel of his hand in mine in the bar. His penis against my leg. It's not fair.

'Got time for number seventy-eight?' Reuben says, gesturing to the list on our blackboard.

Written in red chalk, it's the top one hundred movies of all time, according to some worthy poll. We are rubbish with films – a rite of passage we both somehow missed during our teens. I was too busy overachieving – studying and amateur dramatics and ballet and clarinet – and Reuben was becoming Reuben; learning. He's the most well-read man I've ever known. Can give you chapter and verse on Lacan, Marx, Kant. He was adopted as a baby into a very scholarly family who ran a pub. His entire childhood was spent reading books in the rooms above the bar. Even now, when we go to visit them in Norfolk, they talk about economics, politics. The bar is littered with paperbacks they're halfway through.

And so now we're watching the films together. A few a week. We just watched number seventy-nine, and I see that the next one is *The Exorcist*. When we started, Reuben bought a blanket that we always get out now, and snuggle under it. Every now and then, while we're watching, he will pause the film and say, 'Are you listening?' and we'll laugh when I am not.

A siren goes off in the distance. I can hear it getting closer and closer. Reuben is looking at me. I can't look back. I can't speak until I know whether or not it's for me. It gets louder and louder and I expect it to cut off. There'll be two strapping policemen getting out, wearing heavy boots and carrying batons. They will ring the doorbell. Any second. Any second now.

Only, the siren continues again, into the distance, getting quieter and quieter, orbiting away from me. It's not for me. This time.

I gulp and look at the wintry blackness of the window.

Is this how it's going to be now? Will my London – the London Reuben and I love so much – become a kind of waiting room for my . . . for my what? My capture? I shake my head. I can't think of it.

'I'm not really up for *The Exorcist*,' I say with what I hope is a gentle laugh.

'We said we'd do them in order,' Reuben, a stickler for rules, says. He turns away from me and indicates the board.

He's standing at the end of our long, narrow kitchen, and the way the light catches him reminds me of our wedding day. Reuben was half in shadow at the end of the aisle. I'd spent so long imagining our wedding day – the planning and organization almost killed me – that when it finally arrived, I spent the entire day pretending it was somebody else's, and that I was simply a guest, instead. I could enjoy it better that way.

I remember the kiss he gave me. Our first as husband and wife. Perhaps he was just embarrassed to be kissing me in front of a handful of people. Or preoccupied with the life commitment he had just made. Or maybe he thought I pulled away, first. But I remember that kiss. It was dry, formal. Not like his usual kisses. I've never asked him why. But I've always remembered it.

'Okay,' Reuben says, leaving the room with his wine. I hear him go into the bedroom.

I stare at the kitchen counter after he's gone. Something is folded neatly in half in the letter rack. I pick it up, trying to distract myself from the seismic swirl of thoughts just off stage-left in my brain. It's an application form. I frown, looking at it. It's my handwriting. I pull it out, unfolding it. It's my application for a creative writing course. How could I have forgotten? I hold it up to the light. It's like a relic from my life Before. It had seemed like the answer, last Tuesday, when I printed it out and filled it in and then forgot to post it. Reuben's attached a stamp to it, neatly, with a paperclip. It's exactly the sort of thing he does: hands-off, but helpful.

He arrives back in the room and I leave the letter on the side and join him on the sofa. 'Thanks for the stamp,' I say. 'But I'm not sure creative writing is the Thing.'

Reuben nods, putting the paper down he's reading, and looks at me. 'You don't need a Thing,' he says.

'No?'

'I got halfway through the sudoku,' he says to me. He flicks the paper to the back and shows me.

I look down at it. 'That's an eight and that's a two,' I say.

'Too smart for your own good, Murphy,' he says. 'Coming to bed? Bring the wine. We won't be able to do this when baby Oliva's here.' He, too, has been talking more and more about babies. Soon, we keep saying, wanting to enjoy the last of each other, like we are on a decadent night out we're not quite ready to finish yet.

'Yeah,' I say. I can see Sadiq again, in my mind, lying face down on the ground. I'll go to bed with Reuben, reading my book while he spoons into me, and in the morning, I will tell him.

'Aren't you going to tell me?' Reuben says as I climb into bed beside him.

'Tell you what?' I mutter, not looking at him. Instead, I am eyeing the blinds, waiting for them to flash blue as the police arrive. I am looking at my phone, waiting for it to ring.

Nothing happens. I can't believe I am going to bed. I'm really doing it. Really not going back.

'You know . . .' Reuben says.

I instigated the game, but he is fully on board now. It's become a thing we do seamlessly, like locking up. Like brushing our teeth.

'No,' I say.

Reuben looks at me in surprise. 'We've not missed a day,' he says.

'I just can't,' I say. 'I can't think of anything.'

Reuben's expression darkens, but he doesn't say anything more.

Ten minutes later, I open the drinks cupboard with my good hand in our tiny kitchen and find another bottle of wine. I'll just have a few glasses. To take the edge off. And, I think darkly, to try to forget. I hope drunken amnesia might be a kind of blur across the night, obscuring everything, right back to the moment when I pushed Sadiq.

My hand is shaking as I plunge a corkscrew into the bottle, steadying it between my knees, unable to use my injured hand, stabbing the cork through the heart.

I dream of Sadiq, while dozing on and off, and during the night he appears, standing in the doorway, a black, death-like figure, a foot nearer to me every time I blink.

By the third blink, he is right in front of me, his face to mine, his hands held up like they were in the selfie we took, but bloodied, red rivulets running down them.

When I next wake up, it's light outside. Reuben is sleeping peacefully, on his side, facing away from me.

39

I don't remember immediately. It takes an effort, like waking up in a strange bed and having to piece together, for a few seconds, where I am.

Bad dreams. I recall the bad dreams first. A man in the corner of the room. His bloodied hands up close to mine. His breath on my face.

But no.

Not all of this is a dream.

A dark cloak of fear draws around me. I feel the blood seep from my face. It was real.

It was real.

My left hand is clutching at the duvet and it throbs as I flex it. And then I recoil. Those hands. Those hands that pushed that man. That body and mind that left. That hand that got twisted in the road, in my haste to flee the scene. *The scene*. I'm walking across the bedroom, still half asleep, and into the bathroom. I want to look at myself. To see myself. To check I am real and not changed, and to piece myself together.

In the mirror, I trace a finger down my cheek. It's almost imperceptible – barely there, but I can see it. A dried bit of white stuff: salt, a crust. In an oblong shape on my cheek. A dried tear. I've been crying in my sleep.

I gulp. I have to tell Reuben.

I peer out of the bathroom. My head turns towards him, like a flower to the sun. The morning light has caught his features, making them rosier than usual. I can't stop looking at him. His beard shines auburn. His eyes are closed. Soon, those beautiful eyes will look at me differently.

4

Reveal

I am shivering as a female police officer approaches. She's heavily made up, which surprises me. I wonder what she looks like beneath the thick layer of foundation, slightly too pale for her, and underneath her coarse, spiky lashes, the blue eyeshadow.

I draw my coat further around me.

'Joanna,' she says to me.

I look up at her. She will surely realize it was a mistake. An accident. Not intentional. Woman to woman, we can work it out. I look closely at her. I wonder what sort of bedroom she stands in as she applies her make-up. Minimalist? Or maybe one full of curated *pieces*? I wonder what led her to the police and if she finds it difficult as a woman. I wish we could talk about this; that we'd met incidentally, at a hen party or a christening.

'Joanna Oliva. Yes,' I say, my eyes still running over her features.

She lets out a sigh, a short, sharp exhalation through her nostrils. And then she shifts her weight. She's bored. I am just another case in a long line of night shifts. How peculiar that two people would perceive the same event so differently.

The man – not-Sadiq – is coughing in the recovery

position as the paramedics are working on him. Relief floods through my arms and legs like liquid happiness. He's okay. And so I'll be okay.

I look back at the police officer. She's still staring at me. The relief opens my mouth for me and pulls the words out. 'We were in there,' I say, pointing in the direction of the bar with my thumb. 'Well – actually, we weren't. But I thought it was him when I pushed him.' It's garbled. I'm babbling. But I trust her, this woman with the blue eye-shadow and the professional job. She is here to help me.

She holds a hand up, like a mime. Her nails are long and pointed, painted a strange matt that doesn't catch the street lights. I bet she does them herself, has bought the UV light machine and makes a bit of money on the side. Maybe she's obsessed with nail art and puts her designs on Pinterest. I could never manage that. I am so messy. I paint the edges of my fingers, too, and just hope it'll wipe off.

The gesture cuts me off. My next words die in my throat.

'Okay, Joanna, I need to stop you there,' the police officer says, her hand still held up in front of her. She points back to Sadiq – no, not-Sadiq – on the towpath. The ambulance crew are lifting him up, on a stretcher, a bag over his face like a blown-up rubber glove that one of the men is squeezing. He's not conscious. That much is clear. There are vehicles everywhere, parked on the road above us. An ambulance. A first responder in a green and yellow car. And the police. All for me. For us.

'Joanna Oliva, I am arresting you on suspicion of assault contrary to section eighteen of the Offences Against the Person Act 1861.'

'What?' I say, flabbergasted.

'You do not have to say anything,' she is saying to me.

The words are familiar, but it takes me a moment to place them. It's not a hymn or a song lyric or a phrase. No. It's a caution. The caution. All the crime dramas I've ever watched – *The Bill* while my mother was ironing, *The Bridge*, after which I applied to be a Police Community Support Officer and then didn't attend the interview – blur together in my mind as I realize what's happening. I am being cautioned. Arrested. Me.

I could make a dash for it. Down the canal. I start to plot a route. Past this woman, down the towpath, along the canal, up those steps. Back into central London. Into any number of alleys and nooks and crannies. Any bars or the toothpaste aisle of a Tesco Express or a phone box decorated with prostitutes' business cards so the sides are made opaque. I could go. Now. It must be the drink talking; I always did get the beer fear. I shake my head, but my vision blurs as I do so, my surroundings moving like liquid.

She's still speaking. 'But it may harm your defence if you do not mention, when questioned . . .'

The funny thing about your life changing in a moment is that you are the same person after the change. I, Joanna Oliva, wife of Reuben Oliva, still wonder how long it took her to memorize the caution and whether or not she felt a frisson of power the first time she said it to somebody. My main thoughts are still what Reuben will think of me, and whether or not he will look at me differently, even though it is trivial against the backdrop of what I have done, like a cancer patient worrying about losing their hair in the face of a life-threatening disease.

'. . . something which you later rely on in court . . .'

The night seems to become colder around me and I draw my coat sleeves down over my hands, even though the action strains and pulls at the wool.

'. . . anything you do say may be given in evidence . . .'

And, with those words, I begin the process of no longer being myself. I've gone through the veil, to the underworld. I'm not myself any more. I'm not Joanna. I can't go home and sit in bed with Reuben and play our end-of-the-night game.

'Do you understand,' the woman is saying to me, 'what I've said?'

I nod because I don't know what else to do. And they load not-Sadiq into the ambulance and close the doors with soft clicks in the night.

'You'll come to the station,' she says. It's not a request.

'Of course,' I say, wanting to please her, momentarily distracted by the glint of her wedding ring.

Reuben and I didn't choose rings, in the end. He thought they were clichéd, which made me laugh. Laura was impressed. She loved the unconventionality of our wedding.

The policewoman searches me then. She gestures and, just like airport security, pats me down. 'Do you have anything on you that might cause danger to you or others?' she asks.

'No.'

The policewoman tries to lead me by the arm over to their car but I walk willingly, like a well-trained dog keen to please. I get into the back of the car myself. The door handle is slick with rainwater.

She sits next to me in the back seat. I daren't touch my mobile phone, though I want to. Reuben will be worried.

I close my eyes and pretend I am in a taxi, that some chatty Uber driver is talking to me. The other police officer gets in the driver's seat and stalls the car before pulling away. I wonder if she took lots of attempts to pass her driving test, like I did.

My brown leather handbag is resting at my feet. I could reach it. Touch it. But perhaps that would be a crime.

'Which station are we going to?' I say. I wait a few seconds before looking up at them.

They don't answer. They don't speak. We just drive on in silence, the night streaking by.

I feel less and less human for every mile we travel.

It is only a ten-minute journey. The car comes to a shuddery stop and I reach to get out, but it is locked. The woman walks around to my side of the door, opening it like we are at the BAFTAs. She doesn't look at me, just stands aside like a footman. I look up at the building. Paddington Green Police Station. I've never been here. I'd never been to Little Venice before tonight. And now they will be significant to me.

I step out of the car. The police station looks more like a hospital. Wide and flat and sprawling with a tower on its top like a growth. My eyes track it upwards. Floor after floor. What are they? Offices? Cells?

We're around the back of it, in some sort of secure area. I hear the gates closing behind us.

'This way,' the woman says to me.

She doesn't have a name badge and she doesn't speak into a radio. She walks next to me, her right hand extended, ready, I guess, in case I make a sudden movement. I look up at the sky instead, taking in the grey expanse of it, before I am *inside*. I try to send Reuben a message with my mind. He's always known what I'm thinking better than anybody. *Reuben*, I say into the night, looking at the low-hanging orange moon, *I'm in trouble*.

The air is cold against my face as I walk. My heels on the tarmac sound like bangs in the night. I can't believe I'm still wearing them. What must I look like?

The policewoman pushes a side door open. Immediately I can smell something familiar. I feel nostalgic when I realize that it's the old people's home that Mum's mum was in. Urine mingled with the smell of overcooked stew and dumplings; a sweaty, potatoey, clammy smell.

We enter a brightly lit room. Everything is some shade of blue. The chairs are navy. The desk is teal. The walls are sky blue. I am walked through a scanner, like at an airport. A man is standing there. He's swarthy. Maybe Spanish. Italian. There's something catlike about him. Slanted eyes. He smiles at me, which surprises me, and he has pointy incisors.

The machine beeps loudly, three times.

'Coat off. Why's she still got her coat?' a cockney man behind the desk says to the woman who brought me in.

'Hang on,' the woman says.

'And your bracelet,' the man says to me, rolling his eyes.

My fingers trace over my wedding bracelet. 'Oh, I . . . it doesn't come off,' I say. My words sound slurred.

'Got to come off.'

I show it to him, wordlessly. It catches the overhead strip lights.

'It's got screws,' he says, seemingly to himself. 'Too risky.'

He disappears down the corridor and comes back with a screwdriver. One by one, he removes the tiny screws I didn't even realize were there, and my lifetime bracelet is off, my arm feeling bald and raw underneath it.

The woman swings my handbag on to the high desk which another woman sits behind. My eyes are drawn to the side pocket where I saw her put my phone. I can see it poking out, on a bed of receipts and chewing-gum packets and a notebook.

There's an annex behind the desk, a small room, and it's got a whiteboard in it that a man is writing on. It's divided into grids, with times. The man is writing my name down, which he's reading off something that has been given to him. He's in full uniform. White shirt with black shoulder pads with numbers on: 5619. A black tie, embossed with a crest at the bottom.

There's something behind him, too. I crane my neck to see. Three miniature televisions are suspended from the ceiling on sturdy brackets. Some people must try to pull them off, I presume. Something opens up in my chest. A hollow feeling. Fear, I suppose. The televisions are CCTV. Of the cells. Little people moving around in the greyish-green boxes, like tiny captive holograms. I close my eyes.

'Let's try scanning you again,' the man says. He's holding my coat.

I walk towards the scanner. Finally, it doesn't beep any more. As if this triggers something, another woman appears by my side.

'I'm the Custody Sergeant,' she says.

47

I look at the clock. Midnight. Reuben will be frantic. That phone call. And then nothing. I have hardly thought about it since I called the police. Why didn't I call him again, before it was too late?

I look back at her. She's blonde, with inch-long mousy roots. She's in her late thirties, maybe. She's wearing reddish brown eyeliner which has clumped together in little brick-coloured balls at the roots of her lower lashes. 'I'm Sergeant Morris. You have the right to a solicitor –'

'Okay,' I start to say. Do I know any solicitors? I think of all my friends. Reuben says I've got so many. But no solicitors, I am sure.

'You have the right to have somebody informed of your detention,' she says, talking over me like a robot. 'You have the right to consult the Codes of Practice. Do you have any questions?'

'Sorry,' I say. 'How do I get a solicitor?'

'We can contact the duty solicitor or you can call somebody else,' she says, 'so long as it doesn't interfere with our investigation.'

My mind reels. 'I get one call?' I say.

'Yes.'

There's no question who I will call: I need only him.

Right in the corner of the custody suite, still in the open, in full view of everybody, is an old-fashioned telephone. There's no seat. Three policemen are sipping tea, right next to it, out of cardboard cups with *PG Tips* written on the side. The phone's handset is weighty and black with a heavy silver coil like a snake.

I call Reuben's mobile and listen to the tinny ring. He never usually answers unknown numbers. He wouldn't be intrigued by them like I am. But, nevertheless, I hope he does. I want to hear his voice.

He answers almost immediately, unusually for him. He must've been worried.

'It's me,' I say.

'Are you okay?' he says.

'There's been an – I don't know. An incident,' I say.

'Are you okay?' he says again.

'Yes. I am.' I look over my shoulder. The entire suite is still full of police. I can't explain. Not here. 'Look – I need a solicitor,' I say.

I may as well have said I have flown to another country, or given birth. I can hear his stunned silence, heavy down the phone line. 'A solicitor?' he says eventually. I hear a faint rasping. He will be rubbing his stubble. 'Where are you?'

'In the police station,' I say in a low voice, although it is not those around me who will be embarrassed for me.

'*Where?*' Reuben says, and in his tone is a stunned note of incomprehension. It is almost funny.

And then I hear it. Not in anything he says, exactly, but in a beat he leaves between words. A beat that sounds a lot like judgement.

'What . . .' he trails off, then lets out an exhalation.

I have blindsided him. I have shocked my calm, stable husband.

'Jo – what's happened?'

'I pushed that man.' I say it again, without thinking.

'The one following you?'

I close my eyes. 'Yes,' I lie. It's too complicated to go into now. I'll tell him later. 'He's . . . injured.'

'Okay,' he says. 'I'll come.'

49

For once I love his brevity. 'It's Paddington Green Police Station.'

'I know it,' he says softly. Of course he does. His clients must be here often. 'I don't know a solicitor well enough. Get the duty one.'

'Okay.' I'm lost in our conversation, and I jump when Sergeant Morris appears right by my side. 'I've really got to go,' I say.

'Shall we . . . shall we do the things?' he says.

'You first,' I say with a little smile, grateful, pathetic tears budding at my eyes.

'Your . . .' He must be thinking hard. I hear him swallow.

We started this charade two months into our relationship – Reuben reluctantly, at first. And now he's the instigator, like a child told their bedtime routine; expectant. We're on number 2,589. Over two thousand five hundred facts we love about the other. We've never missed a day.

'The piece of hair right by your temple that never, ever goes into a ponytail,' he says.

'The way you file your post immediately,' I say.

'I'm sure you've used that one before.'

'Nope.'

'Two thousand five hundred and ninety tomorrow,' he says.

I hang up first.

'In there,' Sergeant Morris says to me after the call.

'Where?' I say.

She points to a room next to a toilet. I go inside and a Forensic Scene of Crime Officer introduces himself to me.

It's a blur, what happens next. Fingerprints. A DNA swab, hard and dry against the inside of my cheek. A breathalyser. A photograph. Just like in the movies. A blood sample. The underneath of my fingernails are scraped, even though I tell him I was wearing gloves.

'Take off your shoes,' he says, when I think we're done.

'My shoes?' I say dumbly.

'Yes.'

I take off my silk-covered heels and hand them over.

He delves into a basket nearby and pulls out a blue blanket stamped with *HMP*. I see that, bundled up with it, are a pair of grey tracksuit bottoms, a T-shirt and some black plimsolls. 'We need your clothes, too.'

'My clothes?'

'For forensics.'

'Right . . . okay,' I say.

When I'm finished, and in prison-issue grey clothes, I emerge into the custody suite and am given back to Sergeant Morris.

'Do you want to look at our Codes of Practice?' she says.

'No,' I say blankly.

'Okay, then,' she says, in the tone of voice of a weary mother letting her child spend all their birthday money on sweets.

I look over my shoulder as we walk. Am I supposed to read the codes? Should I want to read the codes?

She leads me down a corridor. The vinyl flooring – a kind of rainy blue-grey – squeaks underneath her shoes as we walk.

I don't know where I'm going and I don't ask. I wonder if my mobile's in a clear plastic bag in a locker somewhere, buzzing sadly. If I ever leave it alone for more than an hour I come back to hundreds of texts and tweets and WhatsApps and Snapchats and emails. Reuben despairs of all the noises it makes; he says that every day I am in touch with everybody I have ever known.

Our surroundings get grimmer as we walk. Along two more corridors and through heavy doors – painted blue, just like how a child might draw a police station, a *nick*. She holds each door open for me, not in a polite way, but more so she can watch me go through and make sure it locks behind us.

We round the corner and I see that we are into the female cells. It's exactly how you'd imagine it. There are rows and rows of them. My eyes trail upwards like I am watching rocket fireworks. There are more above those. And more again above those. There are bars. Bars everywhere. Metal flooring with holes in so that I can see right up. I feel vertiginous. We walk up a flight of stairs, on to the first floor, and along a corridor.

We come to a stop outside a door with a '13' written on it. It has a blackboard outside it. On it she writes: *J Oliva*.

I can hear someone retching. I turn my head to the sound. A groan, a guttural noise, and then a splash. And, like I've opened the door to it, I notice all of the other noises. Moaning. A woman shouting. Like we are in a closing nightclub at the end of a particularly violent happy hour. I draw my arms around myself. I pretend my arms are Reuben's.

I breathe deeply, trying to calm myself, but it only enhances the smell of the place. Wee. Old, sweaty food. Vomit. Stale alcohol.

'In,' she says. 'Time twelve-o-six.' She makes a note in a book.

'In?'

She pushes open the door. I haven't thought about it. About where we are. About where I'm being *put*. I didn't think . . . there were no handcuffs. Nobody forcing my head down as I got into the car. I didn't think I would be here. It's a complete shock to me.

There's a blue plastic mattress on the floor. No – mattress is too grand a term. It's of the type we used to lay down in PE for gymnastics and tumbling. There's a smaller one, too, which I guess is supposed to be a pillow. There's no window. There's a tiny vent in the wall, top left, next to the high ceiling. There's an arrow on the ceiling, pointing left. It's huge and black and I must be staring at it, because she says, 'It points to Mecca.'

She passes me the blanket.

It smells strongly of urine, much worse than outside.

To the left there's a toilet. No lid. Metal, like on a train or an aeroplane. I remember when Reuben and I flew to Berlin and I used the toilet during turbulence. It stinks. That synthetic cleanness combined with all the dirty things that have gone down it, so they become interchangeable. The bleach and the dirt. They smell the same. There is no toilet roll, and no flush. I blink, looking at it, until I realize Sergeant Morris has left me. The door slams shut and I jump, and then I keep shivering as the word for it reverberates around my brain.

It's a cell. It's a cell.

It's my cell.

5

Conceal

I haven't told him. I haven't told him, I haven't told him, I haven't told him.

I look at him as he stirs our porridge on the hob.

He is always cooking. He does the cooking, and I do the washing. Two years ago we divided the chores up to stop arguments. Needless to say, the dishes are stacked neatly, the dishwasher never used to store dirty plates, while the laundry basket is overflowing, belching washing like a drunkard by the side of the road.

My hand is getting worse. It is damaged and dysfunctional. It doesn't do what I want it to. It was stiff this morning.

Reuben is serving the porridge. The kitchen and living room of our flat are open plan. It is basically a studio, even though it has two bedrooms. But we love it; we don't care that we can hear the upstairs neighbour come home in her high-heeled shoes at three o'clock in the morning. We like the unapologetic griminess of it, of London. The artificially warm air; the hot dust smell of the tube that tells me, after a holiday, that I'm home again. That my feet in flip-flops go black in summer from the smog. The way everybody looks like utter rubbish on the underground at the end of a night out, all pale skin and smudged eye make-up in the bright, harsh lights. That, once, we saw a man with a snake on the night bus, and nobody even stared. All of it. All worth the price tag and the lack of space. Our parents don't understand it. Reuben's wonder why we don't sell up and get out of there. *There are other economies*, his dad will say to us.

A picture of our wedding day is hung on the wall opposite the cooker. It isn't staged. 'I don't want a massive, pretentious canvas of us grinning,' he said to me soon after he proposed. And, after all, we didn't even end up having a big wedding. It wasn't the best day of our lives. We were pretty nonplussed by it all, after his non-proposal ('I don't want to patronize you . . .' it began). It was a small affair. I wore a knee-length dress. We went out for a boozy lunch afterwards, at Ask. He drank too much red wine and didn't remove his hand from my lap even once, ate his pizza one-handed. And then, out in the courtyard – he used to smoke – we had a moment I'll remember forever.

'We did it,' I said.

He nodded, vigorously, his cheeks hollowing as he sucked on the cigarette. 'We did the thing we wanted to do,' he said plainly, summing up my happiness exactly.

That simple joy of living our lives for us. Sod everyone else.

We held hands, then, under the umbrella, as he smoked in the rain. I wore red shoes, and felt luckier than I thought it was possible to feel.

I stare at the photograph now. It's candid, both of us facing each other. I'm laughing gleefully. Reuben's eyes are raised heavenwards, but there's a tiny smile on his face.

How could I tell him? He would stop looking at me in that way. That tiny, knowing smile of his. I'm one of the only people he likes. And so how can I tell *him*, before anyone else?

It gets too much at four o'clock in the afternoon. I've escaped into the bathroom twice and dialled 999, then stopped myself at the last moment. My hand is still throbbing. It looks just the same – no bruising – but my wrist still feels weak and useless. I will see if it gets better. And then I will go to the doctor, once all of this is sorted.

I tell Reuben I'm going to go for a walk. I'm light-headed – I have hardly eaten – but I put my jacket on anyway to leave. Reuben looks out at the twilight but says nothing. I look both ways before ascending the stairs out on to the street, as though the police might simply be waiting there for me, too worried to knock.

The cool night air is chilled inside my lungs. I thought I would feel calmer, after a few minutes, than I did in our hot flat, but I don't. Nothing helps. My stomach churns and I can feel a weight across my shoulders. Everything seems scary, on the walk – out, by myself. The distant sound of sirens. The street lights that seem too bright. It is the beginning, I suppose. The beginning of living in fear. I'm not happy out. I'm not happy in – holed up, inside.

When I let myself back into the flat, Reuben is playing the piano in the box room at the back. He only ever does it when I am out. I stand for a second, then shut the door behind me. As expected, the playing stops. He sits uneasily with that talent, does Reuben. It is too extravagant for him.

He appears in the doorway. I have always loved the proximity our flat affords. I like being able to call Reuben from anywhere, to make casual conversation with him when I am in the bath, when he is cooking.

'Number two thousand five hundred and eighty-nine,' he says, still standing in the doorway, 'how cute your cheeks look when they're red. When you've just come home from a crazy walk.'

I never even have to think about the list of things I love about him. It is endless. I love how shy he is about his brilliant, artistic, instinctive piano-playing. How he is forever crossing boundaries with his clients, bringing them home, taking them on trips, when he shouldn't: how much he loves those messed-up kids. How he once told my brother, Wilf, that he was being condescending to me.

I should respond. I should offer up something I love about him. Or cross the room and say thank you. A full hug. The length of our bodies pressed together. I should tell him how happy the sound of his piano-playing makes me feel when I get in.

But I can't.

Because if I do that, then I'll tell him. I know I will. Or, worse: he'll know. He'll see the blackness at my centre. He'll guess. And he'll hand me over.

He's still looking at me, almost expectantly. I avoid his eyes, looking down.

What he's not expecting is my rejection. And so it makes it worse when it comes. When he realizes I'm not going to answer, I sense his gaze shifting. He's embarrassed for me to see how hurt he is, and so he turns away from me, messes uselessly with the plants on the window-sill. He starts watering them, not looking at me.

The water trickles, the only sound in all of London, it seems to me.

We take it in turns to make coffee in the evenings. It was his turn this evening, but I followed him, not wanting to be alone, my body fizzing with acid.

I promised myself a day, but now's the time. We are alone in the kitchen. This is the moment.

'I didn't even tell you about my Brixton boy,' Reuben says, looking up at me as he packs ground coffee carefully into our stove-top espresso maker.

'No?'

'You know the one – the boy who got out of the gang stuff, last Christmas? Behaved himself?'

'Yes,' I say woodenly.

'Well, he's been out with other lads . . . torching cars.' He leans against the counter. 'I can't work him out – it was all fine.'

Reuben is often bewildered by things like this. I suppose it is a symptom of having a steady mind. If you remove the boy's problems, the boy will behave. Very logical, but untrue.

'But don't you remember being a teenager?' I say, with a tiny laugh, turning to look at him, grateful for the distraction, for the chance to emerge out of my own head, even if I have to fight while doing it, like climbing a rope with no support, burns on my hands.

'I was just . . . I was very boring,' he says, flashing me a small smile.

I wish for a moment that other people could see this Reuben. That he would let them.

'But you of all people had reason to be – to be angry,' I say.

'My adoption was hardly personal.'

I can't hide a smile. 'You are very blessed to have a sound mind,' I say, reaching to touch his hand.

He pulls me to him, immediately, and I step back. He leans his weight against the kitchen counter, looking thoughtful. The coffee maker is on the hob and the second it starts to bubble he turns the gas off. 'Don't want burnt coffee,' he says, looking pointedly at me.

'He's not happy, then,' I say. 'Even if he's out of the gang and with functional people . . . he's not happy.'

'Why not?'

I shrug. 'Some of us are screwed up. We sabotage our lives. We don't know why.'

He gets the milk out of the fridge. 'You're my people person,' he says, reaching a hand out to me tentatively. It brushes my stomach and I move away from him.

He's always called me that. His 'people person'. One of his many nicknames for me.

He turns his eyes to mine. There's a question in them. 'You alright?' he says. 'You sound sad. You're not a screw-up.'

'I am,' I say hoarsely.

He looks at me. 'You're holding your arm weirdly,' he says.

This is surely the moment. I have put it off and put it off. But now I have run out of excuses. My deadline is upon me and I have yet to begin. It is the story of my life.

He sits down at the kitchen counter, at the breakfast bar that divides our kitchen from the living room, but turns towards the television, sipping his coffee. He has the BBC News Channel on. He always does, even though it irritates him.

I open my mouth. In some ways, it would be so easy. They're just words.

My mouth stays open, like I am waiting for something. Waiting to feel ready. Waiting to be sure. I am never sure about anything. It is easier to do nothing. I glance at the window, out on to Edith's yard, and then back at Reuben. My gaze slides away from his and towards the television. Focusing in on it like a camera lens, I see the news bulletins. They flash up, narrated, and interspersed with music:

Surrey MP in expenses scandal

A passing doctor has delivered a baby born in central London's flagship Topshop store

How London is dealing with the growing migrant crisis

I turn towards Reuben as I hear the final headline. It's almost like I'm waiting for it. A bong, and then:

London canal-side attack

I know before I know. I know before they've said it. I know because of that bong, as though it is meant only for me. Unthinkingly, I grip the counter, scratching it with my nails.

The news has moved on, back to the first story. Some politician fiddling his expenses. I don't care about that, I don't care about that.

London canal-side attack. I repeat it, over and over, to myself.

My body contracts as though I'm in labour. I feel it right in my heart, moving down my arms and legs. I don't respond to Reuben about my hand.

He has turned back to the television. 'We're ruled by the corrupt and nobody even gives a shit,' he says, gesturing to the screen. 'How am I supposed to teach young kids to stop lying and cheating when the people who *run the country* do it? How hard is it to think "I'm not going to fiddle my expenses now I'm an MP"?'

It is one of the only topics he is verbal about; he is often sounding off at parties while people stare awkwardly into their glasses. The day Laura met him, she looked knowingly at me and said, 'There is nothing as sexy as a socialist.'

I usually sit there and think: *I am glad my husband is the moral one, the uppity one, the one who actually does practise what he preaches, and not the one who finds it awkward.* Like the time he said he thought women never lied about having been raped, and the room went silent. But now I don't think anything. I can't. I am hot and panicky, feeling as though Friday night's act is written across my forehead, that my thoughts have materialized right there in the living room in front of us. I have turned around and am staring at the television, waiting.

'Lying,' he continues. 'They call it these stupid names. Bespoke offences. No one calls it what it really is. It's not an *expenses scandal*. It's *lying*.'

I raise my eyes up to the ceiling. What is the universe telling me? Should I keep quiet because I have already told lies, or fess up to stop myself telling even more?

I sit numbly on the sofa.

I try to control the wild anxiety. It might not be about him. It might be somebody else. Yes. A stabbing. A shooting. It's London. So what if it's by a canal? How many canals are there in London – miles, isn't it? More than Venice – or is that Birmingham? I don't know. I don't know anything. Oh God. How am I supposed to get away with a crime?

Attack. It's so presumptuous. They don't know. They don't know how it was. He threatened a woman. She was frightened. She fled.

'I mean,' Reuben says, gesturing with his coffee. It sloshes on to the wooden floor, fawn-coloured liquid seeping between the cracks. 'Shit,' he says. He immediately puts the cup on the table and goes to find a cloth. 'I always thought power corrupts,' he says, as he's wiping up the stain.

The presenter cuts to the baby news story, interviewing people who saw the woman's waters break in Topshop. 'Not sure why she was shopping,' one of them says with a laugh.

I'm half aware that Reuben is wiping up beneath my feet, but my whole mind is turned towards the television, and that last news story.

'Don't know why we put up with this shite for news,' he says, standing up and reaching for the remote. 'So what if she was shopping?'

I go to stop him, then admonish myself. I can't do that. No – I can. I've got to tell him. 'Leave it on,' I say, my voice casual. I'll tell him when it comes on. I've got two minutes, max.

'Can't deal with this drivel.' He ignores me and flicks to a cooking channel.

Reuben does this every day. Puts the news on. Gets annoyed. Turns it off. He's not very good at listening to my preferences.

A man's preparing to skin a rabbit.

'Jesus,' I say, involuntarily. I inch my fingers towards the remote control, wanting to switch back. It gives me the perfect excuse to put the news back on. But, as I press, a thought chills me.

They know.

It's not on the news because they don't know, but because they *do*. Soon, a grainy image of me – on CCTV, maybe, or a photofit – is going to appear. I really have only got two minutes left. Two minutes here with this man, in Before.

I curse that I've spent my entire adult life scrolling in front of laptops and telephones and not paying attention to anything. Daydreaming. Thinking of career swaps I could do. Making up backstories for people. Not looking and listening and learning. Does it being on the television mean they know it's me? Or does it mean they definitely don't?

They're talking about the Calais migrant crisis. It goes on and on. I sit, rigid, like I am on a bench outside in the cold, not in my warm living room with my husband.

And then. And then. It is my headline's time. No, not mine. *Not mine.*

A man was discovered by the side of a canal in Little Venice in the early hours of Saturday morning.

It's as though I have been plunged into a vat of hot

acid. My whole body fizzes. I can't believe it. I just can't believe it. That this is happening. That this is my life. What have I done?

Caroline Harris, our correspondent, is at the scene.

They cut to her, right close up to her face.

'I am standing at the scene of a strange attack,' Caroline says, her voice clipped.

The camera pans out slightly, and I feel the contraction again. Just don't think about it, Joanna. Just ignore it.

But I can't ignore it. It's right there in front of me.

'A seventeen-year-old man was discovered at the edge of the canal at six o'clock this morning by a dog walker.'

I sigh with relief. It can't be me. Seventeen? Sadiq was not seventeen. There's no way.

And then the camera pans out further. And she's right where I was, just eighteen hours previously. There are the steps. They're no longer wet. They've dried out. The weather's clear, the sky a navy blue. The reporter's breath blooms in front of her, just like mine did. The police tape flickers in the breeze. It's blue and white. A yellow and white tent sits inside the cordoned-off area. What on earth is that? I think, looking curiously at the television.

'God,' Reuben says. 'Reckon it was that nutter?' He has a fantastic memory for details, and I silently curse it.

'What nutter?' I say, hoping to throw him off the track. To pretend me and my nutter were somewhere else.

'The one who followed you!'

Reuben is looking at me, an expression of disbelief, almost derision, on his face. 'You look mad,' he says in his blunt way.

I nod quickly, looking at the television. I can't speak.

It's like I've only got so much brain power, and it's all focused on one thing.

The woman is still speaking, the yellow and white tent – *tent?* – quivering in the wind.

I frown. Why was he only found at six o'clock? Was he drunker than I thought? He must have been freezing.

And then I replay the sentence in my mind. *Discovered.*

Goosebumps appear all over the back of my neck and on my shoulders. *No.* Please, no.

'It's always a dog walker,' Reuben says. 'Some scumbag's left them traumatized.'

Some scumbag. That's me.

He stands and goes into the kitchen, his empty coffee cup in his hand, and swills it out before putting it in the dishwasher.

'The man was taken to hospital at six o'clock where he was unable to be resuscitated. The police are treating his death as a murder enquiry.'

Before I know what I'm doing, I am sliding off the sofa and am face down in our rug. My left hand protests at the bent angle, but I don't care. I'm not crying. I'm doing something else. Something a wild animal might do. Keening. Rocking forward. My mouth open, but no sound coming out. The regret washes over me. I don't care. I don't care that Reuben is just over there, his back to me, pushing the dishwasher drawers into place – I'll have to tell him now anyway. The dishwasher must be full, because he puts it on: he is so good, and so good to me.

Died.

Died shortly after.

Killed.

Murder enquiry.

Just like that. A life snuffed out. A few moments before, he was alive; a mesh of thoughts and hopes and views on music and books and the housing market. And now. Nothing. The machine off.

Reuben is living with a murderer. If I tell him, he will march me straight to the police station. Asking him not to would be like asking him to write with the other hand. Like telling him to vote Tory. To rob a bank. To smack a child.

And that bloody MP work he's doing. How could he do that? Help his local MP out, while living with a known criminal? There's no answer, I think, getting up off the rug and sitting down on the sofa.

It's not even that. No, it's something else. It's because he would – privately, alone, so as not to upset me – quietly wonder at me. He loves me – in all my fecklessness, my messiness, my disorganization, my crap job – and this would give him pause. He'd never let on, but I know it would happen, like coming back into a hotel room and seeing it's been cleaned, the towels re-stacked, the toilet paper folded into a point. You wouldn't know unless you were looking for it. But I would know.

Reuben's standing in the kitchen, his back to me. He turns, looking thoughtful. 'There but for the . . .' he says. 'Imagine if you'd been a few hours later?'

I start to feel the same panic I felt in Little Venice. A pounding heart. My hands involuntarily making fists. A cold sweat over my back and shoulders. I wouldn't be surprised if, when cut open, I saw that my blood was black, congealing, or that I was full of cockroaches, or had an anvil, nestled weightily in amongst my organs.

How can I tell him now? Now that it's murder? It will ruin him. I will be the worst person he knows. An enemy.

And, in the back of my mind, right in the recesses, among the archives and the distant, half-formed memories, is something else. Seventeen. There is no way Sadiq was seventeen. And so . . . perhaps it was not Sadiq.

I can't let myself think it. It *was* him. I was being pursued.

And that is why I killed.

That has to be true. Anything else would ruin me.

I fall asleep on the sofa in the early evening. My mind must be exhausted, but napping isn't exactly unfamiliar to me: I spent my entire time at university taking illicit naps. My natural reaction is to switch off. To ignore. I sleep deeply, but dream of Sadiq.

Reuben wakes me with another coffee – he drinks so much of it, although it never seems to affect him – and walks out of the living room, probably going to his piano room to write up case notes. As he leaves, he says over his shoulder, 'I don't think I've ever known you to sleep talk.'

'What?' I say.

He laughs under his breath, as he walks down the hall, and says, 'You were talking absolute rubbish.'

I can't ask him. I can't press him. But what if it was something damning? I draw my knees up to my chest and hope that it wasn't.

I stare at the news, even though they've moved on from my story. I hear two sirens rush past, and jump both times, a layer of sweat materializing between my skin and my clothes. There are so many sirens in London.

I have never done anything alone in my life. I've led it by committee. Asking everybody's opinions on how to have my hair cut and where to rent in London. Facebook and Twitter were devices where I outsourced my decisions to others. And now: I'm alone.

I have almost finished the coffee when Reuben walks back in. 'You were apologizing, in your sleep,' he says, as if no time has passed at all.

'What for?' I say.

'Don't know.' He throws me a strange look. I must look guilty. 'You just kept saying *I'm sorry*. Over and over.'

I should laugh it off, but I can't. All I can think of is what I am sorry for.

Murder. I am sorry for murdering a man.

I meet Reuben's eyes again. He is looking at me slightly quizzically. The slightest of frowns crosses his features.

'Oh, right,' I say faintly. 'How strange.'

'Unlike you,' he says.

No.

Nobody must know. Not even Reuben. Especially not Reuben.

6

Reveal

I have been on my own for what feels like fifteen minutes. I've been given a cup of tea that tastes like cigarettes.

I wonder what the other people do in these cells. And then I see their sleeping forms in my mind, on those little screens in the custody suite. I look up, above the door, at the grimy ceiling – how did it become splattered with brown liquid so high up? – and I see it: the CCTV camera, white, like a robot, pointed down at me. I, too, will be on those screens. Being watched.

The hatch opens, and I jump.

'You've eaten, I presume?' a man says, and I shake my head.

'We were going to eat after,' I say.

Kebabs ;) Laura had WhatsApped me, when we were planning our night out.

'And you've been drinking.'

I can't answer him because he huffs as he slams the hatch, like I am an animal in a pen.

He appears again after a few moments. My body has begun to shiver and jerk. It was an accident, I want to tell him. I hear the hatch slide open and he peeks in.

'All-day breakfast,' he says.

He pushes a box through to me. If I wasn't there to

catch it, it would've dropped on the floor. It's in a white plastic tray that's steaming. It hurts my hands and I carry it by its rim over to the mattress. There's no table.

He leaves again, and I remember a few weekends ago when I tried to make sweetcorn fritters. They came out like chicken feet, Reuben said.

Even through the heavy door, I can hear somebody say, 'We've got a probable section eighteen in there. Worse if . . .'

A section eighteen? I wonder what that is. Maybe it's police speak for somebody who is incorrectly detained; who will be released just as soon as her solicitor arrives.

Hypothesizing makes me uncomfortable, and I automatically reach for a mobile phone I no longer have, am no longer allowed to look at freely. It has been years since I have sat with nothing to do. I can't even imagine eating my dinner without some device playing in front of me.

There's no clock, and no sun, and so I eat, and I look at the items in the room – the *cell* – with me. The circular fluorescent light. The inside of it is lined with dead flies. The black arrow. It's painted so neatly; somebody must have used a stencil.

The food is awful. It's as if somebody has blended an all-day breakfast into a liquid, then cooked the whole lot. Marbled through the eggs and bread are occasional chunks of bacon. It's cold in the very middle. The eggs feel like jelly in my mouth.

As I finish, lacking anything to do and having run out of thoughts, I reach my hand out in front of me and trace a finger down the blue wall. It's cool. The cheap paint bobbles underneath my fingertip.

The eggs catch in my throat as I start to cry. I'm crying for lots of things. At my unluckiness, I suppose. At where I find myself, aged thirty. But mostly for Reuben. Because I miss him. Because I know he'll be missing me. But also because of that judgement. That beat of judgement I heard the second after I told him. I didn't imagine it. I know I didn't.

When Reuben and I first met, he was standing at the edge of an end-of-university party, observing coolly, not speaking to anybody. At first, it was his height that caught my attention, but by the time I was uncapping a bottle of Jack Daniel's, it was other things, too. The way he wasn't talking to anybody. The way he was simply standing at the bookcase in the bay window, running his finger along it.

'I'm Jo,' I said boldly.

After a few minutes' chat, he inclined his head, led me to the stairs perfunctorily. They were quiet – he preferred them, he said. I liked that he wanted to sit on the stairs and talk about books with a girl he'd only just met. I liked that he didn't give a shit what anybody else thought of him, that he'd been obviously bored beforehand. A man called Rupert walked past us, talking about where he was going to be *summering*, and Reuben and I, as naturally as our hearts were beating, exchanged a glance.

'I hate Oxford,' I said, and his green eyes lit up.

We slagged off Oxford on the stairs. I made him talk, he kept saying in surprise. He hated talking, but he liked talking to me. Only me.

I saw him the next day. We'd been texting all morning and, when I rounded the corner to him, he nodded, a half-smile on his face, like he was remembering something enjoyable, but he said nothing.

'Duty solicitor,' a male police officer says now.

He jerks me from my memories. It can't have been more than an hour since I requested one. I hope he's good. Diligent.

I'm taken to the same phone I called Reuben from, the handset dangling like a noose. I thought it would be nice to be out in reception, but it's not.

My knees shake as I pick up the phone.

'Joanna?' my solicitor says.

I'm momentarily surprised it's a woman. How awful of me. 'Yes. Hi.' My voice is hoarse.

'Hi. I'm Sarah Abberley. Don't say anything, please,' she says crisply, her voice clipped. 'The police are very likely listening.'

'I just need to explain myself,' I say desperately, my voice hushed, into the phone. The receiver is sticky against my chin. 'Clear it all up.'

'Don't say another word to the police. No doubt you've said some things. They'll be standing there drinking their tea, but listening . . .'

I look over at them. They're just sitting at the desk, mindlessly watching the CCTV monitors. 'Um, okay,' I say, sceptical.

'I'm afraid I am serious, Joanna.'

'When will you be here?'

'Soon – they have to . . .' I hear a tapping sound.

I picture her in a slimline suit, cigarette trousers. Geek glasses. Dip-dyed hair. Tapping a pen against a minimalist kitchen counter. A man behind her – tall, a wiry-looking academic, maybe – making avocado smash. They eat late, most nights.

'They have to just get the CID sorted,' she is saying.

'CID?' I say absent-mindedly.

'Criminal Investigations Department. And you can't be interviewed until you're sober.'

'I am *very* sober,' I say.

'Best wait until the morning. Be there as soon as I can,' she says.

I like her brevity. Reuben would like her.

'You have twenty-four hours – anything more than that and they need the superintendent to sign it off. Do you have everything you need – are they feeding you?' she says.

'Okay. Yes,' I say, my voice small, imagining all night in that horrible blue room.

'You won't know it,' she says, 'but I am doing all I can for you. Here. Promise.'

'Okay,' I say. It is almost the only word I have said during our call. She must think me an idiot.

She rings off. The receiver feels heavy in my hand without her on the other end of it. I put the phone down, then stand aimlessly for a second, hanging on to the mild freedom. The different smells out here.

Sergeant Morris arrives again and I consider what the solicitor has said: they were listening. I shiver in the foyer, glancing at her. Not my ally. An enemy.

I am led back to cell thirteen. Soon, the police will go home to their families, and I'll be here alone. Others will take over. Sergeant Morris will go home to her husband who'll complain about her hours while he stirs baked beans, cooking on the hob. Her pyjama-clad children will already be in bed.

I tilt my head back and look at the Mecca arrow. Anything could have happened outside – a world event, a death – and I would not know.

I sit still for a while and engage in one of my favourite games: imagining my future babies. Perhaps they might inherit Wilf's long nose. I play with one baby, in my mind's eye. She has Reuben's ginger hair but my imagination. We're playing with a glockenspiel together. Oh, why have we waited this long? I am ready now, Reuben, I think.

I am checked every half an hour. I can tell by counting. It's useful to know how much time is passing.

They shout at me through the hatch, their hands closing it before they've finished properly looking. It's perfunctory. They call my name and then, when I look up, they leave.

I wish they would just open the door and I could glimpse the outside; look at a new light or furnishing, or even the flight of stairs I ascended a few hours previously, unknowingly walking to my confinement.

At what must be two thirty in the morning, I ask why they keep checking. An embarrassing hangover is beginning to set in. A sensitivity to the light as the hatch is drawn back. A tightness across my head. A dry mouth. Shaking hands. 'Why won't you let me sleep?' I say, sounding pathetic.

'You were inebriated, so you're a category-two check,' the woman says. She's new to me, but no less brusque than Sergeant Morris.

'Category two?' I say.

'One: keep an eye on, routine only. Two: check every half an hour. Three: constant watch. You're in the drunk cell. Mattress on the floor instead of a raised bed.'

'Wow,' I say, craving a chat, some reassurance, a kind word, but she closes the hatch. I call out, involuntarily. 'Has my husband been?' I say, and the hatch is drawn back, just an inch. I see an eye, the side of her mouth. It's not smiling. She clicks the hatch shut, and that's that.

Something must have happened, once, for them to check people like that. I reach my hand out and touch the wall again, next to my head. Perhaps it was in this cell. The person they didn't check.

I tidy up my three belongings. I straighten the pillow. Make sure the mattress is right up against the wall. Put the empty meal box in the corner of the room, next to the toilet.

I will look back on this and smile, I think to myself. It will be added to the list of feckless things I have done, which my family and occasionally Reuben roll their eyes at. *Remember the night you left the bath running and flooded the flat?* Reuben will say, tipping his head back and laughing. And I will say, *I think I topped that by going to jail for the night.*

I lie on my side, waiting for the three o'clock check. I imagine him next to me, his long arms drawn right across my body and around my shoulders in an X-shape. I look at the wall and wonder if he's doing the same at home.

When a new police officer brings me some more water, through the hatch, I ask him about visitors.

'When can I see anybody?' I say. 'Do you have visiting hours?'

'This isn't a hospital,' he says.

He's older, with white hair and a pink complexion. I can't see anything else: his mannerisms, his height. It's a strange, contextless interaction.

'I thought it was like a prison,' I say, swallowing hard. I can feel myself sitting forward, eager, like a dog waiting for its owner to return. *Please don't close the hatch. Please don't leave me here.*

'Get real.'

7

Conceal

I stand idly on the scales. Then get off, and then step on to them again. Nine stone two. I was always, always nine stone seven.

I pull my pyjamas on, and I see that they are loose. I must start eating.

We have just climbed into bed when my phone goes off.

'You haven't read in months,' Reuben says, pointedly looking at my phone.

I sleep better and read more books when I charge it in another room, but for every time I learn this lesson, I forget it again, sneaking it back into the bedroom, scrolling and scrolling for hours until my eyelids are slowly closing. I can't deal with any of that tonight. Personal improvement goes out of the window when you're dealing with something like this.

Reuben shifts in bed next to me, sliding a foot to cover mine. His feet are always icy cold. I call them dead man's feet. The thought now makes me wince. I wonder if Sadiq is . . . no. I stop myself there. I can't think about him, though images flash through my mind. His feet. Trainer-less, now, in a morgue. Bloodless and cold.

The message on my phone is from Laura. I am holding it with both hands – my left hand is working better, but it still aches. Laura's WhatsApp avatar is a close-up selfie. Her hair styled upwards, in an almost-Mohican. She's grinning at me through the phone's screen, her eyes squinting attractively into the sun.

Heh — a non-uniformed police officer (not sexy; really weird) just came to my door asking me about Friday. WTF?

She's sent a string of emojis, ending with a man in police uniform, and I blink at the phone, my heart beating in my ears.

She sends a photograph, after that. It's a new painting she's done. She often sends them over to me for my opinion before they're finished. It's a photographic-quality portrait of a woman with armpit hair. For the first time, I ignore her art.

What do you mean? What about Friday? I send back.

One grey tick. Sending.

Two grey ticks. Delivered.

Two blue ticks. Read.

I fight the urge to delete myself from WhatsApp, Facebook, everything. To disappear.

Reuben shifts next to me. Our mattress is cheap, the bed an IKEA double. It feels small, and I bob like I'm at sea as he moves. He's reading something highbrow. One of the classics. There are too many great books in the world to read shit, he will say, and I will feel guilty when I sneak a romcom into the bath.

Instinctively, I hold my phone away from him. A sharp pain radiates up from my wrist.

The police are coming. No doubt. Surely, I have to tell him. To pave the way for the lies I will soon tell.

'Look at this,' I say, surprised by how shocked my voice sounds.

I would never have said I was an actor, but perhaps I am. I was always changing. Reuben's the only person I've ever been myself with. I'm a free spirit with Laura. A naughty younger sister with Wilf. My opinions become those of the people I'm with, as if the fabric those people are made of rubs off on to me. And, underneath it all, who am I? Who is Joanna? I am opinion-less, formless, smoke.

But here I am, forced into a starring role I never asked for.

'Not up for chatting,' Reuben says.

And, despite myself, I smile. People think he is gentle, shy, but there it is: that steely core. There is nothing people-pleasing about Reuben. It is one of the very first things that attracted me to him. His autonomy. That he can say to me: *no thanks*, and not mean it offensively. It makes it all the better when he asks to join me in the bath, or sits up all night chatting with me, like we did just a few weeks previously, playing old indie songs we loved. Because I know he truly wants to.

'No, look.' I hand him my phone.

And then, after a second – he is an exceptionally fast reader – he drops it on the duvet, face down, still lit up, so it tinges the edges of the quilt a bright, lit-up white.

'What about Friday?' he says.

'No idea.'

He rolls over, away from me, withdrawing his cold foot. 'That bloke,' he says sleepily.

'Oh, yes. Must be that,' I say. 'The follower.'

'No. The one from the news. You should tell them. That something suspicious happened to you.'

I close my eyes. How wrong he is. But how could he know?

'Maybe,' I manage to say, feeling the blood moving around my head. It thunders past my forehead. I have to tell the police. I have to approach them. But how could I?

I need to let Reuben think I have.

He rolls over fully now, right on to his side. And he doesn't ask. He doesn't ask me whether I saw anything. Whether I know anything. He believes me, implicitly.

I lie awake, fizzing, watching the top of the WhatsApp screen that says: *typing*.

Laura replies.

So he arrives and says there's a man found by the edge of the canal, believed that he hit his head and died that night (on the news? IDK). He says he saw from the CCTV that I walked nearby – did I see anything? How bizarre?

CCTV. CCTV. CCTV.

I bet it's everywhere. CCTV. I have never thought about it. Perhaps they cover the entirety of London. Maybe it is a matter of time, for me. Perhaps they're producing a photofit as we speak. Perhaps, as I was dithering, I turned and looked right at a camera. Staring into its eye, unknowingly. They will be here at any moment.

Was it accusatory? I type.

And then I delete that. I am unconsciously preparing my own evidence.

How strange, I type instead. *I'll let you know if they come calling here . . . shame he's weird and not hot.*

The banter comes easily to me. The lies.

I put my phone on the bedside table and make a list of

evidence in my mind, the light off. I am ostensibly sleeping, and Reuben's breathing becomes even.

I try to reason with myself. CCTV might not have found me. And I can't do anything about it. What could I do – sneak into buildings and wipe it? I almost laugh. I wouldn't even know how. And I don't want to. I don't want to get away with it. I want it to never have happened.

What else? I try to think. A hair at the scene. My hair is forever falling out, clogging drains and brushes. But – would they know it's mine? My mind isn't clear. No. Not unless they suspect me, and test me. They wouldn't know. I don't think.

What else?

No fingerprints. But fibres from my glove on his chest.

The tread of my heels. Was there mud, or just concrete? I can't remember. It stacks up against me, the evidence. There is no point trying to stop it. They are coming. I lie, rigid, listening for sirens, for the knock at the door.

The anxiety seems to bloom across my body, as if an elephant has taken up residence on my chest. It shifts around as I think, harder and harder, about what I've done. I've ruined my life, and ended another's, with that push. That reckless push. I will surely never be the same again. I've killed a man. It feels so abstract to me, here in my bedroom.

The right time is now, isn't it? Before they find me, and after I realize that it's over for me. That there is too much evidence. That I am too unskilled to pull it off. That the stakes – *murder* – are too bloody high.

I sigh, trying to shift the elephant, and I roll on to my side. Instinctively, Reuben reaches out for me, scooping me up and pulling me close to him. The duvet's too hot and his arm's too heavy. I can't take it, and so I shift away from him. He makes a disgruntled, disappointed noise; a sort of *ohh*. But I ignore him.

And then it is morning and Reuben is cooking downstairs like everything is normal. But in the bedroom, I am a prisoner, inside myself.

I can't believe I've gone back to work, but I have, and I've managed a day.

Ed often drops me home, then takes the bus back to the garage to fill it up with petrol and park it, safely under cover, for the night. That's how it works. He is nice like that.

I used to find the library bus comforting, being surrounded by the pages and pages of other people's thoughts: whatever you're going through, I would think, somebody has been there before you. I don't think that today.

I have gone to tell Ed three times today, during our proximity together on the bus. He has always brought out a confessional quality in me, like a priest. He would be less judgemental than Reuben – of course – but he has almost too much perspective sometimes. If we're not in war-torn Syria, if we have a roof over our heads, there can be no problems in his world.

We met six years ago, when he hired me. He never asked once about Oxford, and never has since, even though I mention it often. It's one of the things I like most about him. He observes me dispassionately. He brings me in a cake on most Mondays – he bakes on Sunday night, to stave off the pre-work feelings, he says. We eat it and peruse the new books that have come in. I have become used to always having a copy of the latest best-seller, for free. A few years ago, that would have been all I wanted from a job.

We pull up outside my flat. It's in darkness. Reuben's at his youth club's Monday meeting.

Ed has left the engine running, is waiting for me to collect my bag and go. It's just after five thirty, and pitch black outside.

'You have guests,' he says mildly, gesturing with a liver-spotted hand to my door. His glasses glint as he turns to look at me.

And that's when I see them. Two figures at my door. I can only see the tops of their heads, one dark, one blond, lit up by the street lamp above them. They're at the bottom of the stairs to our basement flat, their legs disappearing into the shadows. It's the police. It must be.

I wonder how they have walked down past all the plants I bought recently on a whim.

And then the panic sets in.

The sweating is back. The late-night animal is sitting heavily on my chest again.

I can't make Ed drive me back now. I can't raise his suspicions. I try to think of a story, a reason to go back, but my mouth is parched, the well of lies dried out.

'Oh, I know what that is,' I gabble.

'The pigs,' Ed says mildly. He looks at me, his eyes moon-like in the darkness.

'The what?'

'Police,' he says, gesturing down at the men.

They're not moving.

'How do you know that?' I say.

'Oh, two blokes. A Vauxhall Insignia. A second rear-view mirror. Pretty obvious,' he says.

His voice is toneless, no judgement, no suspicion – and no derision that I didn't know myself. That's Ed's way. Once again, I am struck by how much the people in my life trust me.

'You're expecting them?' he adds, looking closely at me.

I realize I have already shown my hand, already said I knew who they were. I try to think of benign offences, but my mind is blank.

'Three,' I spit out, after an embarrassing silence. 'Three burglaries in two weeks on our street. Must've been another.'

'Oh, Jo,' Ed says, his eyes full of compassion. 'How scary for you, in the basement.'

My eyes fill with tears at how much he cares about me.

I grab the door handle with my good hand and leave without saying goodbye, walking towards our flat. I can't speak to them. I must hide.

I hear Ed pull away, the engine fading as he disappears down the road, leaving me alone, trusting that I am not trying to dodge the police who wish to speak to me, that I am not – whether I intended to be or not – *on the run*. How slippery that slope really is.

I don't want to walk past them, and Ed dropped me almost at my door, so I have no choice but to ascend the steps two doors down from mine, not looking at the police, looking only straight ahead. I don't press a buzzer. I don't try the door. I merely stand in the alcove, hoping I am in complete darkness, an anonymous figure the police don't want to speak to. I can hear them murmuring, two doors along, beneath me at my basement door, but can't make out their words.

My back is flat against the blue door, and my heart is thudding heavily in my chest. I close my eyes and pray for them to leave. To give up. That nobody comes out of this door, expresses surprise, calls me by my name. I stand there in silence, hoping I haven't been seen, and wait.

It is ten minutes before they leave.

It is a further five before I come out, my knees trembling. They have left me a note. Please call them, it says.

8

Reveal

The solicitor arrives at nine o'clock in the morning. Sergeant Morris is back – I don't understand her shift patterns – and she comes to get me from my cell. I leave my cell in my prison-issue wear and meet the solicitor in a large interviewing room.

I am hung-over. I have had half-hourly wakings for seven hours. The one time I didn't acknowledge my name being called, the police officer came into my cell and shook me awake. Every time I fell asleep it was time for the next one.

Sarah is not how I imagined her, but she's not far off either. Long, dark fluffy hair. Tall and willowy; perhaps as tall as Reuben. There is an air of chicness about her. Red lipstick to start the day. Crooked teeth, but very white.

'Joanna – the duty solicitor, Sarah Abberley. Sarah – Joanna.' Morris turns and leaves without another word.

'So,' Sarah says, once we're alone.

I like that proactive *so*. She explains the caution to me. She breaks down all of the words, even though I know what they mean.

'You've been assigned to the CID, who are for serious crimes,' she adds, when she's finished.

'I just . . . what's happening? It was just a push.'

She looks up at me sharply. Her eyes are blue, and incisive, like a hawk's. They move quickly, darting around, taking in my clothes, my shoes, my shaking hands.

She gets out a pen and a branded notepad from her law firm.

She is looking down at the pad, taking down my name, the date and the time, but then she raises her eyebrows to me. They're plucked but not overly so. Smooth, angular dark lines.

'What happened?' she says simply.

I start from the beginning.

Sarah writes notes occasionally, but she mostly just sits, looking at me. Nodding and mmm-ing.

I tell her everything.

Except one thing.

It's not even a lie. Not really. Simply an omission.

I don't tell her of my pause. My tiny pause as the man in the street lay in that puddle. I can't tell her; don't want her to know that I dithered. That, in another life, I might've fled. I tell her I got him out of the puddle immediately.

When I've finished, she says, 'Look, they won't give me any disclosure. So you need to give a no comment interview.'

'No comment? Why would I do that? I have lots of comments,' I say. 'I want to explain.'

'I know. You have a strong defence. But they are being obstructive. They won't tell me anything. What you said at the scene. The position the victim was in. His injuries. If they have witnesses.'

'I . . . he was at the bottom of the stairs. I said I pushed him –'

'My advice is to give a no comment interview,' she says, her voice razor-sharp, cutting me into ribbons.

Embarrassed, chastened, by her tone, I look around the room. There's cladding on the walls. Grey-green, the colour of a dirty pond. It's spongy, and makes the room look smaller. Soundproofing, maybe. There's a gap in the cladding, like a dado rail, only it's white plastic, with a red strip running around it. I extend my fingers towards it.

'Don't,' Sarah says, reaching a slim arm out to stop me. 'It's a panic alarm. You'll send a load of police in here. The last thing you want.'

'Okay. I'll give the no comment interview,' I say after a moment's thought.

'Good. Now, Joanna. I think they will be talking about causing grievous bodily harm with intent.'

'What's causing grievous bodily harm with intent?'

'It's very serious.'

She passes me a sheet of paper, an Internet printout. It has *Offences Against the Person Act 1861* written across the top.

Offences Against the Person. 'Sorry,' I say. 'I'm still not really understanding.'

'Okay,' she says, grabbing a blank sheet of paper and a pen. On a page she writes *murder,* followed by *attempted murder, manslaughter, s18 (GBH with intent), s20 (GBH), common assault.* 'These are in descending order of seriousness,' she says. 'Killing, trying to kill, killing with reason or excuse.' She points to the words as she runs down the list.

'But I didn't kill anyone.'

'Section eighteen is causing grievous bodily harm with intent. Section twenty – causing grievous bodily harm. GBH.'

'Right.'

'Lastly – common assault.' She taps her pen against the sheet of paper.

I wonder dimly if she loved law school; if she always wanted to be a lawyer. If the bureaucratic justice system disappoints her. I'd never thought of being a lawyer. But perhaps I should have. I would like to do what she does. Turn up on weekends and save the day in a pinstriped suit.

'Causing grievous bodily harm with intent. Just below attempted murder,' I say, tracing a finger over the words. She's pressed hard with the ballpoint pen, and the letters feel three-dimensional, the paper curling underneath them. 'I didn't have any intent,' I say.

'You pushed a man.' She says it kindly.

'But . . .' I say. 'He was . . . Sadiq was . . .'

'I know. And we're going to run that. We'll say it was self-defence, but back it up with another legal doctrine. Called *mistake*. It says if you believed the mistake you made – genuinely – then the court will treat you as if it were true.'

'Good,' I say.

Causing grievous bodily harm with *intent*. What intent? Am I a monster? I wish there was a mirror in the interview room that I could look into and inspect myself. To see if I have changed. I haven't seen myself since Friday evening.

She pushes her hair back. It's flyaway, fine, like mine, and it falls forward again, like grass swaying in a spring breeze.

'Okay, Joanna,' she says, leaning forward. Her foot

squeaks against the linoleum underneath us. 'Let's talk worst-case scenarios.'

She's levelling with me. Making the mistake that – because I am well spoken and intelligent looking – I am not a mess: a fuck-up. That I deserve to be levelled with.

'No, I . . .' I say. 'I don't want to know. I don't like worst-case scenarios.'

I don't add that I prefer to bury my head in the sand, that I have lost jobs and failed exams and simply not turned up to things when it mattered. That I have quit things that just seemed to be – somehow – too hard to continue with.

She sits back now, looking at me with those bird-like eyes. 'No?' she says. 'I would want to know.'

'No.'

'What do you do for a living?'

'I work in a library,' I say. 'A mobile library.'

Already, that life – my job – feels like another universe. The regulars who I would nickname. Quiet, calm Buddhist Ed, the librarian and my manager. The children I help to discover reading; a world of complete magic. I love lots of things about the job. I love sitting in the sun under the skylight on quiet days. I love recommending my recent favourite thriller to people. I love meeting everybody: babies, elderly people. Lonely people.

Sarah nods. 'There are some things in your favour, anyway,' she says to me. 'Some good news.'

'Yes?' I say.

'You stayed and called 999. You did CPR. The court like all this stuff.'

'Yes,' I say, not telling her how close I came to walking

away entirely. How easy it would have been. How much I regret it. 'Is it very serious?' I say after a pause, wanting her reassurance.

But, just like her steel-grey bag and her stern red lipstick, she doesn't hold back. 'Yes,' she murmurs. 'I'm afraid so.'

I look down at her papers, avoiding her eyes. She keeps staring at me. Not intensely. Just thoughtfully. Impassively. My eyes run over her notes, and I avert them after a second, in shock.

I look at the wall, at the door, down at my hands. Anything to stop my brain from processing what I've seen, like a partner in denial about a text spotted on their other half's mobile phone.

But I can't forget it.

I can't un-see it.

A printout from the Internet. The CPS Sentencing Guidelines. *Three years* was written at one end of an arrow.

And at the other, there was simply one word.

Life.

9

Conceal

Reuben's made a fry-up. The smell turns my stomach. I am now nine stone.

'Alright,' he says as I walk, ghost-like, into the kitchen. My pyjamas are damp from sweating all night. I have made lists in my mind, lists that I am too afraid to commit to paper for fear of creating evidence.

Tread marks. Hairs. Glove fibres. CCTV.

Reuben kisses me on the top of my head. Unconsciously, I duck away from him, jerking my head away as though I am infectious, poisonous, and he might catch it from me. And isn't that true? I can't believe we were on the verge of making a baby together.

He looks at me in surprise. I have never done anything like that – have always been the needy one, the clingy one; childlike in my need for cuddles.

'Made you eggs,' he says, instead of asking me what's wrong.

I don't reply for a second. He hates eggs. He never cooks them. 'Tuesday morning cheer-up eggs.'

I can feel tears waiting in the wings, but they won't come. I am too frightened to cry. I can't bring myself to say anything, either. I have become almost mute with guilt.

'Really,' I say eventually. My voice is hoarse.

He knows I need cheering up. What else has he noticed?

'Look,' he says, flopping a fried egg out of the pan. I nod, once. He's still staring at me, but I ignore him and silently take the plate to the breakfast bar.

I push the egg and beans around my plate. They leave orange smears that start to congeal.

Reuben's silent, too. He's hurt, I can tell. He would never say so, would never be so petty as to pick an argument over *eggs*, but I can tell.

'I can't eat this,' I say. I can't force it down my dry throat.

I stand and scrape my egg into the bin. Right there, on top of the other rubbish in the bin, is another floppy white disc. Another egg, already in the bin, slightly blackened underneath. He must have burnt the first one. Made me a second.

Sky News is on a silent loop in the background as I dress. I try to use both hands, but my left is still useless; stiff, now, more than painful. We have a TV in our bedroom. Reuben resisted it, at first, said it was dysfunctional, but I like to watch *Don't Tell the Bride* and scroll through Instagram on my iPhone before bed. I loved that time.

My top hangs off me. I can see my ribs, just below my collarbones.

I avert my eyes from my changing body and reach for my mascara. I have to leave in half an hour, and all I am thinking is that I shouldn't be putting make-up on. Maybe if I hadn't worn mascara, hadn't worn those shoes ... maybe Sadiq would have left me alone. Maybe he'd have approached Laura instead. Or somebody else entirely. Maybe I looked *up for it*.

And then he wouldn't have followed me.

And then it wouldn't have happened.

And now I wouldn't be hiding.

Just as I apply the last stroke of mascara, the news bulletin changes again.

'The body of a man left for dead by the side of the canal has been identified by his sister. It is that of Imran Quarashi.'

I am staring at the television. Waiting.

A photo pops up. *Imran* in a field in the summer. They zoom in, cropping out a woman. He's smiling. Happy.

I can no longer ignore it. No longer deny it. I killed the wrong man.

'He was found, face down, in a shallow puddle in the early hours of Saturday morning. It has now been confirmed that he died from a lack of oxygen reaching his brain during this time and catastrophic head injuries sustained from a fall. He had been out jogging.'

It feels as though my body's not mine any more. My hand holding the mascara wand. My feet nestled in the carpet. They do not belong to me.

It could have been prevented. That's the worst thing. I keep thinking that something is the worst, and then finding something else, like a layered onion with a rotting core.

They cut to a video of a woman standing nervously outside a white building. I can't make out where it is.

'Now we're speaking to Imran's sister, Ayesha,' the news presenter says.

'We're so sorry about Imran,' another presenter says.

There they are. The people I have tried to avoid.

'I am – *was* – his sister,' the woman says carefully. She's beautiful; petite, with huge eyes, a turned-down, full mouth. She has a mole, right in the middle of her cheek. A beauty mark. 'Our parents are back in Pakistan. It was – it was just us.'

I can't stop looking. At this woman whose life I have ruined. If only . . . if only I could reach out into the television and touch her. Tell her how it was. My cataclysmic mistake.

Imagine if I had handed myself in. Dragged him out of the puddle. Explained myself. They might've let me go. Surely they would have, once they'd seen that I was good. But I am not good and he is dead and I have no choices left: I have run out of them.

I finish applying the mascara, mechanically, like a robot.

Outside, sleet flurries swirl around an illuminated halo of a street lamp. It's still dark. Edith has put fairy lights up. She does it every year. Reuben says it's tacky, but I like it. She puts them around the Hammersmith and Fulham Council parking meters and along the steps leading to the front doors. I can hardly believe the world is continuing.

I wonder how many other near misses I have had. How many times have we laughingly crossed the street and not seen a car speed past moments later?

Reuben comes into the bedroom, his keys in his hand. 'Be back late,' he says. 'Got a thing.'

He is always mysterious about his work; will hardly ever tell me exactly what he's doing.

'Okay,' I say woodenly, but my voice catches.

He stops, his hand on the door, and looks at me. 'You alright?' he says softly. 'You seem kind of . . . down.'

'Yes,' I say, thinking, *Don't come near me. Don't reach out to me. I'll tell you if you do.* I nod quickly, looking off to the left, not meeting his eyes.

'Hey,' he says, dropping his keys on the bed and coming close to me. In a single movement, one we have practised again and again, he wraps me up in his arms. My head slots neatly into the place between his shoulder and his neck. His hands come around my shoulders. 'Jojo,' he says.

It wasn't Sadiq. That is all I can think about while the man I love holds me close to him.

I have killed without reason. It was bad enough before, but it is worse now. Somebody innocent has died at my hands.

'What's up?' Reuben says.

Perhaps I could . . . perhaps he would help me. Stand by me. Make it better. My confession looms tantalizingly in front of me.

I lean back and look into his eyes for what feels like the first time since Before. 'Nothing,' I say glumly.

'Tell me your worries,' he says; a sentence he's uttered many times before.

I keep staring at him, and he raises his eyebrows, just a fraction, like somebody encouraging a frightened, unsure toddler to take its first steps. He raises them further, then gives me a tiny smile, a smile just for me, and it is as though my chest is expanding and letting all the good feelings in again: hope and optimism and forgiveness and love.

'Something happened on Friday,' I say slowly, wondering what I'm going to say, unable to stop thinking about the intoxicating relief of telling him.

He steps back, but runs his hands down my arms, as if warming me up, then takes my hands in his. 'What?' he says. 'With the man?'

I nod. I'll start at the beginning. I'll tell him – properly – about the bar. And then . . . and then I'll see.

'Yes. Sort of,' I say, taking a deep breath. It wouldn't be just mine any more. It would be our secret. Shared. He would help me. 'I did something bad.'

There. It is out there. My confession. My half-confession.

'What?' Reuben says gently. 'It's okay.'

'He had . . . he'd grabbed me. In the bar. I felt his . . .' I'm surprised when the tears come. This isn't about that. And yet – isn't it, all the same? 'He grabbed my bum,' I say. 'It was really full on. Worse than I made it out to be. I was very scared.'

'Shit,' Reuben says. 'I'm so sorry, Jo. You should've said.'

'I know, but – but *after* that –'

'Yes?' he says. And then, because he works with youths, and always knows the right things to say, he looks me directly in the eyes and says, 'It wasn't your fault. You did nothing wrong. It's never okay to do what he did. To grab you and to follow you.'

I nod again, but now the moment is over. I can't tell him.

It *was* my fault.

It was *all* my fault.

We break apart soon after that.

10

Reveal

'Interview tape is running,' Detective Inspector Lawson says. 'Video on.' He cautions me again.

I can see myself reflected in the lens of the video camera.

'Can you please state your name for the record?' Lawson says.

I lean forward. 'No comment,' I say.

It's what Sarah told me to do; it's what we decided I would do. To buy us time to build a defence. So that I wouldn't incriminate myself. It was for the best, she said, until we knew what we were up against.

'And please can you state your date of birth for the record?' the other detective, Detective Sergeant Davies, asks.

'No comment.'

'And can you give us your address, please – otherwise we won't be able to process this interview at all.'

I dart a look at Sarah. She's looking intently at me, and then the police officers, and then me again. She nods her head, just once.

'No comment.'

'What happened that night, Joanna?'

'No comment.'

'If you explain, we might be able to end things here.

We'll release you. You can get some sleep. If you cooperate, Joanna, things will be much easier for you.'

'I . . .'

The CID both sit back, together – they are like one unit, with the same body language and expressions, one a paler, taller version of the other.

'No comment,' I say, feeling like a clown in the middle of a serious meeting.

'Let's just cooperate, Joanna. I take it your silence means you're thinking about it? Pleading guilty?'

'*No*,' I say.

'The victim's name is Imran Quarashi.'

'Imran,' I say. Who is he? What does he like? Where is he now? Will he get better? I can't ask these questions, of course.

Sarah shoots me a look. *Do not say anything except no comment*, she counselled me. I've failed already. I smile apologetically at her, but she ignores me.

'How did you injure Imran, Joanna?'

'No comment.'

'You pushed him pretty hard, didn't you?'

'No comment.'

'And he was in the water, wasn't he? Do you know he's on a ventilator?'

That's the question that does it. I can't handle it. I can't let this go on. These useless no comments. These accusations. It's the truthful accusation that hurts the most.

And so I tell the lie. The same lie again.

'I got him out of the puddle straight away,' I say. It doesn't really feel like a lie as the words come out. They rasp from the back to the front of my mouth, feeling urgent and correct and true.

Sarah's eyebrows shoot up, and she reaches a hand out, as though I'm a volatile dog about to bolt. 'A moment,' she says, rising.

We go into a side room on our own.

'Not a word,' she says.

'But –'

'I know,' she says, and her eyes are flashing. The whites are clean and pure looking, and I wonder if she self-medicates with eye-brightening drops, late at night, at her desk – like they might do in *Suits* or *Law and Order* – and she looks so angry that I can't bring myself to tell her. To tell her that I have lied.

It's okay, I am thinking. Nobody will ever know. Nobody knows. Perhaps I can mould time – the sequences of events, the pauses, as the man lay there – like they are plasticine.

We have to go back into the interview room. Sarah leads.

'My client was not made aware of the extent of the victim's injuries,' she says.

I sit back down in the hard plastic chair, which is warm with my own anxiety, and close my eyes. I have no idea what any of it means. I try to block out the two doors, opening one after the other, even though they're only a centimetre apart, and the panic strip and the soundproofing and the tape recorder and the video and the threadbare carpet and the policemen, and I hope – just hope – that if I think hard enough I will be able – just this once; oh, please, just this once – to go back.

I've been back in my cell for an hour when Sergeant Morris comes to collect me. 'Out,' she says to me through the hatch.

Sarah and the two CID officers are waiting in a new room. She still looks immaculate. If things were different, I'd ask her what she uses and how she applies it. Perhaps she uses a heat-protecting spray.

It simply says *Private Room* on the front of the door, just off the custody suite. Three polystyrene cups are littered around, teabags clumped stickily in the bottoms of them.

Sarah looks up at me, and I think I see a hint of an apology in her eyes.

'Joanna Oliva,' the blond CID officer says.

'No comment,' I say, and I see a ghost of a smile on Sarah's face.

'You do not have to say anything,' the blond man says, 'but it may harm your defence if you do not mention, when questioned, something you later rely on in court. Anything you do say will be given in evidence.'

I turn to look at Sarah again, confused.

'You are charged that on 4th December you did cause wounding or did inflict grievous bodily harm with intent on Imran Quarashi, contrary to section eighteen of the Offences Against the Person Act eighteen sixty-one.'

In my mind's eye, I see Reuben's eyes widening in shock. I don't know why I always imagine his reaction, and not my own.

I drag myself back to now.

Charged. I'm charged. There's to be a trial.

I will be cross-examined by barristers in wigs, intending to catch me out. I'll stand in the dock of the Crown Court while a jury sits and judges me. Will this be on my record forever? I think of the Open University course in social work I considered doing. I see us turned away from a flight to America. I see Reuben, standing by me, because it's the correct thing to do, but being aghast at what I've done, at the change I've inflicted on our lives. The image is so vivid, it is almost real.

It goes on: Reuben telling a nameless, faceless colleague that he's off to visit his estranged wife in prison. The colleague will offer him a drink. *One for the road*, she'll say. He'll accept it, unwillingly at first, and then one drink will turn into two, and he will miss visiting hours, and spend the night telling a blonde woman how much he used to love me.

That thought takes root, right in my stomach, able to germinate in the hollow left by the crime I committed.

The Offences Against the Person Act. Eighteen sixty-one. I turn the words over in my mind like somebody milling soil, uncovering the plants underneath it. Eighteen sixty-one. I've done something that a government in Victorian times thought was wrong. Something that's been wrong since almost the beginning of time. A rung below murder, attempted murder, manslaughter. It sends a shiver through me.

'Do you have any comments?' the police officer says.

'No,' I say. 'None.'

I am released on police bail. I'm to return to court on Monday for my bail hearing, proper.

Sarah says, 'See you then,' in a businesslike way, as though we're merely meeting for a coffee, and leaves.

I am given my charge sheet, and there, as I walk into the reception, is Reuben.

He's leaning against a wall. His legs are crossed at the ankles, and he's raking a hand back through his hair. He's wearing dark blue jeans, white trainers and a navy-blue coat with fur around the hood. He looks serious, his grey-green eyes raised to the ceiling. He is a tableau of somebody waiting for bad news. It feels like years since I have seen him.

'Hi,' I say, which comes out more like a croak.

'Jo,' he says, and the tone he uses is gentle. Kind. He extends a hand towards me, and it envelops mine. It's cold. 'Let's get the fuck out of here,' he says.

I close my eyes, drinking in his tall, assured form. When I open them again, he's looking derisively around the reception. It won't be snobbery; it'll be something else.

Sure enough, he turns to me and says, 'So this is where they *process* everyone.'

I nod once.

His tone is the same as the last time he came with me to see my parents and they were going on and on about a Sancerre wine, pouring it and wafting it and tasting it. 'You don't know about wine, do you, Jo?' Mum observed, and Reuben said, 'Why would you? Pretentious wankers,' into my ear, which made me laugh.

I'm given a plastic bag containing my things. My bracelet. My purse. There's nothing else in there.

'Where are my clothes . . .' I say. 'My phone?'

'They're staying with forensics,' a police officer says.

I can feel a heat spreading across my cheeks. Forensics. Bail hearings. The future isn't stretching out in front of me any more. The road's turned; headed off at a right angle. It's become overgrown, wild with trees and weeds, so thick we can't see our way. There is no normal path. No house in the suburbs. No children on our horizon, though it pains me to think it.

'Oh,' Reuben says, reaching over and sliding open the Ziploc of my things. 'This can't wait.' He gets out the bracelet, my wedding bracelet, and manoeuvres it on to my arm. It sits loosely, it's screws removed, but I don't mind. His gaze holds mine the whole time, the same look on his face – a kind of serious happiness – as on our wedding day. I understand the message immediately.

We walk out of the police station and the cold winter wind feels glorious against my face. I close my eyes into it, like a dog on his first walk of the day, my face held up to the sky, just smelling and feeling the clear air and the space and the freedom. Reuben stands next to me, silently, holding the Ziploc bag, not saying anything. I breathe in the smell of the London car park. The pine trees. The minty-cold winter breeze. The exhaust fumes. It's overwhelming after twenty hours of the same cell.

When I open my eyes and look at Reuben, I expect to see sympathy – my heart lightens in anticipation of it – but instead there's a strange expression on his face. And then it occurs to me: he can always see both sides of things. He will always defend the party being slagged off at a dinner party. It's his way. It annoys my friends, my family, but I like it.

So what if he sees it from the victim's side?

I can't think of that. Not now I'm out; free. Who knows how long this freedom will last? I must try to enjoy it.

And, like a woman whose husband has left her, or who's just been sacked unceremoniously from her job, I don't think about where that road's going. I will just concentrate on going home, tonight, with Reuben. To my own bed.

Tonight, I will dream of the hatch. I know I will.

*

Reuben pours a cup of tea, milk in first, amber steaming liquid second, and passes it to me. Edith is outside, coming home from her dog-walking with her daughter. Edith's in the wheelchair she sometimes uses. The dogs look older, their beards whiter, their legs rangy.

I turn away from them, cradling my tea, and Reuben looks at me, his eyes watchful, and waits. He doesn't need to say anything further. I hardly ever owe him anything, and he hardly ever asks anything of me. But he wants this, tonight: an explanation.

And so, without waiting any longer, I tell him.

He listens, not saying a word. He's always been a great listener. He barely breaks eye contact, even when he sips his black coffee – he never drinks tea.

At the end of it, he sits back. 'Jo,' he says.

I wait for the tough love. This is how he does things. He listens silently, then sums it up in one sentence; usually a sentence nobody else would be able to get away with saying to me. *You need to stop seeing your fucking rude parents*, for example. Or, *Stand up for yourself, then.*

'It will . . .' he says, 'it will be okay.' He taps my leg, ever so gently, and that's that.

'And then after that,' I say.

'After it all . . . babies,' he says with a nod, confirming that we are on the same page, even in a crisis.

'Ginger babies,' I say.

'Steady on,' he murmurs.

The relief is overwhelming. Both at his acceptance of our situation, and the reassurance he would never usually give. It's so overwhelming it becomes intoxicating. I creep closer to him on the sofa. Maybe it will all be okay, I am thinking. Maybe this will be behind us in a few months' time. Not laughed off, not minimized in the way that I'd hoped, but behind us nevertheless. Reuben is always right, and so I believe him.

And that's what makes me want to tell him.

'I was talking to Sarah about how long the guy was face down in the water . . .'

'In the water?' Reuben says.

'Yes.'

He doesn't say anything, but something in his body language changes. It stills. I am about to tell him, but then he is looking at me peculiarly. It is as though he is reassessing me.

'And how long was it?' he says.

'No time, really,' I lie. 'I got him out straight away. But she asked,' I add uselessly.

Reuben nods, once; a firm, downward movement. 'Good,' he says. 'She probably just . . . she's probably just checking.'

'Yes. It was immediate.'

He doesn't say anything else. I give it a few seconds, but he sips his coffee, swallows audibly, and then sips again. Not speaking. Not quite looking at me.

But I can read his features so well, even though what I see on them now surprises me. He is usually sympathetic to the wrongdoer; the underdog. But now I see his brow wrinkle, his top lip curl up slightly, and I know that he is thinking, *How could you do this, Jo?* But he doesn't say it. Why would he?

11

Conceal

It's all over the newspapers.

I can't google it. Can't ask anyone. Can't browse BBC News on an iPad, for fear of leaving an evidence trail, but I can read it in the papers that come every morning – the papers Reuben devours with his coffee.

I grab the local newspaper before he can and spread it out in the sunlit kitchen. It's stopped sleeting, finally, and outside the frost sparkles in the light.

The police are treating his death as suspicious, an article on page nine says. I read that sentence over and over. *They are appealing for anybody who was in the area that night to come forward. The funeral will be next Monday*, it adds.

I go to bundle the paper up, to throw it away before Reuben sees and asks me if I have volunteered what I know, but then I see the quote, in bold. **Imran will be missed**, it says. It is signed off *Mohammed Abdullah, Imam, Paddington Mosque*. He will be missed. Because of me.

I screw the paper up and take it outside, putting it in Edith's recycling bin. My left hand aches as I do so. I call the GP. I'll make something up, I reason. I make an appointment. I'll get that hand sorted, if nothing else.

*

The next day, I swing my legs out of bed. The ever-present sweat evaporates off them, feeling like needles on my skin.

I haven't hidden any evidence yet. I have been watching endless Netflix episodes in the night when I can't sleep and not doing anything about my problems. *It is Classic Joanna*, Reuben would say, if he knew. Vintage Joanna. Not in a disparaging way. Just in a factual way: it is what I do.

Only, I'm not able to ignore it completely. I don't know what's wrong with me. Usually, I have no trouble ignoring things. The huge gas bill we got that quarter when I had the heating on constantly. I just hid the bill under the bed. The lump in my armpit I had for over eighteen months but never saw the doctor about. It went, in the end, but what if it hadn't? And yet this – *this*, I can't ignore. It keeps popping into my mind, making me sweat and shake intermittently.

I've got to get rid of the evidence. That's the most important thing. I'm not *trying to get away with it*. Not yet. I can't decide that. The guilt is too bad. But I need to protect myself. For the time being. And that starts now.

I call work, speak to Daisy in the office, say I'm at the doctor's. I'll go in later. Nobody is surprised. I've got form for this unreliability, sadly, a fact Wilf – who has never called in sick once – finds astonishing.

We were the Murphy siblings. Off to Oxbridge. Ruling the school, in the musicals and the orchestras and the swimming teams. We were almost famous. We used to be so similar. We were high achievers, but we were also piss-abouts, behind the scenes. Used to do our homework reluctantly so we could be free to find our Narnias in the back garden (Wilf once did a wee in the bushes and Dad told him off for being vulgar) and bounce on our beds. We were allies against our oppressive parents and the silent, huge house. And then he changed. Or rather, I floundered. I went to Oxford and couldn't do it without somebody cracking the whip, and Wilf . . . well, he rose to it. Becoming the kind of person who enters six marathons a year and talks endlessly about *training runs*. The kind of person who has extreme opinions about the stock markets and discusses them in Zizzi on your thirtieth birthday – for example.

And so, despite what he'd say, I feel no guilt in calling in sick. I'm not even a librarian. I am unqualified. It hardly matters. Besides, it's Ed's day off today, thank God. Hopefully he'll never realize I have been off, too.

I can't make a list, and so I sit on the end of our bed and consider the evidence. I itemize it in my mind.

My coat.

My shoes.

CCTV.

My gloves.

My scarf.

My appearance.

Witnesses.

DNA?

I catch sight of myself in the mirrored wardrobe doors and wince. It's all so amateur. If this had happened to Reuben – not that any of it ever would have, I think with a frown; not only because of his morals but also because of his *gender* – he would have had some idea of what to do.

Do police look at the tread of a shoe at a crime scene? Do they check every CCTV camera, question everyone in the area, search for minuscule bits of DNA that might have drifted down on to the steps? Or would they think: this is unexplained; perhaps this man tripped? I have no idea. None.

The first thing I must do is get rid of everything I was wearing.

I can't burn them. It would draw too much attention. I don't want to bin them. I would worry about where they'd end up, that they could be traced to me.

Sainsbury's, I think. There's a clothing bank. I could put them in there. They will become anonymous, tangled with all the other clothes. I get in the car, having stuffed the clothes and shoes – those beautiful shoes, with their cream ribbons, worn once – in a bag for life, and drive there. My hands are slick with sweat on the steering wheel and leave an imprint on the plastic door handle as I get out.

I stand next to my car, the milky winter sunlight in my eyes. A man is ahead of me at the clothing bank, meticulously opening and closing the tray as he loads blouses and skirts on to it. I cannot help but stop and stare at him. It's not what he's doing. It's the look on his face. I think he's trying not to cry. His chin quivers violently. His hands shake.

I can see the clothes from my position by the car. A sage-green blouse. A creased-up linen skirt. A pair of pointed shoes with a heel. As I stare at him, he clutches a cream blouse and brings it up to his nose.

They're a wife's clothes, I find myself solemnly

thinking. No wonder his chin shakes. I wonder how many weeks or months it has taken him to accept it. To clear out her side of the wardrobe – to bring the clothes here – and to donate them.

How could I possibly go over and interrupt that? Not only interrupt it, but taint it, with my sordid activity?

What if I am found out? And he – a widower – is called to court, because he witnessed me burying evidence, and is forced to relive the day he finally summoned the courage to throw his wife's clothes away? I couldn't make him do that.

I stand in the cold sunlight and continue to study him. He's well dressed, with a nice car. They had a nice life, I think. Barbecues every Bank Holiday Monday with their friends. Three children who visit all the time, not like me and Wilf; weirdly aloof but needily competitive, too. Little bowls of Maltesers and M&Ms around the house, and not just at Christmas. She will have loved Glade plug-ins and I bet he would have been irritated by their synthetic smells. I can picture them now. I turn away. I can't bear it. His sadness.

I shouldn't put all of the clothes in one bin, anyway. I should spread them out.

I'll take them somewhere else.

It is the first time in my entire life that I am being meticulous. That I am thinking and planning and going over things. And it is to get away with murder.

It would surprise everyone. This attention to detail I'm exhibiting. Everyone except Reuben. He wouldn't be surprised at all.

'That brain,' he had once said, almost sadly, to me, at

Wagamama's for lunch when I seamlessly ordered eight dishes for everyone from memory.

Wilf was looking at me carefully.

'Joanna's brain?' Mum had said. 'Silly Joanna?'

Silly Joanna has its roots in a phrase Mum, Dad and – sometimes – Wilf used to say, while laughing. They would laugh when I admitted I didn't know whether Germany had a coastline or confessed that I wouldn't know how to start a fire. *Joanna could never survive on a desert island*, they would say, while laughing at the very thought of it.

Reuben's expression had darkened at that. In the car, on the way home, he had said, 'Do they always do that?'

'Do what?' I'd said.

'Drag you down.'

'They're only joking,' I had said meekly, and he'd looked at me, aghast.

I smile faintly at the memory now. He'd be proud of me, if it weren't for the subject matter.

I am facing Sainsbury's, away from the man, still holding my bag of things, not really looking, when my eyes land on it.

On the side of the building. Like a webcam. White, with one black eye. A CCTV camera, it must be. My eyes trail across it. There's another. And another on the far corner. I crane my neck, leaning out of the car window. I see them, different shapes – some rectangular, some like domes, some shabby and rusted – stuck to the buildings on the other side of the street. A café. A deli. A card and gift shop. It's like the whole world is opening up in front of me. I've never noticed before. CCTV. CCTV. CCTV. It's everywhere. Like ants in a nest, the more I look, the more I see. It's everywhere. It's absolutely fucking everywhere.

It is only a matter of time before they find me.

People do not get away with murder. And this is one of the reasons why.

I see my attack framed in the lenses of a hundred cameras, a kaleidoscope of Joannas and Imrans. My back to the camera, as I push him. A side view of my hand lifting up, striking his. A view from down the canal, Imran tumbling down the steps. My mind skitters into irrationality. A view, close-up, of Imran's face as he dies, as he breathes in the water. A view from inside as he struggles for breath. From inside his cells as they die. From inside those cells' nuclei as the lights go out. From inside his brain as his memories die and become nothing at all.

It's remarkable that here I am, a killer, and I am still outside Sainsbury's. That Sainsbury's even exists.

I go inside, just in case anybody's keeping an eye on me. I'll buy something. Anything. So as not to arouse suspicion.

I pay at the kiosk, holding a pint of milk, trying not to think. The handle cools my fingers.

A paper catches my eye as I queue. I almost rub my eyes in astonishment.

CANAL-SIDE RACE HATE

Race hate? Race hate?

I shift closer to the paper, trying not to draw attention to myself. I can't buy it, of course. I can't even reach and touch it – there's probably a bloody camera right behind me – but if I shift a bit, I can read the front page.

I scan it quickly. They think it was racially aggravated. Because he was Pakistani, Muslim, I think dully. That area of London had been rife with racial unrest.

I stand, staring at the paper, holding my milk, and thinking of Reuben. He is always my first thought. Poor Reuben, and the work he does for his charity.

I pay for my milk in cash. 45p.

How can they decide it was racially aggravated when it wasn't? How can they unilaterally tell their side of the story? What about mine?

But then, I think, as the automatic doors open for me, why wouldn't they? This is the price I pay for anonymity. I have no right of reply. No right to even ask them why they think that. A man is dead, because of me, and living with people's assumptions about my motivations is surely part of my punishment. I can't believe I'm even thinking it. I have no rights in this situation, and nor should I. None at all.

I get in my car again and stare at my mobile like it is a snake about to attack me. I could call now: 999. Or google the number for the nearest police station. Drive there, and end it all.

I reach over and hold the phone in my hand. It's weighty. One call, and I would likely go to prison for life. Life. It's said so casually on the news. But – life. One call, and I could explain, to those dear to me, how it happened. That I was frightened. That it wasn't about his race. That I didn't leave because I didn't think . . . because I didn't think that his Pakistani life mattered.

There are a million reasons to call, of course. To do the right thing. To make amends. So the family can finally know what's happened. To trust in the justice system that it won't punish a good person for making a bad mistake, and let it decide my fate for me. So I can stop lying to Reuben. So I can stop living with it; stop waiting for the police to knock the door. All those pros, listed out in my mind. All those pros, and then just one con, but with a weight as dense as mercury: I would more than likely go to prison. Jail. *Inside.* Just one con, but it matters more than any of the others.

I turn the car's ignition on, the bag of soiled clothes with – no doubt – Imran's DNA on them sitting next to me like a bomb.

That afternoon, I think, *I'll put them out.* For charity. I'll go through the donation bags left over in our kitchen, and then the incriminating items will be gone, jumbled up with everybody else's, like unidentifiable faces in a crowd.

I'll say I was having a clear-out, if anybody asks. Only those close to me will know how unlikely that is. I'll tell them I read an article recently about minimalism. And even if they don't believe me, confusing my loved ones is the best option I have now.

It's better than the alternative: keeping the clothes, hanging, like spectres in the back of my wardrobe.

Reuben's father sends me a text. He texts me often. He started tentatively, when he got a mobile, but texts in earnest now. It's always overly formal, and almost always signed off with a 'P', but I like them.

I don't open the message now. Can't look.

It's already after two in the afternoon, and I am rifling in our kitchen drawer for four charity bags that I will distribute evenly along our road, each containing a contaminated, criminal piece of clothing. I should be at work, of course. No doctor's appointment takes this long. Much longer, and they'll request a note, but it's hard to care.

The gloves in one. Cancer Research. The scarf in another. Barnardo's. Laundering my possessions through a charitable system. I disgust myself.

I pause over the shoes and the coat.

The shoes. Ordered Before. An emblem of my life as it once was. An ASOS order I knew would irritate my husband. Frivolous shoes before a much-anticipated night out. My only problems the credit card bills and the pinching sensation the shoes produced in my toes.

The coat. Filled with duck feathers. A present from Reuben, for my thirtieth. I have no idea how much it cost. I expect hundreds. But I was always shivering, on the way to work, in a stupid trench coat, the skin on my arms cold to the touch when I arrived. I didn't think he'd noticed. And then, in August, the day I turned thirty, he placed a squishy, large package on the bed. It was the coat. 'Ready for the winter,' Reuben said. I have worn it every day. It's like a duvet. Wrapping me up, reminding me of him as I walk to work.

I ball it up, bringing it to myself like it's a baby, squeezing it tight. The feathers inside it crinkle underneath my arms. I bury my head in it as though it is his and he is long gone. Just like the man in Sainsbury's did. Only, I am saying goodbye to myself. To the Joanna whose husband bought her thoughtful birthday presents.

I shove it in the last bag. Macmillan.

I put the bags in my car. I'll deposit them along another road, next to bins and by doorsteps.

But first: the shoes. They are too distinctive. I can't risk it with those.

I drive to the tip on a whim, the shoes sitting on the passenger seat next to me. I look at them as we sit at traffic lights and at junctions. Right outside the recycling centre, I see the sign.

This waste disposal centre is monitored with 24/7 CCTV: Smile – you're on camera.

I loop back around, driving past the sign, pretending I was never going in. My lower back is sweating against the seat. My legs tremble so much my feet slide off the pedals. There are cameras everywhere. It would only take one, to see me acting suspiciously, *disposing of evidence*, for them to know. I can't go to the tip, and I can't put the bags out, either.

I return home with the bags and the shoes and shove them in the back of my wardrobe.

12

Reveal

Westminster Magistrates' Court is not how I imagined. We are here for my bail hearing. This happens at the Magistrates' Court. The trial happens at the Crown Court. Mine will be at the Old Bailey, Sarah tells me.

The Magistrates' Court looks like a sixties office block, the grandeur only apparent if you get closer and can see the crest with the lions on it. Otherwise, it's an unassuming building in central London where, inside, people's lives are changed forever. If it wasn't me, if it wasn't my bail hearing, it would be so interesting. These people at the heart of the justice system, at the juncture between freedom and imprisonment. The lawyers in robes sweeping by. The divide: between the suits and the lay people who have wronged, or are unfortunate enough to know somebody who has.

I called in sick to work. It was the best I could do. Ed was nice about it, as he always is, and I was grateful for that.

Sarah is waiting in a meeting room for me. She's wearing a black skirt suit and a white shirt. She keeps shifting within its confining fabric, while it remains stiff around her neck, uncomfortable. Her face is less made up than it was on Saturday, and her eyes look smaller and more tired.

She hands me a machine coffee. It tastes like burnt toast.

We haven't told anybody yet, Reuben and I. It could be on the television or in the newspapers. I have no idea. But it's like there's no room for it in my head. I should have told Ed. My parents. Wilf. Laura. But I can't. Not yet. Not when I could be imprisoned within the hour. Reuben will have to do it.

'I've got all of your mitigation,' Sarah says, indicating a pad.

She's changed her nail colour. I wonder if she removed it last night, scrubbing frustratedly at it while talking to her other half, then slicked on a new shade while he made them liqueur coffees at a stainless-steel breakfast bar.

'And you have no aggravating features,' she adds, interrupting my chain of thought.

'No,' I say softly.

'No previous. Good character. No flight risk.' She is rattling off her checklist.

I can see Reuben, through the windowed panel in the door, standing confidently, assessing everybody. He comes to court a bit, for work. He looks at home here.

'You must be wondering at the likelihood of bail,' Sarah says.

'No,' I say. 'I don't want to know.'

I can't be worrying about likelihoods of imprisonment. I don't understand it: I am currently free to wander down the road and buy breakfast from Pret. If there is no risk now, what is the risk in a few hours' time? But then, what is the risk *at all*? If I am bailed now, why put me in prison later? I raise my eyes to the marble carved ceiling and pretend for a second that I am merely in – where? Where looks like this? – the Natural History Museum, maybe, and Reuben is earnestly explaining the dinosaur exhibits to me.

What is the point in any of it? I have learnt my lesson, haven't I? I am not going to do it again. I will never so much as touch another person again, I tell the universe.

We walk out. I'm listed fourth in Courtroom Two.

The foyer looks like it's made of marble and glass, with rows of benches fixed into the ground, like in an airport. But it's the people who sit at them; they're the people I would like to talk to. Or maybe to write about. They are like personifications – is that the right word? – arrayed on those little benches. A man whose shoulders are back, gesticulating at his lawyer. Defiance. A man in a tracksuit, elbows resting above his head on the wall, forehead against the cement right next to the justice crest. Grief. Or maybe Penance, or Regret.

I have no idea what I'm doing here in my Boden blazer, my husband's hand in mine. None at all.

We have a three-hour wait. I watch Reuben. Looking at him calms me down. He never fiddles. Never gets his phone out. I like to stare at his slow movements, his green eyes raising upwards as people approach; at how he slides his leg closer to mine, lays a hand in my lap just like he did on our wedding day.

But, eventually, we're called; my name is announced on an electronic screen above the door to Courtroom Two, as if I am in the GP's surgery or at the dentist (if I hadn't avoided the dentist's for the last ten years).

'All rise,' a clerk says.

I immediately think of the Blue song. I am still a silly, immature thirty-year-old who would like to snigger in court; my mind hasn't caught up with the fact that I am the defendant, and it is me in the wooden dock fronted by the bullet-proof glass.

I hardly understand a word of the proceedings. The lawyers and the magistrates refer constantly to a big black book, which they all have open on the table in front of them. The magistrate puts her glasses on to look at it. Their words are a rainstorm of legal jargon: mitigating circumstances and aggravating features and flight risks and CPS sentencing guidelines and referrals to the Crown Court and provocation and reasonable force and premeditation and grievous bodily harm and *mens rea*.

I understand the facts, but the facts seem to be a backdrop, at best, to what is being discussed. They are not talking about how I was walking home alone. Or that he came up behind me. Or what I did. The push.

It's other stuff. Logic and argument and *theory*.

I stare at the immaculate glass. It isn't smeared. Why not? I wonder. There's a security guard behind me, in a navy-blue uniform. He's making sure I don't move, bolt, make a run for it. Because, once again, I'm no longer free. Not for now. Not for these minutes.

My whole body is covered in sweat. I try to calm myself, try to imagine placing my hands against the panes. Perhaps I'm just at SeaWorld, or at the zoo – the penguin enclosure cool against my palms. We'll get an ice cream and then drive home. I close my eyes with the ferocity of my desire. If only I had walked away. If only it had never happened.

'Joanna Oliva, please stand again,' the magistrate says.

Her voice was clear at the beginning of my bail hearing, but has become muffled and raspy-sounding, as though she can no longer be bothered, by twelve forty on a Monday afternoon. There are three of them, the magistrates, but only she speaks.

Oliva. I was so happy to have his name. To ditch my plain name, and take his interesting one. 'No, it's O-*lee*-vah,' he's always had to say, and now I do, too. I liked it. And the rest; his *family name* and all it stood for. That he was adopted, and they all loved each other, it seemed to me, without conditions. The Oliva pub, where he spent his teenage years getting a fantastic alcohol tolerance and a brilliant poker face and an education in all the classics. R. Oliva, occasionally quoted in the press on issues of social justice, London gangs. I loved all of it. Joined it readily. The Oliva clan. And now, here I am, tarnishing it.

I look up, my eyes trailing past the bench, past the justice crests, past the high, barred windows and beyond, up to the strip lights. They're the same as in the police cell, and the panic washes over me again, less like a wave and more as if I have jumped off a boat and sunk fifty fathoms deep.

I haven't even been thinking about it. Haven't been working it out. But my brain has, ticking over in the background like a radioactivity monitor nobody knows is working, totting up numbers all on its own.

There are five and a half thousand nights in fifteen years, a life sentence, I think suddenly to myself. *And I did just one.* I can't do it. I can't do it. I can't do it. I want to break free of my enclosure, rip out the glass.

The magistrate is speaking. I don't understand – can't understand – the words she's saying, but I like the tone. It reminds me of when Wilf and I would watch the football scores coming in, on our tummies in front of the television, and we would try to predict the results from the tone of the announcer's voice. I can hear it. *While this is serious* . . . she's saying. The rest is currently unsaid, but I understand what it'll be. The State: nil, Joanna: *one*.

She is listing the things I haven't done. I didn't flee the scene. I have not attempted to conceal evidence. I have not ever committed an offence before. And then she says: *The defendant sought immediate help.* I ignore this, not letting my mind look at it, like trying to hold still a mechanical toy.

'And so I am minded to think that, although this carries with it the risk of a very long prison sentence, I am not of the view that the defendant needs imprisoning pending trial.'

I look across at Sarah, wondering if what I'm hearing is correct. Her back is to me, her head bent, intently listening to the magistrate. I look at Reuben instead. He's looking directly at me. He's wearing a shirt and tie; he hates ties, always pulls them off at the earliest opportunity, always looks slightly scruffy, even when he's trying hard not to.

The magistrate moves on to bail conditions. I don't listen to them. I am daydreaming about how I am to be – temporarily – free. I don't want to think about the tomorrows; the trial, the aftermath. I will think only of right now, I tell myself. The sky beyond those windows. The weather. Our tiny basement flat. Reuben. All mine for a few more months of borrowed time.

13

Conceal

The GP thinks my hand and wrist need strapping. I enjoy her tender touch on my arm and hand, her concerned expression when I tell her I have had a lot on, that I fell when hurrying.

'Be kind to yourself,' she says, in the tone of an exasperated schoolteacher.

When I get home, Reuben stares at the strapping, and I tell him the truth: that I fell over.

I only omit to tell him when, and why.

I don't check the work rota much more than a day in advance – a fact which irritates Reuben – so I don't know until the Monday – ten days After – that I have the Tuesday off.

I kiss Reuben goodbye as he leaves. I haven't kissed him since it happened, and a faint frown crosses his face as his lips meet mine, which I try to ignore. But I can't un-see the way he draws me to him, wanting to extend the kiss like someone on rations might bulk up a meal.

'You've got so thin,' he says.

'Oh, really,' I say, self-consciously patting down my slim hips. The bones protrude into the palms of my hands. 'Good.' I want to disappear.

When he's left, I go out and walk, crunching around in the winter frost. Walking's the only thing that seems to work for me. The only time I feel okay. The rhythm of it. The lack of thought. The cold, harsh air. Who knows what I'll do when it's warm again?

Of course, I find myself walking towards Little Venice, but I steer myself south.

It's no longer snowing but it's still bone-cold – the worst winter on record, the newspaper headlines scream – and I wrap my thin trench coat around myself, walking alone along an A-road in Paddington. A bizarre, sixties building with an extra bit on the top of it sits to my right, and I turn instinctively towards it, crossing the road, turning down a side street towards central London. I will go and look at the landmarks, I think. Look at my London: one of my favourite things to do.

I wander for hours. And then, before I know it, without realizing how far I have drifted, it is there in front of me, a white, square building, a golden dome: the Paddington Mosque. I stand in front of it, blinking, and I know why I have arrived here, almost unconsciously, without quite knowing myself. To pay my respects. To say sorry. To express my regret. I'll do it alone, and quickly. I think back to the news article. He was buried yesterday. I won't be disturbing anybody. I'll nip in. Find his grave. Leave. Nobody will know. It is necessary, I realize, for me to do this.

I let myself in through the door – my left hand hangs by my side, strapped and useless – knowing just enough to remove my shoes and hold them in my hands as I cross the carpet of the women's section. I cover my hair with my scarf.

The mosque, on the inside, is nothing like a church. More like a living room. The carpet is red and swirling and the edge of the room is lined with pillars. Otherwise, it's almost entirely empty. A chandelier hangs from the ceiling and it seems to sway slightly in a breeze that must be coming from outside. A few men are praying around the edges of the room, and I cross it silently, putting my shoes back on when I reach the door. But, after a second, I realize there's no graveyard here. I ask someone, and she directs me to the cemetery over the road.

It's frosty and the grass crunches underfoot. My breath steams out in front of me, eddying like bathwater in the frigid air.

The cemetery is completely empty. I take a deep, chilly breath. I am alone with him. He's here somewhere. Imran. I'll stop a grave or two away – I can't risk going right up to him – and pay my respects to him from a few feet. I'll pretend to be visiting someone else.

They are different to Christian graves, to secular graves. The headstones are mostly smaller, but some of them have entire tombs, crypts, shining white in the sun. They are all pointing in the same direction, I notice immediately. It gives a strangely uniform effect. Rows and rows and rows of them, evenly spaced, like somebody has neatly laid out piles of paper.

I find his grave – marked with a wooden stake. I don't know how long I stay there for. Just looking, three along from his grave. This is close enough. If he could see me now, he would know. He would know that I'm sorry. *He would want you to hand yourself in*, a voice inside my head says, but I gulp back tears and ignore it.

Instead, I just stand there, my feet cold in the frost, breathing deeply, apologizing with each breath.

'Rubbish, isn't it?' a voice beside me says.

I turn and see a woman standing next to me. I didn't hear her arrive. And, then, with a panicked lurch, I realize that it is obviously, unmistakably *her*. Ayesha. His sister. Her face is more drawn than it was on the television, but I recognize the turned-down lips, the mole. I can see hollows underneath her cheekbones. Like she is biting her cheeks.

I want to back away, to turn and run, but I can't. I can't do that to her – scare her in this peaceful graveyard, where her brother rests. So recently buried.

'I'm not supposed to be here again so soon,' she says. 'But I can't stay away.'

She raises her face to the sun. It kisses her features – lighting her forehead and shadowing underneath her bone structure – and I look away, embarrassed.

It wasn't right to come. It wasn't right at all, I think, wanting to run far away. I am a monster, a killer, following the same murderous instincts that have preceded me for hundreds of years. Returning to the scene of the crime. Coming to the grave. Stupid. Selfish. Predictable.

'I – I'm sorry,' I say. 'I'm here to . . .'

She's looking at me expectantly and I wonder why I spoke at all. I can feel my eyes darting around the graveyard. I can't pretend to have known him: that is a step too far. I will just . . . my gaze lands on a gravestone bearing the inscription *Hanna Ahmed: lost too soon*. It has this year's date on it. She was born in 1983.

'My brother's girlfriend died,' I say, the lie escaping my

lips before I can really stop it, thankful for my fast brain, always good with numbers right from when I was young. 'I'm just – I'm so sorry to have . . . disturbed you.'

Her expression is soft, and I realize she wasn't asking me. Her expression looks questioning, but it is only grief. Hollow grief that I have caused. Her eyes meet mine. They're a dark brown, almost black, the pupils lost inside.

'I'm sorry,' she says, gesturing to the grave, almost as new as Imran's, the earth piled on it, covered in plants and flowers. 'About your brother . . . about his girlfriend.'

I wave a hand, like it doesn't matter, which she must think is strange.

'They're at rest now,' she says, looking out over the graves. 'Mecca's somewhere that way,' she says. 'You know?' She looks at me. 'I never believed all that, but he did. I think.' She speaks with a cockney accent.

She doesn't care that I'm not answering. That I'm thinking about Imran and every grave in here. She leans down, looking closer at Hanna's grave. 'She was young, too. Did they bury her fast? As soon as the post-mortem was over, we got the body. It's hardly been any time at all.'

'I don't know,' I say, a blush creeping across my cheeks.

I take a step back, the panic descending again. What am I doing here? I have to get away. I can't be doing things like this. Risky things. Cruel things. Things that don't make any sense.

I take two steps back, but, as I leave, I can't help but wish her well. She nods gratefully, her eyes still on me.

*

I dream of Imran again and wake up sweaty.

I shower, my arm feeling wasted without its splint on, ashamed at the strange concoction of emotions inside me. Sadness — it's almost all sadness. But there are other things, too. Sadness is the main course, but there is a starter of guilt. No, make that a sharing platter.

But then also, right at the end, after pudding — a biscotti on the side of the coffee, maybe — is something else. I see it for what it is, and wince as I realize.

It's relief. A chink of relief, because, as each day passes, it's looking like I might have got away with murder.

I am despicable.

14

Reveal

Reuben finishes playing for me. His head is bent low, the fingers finishing the piece with the softest, quietest, most understated ending. A musical sentence, trailed off.

'Calmer?' he says, turning to me with a smile. He hardly ever plays for me.

I nod, but I'm not really. 'Yes. No,' I say. We are about to leave to go to my parents'. Wilf has said he will be there, too. We're telling people. We can't avoid it any longer.

Nobody saw my bail hearing in the press, of course. They wouldn't have believed it if they did; would think it was a coincidence. Somebody with the same name. That's what I would think. It would be too far out for me to even consider it.

'They'll think I'm pregnant,' I say, as I take my trench coat from the hallway.

'Fuck 'em,' Reuben says, as I walk back into the spare room.

He closes the lid on the piano keys. As he does it, I think suddenly of Imran, on some life support somewhere. I think of him dying. I think of my charge changing to murder.

*

Mum and Dad live in Kent. They call it London, but it isn't. Not proper London. There are open, green spaces and its own town centre, and houses, not flats. There are no London buses or tube stations or constant sirens. There are no jaunty, confident urban foxes or pop-up yoga studios or night buses. It is not our London.

Reuben's father texts on the way. Reuben got me a new phone, this afternoon. It's a different type, and I'm not used to it. Transferring my number over was a pain. Reuben glances across as it beeps.

'Does your dad know?' I say, before I open the text.

Reuben nods, his hair flashing, orange and then auburn, orange and then auburn, as we pass underneath street lamps.

He doesn't defend telling him. I'm glad he doesn't. But . . . there is something strange about it. I would have liked him to have asked me, maybe. But no. I won't let the thing that I have done create a space between us. We are seeing my parents and it is only right that Reuben's should know too.

I look down at the text. *Hope my boy is treating you well*, it says. I frown. He has never sent such a text, has never needed to. Reuben has no temper, no moodiness, no edge. Not with me, anyway.

I tap out a response, not looking up at Reuben. *Always, of course xx*, I say.

You know where I am. All sounds very unfair to me, Jo. Hope R is good to you. You know how he can be, he writes. I feel my mouth slacken, my eyebrows knit together. *How he can be?*

I can't ask what he means by that. *You know how he can be.* It would be awkward. And so I don't; I avoid it, but I do think about it as I watch London spread out as we travel, like the universe is expanding as we drive. Perhaps he means because he can be blunt. Perhaps he means because Reuben is always completely honest about what he thinks of people and their actions, is moralistic. But he's not, with me. No, not really.

But none of these things really makes sense. There is no *obvious thing* that would necessitate a text like that.

'He alright?' Reuben says while we are paused at a set of traffic lights.

'Yeah,' I lie. 'Just – chat.' I like to chat to Reuben's father, and he respects that.

Mum opens the front door when we arrive. She is tall, unlike me, and has her hair in a conservative up-do. She looks just like Wilf: lithe, with bulbous eyes. They both have the same exaggerated mannerisms. They're heavy-footed; when we stay over I can always hear her and Wilf stomping around upstairs. The occasional time she tells a story she thinks is actually funny, she juts her jaw out as she tells it, self-consciously, as though she shouldn't be laughing.

'What's all this?' she says.

The tone immediately annoys me. As though I am being a nuisance. Creating drama. That's the assumption they always make about me. I try to catch Reuben's eye, but he's staring fixedly down at the welcome mat. I once told him off, in the car on the way home, for huffing throughout a Christmas dinner with them, and he behaves differently now, less antagonistic and more mournful.

Wilf is sitting in the dining room, at the head of the table, and Dad is pouring wine from an actual carafe. Reuben nods to them, not saying anything, and sits at the other end. I sit next to him, and his hand lands on my knee, squeezing gently. Mum and Dad sit, too, opposite each other, and look at us expectantly, slightly impatiently. I find myself thinking I'm glad that I'm not pregnant; that I don't have to tell them like this. I could just imagine their tight smiles, their tiny congratulations. They don't know how to be joyful. They would say they gave us a happy childhood, my parents. That they took us to meadows where we ran amongst the wildflowers. But those tiny smiles, the condescension, their *Oh, Joanna*s – they erased it all. Only, I am not brave enough to ever say. I might be wrong. Wilf seems happy enough. And so it's not legitimate, my suffering. It doesn't feel it, anyway.

I look across at Reuben. I can't do it. I can't say it. But I know he can. They trust him. But I become different around them. No, not different: a worse version of myself.

'On Friday night Jo was harassed by a man,' Reuben says.

He omits the *bar*, and the *night out*. I'm glad of it. I'm glad of all of it. That he's explaining, and not me. He legitimizes it somehow. It's not right, but it's the way it is.

'Right,' Dad says, his eyebrows drawing together, not in concern but in confusion.

'She thought he was following her, but it was another, similar-looking man,' Reuben says. He swallows, withdrawing his hand from my knee.

Mum picks up a coaster and starts turning it around rhythmically, so that its square edges bang against the table, one side, then the next, then the next. It's a sound I remember from a thousand awkward childhood dinners. We ate good food – organic food, balanced diets – but we had no conversation. Not real conversation, anyway.

Wilf is sitting back in his seat, his body language languid, but his face serious, appraising mine. He's grown a goatee. It looks ridiculous.

'When he got too close she pushed him, and he's injured and in hospital. The police are involved . . .'

It's the best he could do with a bad story. It's factual, unemotional; exactly as I want it to be.

'Involved how?' Mum says sharply.

'They've charged me,' I say, breaking my silence.

'With what?' Wilf says, speaking for the first time.

He's a City worker. Something in finance. I have no idea what. But he seems to know things about the world. True to form, when I say *causing grievous bodily harm with intent*, his eyebrows raise, and he says, 'Section eighteen?'

I cringe when I recall thinking a section eighteen meant I was going home without charge. How do these people know so much more than me?

'Right. Well. When's all . . . that?' Mum says, awkwardly swirling wine around her glass.

'The summer,' says Reuben, before I can. 'Early June.'

'Well, there must be something more to it than that,' Dad says. 'It's preposterous for them to charge you for self-defence.'

I suppose his indignation is on my behalf; that it has its roots in sympathy, somewhere, hidden deep.

'It wasn't self-defence. Because I was mistaken,' I say.

'How badly injured is he?'

'Quite,' I say. 'He was . . . I didn't realize it but he was face down in a puddle –'

'For a few *seconds*,' Reuben interjects, and I swallow hard.

'They must think you did something else,' Dad says.

He was always this way; sure he was correct even in the face of overwhelming evidence to the contrary. About immigration and benefit claimants and London's knife crime. Reuben used to try to tell him, in the early days, until every visit ended in a row and he stopped.

'They must,' Dad says again.

Mum nods ferociously next to him and I see now: this is how it's going to be. Everybody will have an opinion on me, on what I did, and on what the State did to me in response. Everybody is wearing lenses, and they see me through them now, filtered through their own views of what constitutes violence and self-defence and the law. Even Reuben does it. I see him looking at me sometimes, when he thinks I am engrossed in something else. His expression is puzzled. Incredulous, even.

I am public property. Nothing is private any more. My life has been blown up, projected on to a wall for everybody to watch. A decision I made late at night after too many drinks is being played out in front of us like a tragedy on the stage. I'm not sure even I would defend that reckless, quick decision I made, and yet I have to, to stay free.

'That sounds really unfair,' Wilf says. 'It's an honest mistake. And you're . . . you know.'

'Well, quite,' Mum says. 'Your imagination. You were always . . . imaginative. Your make-believe world.'

Reuben's head snaps up and then he lets out a derisive snort. 'That's the best you can come up with?' he says. 'That's your sympathy?' I put a hand out to stop him, but he stands up. 'I knew you'd be like this,' he says. 'Can't you see she needs . . .'

He walks across the dining room and I follow him, not out of anger for myself but out of loyalty to him.

Wilf catches us in the hall. Reuben's hand is on the door, wrenching it open.

'I meant because you're a woman,' Wilf says. 'I know . . . I've seen those viral videos. The catcalling. Stuff like that. I know it's different for you.'

'I know,' I say, looking up at him. 'Thank you.'

I remember the fear I felt that night. Sadiq's body pressed against mine in the bar. His hand shackled to mine against my will. I remember how it felt when I thought he was following me. Like feelings I've felt a thousand times before. But bigger, this time.

That everyday sexism. The builders who yell at you – abuse or flirtations – and the men who sit too close on the tube, spreading their legs suggestively. The bouncer who follows you down a side street, telling you what he'd like to do to you. The eager man at the party who thinks it's romantic to repeatedly pursue you. Are women not always pleading self-defence? Are we not always provoked?

'Thank you,' I say to Wilf again. Reuben is standing outside, pointedly waiting – not unusual for him – and I turn again to my brother. 'I had better go . . .'

'Yeah,' he says. 'Shame.' He reaches out and punches my shoulder; something he's never done before. 'Was going to fill you in on my failed love life.'

It's a rare moment for Wilf. Usually, he's all about keeping up appearances. Complaining about capital gains tax. Worrying about having to sack his cleaner. That sort of thing. Things dressed up as complaints, but ones I can see behind. I have no idea what his hopes and dreams must really be. It's impossible to see, with all that rubbish obscuring them.

'What happened?' I say, wanting distraction. Wanting, for just a moment, to judge someone else's life, the way I used to. Before.

'The latest binned me off. Said I must be posh to live in Wimbledon.'

I almost roll my eyes. Of course. Not a true love life disaster. Something else.

Wilf bought well in the London market and it's changed his life. His flat made him £150,000 in just over a year. He now owns four London properties. Buy to lets. He whinges about his tenants.

'But more another time,' he says.

I close the door softly behind him. Reuben walks straight past the car.

'What . . .?' I say.

He doesn't answer me, just keeps walking, reaching behind him for my hand. We walk together, to the end of my parents' winding road, and he turns to face me and gestures towards me. I step into his embrace. His hands encircle my shoulders and I can feel the length of his body against mine. It's a proper hug. The kind we couldn't have in the car.

'I'm so sorry,' he murmurs. 'I'm so sorry they're such utter shits.'

'Me, too,' I say.

Later, on the way home, I turn to him. The heating's on high and he drives so carefully, so slowly, that I feel utterly safe. Almost asleep.

'I was unlucky, wasn't I?' I say. I can't help myself.

'No doubt,' he says immediately.

'Would you prosecute me?' I say. 'If you were the police?' I can't avoid asking that, either. Usually, I would prefer to never ask, to choose never to know, but something's changing.

'How could I?' he says. 'You're my *wife*.'

Even after two years, the word sends a frisson up and down my spine. His wife. The only one he chose. For life.

'But if I wasn't?' I say.

We're approaching a roundabout. Reuben hates this junction. He hates driving in London. He doesn't hear me, is navigating around the traffic island, checking his mirrors methodically. He looks over his shoulder as he changes lane, his gaze alighting on me. Just for an instant.

I tell Laura, too. Before she hears it somewhere else. It might be on the news, Reuben says. Depending on what happens to Imran in hospital. I press 'call' with shaking fingertips on my phone.

'About Friday,' I say as she answers. My tone is brusque, trying to cover the embarrassment of not having told her sooner, of having an incident involving her lead to one that's just about me. Laura wouldn't have done what I did. It is better I tell her now, anyway, before Sarah requests a statement from her.

'What about Friday?' she says.

'I thought I was followed – after we left. By that bloke. Sadiq.' I try to do it how Reuben did, but I fail. The edges of my vision darken as though somebody has dimmed the lights in our living room.

'Yeah?'

'And – I mean, it wasn't. But I thought it was . . .' I swallow. How am I going to be cross-examined on the witness stand if I can't even cope with explaining it to my best friend?

Laura, as ever, says nothing, waiting. I can imagine her hand raking through her cropped hair, her eyes squinting as she tries to understand what I'm saying.

I tell her the rest. What I've told Reuben. What I told the police. Omitting my lie.

'They can't do that,' Laura says. 'Surely it's just – surely it's just an innocent mistake.'

'It's the law.'

'Well, the law's wrong. What should you have done? Wait to be killed?'

'Apparently.'

'God. I can't believe it,' she says.

'It wasn't the best night ever,' I say with a weak laugh.

Laura doesn't speak for a while. And then she says, 'Well – I just went home and had a pizza.'

We both laugh, and I love her for that.

Reuben told my work, and they requested a meeting for the day I return. Today.

I'm only half aware of all of these things. They happen on the periphery of my vision, like planets orbiting the sun. Reuben asked if he should tell them, and I remember saying yes, but what I remember more vividly is eking the tea out of the teabag as I squeezed it against the white cup, and being struck with the notion that I might only have a finite number of cups of tea left in the outside world. In freedom. That, after a few hundred more, or maybe fewer, my next tea might be a prison cup of tea. I poured it down the sink, suddenly terrified.

News travels fast, and a colleague texted me. *I'm outraged on your behalf*, she had written. She went on to say she couldn't believe I would ever be charged for that. I didn't know what to say back.

We're both silent as we approach the Hammersmith Library and the offices behind it. We both know. Of course the government library service isn't going to let me work for them. The government is charging me with wounding with intent, after all.

Reuben stops, a hand on the door handle, his eyebrows raised. I nod. I want him with me.

It is quick and painful. I am suspended. I am not innocent until proven guilty. It is quite the opposite. Ed looks at me with what I first think is embarrassment, but later — in bed, at 4 p.m. — I realize was actually fear.

He is afraid of me. And of what I might do.

The next day, I report to the police station at noon. I have to go at noon every day.

It's snowing again.

There is already somebody at the desk, wearing an ankle tag, and I sit down on a bank of grey chairs affixed to the wall. The tag is a wide, sturdy band, like a Fitbit. It has a grey face with an eye on it, like a webcam. His skinny jeans ruck up around it. Evidently it is new to him, because he asks how he'll shower, gesturing down with his right hand, cocking his leg like a dancer. The woman at the desk tells him in a bored tone that it's waterproof. He swears at her, and she threatens to report him.

He makes a loud phone call on the way out. 'Finally done. Some bitch all up in me,' he says.

I blink, trying to ignore him. I wonder if they prefer me, here, at the reception desk, sitting primly with my handbag.

I have no tag. No conditions except this reporting. This endless reporting. Every day. Even weekends. Just to prove that I am . . . here. It is tautological. Pointless.

Two women come in as I'm at the desk. They're both skinny, ill looking.

'This, then methadone, then to the shops,' one says to the other.

I start, my body jolting, then stare at them. And then I feel the strangest dart of emotion: envy. I am envious. That this is not shocking to them. That they don't think their lives are ruined. That maybe court appearances and bail conditions are routine – a nuisance, an annoyance, like flies in the summer heat.

'I heard about you,' the woman behind the desk says to me. 'For what it's worth, I'm on your side. He deserved a lamping.'

I don't correct her. I don't remind her of my mistake. I simply nod, and say thank you.

'Mum called,' I say.

I am sitting by the breakfast bar while Reuben chops an onion. How many thousands of onions have I watched him chop, sauté, serve? I usually love it. The warmth of it. The distraction of the cooking. The smells and the creativity and his flair; that piano-playing flair he some-times demonstrates. It's one of the many reasons we won't move: we love the closeness, the proximity our tiny flat affords.

He doesn't answer. This is his way. He lets me talk, if I want to. Or not, if I don't.

'The landline,' I say.

Reuben glances up, catches my eye, smiles briefly. 'Of course.'

She always telephones the landline. I wish she would get the hang of emails, of texts, so that I could politely ignore them, or that she would call my mobile so that I could screen it, but she never does. I answered unthink-ingly, hoping it was good news – from the police, from my lawyer, from the victim, saying he wanted to drop the charges – but it was her.

'She didn't apologize. But she invited us again, this weekend.'

He looks up at me at this. 'Why would we go back to their house when they were rude to us?'

'Because they're my family. I might need them,' I say uselessly, my mind spiralling over past news stories I have ignored, but whose details have entered my psyche some-how. Alienated prisoners, released with nowhere to go. Not just because the probation system has failed them, I bet, but because their families have, too. I can't let it happen.

'You don't need them,' he says. 'Bunch of twats.'

'I think she understands – a little bit.'

'She's a woman,' Reuben says, nodding. He gets a sec-ond onion out of the bag.

I am sure he ordinarily wouldn't, if he weren't angry. It'll be too strong, whatever he's cooking. An onion husk skitters to the floor and he picks it up and puts it in the bin, then bends down and picks up a tiny, almost invisible piece and bins that too.

'Don't be such a misanthrope,' I say. It comes from nowhere.

'I am a misanthrope.' He shrugs as he says it, the knife jarring in his grip.

Outside it's sleeting. We have a round window in our kitchen. When Reuben's not around I pretend our flat is a ship, narrate the shipping forecast as the kettle boils. I love to watch the weather through it, that portal. In the summer, the outside world looks like a terrarium, and I pretend I am a lizard.

He looks at me now, and adds, 'Don't go if you don't want to. Do what you want.'

'It's not that easy,' I say, though I don't explain. Things are simple in his world. Things that are right are right and things that are wrong are wrong. Nothing is ever tangled. I look up at him as he tops and tails the onion.

He looks tired as he rubs his beard. On another day – in another life – I would have poked fun at that orange beard, said he looked like he'd been eating too many carrots. He would have smiled his small smile, shot me a mock-warning look.

'Who have you told now?' he says, sidestepping my irrationality like it is a smear on the pavement he wishes to avoid.

I am grateful for it, though it seems distasteful,

somehow, too. His words remind me of a very specific period of my life, when I was seventeen.

Who shall we tell? Dad said when I got the letter. It was our favourite thing to do. He came up to my bedroom with the cordless home phone and his address book and we went through every contact he had. *Joanna's got into Oxford*, he said, over and over again. It was nice, that night, that one tiny night in my teenage years that's come to define them.

I look at Reuben now, his gaze wary, his body language braced. 'Laura,' I say. 'That's all.'

He nods, his mouth turned slightly down, his eyes on me.

He understands, I think. My shame.

'What else did you do, today?' he says, making small talk, so unlike him.

He's moving the conversation along like it is a reluctant child who doesn't want to go to school, who's being hurried along against their will.

'Went to the police station. That's about it. It takes ages.'

His expression changes. It's just a flash, but I see it. Judgement.

You know how he can be.

I turn away from him, unable to look at that expression any more. For the next six months I will have to check in. After we go out for brunch on a Sunday. Instead of work. It is where I will go every single day. Through winter colds and flu and vomiting bugs. And he will know about it.

I won't be able to get up at eleven in the morning and have a shared bath. It has become the lynchpin of my day.

I go and sit in Reuben's office, opening my laptop

uselessly. It springs to life, and there's an application for an arts grant open on it that I evidently couldn't even finish. I was going to try to write a literary fiction novel. I had even opened Word, written a 'I' at the top of a blank page, and nothing more. It's embarrassing, and I shut the laptop again, turning in the chair and looking at the spare bed. I can hear Reuben in the kitchen, and then I can hear him coming along the hallway to me.

'Fancy a walk?' he says. 'While things cook?'

I catch his eye through the slice in the hinge of the door. One of his green eyes is visible, half an eyebrow, but nothing more.

'Okay.'

'It's freezing,' he says.

'Yeah.'

He opens the door. 'Got your thirty coat?' He looks past me at the laptop.

He has probably seen the arts grant. We use the same laptop. But he would never say, would never want to embarrass me, says he's happy if I simply do sudoku for the rest of my life if I want to.

'Forensics have it,' I say. The coat he bought me for my birthday. That beautiful coat.

He winces, like he's made an awkward faux pas at some work event, not offended his wife of two years, his partner of seven. 'Sorry,' he says, shifting imperceptibly away from me.

'No, I'm sorry,' I say, trying to reach out to him.

I step towards him, but he steps back further. His eyes are wary as they meet mine, his head tilted back slightly. I wonder if he fears me, too. If everybody does. If they are all secretly wondering what else I am capable of.

Suddenly, there in the spare room, I want to feel his skin on mine. His hands around the back of my waist in their protective way. His warm cheek against mine. His soft, full lips – I love those lips, the way he speaks right before he kisses me, sometimes, and it's as if the gravelly, quiet words are just for me, breathing his air out into my mouth. I step towards him, placing a hand on his arm, wanting him to step forward, open his arms, his body, and hold me tight despite everything. For him to love me in spite of myself.

And he does hold me. But before that, there's just a beat. It's hardly noticeable, but I spot it. He hesitates. He doesn't want to. But he weighs up his options and he knows that he should.

His body feels stiff against mine. Unimpressed. Unyielding. Conditional.

When he's holding me, I feel his head moving. I can see it, too, in the mirror that hangs above the bed – the mirror I bought when I read it would make the room look much bigger, when I wanted to *do up* the spare room in a minimalist Scandi style after reading a spread in *Elle* about it.

'What's up?' I say.

'Nothing,' he says, predictably. 'Nothing.'

15

Conceal

I am eight stone ten.

I have started weighing myself regularly, watching with a strange fascination as the secrets build up inside me and the weight falls off. I stop looking at the numbers and go to work, eventually.

It should be my dream job, being a librarian. I have loved reading forever – there is always a curled-up paperback on my bedside table – but I have always wanted something . . . more. Something more than books and checking people's fines and remembering to fill the bus up with petrol at the end of the day. Loving books isn't enough.

I have driven to work. The clothes are back in my car, transferred to the boot. I have decided I want to hide them in the library's offices.

The coat. Scarf. Gloves. I have decided I am going to put them into the lost property, like laundering money through an otherwise clean system. Nobody checks the lost property; Daisy just bins it annually, every summer, without looking. As long as I bury them deep, nobody will know. My coat is warm, with its filling, but isn't distinctive looking, and if they ask me if it's mine, I will deny it. None of them has ever seen the shoes, so it doesn't matter that they are distinctive. They were brand new. Are unconnected to me. So they'll be thrown away eventually and, until then – well. I know exactly where they are, but they are not in my house, and not discoverable by someone with the ability to connect them to me. But I can keep an eye on them. I do not have to worry about them being discovered by a stranger, uncovered, found by the police: they are hidden in plain sight.

The winter is rushing by, but the animal on my chest isn't diminishing. If anything, it is growing in size. Maturing. Becoming the biggest animal in the world. A blue whale on my chest.

It is the shortest day of the year, which I would be pleased about if it wasn't also the longest night. The shortest day would be welcome, gone in a few seconds, and the next, and the next, too.

December's always been a good month for me, and 21st December a good date in particular. Don't we all have lucky dates? As each year wheels around, I spot them.

Good things seemed to happen time and time again. On 21st December, I passed my driving test – a sweaty, gung-ho girl on my fourth attempt. It was when I was good, back then. I was the straight-A student. Everybody knew me; I was off to Oxford the next year. I played Sandy in *Grease* at school, won the swimming competition, was captain of the hockey team. I was an all-rounder. Now, I am a jack of all trades, but a master of none. Everyone's interests seem to have narrowed to one, except mine. Mine have widened, dispersed, to almost nothing. I do nothing. I am nothing.

And then, on 21st December, almost a decade later, Reuben proposed. I'm glad it was after all of that, and after Oxford; that Reuben asked me to marry him in my second guise, and not my first. That his love seemed – to me – to be unconditional.

And now here we are, and the wheel has turned again, and everything is different.

It's sleeting, hardly daylight, and the traffic is slow moving. It takes us longer than usual to get to Brentford. Sometimes, when traffic is bad, I pretend I am a celebrity in a slow-moving convoy. Reuben thinks it's ridiculous; Ed doesn't know.

It's 11.03 a.m. when it happens. We've just pulled into our stop and there's somebody already waiting. A tall woman, holding a little boy's hand. He has floppy dark hair, a turned-up nose. Plump cheeks, like a hamster. She's wearing bright green trainers and a black leather jacket that's spattered with sleet.

I think I know immediately, but I pretend not to, organizing library cards in their filing boxes, ignoring it. Ed opens the door, letting in a blur of cold December air. And then they're here, on the bus, and I can't ignore it any longer.

'Alright,' she says, clambering up the stairs, the boy behind her. She has long, angular legs, like a grasshopper, and takes the steps two at a time.

I am standing against the counter, listening to the sleety rain on the skylight. Deliberately looking up. Up, up, away from her. When I glance back, she's looking at the boy, who's standing on the top step, holding his tiny hand, palm up, to feel the flakes on it. Slightly impatiently, she reaches out and grabs him, like pulling on a dog's lead when it wants to stay and sniff the grass.

The child joins her, and when she turns her face to me, I have to acknowledge it. Those dark eyes. That mole. Her grief, worn like a layer of foundation slicked across her skin. Underneath her eyes. Across her forehead, which is furrowed, more lined than before.

And, as if my body remembers, too, it's as though there is a Catherine wheel of fire in my stomach. It churns so much I feel as though I might vomit, but it also creates a heat of its own, radiating outwards. Sweat forms in strange places. The small of my back. My upper lip. My sides, trickling down from my armpits in rivulets. She is here for me. It is over.

Ayesha. The surviving relative of the man I killed. And a child. Whose child?

'Hi,' Ed says, stepping towards her. He glances at me.

It's only a momentary look, but I know what it means. He's wondering why I am standing, stock-still on the bus, instead of serving our only customer. He is probably wondering why I am staring so intently at her. Perhaps he's caught my expression. He is very perceptive. Spends his time, like me, people watching. We used to discuss people together. Before.

I don't care what he thinks. I have to get off the bus. Away from her. Out into the cold air again.

'I've been sick and I'm going to be sick again,' I say in an undertone to Ed, which isn't too far from the truth.

'Um,' Ed says, dithering. A book of mindfulness is

splayed open on the counter behind us, which he's been reading during the quiet stops – now that I don't talk to him, I suppose. 'Do you need to go outside?' he says.

'Yes.'

I clamber down the steps and out into the cold. What's she doing here? Who's the boy? My breath clouds up the wintry morning air. Sleet pours down, as cold as snow but as fast and needle-sharp as rain. I'm cold, but I don't care.

I can hear Ed serving her. I cock my head, trying to listen.

She's trying to get the boy – Bilal – into reading. They've had some family problems recently, she explains in her south London accent. I'd forgotten how husky her voice is. 'Very recently,' she adds, as I listen. 'Only two weeks ago, but it's never too soon to try new things, is it? Maybe reading picture books will help him to – forget?'

Ed is silent as she talks, which is his way.

'So you'd like picture books?' Ed eventually asks, mildly. His voice is more muffled than it should be. He'll be squatting down, his knees clicking, as he tries to find the right age books for Bilal. I'd deal with them much better than Ed is doing. For all his compassion, his calm silence is unnerving. I'd find out what Bilal liked. Adventure. Colourful picture books. Escapism.

'My brother was – well. We don't know what happened,' she says. 'Bilal wants – his uncle was – I think he should be ... aren't books supposed to be a great distraction?'

Blood pounds in my head. Bilal's uncle. Guilt and regret hit me like a first frost. I feel myself withering underneath it. I think of all the things he might miss out on, with the uncle that he'll never really know. The sharing of a cheese platter late at night while they watch *The Godfather* together. Phone calls about things he couldn't tell his parents. Those things. Those adult, uncle–nephew things. I can picture the scenes so vividly, they may as well be playing out in front of me. Poor Bilal, I think, my back to them as I look out across Brentford, feeling sick and repulsive.

'Distraction sounds good to me,' Ed says.

'Yes,' she says softly, so quietly I can barely hear it.

Perhaps . . . perhaps she is not here for me. Perhaps she doesn't know. Maybe it really is simply about books, and the things they can do for people. I would turn to a library in grief, in tragedy. Why not her?

To my frustration, Ed says nothing back to Ayesha. Couldn't he console her, where I can't? But then, this is not Ed's way. How many times has he sat silently, munching on pick 'n' mix, back when I have had problems, and said nothing? (He loves sweets, and is one of those people whose preferences seem to dominate, and so all we ever eat on the bus is pear drops and bonbons and foam bananas.) Hundreds of times. He just listens, does Ed. Without judgement, and with compassion. I am never usually irritated by it.

I keep breathing in the winter air until I hear them coming down the steps. Bilal's clutching two picture books. Ayesha has a few more. She glances at me, just briefly, but I see it. Ed waves them off, then perches on the top step where Bilal had stood, catching flakes of sleet, looking at me carefully.

I avoid his gaze, walking up the stairs and squeezing past him. My bad hand brushes the door frame and I wince in pain. Ed leaves it. He'll choose his moment. He tilts his head back and I see his huge, thick glasses blanch white as they catch the reflection of the skylight. We are both silent for a moment.

And then, suddenly, she has appeared again, right at the bottom of the stairs, looking up at me, her nose scrunched.

'Hey,' she says, her tone upbeat, her voice higher than usual, for just a second.

I freeze, knowing almost before it happens what's to come.

'How's your brother doing?' she says.

Ed looks at us, his head moving left and right, from her to me and back again.

'I thought it was you, when I saw you – when we were coming out,' she adds.

'Oh,' I say, wondering if I can deny it.

I had my scarf around my hair in the mosque. Perhaps I could get away with pretending not to know her. No. I can't. She hasn't asked if I'm the same person: she knows. I can't lie. I won't get away with it. The sweat is back, the heaviness on my chest, and I shift, gulping as I loosen my scarf. The same scarf. Stupid Joanna. Why did I go? How could I have been so foolish?

'My brother,' I say.

She's nodding, encouragingly, a faint frown crossing her features. She wishes she hadn't asked. She has embarrassed me. And that's what stops me lying – trying, and failing, to be good. It's not fair to pretend I don't know what she's talking about. It is strange, this new world I inhabit with its contradictory rules.

Ed is still in his own world, looking up at the skylight, and so I answer her.

'He'll be okay,' I say. 'I hope.' I give a worried, hopeful shrug, playing the role of my life: the sympathetic sister. Sympathetic over a fabricated death.

'I hope so, too,' she says, bobbing on her toes. And then she takes Bilal's hand, shifting the books to her other arm, and leaves again. 'We'll be back next week,' she says.

My body is flooded with cold, cruel fear. I never realized it before, but fear is the worst of all emotions. With sadness, you cry. With grief, you miss somebody. But fear. Fear gets under your skin. And you can do nothing but feel it. Worry about it.

She will be back. There's no getting out of it. I have to keep the lie going. Package it up, as though it's the truth. Absorb it into the regular rotation of lies I have told.

I look back at Ed. He's still looking up at the light, but his eyes are on me. The effect is strange. Almost animalistic. Very slowly, he raises his eyebrows, his expression opening, becoming expectant.

'Wilf's girlfriend died,' I say.

'What?' Ed says. His head drops, his mouth opens.

'A while ago,' I say, wondering how I will explain it away. My colleague, my friend. There's no way I wouldn't have told Ed. 'He hardly knew her, actually. It was all very early days.'

'Jesus,' Ed says. 'How?'

'Car crash,' I say, recalling some statistic about the most likely way to die.

'God,' Ed says.

He turns away from me, sorting out the children's shelf, which is messy and disordered from where Bilal has pulled books out randomly. There are gaps, like missing teeth, making the bookcase grin weirdly. 'How serious were they?'

'Just a few dates,' I say.

Minimize it. Isn't that what you're supposed to do? To dampen the effect of the lie, like slowly, slowly putting out a fire. Next week I'll tell him it was just *one* date, actually, and soon he will have forgotten it, like a tattoo gradually getting lasered each week and fading, fading, fading . . .

'When?'

'Just a few weeks ago. I didn't want to – I didn't want to make it into a huge deal.'

'What a shame for Wilf, though,' Ed says musingly as he neatens up the books.

Ed knows Wilf's completely blank relationship history as well as I do; he's forever listening to me moan about how my brother is a workaholic, doesn't value relationships, only things. Mostly money.

'And for you, Jojo,' he says softly. 'I'm so sorry. You should've said.'

I shrug awkwardly. I can't deal with his intense compassion.

'I'm so sorry, Jo,' he says again, glancing at me and holding my gaze.

'I know. Bad luck,' I say, bringing a finger up to my mouth and biting the nail.

*

I tell Ed to drop me back at the office, that my car's there, waiting for me. I tell him I'll lock up. He looks up at me, surprised; he almost always drops me home.

When we arrive, he says, 'I've got loads to do here.'

I realize, then, that my working day usually ends long before his. I never knew before.

'I can help,' I say, following him inside, even though I will have to come back out to get the clothes.

As he gathers up books, I tug gently on the cupboard where the lost property sits. I can picture all of the items behind it. Jumpers and tops and children's coats. There's always loads of it. It will be so easy to hide mine there; they'll be taken to the tip, one day, but not by me.

But the cupboard is locked. Ed's keys are always attached to his belt; he wears them like a janitor. There's not enough time to get to my car and put the stuff into the cupboard without him seeing, anyway. He's busy tidying up, but close by. Always close by.

There's no opportunity. He doesn't leave the office until he's done, and waits for me, expectantly, then leads me out to my car with him.

I glance behind me as he locks up, wistful, looking at the cupboard through the window, at the opportunity.

Missed.

16

Reveal

It is five weeks After when Sarah telephones me. It was the strangest Christmas, full of foreboding instead of cheer. Where would I be next Christmas?

'We have witness statements,' Sarah says. She asks me to go to her office later that day, or the next day, but I want to go now. I can't wait. She says – reluctantly, it seems to me – that she's free.

'Will you come?' I say to Reuben, standing in my trench coat, which isn't quite warm enough for the January chill. 'I don't know what they'll say.'

'Of course,' he says immediately. 'Of course I will.' He isn't looking at me, fiddling instead with his keys, sorting the flat key out from the others ready to lock up.

I hear him make a call while I am getting my shoes. He is cancelling a meeting. He emerges, his face impassive, and then I see that he is wearing a suit. I don't ask what the appointment was. Court, maybe. With a client.

We arrive and sit down in Sarah's foyer. It's run-down, with a shabby red-carpeted corridor lined with boxes. There is no receptionist.

'It's good,' Reuben whispers as we sit. 'It means they're not making too much bloody money.'

It's called Powell's. I've seen it on signs, I remember now. In less than salubrious areas; above high-rise flats and in back-end car parks. It advertises itself on teal-coloured billboards, posters, business cards left on the tube. As though anyone committing a crime might require their help to deal with the aftermath. And isn't that true? Look at me.

Sarah comes to collect us and we go to sit in a meeting room. I like her lack of small talk. No discussion of the journey here, the weather, how I'm feeling. She's wearing a T-shirt, tucked into a skirt suit. It's styled up, with a large necklace, so it's just about office appropriate. Her handbag – a leather one from River Island, according to the logo on the zip – and her keys sit nearby. She has a Sea Life keyring, and I wonder why. Perhaps it was her first Mother's Day present from her child, if she has one. Or an in-joke with her husband, if she has one.

The view from the window is out on to central London. I can see the Gherkin and the Nokia building. I close my eyes and try to imagine that I'm just a high-flyer. That I'm here because I'm smart, not because I am incredibly, incredibly dumb.

The room has a large table in the centre of it, but it's pine, and rickety, not a mahogany boardroom table. There's a display of straggly lilies, which Sarah positions to her right. Cheap tea and coffee machines are off to one side.

'I've traced Sadiq, from the business card you gave me,' she says. 'I'm hoping he will confirm what you have said about that night.'

I breathe out through my nose. 'Good,' I say. 'Good. He will. It was obvious. Laura will, too.'

'It will be excellent if Sadiq confirms it himself,' she says. 'I'm seeing him next week. Anyway. The victim has woken up. He can't give a statement. This is from his sister. And then a second one from his treating doctor, about his current condition, which is evidently slightly worse than we thought. We will get another expert statement about his health, but at the moment they both create a picture of it for us.'

She rattles all of this off as though she is talking us through a complicated but tedious paperwork procedure, like how to get a mortgage or to challenge a parking fine.

'He's worse?' I say.

It hits me then. It happens all the time. In the shower when I'm opening a new bottle of strawberry shower smoothie. Taking a first sip of coffee in the morning. Gazing out of a window. Feeling the cold winter air against my face. If we *lose*, as Sarah puts it, I will be in for a very long time. I haven't googled it. I haven't asked her. But I know, from that one-word sentence I saw in her notes.

Life.

It's ironic, really, when it means practically the opposite of living.

She's not looking at me, concentrates instead on pouring the water from the jug into three glasses. A segment of lemon plops in, splashing the pine table. A drop of water sits there, distended, on the tabletop, and I reach out to squash it with my index finger. Reuben's eyes follow my movements.

I leaf through the statements. None of the words leap

out at me. They all blur together. I glean what I can from them: Imran is brain damaged; to what extent, nobody knows.

I don't want to read on, but I do. The words keep on attacking me, like hundreds of needles across my skin.

Currently, he can't care for himself. He will probably struggle to work. At the very least, he will not be the same again. He is struggling to regulate his emotions. He is forgetful, reintroducing himself to nurses, over and over. He is not Imran any more, his sister's statement reads sadly. He drinks tea, mechanically, with a straw, the cup held by a nurse; he has forgotten, his sister says, that he hates tea. My eyes fill with tears.

In all of that – the injury, the life-changing stuff – it's the tea that does it.

Sarah is watching me reading it. 'It's all just conjecture. We won't know his condition for a while now. Until he's stable,' she says. 'So ignore that. They're getting proper expert evidence. About his prognosis. His injuries. We need to concentrate on what his sister says about what he was doing that night, and link it to your mistake. To make people see how easily you made it.'

She briefly shows me a couple of photographs, taken from the hospital. A head wound, deep and red. A close-up of his face, in hospital, the eyes closed. He looks nothing, I realize with a start, like Sadiq. He has distinctive, high cheekbones, a wide, sensual mouth that turns down at its edges.

'Can I see him?' I croak.

'Who?' Sarah says.

'Imran. What did he look like – before?'

'I don't know,' Sarah says.

Reuben plucks the papers out of my fingertips and lays them, text down, on the table. I look at him gratefully, but really I'm processing the last sentence I read in the witness statement.

Previously, he loved running, dancing, and was undergoing a cheffing course in central London. He suffered from social anxiety but was learning to manage it with exercise and CBT. He was out running that night when . . .

He was running.

He was just running.

I almost laugh. It makes sense in a funny kind of way. I can plot it, like a narrative; my whole life leading up to this point.

When I was five, I thought I saw a jester outside our car in a petrol station while Mum, Dad and Wilf were inside in the services. I swore on it. And that's where it began. The teasing. *Imaginative Joanna*, they would say. *She confuses fantasy and reality.*

I spent my degree making up stories for the strange people dwelling in my tutorials. Everybody at school had looked the same, in hindsight, and suddenly, at Oxford, everybody was . . . different. A man with waist-length dark hair. I used to imagine him combing it every morning. One hundred brush strokes, I was thinking, instead of discussing *Ulysses*. The girl with the bowl cut of curls, the ends of which she dyed red. The boy who had already made so many notes his folder was rammed full of immaculate, tiny writing.

I still do it now with every customer who comes into the library. Or I did, anyway. The man with the little regular scars on his forearms. The woman with the bald patch on the top of her head. The guy with the beard and the wild hair but the wise, kind dark eyes who I privately call Gandalf. Who were they all? I wanted to know. I made things up for them. To get inside them.

And now, here we are. The perfect, unfolding narrative from an imaginative woman. I was lifted up by the fingers of God and planted in the wrong place, at the wrong time, and I imagined that somebody who was merely out running was trying to attack me.

His life is changed, and more than mine. I deserve all of this. Anybody would say so. The State would say so. The law. And that's worse than any of it. His injuries. His life.

Reuben clears his throat. 'What's the point of all of this? She's not *dangerous*. She doesn't need to be *inside*. He probably doesn't even want her inside.'

'No . . .' Sarah says, nodding seriously like my socialist husband hasn't just taken down the justice system in four sentences. 'You don't need to tell me that.' She says it kindly, not dismissively, in a departure from her usual authoritative tone.

'To punish and discourage,' Reuben says, talking over her, using the voice he uses when he's talking to Tories.

I see Sarah shift away from him. What Reuben doesn't realize is that he is never going to change anybody's mind.

'Those are the reasons – for prison – aren't they?' he says.

'Yes, but –'

'She doesn't need punishing. She's not going to do it

again. What's next? Reforming her? Get her a probation officer? As if. It was wrong place, wrong time. Removing offenders from society – that's another reason, isn't it? Because they're dangerous. Well, she's not. I just can't see why . . . it's a hefty prison term, isn't it?'

Sarah doesn't say anything in response to that, only darts a quick look at me. She knows I don't want to know, and so she won't hint either way. She's a good lawyer. Her legs are crossed only at the ankles, primly, and she sits forward in a wave of perfume and looks at us. 'You missed one,' she says.

'What?' Reuben says.

'Justice.'

'Justice?' he thunders.

'This is the law,' she says, spreading her hands wide. 'The prosecution have to prove that Joanna broke the law. Forget about the rest. Just look at the offence. She did not commit it. That's what we're arguing. Self-defence. Mistake. If we prove the mistake was made in good faith, and not negligently, then the law will treat your case *as though it was Sadiq*. Then, we need only to establish that you acted in self-defence.'

Just look at the offence. I repeat it to myself, thinking about Imran and his tea. But quietly, a small voice in the back of my mind agrees with Reuben: what use is it all? What will change for Imran if I go to prison? Who is any of this for? The thought is like a rain cloud, flitting over my consciousness. What's the point of any of it?

'If something's a crime and you do that thing – you deserve the punishment. That's what the UK law is. Whether or not . . . whether or not you're – you

164

know – good. The idea is that the law puts in place all possible excuses and defences. If you don't have one, then you get the punishment.'

I don't say anything. I am not good.

'But it was a mistake,' Sarah continues. 'And there's good, supportive law around this. There's a whole doctrine . . . I think that's your best shot. Though it's not used very often. Sadiq will help. I will impress upon him that it's best just to be honest. To prove your innocent mistake.' Her features soften, and I can see sympathy there behind the facts of the law. Has she ever walked home alone, on an ill-advised jaunt? Perhaps she had dodged the bullet that hit me.

'Mistake,' I say. The whole thing was a mistake.

'So, we'll use mistake to make the point that you thought the victim was somebody other than who he was, and then self-defence after we've got over the mistake hurdle.'

'Right.'

I reach over and finger one of the lily petals in the middle of the flower arrangement. It's plastic. The pollen's plastic, too. They looked so real, until I saw the fine layer of dust.

'We can do this,' she says.

'Okay,' I say.

'We can.'

'Okay,' I say again.

'Let's get to it, then. We need to put your defence statement together. It's your evidence.' She turns to Reuben. 'So, according to the phone records, Joanna called you at eleven thirty-three.'

'Yes,' he says.

'And how did she sound?'

'Well – frightened,' Reuben says, looking at me. 'Of course.'

She looks at me. 'So you hung up, and then you must've walked for . . .'

'I don't know.'

'Your 999 call was at eleven thirty-nine.'

I think quickly, am forced to think quickly. 'It happened at eleven thirty-nine.'

But the reality, of course, is that it will have been eleven thirty-four. Right after the call cut out. The rest was . . . the rest was the dithering.

'So you were pursued while on the phone to Reuben, and then pursued for a further five minutes.'

'Yes,' I lie.

'Right,' she says. 'And where were you when you called Reuben?'

My mind spins. Did I ever tell him I was right by the bridge? I don't think so. 'Outside the bar,' I say, hoping there will be no accurate telephone call records. I thank the stars that Reuben turned off my GPS that one time, said Facebook was tracking my every move.

She writes it down. 'Okay, then.' She looks up at Reuben. 'And you agree with this – you corroborate?'

'Whatever Jo says. That's the truth,' Reuben says, his face open, trusting.

Reuben and I are in the car behind Sarah's office. Neither of us is saying anything. He's not put the keys in the ignition yet. It's one of those January days where it seems as though it's not ever going to get light, the rain beating down like God is drumming his fingers on the roof of the car. I made Reuben come to V Festival with me, years ago, to see The Killers, and it rained like this as we left. *You hated that, didn't you?* I'd said to Reuben in the car. He'd nodded, smiling that half-smile. *Never make me attend a festival again*, he'd said, the car's wheels spinning in the mud. We failed to move, had to call the AA out, left after dark in the end. I was unable to stop laughing on the way home and, eventually, Reuben joined in.

'I can't believe he's so badly injured,' Reuben says now. His voice is low. Gravelly.

'I . . . I know,' I say.

'He'll give evidence. If he recovers enough,' Reuben says. 'So we'll see . . . we'll see him. In court. The man you –'

'I know,' I say quietly. 'I know.'

'I feel like a dickhead for sounding off. I sounded like a victim blamer or something,' he says.

'You didn't,' I say. 'It all seems . . . so unfair. So shit.'

'Yes. If you hadn't been there . . . it's not like you were waiting to hurt someone.'

I can see him grappling with it. My crime. The law. Everything.

'I mean, you hardly did anything wrong. Did you?' he says, and when he turns to me, his eyes look desperate, lined and older looking than before.

I squeeze his hand, not knowing what to say. *Of course I did*, I want to tell him, sadly.

'You made a mistake. But then you did everything you could to fix it,' he says. 'I just . . . I just don't know why they're going after you like this.'

I can't think about it. People may be sympathetic, but it is hardly commonplace. A man is disabled because of me. I swallow. If I had left two minutes later. Two minutes earlier. If he had been wearing different trainers. If only Sadiq hadn't frightened me – surely some of this is partly his fault? – then none of it would have happened. If I had been brave enough to turn my head, just a few degrees. I would have seen.

God, I am so stupid. I have ruined my life. I have ruined his life. I have ruined Reuben's life. The only person winning is Sarah.

'I wish things had been different,' I say, my voice low.

'Me, too,' he says. 'I wish we'd stayed on the line. That we hadn't got cut off.'

'I really thought . . . I really thought it was curtains. I thought he was going to – to . . . to get me,' I say, and my voice breaks. Because, underneath it all, of course, I am a victim, too. Imran is worse off than me, but I am a victim of *something*.

'I know,' he says.

I think of the lie I told. The tiny lie that felt meaningless. *I got him out of the water straight away.* They fight, the instinct for self-preservation and the instinct to tell the truth, like stags with locked horns, both sitting on my chest, their antlers stabbing my heart. And suddenly I am telling him, my husband, and maybe he can help. Maybe he can share the weight.

'God,' I say, wishing – foolishly – to downplay it. To mislead. 'I wish I had got him out of the puddle immediately.'

It's as though a silent bomb has gone off in the car. Everything looks the same. The gear stick. The Yankee

168

Candle hanging air freshener left over from the previous Christmas, now faded to a light pink. The rain running down the windows, the drops with trailing tails. And yet everything has changed. The air crackles with it, like that moment between lightning and thunder, like the moment between the two final chords of a piano concerto.

'What?' Reuben says softly, slowly, a note of danger in his voice.

I turn and look at him. His stubble has become a full beard, the strands a dull auburn in the fading winter light, stark against his white shirt. Of course, he's not misled.

'What?' he says again.

'I didn't get him out of that puddle as soon as I said. I was . . . I was so scared. I wasn't doing anything.'

'How long? So those call records – so your account of it? It's wrong? My evidence is wrong?'

I ignore his other questions. 'Minutes. I almost called you again. I almost . . . I almost walked away.'

Reuben makes a sudden movement, towards the gear stick, his left hand reaching to grab it. He grips it like it's an enemy's hand.

'You almost left?'

'I was so afraid. I thought he was going to kill me. And then I was so afraid . . . of what I'd done. I was in shock. You've no idea. You've no idea how something like that – it changes things.'

'I've some idea,' he says.

It has the desired effect: it reminds me that this isn't happening only to me. That it isn't my life alone that's changed forever.

'Yes. I was just . . . I don't even properly remember,' I

say, although I do. I remember absolutely everything: the descending mist. The bright, lemon yellow of the street lights. The man I thought to be Sadiq lying at the bottom of the stairs, his limbs bent at strange angles. How wet my clothes got. My hair clinging to my neck like snakes. How I was paralysed. With fear of him, of course. But also with shock. At myself.

'Can't you see?' I say. 'I was terrified. I was dithering.'

Reuben says nothing.

And so I add, 'Nobody knows.'

I shouldn't have told him that way. I should have been straight with him. Looked him in the eye. A full and frank confession. I could have told him I was ashamed of it. Paved the way. Not this. This selfish, stupid, offhand confession. I went in the back door instead of the front way; I surprised him, like a burglar in the middle of the night, and now he's surprising me back.

'Wouldn't you ever consider leaving? Wouldn't you dither for just a second?' I say.

His gaze swivels to me. That green gaze.

'Did you know?' he says. 'About the puddle? That he couldn't breathe?'

'No. *No.*'

He nods.

'But wouldn't you ever consider leaving?' I push, pressing him, ransacking his mind for a grain of forgiveness, of understanding. But it's not there. I am opening drawers and cupboards that I have already looked in, searching for something I am never going to find.

He doesn't answer me. He puts the keys in the ignition. The car into gear. Checks each mirror. Methodically. I wait. I wait to hear, but nothing comes. Only the sound of the rain, like a timer, ticking down.

'No,' he says, after a few moments have elapsed. 'I'm sorry, but – no. That's a life. There. In the puddle. While you waited. While you stood and did nothing.'

Conceal

Reuben gave me an extravagant gift for Christmas: a weighty, thick butter-coloured candle scented with cloves, which I burnt all through December and into the New Year, not enjoying a second of it, merely staring at the flames and feeling guilty.

It is January, now, and it is just as I walk into work, feeling the cold across my ribs, considering whether I can get a set of keys to the offices so I can get in and hide the clothes, that I see them.

The police.

They are here.

Waiting for me.

I should be surprised, after all these weeks, but I can hardly muster it.

'Men here for you,' Ed says mildly as he starts organizing things on the bus. I walk past him and head towards the offices.

He's in the driver's seat, with the door open, when they say to me, 'We hope you don't mind us coming here – we haven't been able to track you down at home. We did leave a note. We need to talk to you about an event that occurred on a Friday in December.'

As I walk with them, into the office, I see Ed's head is

inclined just to the right, slightly cocked, as though he is listening intently.

'Detective Inspector Lawson, and this is Detective Sergeant Davies,' they say, when we are sitting inside a shabby meeting room.

I go and make us tea from the machine, my hands shaking the entire time. I get the impression Lawson is in charge. I wonder if they're friends; if they find the boss–subordinate relationship tough. Maybe Lawson is a stickler at work but nice in the pub, and Davies finds it confusing ... Davies's hopes are for progression. Lawson's are to lead, to be taken seriously, but also to be liked, maybe. They're peering at me strangely and I place the cups of tea on the table, my left hand aching with the effort.

They're in suits, like lawyers, or the Men in Black.

'Sprained your wrist?' Lawson says.

'Fell over,' I say. 'In the Sainsbury's car park. So embarrassing.'

I don't know where the lie comes from, but it sounds plausible. He nods as I meet his eyes.

'We just want to have a quick chat with you about an incident, as I said, in December,' Lawson says slickly.

I clock the language immediately. Quick chat. Just. He's minimizing it. I meet his eyes. They're so pale as to be almost silvery, with just a hint of blue.

'We're from the CID,' Lawson says. 'Criminal Investigation Department. A man's body was discovered after an assault one Friday night – you might've seen on the news . . .?'

I nod quickly.

So this is it.

It's over.

It's almost laughable, my attempt at getting away with it. I have lasted mere weeks. Of course.

I breathe deeply.

Lawson turns to me, his body language relaxed, open, his elbows resting on his knees. He stares straight into my eyes.

And that's when I think of them. The gloves. The gloves I wore that night – surely with Imran's DNA on them – are in my car, just over there. They loom in front of me, in my mind, like they are dangling in front of us. I am so glad he can't know. That I will still look normal to him. Just the face of a nervous woman.

'We understand you were in the Little Venice area on that Friday night – Joanna. Your friend gave us your work address when you weren't in.'

'Oh,' I say. 'She said you called round there.' But, inside, my mind is racing. She didn't tell me she'd given my work address. But of course – why would she? She is so sure of my innocence, too.

I try to arrange my face into an impassive smile. What would I know if I hadn't been there? I would have seen the news, but that's all. I would remember the date, where I was, because I was nearby – and Sadiq, of course – but nothing more.

'Yes. Yes we did. And to yours. You got our note?'

'Sorry, been so busy, what with Christmas . . .' I lie.

'When did you leave the bar you were at – the Gondola?'

'About half eleven.'

Lawson looks at Davies, who nods. 'Yes,' he says.

'You are on CCTV,' Lawson says. 'Outside the bar.

You and Laura. You part, and you walk in the direction of the canal on the CCTV we have seen.'

It's like a grenade has gone off, and now the air hums with silence. My ears shiver with it. Davies is looking at me. Lawson is waiting for me to speak. I didn't think it through. Another way I'm still the same. I'm not a criminal mastermind. I am still scatty, stupid Joanna.

Where *did* I go? Did I see anybody? *Was* I at the canal? What's my story? Why haven't I taken the time to work it out? It would have taken five minutes. I am a prize idiot.

I can't meet his eyes. Those pale, wolfish eyes.

'We're running out of leads, Joanna. And you were seen – really very near to the scene. It would be great if you could help us.'

'Oh, well,' I gabble. 'I went another way, actually. I went that way and then I went another way. In the end.'

'Right?' Lawson sounds uninterested but his eyes are calm and watchful, looking at me, watching my shaking hand reach for my tea in its polystyrene cup. He is taking it all in.

'So I was going to go down along the canal path, but . . .' I pause. I have to tell them about Sadiq. It's what I would do if things were different. 'A man – called Sadiq –' I add, 'had been harassing me in the Gondola. So I didn't want to walk somewhere deserted.'

It could almost be true. My lies make more sense to me than the truth. The truth is muddy and strange.

The only thing is: it's not the truth.

'I went the long way. Away from the Gondola and . . . along the road. And then across the second bridge down,' I lie. 'Would you like his – he gave me a . . .' I fish around for my purse and find his business card, thinking, *Forgive me, Sadiq.*

'What kind of harassment?'

'Sexual,' I say. 'Predatory.'

Lawson turns the tattered business card over in his hands. 'So bad you went another way?'

'Yes.'

'We'll look for him. Thank you,' Lawson says. He asks me more about how Sadiq behaved, and I describe it simply. Dispassionately. He asks me how he looked. What he was wearing.

'So I was avoiding him when I took a different route. Not down the canal – though it looks like I went that way.'

'Right,' Lawson says with a nod. And then a pause. He sips his tea. And then he looks at me, and says three words. 'Which route, exactly?'

'Which route?' I say. I bet he's been on a course about liars. Hundreds of them. And I bet I am behaving absolutely typically.

We all think we are special. Brilliant liars, if our lives depended on it. But we are all the same. Reuben tells me things he's read (he is always saying *I read somewhere . . .*) and one time he told me about the structure of a lie. It was either that there was not enough detail during the lie, or too much. I can't remember.

'Right – so,' Lawson says, and then he reaches into a kind of satchel that he's placed on the floor and pulls out a piece of paper. He lays it flat on the table. I see after a second that it's a map. A screenshot of Google Maps.

I try to think, but it's impossible under his gaze.

'Show me on here where you went,' he says. 'Take your time.'

I pinch the map and slide it nearer to me. I locate the Gondola with my index finger. That's it, there – yes. Because we could see the canal bridges – just – from the windows.

With my eyes, I trace my real pathway, over the bridge to Warwick Avenue, stopping at the top of the steps. If the CCTV is right outside the club, I must have been seen heading towards the canal. And so, to avoid it, I'm going to have to say I turned almost completely around, left instead of right.

'So I walked this way,' I say, tracing a path from the bar to the road, 'but then I looped over this way.' I finish a path. I hope it works. It goes down a street and over another bridge, but it gets me to Warwick Avenue tube alright, and at about the same angle, because no doubt there's CCTV there, too.

Lawson retraces my steps along the map. 'So if we were to look at the CCTV from here,' he says, pointing to a spot in the road on the map, 'and here . . . we'd find you?'

'Yes,' I say, because I have to.

I try to remember the roads, the shape of them, and I look at them on the map. They're suburban. But there could be CCTV. What do I know? But perhaps he's just saying it, to get me to say something I don't mean. Can they do that, police officers? I have no idea.

'Well, in that case – you're no use to us,' he says.

'I know,' I say eagerly.

Davies starts to speak, then, opening his mouth even though Lawson's gaze swivels to him. 'You saw nothing.'

'No,' I say, thinking that if they were really only interested in my evidence as a witness, and not as a suspect, they would have asked this by now.

A feeling of unease creeps into the meeting room and sits between us. Should I call a lawyer, I wonder? It doesn't make sense, looking at the two men, in my shabby back office room, the disposable teacups. But appearances are deceptive. It doesn't mean they're not here to arrest me, depending on what I say.

'We'll be in touch if we need anything further, Joanna,' Lawson says.

Relief blooms through me like hot air from an oven, but I don't dare relax yet. He could stop, innocently, his hand on the doorknob, and ask to look at what I was wearing that night. My hat. My gloves. My scarf. The tread of my shoes. All just outside, a few feet away in my car.

'That's a weird way to go,' he says as he's leaving. A parting shot, a warning sign, fired into the night.

We're walking through the main office. Ed is sitting on a desk chair, waiting for me, doing nothing at all, as is his way.

'See you later,' I say, my fingers trembling by my sides, wanting them to stop talking, to leave me alone.

'You could've just gone over the bridge. To the tube. It's a totally straight line,' he says. 'And very well populated. If you were worried.' Inwardly, I curse the police's knowledge of London.

'Yeah,' I say dumbly.

'Did you not think to discuss this with us? This harassment? When we're clearly looking for somebody behaving suspiciously?'

Their threat could not be clearer.

And it's obvious to Ed, too, who's looking interestedly over at us.

'I didn't think,' I say.

Lawson nods, once, seeming to understand. And maybe he is trustworthy. Maybe I am being too cynical, too much like Reuben.

This is it, I tell myself. No more. I will work as hard as I can to get rid of that evidence.

Just let them leave. Give me another chance. My shoulders feel rigid with bizarre determination to do the wrong thing as I see the CID out.

They walk to their car just across the street, underneath a spindly tree.

When I get back, Ed is still sitting, doing nothing. Just looking at me. He doesn't ask what they wanted. He doesn't ask what happened that Friday night, even though he surely heard. He doesn't ask if the burglaries were a lie. He says nothing. Simply stares at me, as if waiting for me to say something.

But I don't. Can't.

18

Reveal

We have Laura and Jonty over for dinner. Reuben suggested it, over WhatsApp, without asking me; something he's never done before. He sent it straight to the group we are in, all four of us, and I read his invite like they might. As though Reuben and I are near enough lifelong friends, but nothing more.

When they knock on the door and we let them in, Laura always exclaims how cute our basement flat is, with the plants that make it almost impossible to navigate down the stairs and the herbs that line our kitchen windowsill. We laugh about those plants; the most obvious emblem of my faddishness. She has painted them, before. A beautiful portrait of a child amongst the flowers; a rare, non-feminist portrait of hers.

'Jonty's got mismatched shoes on,' Laura says as soon as she is inside.

Reuben and I look down. He's wearing two Converse trainers, but they're different colours. We laugh, and I'm grateful for the distraction; the normality. It's the first time we've all got together since it happened. It might even be the first time I've laughed.

'They may as well be the same shoes,' Jonty says good-naturedly.

Reuben exhales, a tiny laugh. 'They're different,' he says. 'They're different shoes.'

Laura's dressed unusually, for her. Gone are her normal clothes; the long, flowing trousers that look more like maxi skirts. She's wearing dark, skinny jeans that look expensive, a silk, draped top. A blazer. Her hair is different. Less spiked. Less harsh.

I look at the ship window in our kitchen. It's misty outside and Jonty and Laura have let a chill in with them. I reach to trace a finger down it. It is as though my sand timer is running out twice as quickly as everybody else's. Or I have half as much sand. I wonder if, afterwards, I will remember all these lovely things about my life, or if I will be forever changed, unable to enjoy things, to dream? I think, too, of Sadiq, ready to make his imminent statement about me that might change my life. I think of Imran, lying motionless somewhere. There's an awkward silence as I touch the window, which Reuben – unusually – breaks. He is looking at Jonty with a disbelieving expression; one he has regarded me with, over and over.

'Didn't they look different as you were tying your laces?' he says.

Jonty just shrugs and laughs. 'I was distracted by my beautiful, glittery perfume bottles,' he says, and Reuben laughs, too.

Laura rolls her eyes. 'Very intricate work, painting perfume bottles with glitter,' she says.

'I thought that was just for Christmas.'

'Perfume is not just for Christmas,' Jonty says seriously.

Laura seems distant, and I nudge her elbow. We struggle

to find friend-time, when we're together with the boys. I wish it was acceptable to go on a walk with her, or to have half an hour in separate rooms. There are always things I want to say to her in private.

'You alright?' I say quietly.

'Even the laces are different,' Reuben is saying. He can't leave it alone.

'I don't tie the laces. Just stuff my feet in,' Jonty says.

Reuben smiles at him indulgently, like he is a child, then leads him to the fridge to show him the beer.

Laura perches on one of the bar stools at our kitchen counter. I sit on the other, looking at her. She reaches and picks up the retro salt shaker I bought from Tiger last month and pours a tiny pile into her hand. I stare at it. I'm forever looking for omens, these days. I can't help but stare at the white crystalline pile in her palm.

'You're not working any longer,' she says, sounding strangely formal.

'Well, no,' I say, blinking. 'They wouldn't let me . . .'

'Maybe when the trial's over?' she says.

I nod, although I am thinking, *Long after that.*

She pours the salt on to the countertop. I frown, though I don't mind. Reuben would.

'Your stuff has got me thinking. We're thirty.'

I try not to bristle at that. My crime has got her thinking. The loss of my job. My imminent incarceration. It's changed things for everybody, not just me.

But of course it has. Whether or not it's more important to me, it's still important to her, to Reuben, to Wilf. The human mind is so reliably self-involved. Or, at least, mine is. I can't imagine the life crisis I would have had if it had been Laura who was being tried for causing grievous bodily harm with intent.

I look at her, shifting the salt into tiny piles, wearing her clothes that look expensive.

'I had an interview today,' she says. 'For a grad scheme.'

'Why?' I say. 'You're not a grad.'

'No, but I . . .'

'What?'

'I dunno, Jo. It's time to stop arsing around, isn't it? I want a career. I do. Before I want a baby. That's . . .'

'What?' I say, my voice sounding shrill.

It's as though everybody who used to be around me is prepping, moving on, while my life's on hold.

'Babies,' I say. 'I want them too.'

'Do you?'

'Of course I do,' I say, sounding bruised and prickly all at once. 'But I don't have the luxury of making it happen.'

'Well, no,' Laura says. 'Not right now.'

We lapse into silence, and then she says, 'Marketing.'

'What?'

'It's in marketing. At a bank.'

'Marketing what?'

'The bank.'

'Sounds pointless.'

'It'll be good for me. To join the real world.'

'The rat race,' I say spitefully, even though I do not really mean it.

I am only jealous. Of her direction, but also the luxury of choice. To join a graduate scheme. To not have a planetary problem looming so large that the rest of life merely orbits around it, waiting for the trial, waiting for the outcome. To be able to choose to have a child this year, next year, the year after.

'It'll be good for us. Jonty is going to get one, too. We might sell the boat.'

'Jonty can't even put a pair of shoes on,' I say, and it's meant to be teasing, an emblem of their chaotic lifestyle with their barge that drifts along the Thames, as directionless as they are, and the motley crew of people who stay for a few weeks at a time and then move on. But it comes out as shrill, judgemental, like I am clinging on to a past Laura that she wants to leave behind.

'Yeah, well. It's not too late to learn,' she says, looking at me kindly. Perhaps with pity.

'Are you painting?' I say, thinking of her beautiful, photograph-like paintings. They always make a feminist point, a political point. The most recent set are painted tabloid newspapers, with all of the photos of men in suits as women, and with page three as men.

'No,' she says.

She's had her nails done. Straightened her hair. She looks totally different. And so while we've been making the same jokes, telling each other the same stories about our jobs, she's been getting ready, behind the scenes, like a determined understudy. My life is ruined and hers is just beginning. Soon she'll have all those things; all those proper things. Pensions, cars, a secretary. She would think that was selling out, but I never did. I just couldn't find the Thing I wanted to do.

'You stressed – about it all?' she says, as though *it all* is merely a pressing deadline or an impending redundancy, not the reality that my life is being shaken up like the salt in the retro shaker in front of us.

'Yes,' I say shortly. 'No. I don't know.'

Sat opposite each other, talking over the counter, with the rainy dark world outside the round window, I feel like we're in a café or at a bar. Reuben and Jonty go and sit on the sofa in our tiny living room. I can hear the tread of their shoes on the wooden floor behind us.

Laura dabs at the salt with the pad of her index finger.

'It's just – I don't know. It's time to grow up, isn't it?' she says. She looks excited. 'It took me ages to realize. Years later than everyone else. But I want a proper career. I want to look forward to work – to use my brain. Which isn't useless.'

'No,' I say, wondering whether she thinks mine is.

I can hear Reuben and Jonty talking. They're saying something about July. 'Yeah, sure,' I hear Reuben say, his tone the exact one he uses when he's agreeing to something that he'll later cancel.

Laura's hands are knotted together. She is always worrying; always analysing. No wonder she wants a career. She is nothing like me, drifting, daydreaming, from one location on the library bus to the next.

'It's the sixteenth,' Jonty is saying behind me.

I tune into their conversation instead. It's easier to listen to them than to think of my best friend changing her life because of something I have done. Our flat is so small that I can hear every word.

'Is that a Saturday?' Reuben says, sounding less reluctant. His tone is strange, and I cock my head, intent now.

'Mm, yeah,' Jonty says.

Laura looks lost in thought, dabbing her finger into the salt pile, over and over again, the grains making tiny pockmarks on her skin.

'It'll be just me, probably. If it's July,' Reuben says.

'Oh, right,' Jonty says, sounding taken aback.

I frown.

There's a pause. Laura and I don't speak, and neither do Reuben and Jonty.

And then I hear Jonty again. 'Oh, yeah. Of course,' he says. 'Sorry.'

And it's not the words, or the look I imagine Reuben gave him, which preceded his realization. No. It's the tone. The tone people only speak in when they're talking about my crime. My misdemeanour. As though I've been put on the sex offenders' register or gone to Alcoholics Anonymous. Something shameful. And isn't it?

'Sorry, mate,' Jonty adds softly again.

Laura doesn't say anything then. I keep staring hard at her, knowing she heard my husband talk of my imminent incarceration as though it's a certainty, but she doesn't look up. I scrape all of the salt into the palm of my hand, and feel its weight, then throw it, with my right hand, over my left shoulder. For luck. To get rid of the devil, waiting patiently behind me.

'Jonty was asking about their boat party thing this summer,' Reuben says conversationally after they have left.

I remember their last summer party. Reuben had sent me a very Reuben-like text, across the boat from me, as a very boring woman talked to me about the alternative voting system. *You alright there, or do you need rescuing?* it said. *Rescue me,* I replied, and he came over, and said, 'Sorry, my wife looks very bored.'

'Yes,' I say. I start scrubbing at the work surface, not looking at him.

Reuben is leaning against the kitchen counter and shifts away, looking curiously at what I'm doing. I hardly ever clean.

'I haven't RSVP'd for you.' He says it simply.

He moves to the door frame and leans against it. I can feel his gaze on me. I turn and squeeze water out of the sponge.

'Okay,' I say brightly.

I should ask him why not – because I really can't understand it. At the very least, I should turn around and look at him. Maybe then I would see it in his facial expression: the answer – what he thinks. Is it about prison? Or something else? Not wanting to speak for me when my life is a shambles?

'Jo.'

'Yes,' I say.

He comes over to me, plucks the sponge out of my hand and tosses it in the sink.

'What would happen?' he says simply.

We both know what he means, but I pretend not to.

'What would happen if what?' I say.

His expression darkens. He looks thin. Has he lost weight? He's always been slender, but I can see his collarbones behind his T-shirt, jutting out ever so slightly. I have gained weight, eating as though they will starve me in prison.

'You know what,' he says quietly.

'No, I don't,' I say, taking the theoretical stance: I *might not*; therefore, I don't. It almost seems irrelevant that I do. Why do I do these things?

'What will happen if you get sent down?' he says softly. 'I want to discuss it so . . . if it happens. We don't have to discuss it then, in the court. We have time now. Alone. Together.'

The words shock me. *Sent down.* They're so colloquial. So inappropriate.

'You heard Sarah. Mistake and self-defence.'

Reuben scrunches his nose up, makes a kind of moue with his mouth. As if to say, *That won't work.* But he can't mean that. Surely not.

He's never done denial. Not like I have. Ripped-up, hidden car parking fines simply don't exist for me, but he doesn't think that way. He confronts issues head on, like this. Calmly, not hysterically, not the way I eventually tackle things I've been avoiding for years, taking deep, dramatic breaths and pulling a fine that's become a court summons out from under the bed, and looking at it in horror.

But I can't do it. It feels like facing an oncoming train.

'I can't talk to you about the rent as you're being led away,' he says. 'We need to . . . to strategize.'

'*Strategize.* We're not at a conference,' I say, but actually all I am thinking is, *Led away.*

Will I be led away? I can't handle it. He thinks I might be, like an animal to the slaughterhouse, and what's the difference, really? I am still staring down at the counter, not looking at him. I miss his arms around me and the way we used to list our favourite things about the other in bed. I miss the way Reuben's face would curve into a reluctant smile as I got him chatting. I miss it all. I miss our movie nights. That time we watched *Kind Hearts and Coronets* (number ninety) and Reuben turned to me halfway through and said, 'I haven't got a fucking clue what's going on, have you?'

'There are articles. Online. Have you seen?' he says.

'No,' I say sharply.

'Defending you. Feminist articles. You know?'

'I don't look,' I say, and raise my head.

The briefest of expressions flickers across his face like poor reception on an old television. It's not annoyance, exactly; more recognition. *Of course you don't*, it says.

I grab the sponge again and recommence scrubbing.

'Okay, well, if you want to discuss it, let me know . . .' he says.

And it's a tone I've not heard before. Not directed at me, anyway. I have heard it said down the phone, when clients call at weekends. Difficult clients. Clients who are making poor choices.

I glance up at him, and he's staring at me, like a well-meaning counsellor or head teacher who knows a student's done something and won't confess.

I scrub harder, at stains on the work surface that aren't really there, hoping I can erase them entirely.

19

Conceal

It's late January before I can get a set of keys with nobody seeing. Somebody left theirs in the kitchen, by the tea machine, and I swipe them, quickly.

After that, it's easy.

I text Reuben and tell him I'm seeing Laura and, after Ed drops me home, I walk back to the library, the bitter January air hurting my lungs. It's after eight, and there won't be anybody there, but I look left and right before letting myself in. I look up, too, checking for CCTV. At least I have learnt something.

I slide the key into the lock. Attached to the set of keys is a pink pompom dirtied on its ends, the fur turned grey.

The alarm goes off but I silence it with the four-digit code I've watched Ed put in so often – everyone knows it, even the cleaner – and then it is noiseless, and I am alone inside.

Everything looks eerily different at night. Like an abandoned hospital or jail. The office desks are cast in a strange glow from the street lamps outside and the cupboard creaks as I slide the key in and open it.

The lost property basket is almost full, and I get my items out and add them, right at the bottom. It takes twice as long as it should because of my bad hand.

I can't bear to put the clothes and shoes in a random skip, in someone else's rubbish. It may be crazy, but I want to know where they are. And to be able to check that they are still here – that they haven't been found. That my beautiful shoes are here, and their tread cannot be traced back to me. Nobody I worked with ever saw them. They'll never know they're mine.

I leave shortly after, hurrying across the car park, my head bowed just in case.

Reuben appears in the hallway as I arrive through the door in an old trench coat I took out to wear home with me.

'I've lost my coat,' I say pre-emptively. I am the worst liar in the world.

'You've *lost your coat*?' Reuben says.

His tone is a blend of incredulity and judgement. I know it well.

'Yeah, I . . .' I try to think but I can't. 'I have no idea. It was here and then it wasn't.'

'Did you have it this morning?'

'No,' I say. 'Have you seen it?' I add, which must seem strange. It should have been the first question I asked.

Oh God. I am an amateur. They are going to find me.

'Oh – but it's your thirty coat,' he says. 'I'll check the car.' He opens the door and strides out on to the street where the car is parked.

I stand at the door, still shivering in the dark, watching him. Our security light has gone on. I look up at it. It is strung with dirty cobwebs, the inside lined with dead flies.

I look at Reuben rooting through the car, picking up Sainsbury's bags for life, sweet wrappers and my wellington boots. He hardly ever uses the car and so it's filled with my crap.

He closes the boot, turns to me, and frowns, looking baffled. 'I don't understand how you could have lost a coat,' he says, walking back towards me.

I cringe, not looking at him. This is the sort of thing that drives Reuben mad. Not just my messiness, my disorder, but the illogicality of it. Why didn't I just say I left it when I was out with Laura? Come home without one? I should have thought more carefully. But there's no room in my head; not for these things. Getting away with murder is all I can think of.

Reuben looks back into the flat, a puzzled expression on his face. 'Have you checked the spare room?' he says. 'Sometimes you get in and just dump stuff in random places . . .'

'I've checked everywhere, Reuben,' I say, my tone short.

'There's no need for that,' he says mildly.

I catch his surprised expression. I have wounded our relationship with the crime I committed, and now the collateral damage is materializing in front of us. 'Please leave it,' I say desperately. I'll tell him if he pushes me. I'll tell him. I shake my head violently from side to side. I've got to get away. My secret is sitting right in the centre of my mouth, ready to leap out if I utter another word.

I have killed.

I have hidden evidence.

I have broken into my place of work.

My crimes are stacking up.

His eyes darken. He doesn't deserve this. But neither do I. He reaches for me. His right hand trailing upwards, the left instinctively moving towards my waist. It's a movement we make often, almost like a dance, but I step out of it. I can't. I can't be near him, my head on his shoulder, smelling our shared fabric conditioner. I can't stand with my waist pressed to his, my mouth against his ear. I would tell him. I would tell him where my coat is, and why. It wouldn't be absolution. It would be a selfish, sordid confession that would ruin his life. I've already ruined my own, but it must stop there.

'I thought you loved that coat,' he murmurs.

'I did,' I say.

'But you lost it.'

In Reuben's world, things are simple. If you like your possessions, you take care of them. People are never negligent, or reckless, or unthinkingly careless.

I turn away from him and walk back into the flat. I can feel his hurt gaze on the back of my neck like the warm coat I am missing.

The next day, the Chiswick stop has nobody waiting. Ed parks up, and opens the door, but then gets back into the driver's seat. He's wearing a fleece, and he tucks his slim hands in its front pouch, crossing his legs. My trench coat flaps around my waist. It could fit twice around me, now. The weight keeps falling off.

These days are the slowest. I'm never happy, no matter where I am. Not at home and not at work – but in each location, I think I will be happy in the other.

Ed starts making up the library cards for the recent joiners. He sticks their photographs down, then passes them to me to seal with sticky-back plastic. I hate doing it, usually; I mess them up with little air bubbles and mis-aligned plastic that collects fluff and hairs, but today I quite like the meditative quality of it.

Until he passes me Ayesha's.

My hands become still, hovering over it, as if they are passing through a force field. My thumb seals the plastic over her face, but then remains there as I stare and stare.

Ed brushes past me as I am turning it over in my hands, looking at her library card number, the barcode, scrutinizing her photograph.

'Getting a good look at that,' Ed says, his tone impassive.

I drop the card immediately.

20

Reveal

It is late January and it seems everybody has an opinion about me on the Internet. Reuben was right – it's become a thing, somehow. In the *Daily Mail*. The *Express*. The *Huffington Post*. Some of them say that we have all been there. That every woman has felt her heart speed up when she's heard footsteps behind her on a night out, or when simply walking alone. Some of them say Little Venice has become dodgy, run-down. Others say the effect of men frightening women is cumulative; that the catcalls, the thrown insults, the *mansplaining*, all add up, and many women are merely waiting to be attacked. Of course we *appear* to overreact, the women on Twitter say, because it is always bubbling under the surface. Provocation over decades.

I saw an article about myself, recommended to me on Facebook. I clicked it instinctively, then closed the tab, then reopened it. I couldn't avoid it forever. My trial was approaching. I'd started reading, just the first few sentences. After all, some of the commentators might – as Reuben said – be nice.

I must have used more force than was reasonable. That's what one woman – a lawyer – is saying. I can't possibly have only intended to defend myself. Nobody defending themselves lashes out first, and with such initial force.

They do not know that he was already running, already heading for the steps, already had some momentum. They do not know and they do not care. Was it really possible to make such a mistake? she goes on to ask. Isn't it the job of the reasonable person to check?

There's an article with a photograph of me inserted into the right-hand side. I haven't seen it for years. It must have been taken from my Facebook account. I'm staring moodily into the distance, holding a Starbucks Christmas cup, the winter sunlight behind me.

And, further down, there's one of Imran. I gasp, looking into his eyes for the very first time. They're set widely apart, almost bulbous. He's grinning, a lopsided, self-conscious grin. His distinctive bone structure cuts shadows into his cheeks. He was handsome, undoubtedly.

I scroll past, unable to look at him any longer.

I'm everywhere: on crappy Internet journalist sites and in articles by women for *The Pool* – a woman called Caroline writes so sympathetically about my plight – and the comments section of the *Guardian*. Was I right to lash out? Can self-defence be pre-emptive? Did I have a duty to check? Is it a feminist issue?

There are reams of articles about how women are always being accused of lying in court, and yet rarely do so. We never accuse people who have been mugged of making it up or berate them for having brought it on themselves. Let's believe Joanna, one woman writes passionately. She rescued the man immediately. Let's trust that she made an honest mistake; that if it *had* been the man from the bar, she would have been justified. Let's stop vilifying women, presuming them guilty, and not innocent.

I stare at the article in shock. I have goosebumps all over my arms and back. My face is lit up, blue, by the computer screen. I can see it reflected in the window.

The article is sympathetic and passionate and well written. Only, a small voice speaks up inside me: I have lied. I am lying. I left him there in the puddle while I was procrastinating. While I was deciding what to do. Does just one lie, annexed to the main story like a distasteful extension to a period property, invalidate my main defence? I don't know. I'll never know. I don't know the legal position. I can't ask Sarah.

I close my laptop, and my face falls into darkness, disappearing entirely from the window.

Sarah calls me later.

'I'm meeting Sadiq next week,' she says. 'I'll get a statement from him.'

'Good,' I say.

21

Conceal

January passes. I hardly remember it. The news is filled only with weather – how much snow there's been, how consistently cold it is, every single day – and Reuben sometimes tries to talk to me about that most banal of subjects but I can't bring myself to discuss even the weather with him. I can't remember the last time I looked him in the eye. I don't sleep, and I certainly don't sleep with him. I lie awake most nights, listening for sirens, listening out for the doorbell or the thrum of a text message vibrating on my bedside table. And, lately, reliving it all. The moment I pushed him. The moment I left. But others, too. Reliving it from his perspective. What he might've been thinking as he was innocently running behind me. How it felt to feel his life ending, there in Little Venice, as his murderer stood a few feet away, not caring, not helping.

It's a white February day and Ed is telling me in great detail about his house extension. 'We couldn't just convert the loft,' he is saying. 'Some bureaucracy, you know . . .'

My wrist splint is off, but my hand is not quite the same. I suppose it is because of the delay in seeing my doctor. It still feels stiff and strange.

I stop listening when Ayesha arrives. She materializes

198

just as I am thinking about her, tuning Ed out, thinking about how much I would like to see her.

She looks different. Or maybe she's changed only in my mind. She's more beautiful than I remember. That wide, smooth forehead.

'These are so late,' she says, gesturing to the stack of books she's holding. 'They're the ones I . . . man, it was months ago. I almost nicked off with them, I was so embarrassed,' she says, putting a hand in front of her mouth, 'but then I thought "*No*, Ayesha. Take them back!"'

She is wearing rose-gold bangles up both of her arms. They jangle as she brings her hands up to stop Bilal climbing the steps. 'Sorry, hi,' she says to me.

She tilts her head as she looks at me, remembering. Wilf. That lie.

'Hi,' I say.

Bilal is taller, his limbs having moved from toddler to child in only a few weeks, and he waves at me. His hands are still dimpled, though, little rings of fat around the base of each wrist.

'What's the damage?' she says, waving the books.

'Oh, nothing,' I say vaguely. How could I ever fine her?

She and Bilal head to the back of the bus and, like I am an orbiting moon, I follow them. I am powerless to stop.

The heating's on in the bus and it's at its loudest right next to the vent, at the back. She stands next to it. She's slim, must feel the cold, but all I can think is that I am pleased; nobody can hear us here – the noise will obscure our words. I can ask her . . . things.

Bilal sits on the floor and pulls a Julia Donaldson title

off the bottom shelf and splays it open like a butterfly in his lap.

'Bil,' she says softly, then turns to me, crossing her legs as she stands, so her right and left feet are the wrong way around.

'How are you doing?' I say.

'Knackered. This parenting lark . . . Hey, how's your brother?'

I shrug, trying not to look blasé. 'He'll be okay. He is okay,' I say. 'Better.'

'I wish I was,' she says.

'Yes.'

'Everyone's so angry,' she says. 'It doesn't help.'

'Who's angry?' I say sharply.

'No one cares. You know?' She blinks, then seems to hear my question, on a few seconds' delay, and answers. 'The Internet, I guess. People on forums. Organizations. They think maybe the police didn't investigate it enough – because he was a Muslim. We had a little protest sort of thing, outside the mosque, but only eight people came.' Her expression twists into a bitter smile.

'What're the police doing now?' I say, my tone strangely proprietary, as though I am an interested party. An aunt or a friendly GP, rather than what she believes me to be: a librarian who is sympathetic that her brother died. I'm desperate to know so many things. To know that Bilal is okay. That she is okay. And underneath all of that is something self-serving: I am desperate to know that they do not suspect.

I glance down at Bilal. Is his new slenderness just growing up, or is it something else? He is running his fingers along the tops of the books, lining them up so all of the spines are exactly level. I feel a wave of nostalgia as I recall my childhood trips to the library. Age five, ten, fifteen. When it was all still to play for. Wilf would head to the sci-fi section and I'd go for *Sweet Valley High* and *The Baby-Sitters Club*. We'd reconvene, out the front of the bus, stacks of books teetering in our arms. We walked home that way. We never thought to bring a bag. We'd read one a day, all week. Occasionally lend the other a particularly good one. My brother is still alive. I could call him up right now. I look at Ayesha and wonder how I'd feel if it were me.

'What was he like?' I say softly, the impulse to ask the question a complicated, tangled mixture of curiosity, atonement and sadness.

She gets her purse out and flips it open. 'Here,' she says. She shows me a photo of her and Imran.

It's a selfie. He's holding the camera. Just as Sadiq did, twenty minutes before I made the biggest mistake of my life.

I feel like a rubbernecker, a voyeur, but I can't seem to stop. I stare at his face, his slim, smiling face. He has high cheekbones. A wide smile, with straight, white teeth. He looks like he should be playing soccer in America. Bounding home for Oreos and milk.

'Imran,' I say, tracing a finger over the photograph.

Imagine if she knew. Imagine if she knew who I was, standing here in front of her.

'Yeah,' she says, letting me take the photograph. 'I've got loads. But that's my favourite.'

'Tell me about him.'

'He wasn't perfect,' she says, which surprises me. 'You know when someone is killed –' she says the word easily '– everyone always says they were a *shining light* or something.' Her accent's becoming more London. Getting stronger as she continues speaking. 'He wasn't. He had *mental* social anxiety. He'd go to parties and stuff but come home and tell me everything that he'd said . . . ask me for reassurance. All of that. Did my head in.'

'Wow.'

'Yeah. He was talented, though. Loved food. He was doing a cheffing course. In Central. Used to do those posh food smears on plates, bring them home on the tube.' She pauses, studying her nails, then adds, 'He was good.'

'I see,' I say. There's something in my throat. The old animal that lives on my chest has momentarily climbed up, making my voice sound heavy and husky.

'He was a park runner, too. He got up at eight every Sunday morning. What was your brother's girlfriend like?'

'Oh, no,' I say. 'I'd love to hear more about him. Imran.'

It's hot, here in the back of the bus, and my top clings to my chest under my jumper. The panic sweats are back, but I don't walk away. Can't seem to.

'He was funny,' she says. 'He was *fun*. You know? One of those people who makes things more fun.'

I nod. I know the type. Wilf used to be that way, when we were growing up, before we lost each other. We used to spread the sofa cushions out on the living-room floor when Mum and Dad were out. It was massive, our living room, with no television in it – that was in the den – and they'd have had a fit if they knew what we were doing.

We'd bounce from sofa to sofa, pretending the floor was covered in lava. We called it *electric shock*. We'd shriek with laughter. I'd keep an eye out on the drive, checking for Mum and Dad, and Wilf would almost always nearly wet himself with laughter. So much so that I would have to remind him to use the toilet before we played.

I stare into the distance. How would I feel if he wasn't around any more? I can't imagine the scale of that loss. Not in spite of the fact that we don't see each other much now, but because of it.

'We had a traditional funeral, which he would've hated. But there you go. Mum and Dad came back. From Pakistan. We were living on our own, before that.'

'Are they back there now?'

'Yeah,' she says. 'Just me and Bilal now. Imran's room is empty. Probably get kicked out soon – the bedroom tax, you know?'

I close my eyes, briefly, against this story. I can hardly stand to hear it – their losses.

When I open them again, she's looking at me. 'That's why he was on the cheffing course. He discovered he liked cooking. For us. Well, he sort of *had* to cook for us.'

'I see.'

'I've got loads more things,' she says, opening her purse. One section is stuffed. She passes me two more pictures. Both are her and Imran, again. One on a holiday, tanned against a bridge crossing a river. The other is from when they were little. Their high, distinctive bone structure leaps out at me, like stars in the night sky, getting more obvious the longer I look.

I could tell her now. It would be so easy. She might even

be misled, by me, at first – by my casual tone. She might not realize the enormity of what I am telling her. She'd grasp it soon enough, of course. But maybe I could fool her, for a moment. And I could say sorry, and she'd say she forgave me. And then, afterwards, she'd angrily realize, and turn me in.

My hands start to shake. My eyes fill with tears. I look down as I wait for them to disappear but they won't. They keep gathering, my throat feeling tight.

'But now it's over, you know?' she says.

'I'm sorry,' I say, my voice barely audible.

'He probably didn't know it was happening.'

I think of the reality of his death. He couldn't catch his breath. It would have been freezing. The ground. The air. That water all over his nose and mouth. Maybe he would have thought of her, as he died. Maybe he would have seen his parents in his mind. Maybe he would have wondered, *Who would do this to me?*

I meet her eyes. They're damp, the bottom lashes clumping together.

I can't help but ask. 'Do you know what happened to him?' My voice is raspy and strange. Desperate sounding.

'That night?' she says sharply.

'Yeah.'

She closes her eyes, looking as though she's in prayer. Her skin is flawless, but becoming lined. Not happy lines – smile lines around the eyes, the mouth – but miserable ones. Forehead lines.

Her eyes open. 'No,' she says, blinking. 'The police say . . . they said it was suspicious. But now . . . we don't know. We just don't know what happened to him. Nobody knows.'

'Are you any closer to knowing?' I say, and, to me, my tone is so obvious. So hungry. I marvel once more that people don't know; that they can't tell; that it is not broadcast above my head somewhere in neon.

I move towards her. She backs away.

'Closer?' she says. She looks wary now. Takes another step back. Her rucksack hits a stand of Quick Reads and she reaches to steady it with her hand as it rocks.

'To finding out,' I say.

I brush my hair from my face and notice my hand is shaking. Surely she sees it too. Her eyes stray to it, then back to mine.

She doesn't say anything for a moment. She shakes her head, biting her bottom lip with those white teeth of hers. She glances at my face, her eyes scanning mine. Can she see my tears?

'No, not really,' she says.

And, for a moment, the paranoia is extinguished, replaced by a strange kind of jubilation. This is guilt, I am learning. The odd ups and downs of it. The inconsistencies. The relief, followed by the opposite, because true, lasting relief is no longer possible.

I nod once. 'You can always tell me. Talk to me, about it,' I say.

She just looks at me. Says, 'Right,' and turns back to the books. I have frightened her.

I spin around, then start, feeling adrenaline rush from my heart and down my arms and legs: Ed is right behind me. I didn't hear him. His tread is soft, like a cat's. I should have been more careful, but I look closely at him and see he hasn't heard. His expression is entirely neutral, impassive.

He can't have heard, with the noise of the heating above us. It's like a dim roar.

Ayesha takes out eighteen books. It's more than the maximum, but I let her anyway.

When she leaves, Ed touches my arm very lightly. 'You okay?' he says softly. 'Must be tough thinking about Wilf.'

'I'm fine,' I say.

'You've lost so much weight.'

'I know.'

Later, I should be meeting Laura for our Friday-night tradition. It's still raining, and I'm sheltering in the doorway outside the offices. The air has that grey quality that only February seems to have; like everything is filtered by Inkwell through Instagram.

She said she would text me when she was finished. There's no point walking home when I could get the tube from here, and so I'm standing, outside our offices, even though Ed has locked up. I've told Ed I don't want a lift home, but now I think I do. I can't be bothered to go. What's the point?

She didn't ask to meet; she just presumed we would. We see each other almost every Friday. It would be strange if I cancelled. We won't go to a bar, I decide. We'll go to a café instead.

I picture Laura finishing whatever she's doing – she and Jonty are always doing random things with their collection of people who occasionally live on their boat with them. Dropping them at airports and travelling to Stoke Newington to buy a car for a man called Erik who lived with them for a few weeks. That kind of thing.

But she'll text. I know she will. She's reliable like that, and she'll have been looking forward to it all day. I feel distracted and insane about Ayesha's visit to the bus. Maybe she's keeping tabs on me. Maybe she knows. I'll have to lie to Laura about why I'm distracted, putting up barriers where they haven't existed before; new, ugly, sixties-style concrete blocks in the middle of my most important relationships.

I've got to get home. Away from everyone.

I'll go home – to Reuben. The thought of that curdles my stomach more. Maybe I can avoid him, too. Avoid lying to him. Where could I go?

I don't go to see Laura. I cancel on her. And I don't go home, either. I go to the cinema, alone. I watch some Will Smith film, staring at the screen, not blinking, until my eyes sting. I can't follow the plot, but I don't care. I want oblivion.

Reuben texts me at eleven. *Good time?* he says, and I feel a dart of pleasure. He's been texting me more, recently. Trying to reach me, I guess. And then another appears. Two in a row. *I'm tired. In case you're not back. No. 2,650 – the way you prioritize time with Laura.*

I stare at the closing credits of the movie blankly. He is even wrong in his love for me.

It's half eleven when I get home. This time two months ago, I am thinking. It was happening. It had just happened. That decision that would change everything forever.

Sixty days on. And what have I done to help myself? My clothes are at the library, soon to be laundered through a system designed to get rid of them forever. I wonder if December-me would be pleased that I am *getting away with it*. I don't think so. There's no pleasure in it. It's not my choice, not truly. Like women who have abortions being described as *pro-abortion* by the press. There's no truth in it. We are making the best of a bad situation.

I let myself silently into our bedroom, but Reuben's sitting up, with the light on. I stop, like a burglar, caught, my body language freezing mid-step.

'How was Laura?'

'Annoying,' I say. I don't know why I say it. To add flavour to a night out that never happened. Because I *do* feel annoyed with her, maybe, and with him – irrationally – for expecting our relationships to stay exactly the same when everything has changed.

'Don't bitch,' Reuben says softly. 'She's not even here to defend herself,' he adds needlessly.

'Sorry,' I say, meeting his eyes eventually.

It's not the worst thing I've done, that bitching. Not even close.

I recognize their knock, somehow, when it comes the next day. Reuben is at work, and I'm about to leave. It's an early knock, designed to catch me off guard, I expect.

It's the same two men again. Short and tall. Blond and dark.

'Joanna,' Lawson says.

He lets himself in, really, or perhaps I step aside. I don't know. My limbs are shaking and my ears are rushing and my vision feels blurred. Here they are.

'Hi,' I say.

They go through to the living room and I follow them. Their crisp suits look strange amongst my soft furnishings.

'We have spoken to this Sadiq of yours,' Lawson says.

'Yes.' Fear moves outwards from my stomach and down my arms and legs.

'He says he didn't harass you. He says nothing happened.'

I stop and think for a moment. Of course. Of course he won't just admit it. God. I'm so stupid. 'Well, he's hardly going to say so to two policemen, is he?'

'Maybe not. We could check the CCTV? If he was behaving so obviously badly towards you, maybe he's our man for the attack.'

'Maybe,' I say faintly, thinking, *Surely they know the difference between a sexual predator and a random attacker?* Sadiq may be the former, but I am the latter.

'So, things definitely happened as you said?' he observes casually. 'Sadiq's behaviour in the bar? And . . . after?'

'Yes,' I say, trying to look indignant, as I would be if I were innocent. 'Yes, just as I said.'

'Okay.' Lawson waits, sitting on my sofa, looking at me. 'And your route?' he says.

'Just as I said. To avoid Sadiq.' I stand up, ready to assert myself, to see them out.

'Let us know if you remember anything else,' Lawson says.

'You'll be the first people I call,' I say.

Lawson stops at the door. It must be his trick.

'Thanks so much for putting yourself forward. You're the most important person in this investigation. See you again soon.'

22

Reveal

I meet Sarah in a sterile Costa off a wet high street in Hammersmith. There are winter drinks for sale – bizarre concoctions – and shoppers fuelling themselves mid-trip. Sarah arrives just a few minutes after me.

'Hi,' she says simply. 'Brace yourself,' she adds, which strikes me as a strange thing to say. She stands over me, folding up her umbrella and putting her bag under the table. 'What do you want?' she says.

'Just a tea.'

She lays a small stack of papers in a cellophane wallet, which she's been carrying under her arm, on the table. 'Read while I buy,' she says. She's got a dark, plum lipstick on, but it ages her, showing up the lines around her mouth.

I inch the wallet over to me, then open it.

I flick to the back, to our expert's report on the victim's injuries. It's full of incomprehensible words.

Coup. Contrecoup. Frontal-lobe injury.

Sarah returns. She's in wide-leg trousers that collect the contents of the floor as she strides over.

'I don't understand this,' I say to her.

'Don't worry about that.' She takes the papers off me. 'Experts' reports are always complicated. Imran is awake,' she says.

Something in her expression troubles me. It's only momentary, but I see it. It's the slightest of frowns. Her gaze goes down, then up again as she looks at me.

'Is he – recovered?' I say.

'Getting there,' she says shortly. 'This is what I want to go through with you.'

She takes the front statement off and passes it to me. The back page comes loose, marked SUH1, and I see it's a photograph. She lays it face down on the table and hands me the statement.

I scan the first three sentences, then stop. 'This is Sadiq,' I say. 'Sadiq from the bar?'

'Yes,' Sarah says, a slim hand moving gently across the table towards the statement. She reaches out a fingertip and neatens up the papers. 'I met with Sadiq. But I'm afraid he approached the police, after he spoke to me.'

'But . . . why?' I say.

'He didn't agree with your version of events. He offered to help them. I'm guessing some sort of deal was done. He didn't want them to accuse him of harassing you. So he helped them. He's produced this statement.' She wordlessly turns the photograph over.

Of course. Of fucking course. It's the selfie. The selfie we took.

'He says you were chatty. Friendly. He says you had a bit of a flirt. A hug. And then nothing further happened.'

'But he . . . he grabbed me. He pushed his –' I stop, unable to go on, unable to allow myself to remember. Not only the events that preceded this, my life now, in cafés with lawyers trying to keep me out of prison, but also because of the event itself: a man pushing himself into me, against my will. I haven't spoken about it. Haven't been allowed to come to terms with it.

'I know. And we've got Laura and her supportive statement. But, nevertheless, I got the CCTV,' she says, reaching into the side pocket of her laptop bag and pulling out a CD. Wordlessly, I watch as she boots up her computer, inserts it and finds the file. She turns the screen to face me.

It's three files. The first, the selfie. I'm laughing at something, tilting my body towards Sadiq. Laura is moving away, not me, but I blindly follow her. It always strikes me when I see myself on video how small and meek I look; as though there is nothing going on in my mind when, in fact, it is busy and full. It's strange to see.

The second frame is shorter. In the upper-right corner, in amongst the dancers and the revellers, he grabs me. I see his hands reach for me. But in the video, I look complicit. I do nothing, my face grainy and blank. He holds me while I do nothing.

And then the final frame. He reaches for my hand. My face is open. I hold his hand, doing nothing, actually extending my hand where his went, not fighting back, not trying to attract any attention whatsoever.

'Oh shit,' I whisper as I watch them.

'I know,' Sarah says.

'That wasn't – that wasn't how it *was*.'

'I know.'

'He was frightening. He grabbed my hand so hard I couldn't *do* anything.'

'I know, Jo. I know. But – we've got a battle on our

hands. Proving that. You don't look ... you don't look frightened there.'

'Laura will testify.'

'Of course. Of course she will.'

'And maybe others in the bar?' I say, though I know it's useless.

It looks commonplace, that stupid *hug*. That hand-holding. Why would anybody remember?

I keep replaying the look on my face. That blank look. Stupid Joanna, I think to myself. Pretending I was somewhere else, blanking it out, looking vacant; passive, when I should have been active.

'I'll appeal for any witnesses,' Sarah says, though it sounds perfunctory, as though she's appeasing me. She's not looking at me, is rhythmically drumming her index finger on the table, gazing behind me.

She pushes my tea towards me and liquid slops over the side. They've used full-fat milk; I can see the grease in pearlescent swirls amongst the brick-coloured tea.

23

Conceal

'You didn't come up last night,' Reuben says. He always says this: *up*, even though we've never lived in a place with a staircase. It's a hangover from his old house, his childhood home, the rickety pub with its multiple narrow wooden staircases; the rooms in the roof.

We watched *The Godfather* (number sixty) last night. I said I'd come to bed, but I didn't. Instead, I counted the days. How long since Before.

It's been sixty-five days. Wasn't that how long Jesus spent in the woods, repenting? No – wasn't that forty, actually? I don't know. I should ask Reuben. He's one of those staunch atheists who gets into rows at parties about it, but he's read the Bible. In order to reject it, he told me once. That fascinated me. That somebody would be so dedicated to their private beliefs.

I fell asleep counting the days, on the sofa. It felt safer in the living room, away from his raw, naked form. I told myself that the police were following up on the loose ends because they have no idea who did it.

In the night, dreaming of Sadiq and Imran, I awoke, thinking I heard the police knock again, but they hadn't. As I was awake, I thought about the library keys, still in my handbag. I have been too afraid to return them. Too afraid of being caught, unable to find time alone in the offices, but also not wanting to give them back – in case I need them. It's stupid, but it's true.

My neck is stiff. My hand throbs, too. The dreams are fading from my memory and I feel as though I am sorting through what's real and what's fake, like a child with a shape sorter. Sadiq and Imran were not here, in my living room, as I thought in the middle of the night. But the rest is real.

Reuben is drying a mug. It's his favourite mug. *Trust me, I'm a social worker*, it says on its side. He got it the day he qualified, from his parents. I was there on the last day of his MA. I considered him truly grown-up, that day. The way he rose to the challenges of his course, the volume of work, finding a job at the end of it – and a serious job, a job that mattered. He matured during that two-year MA, becoming – somehow – taller and more muscular. He held himself differently. I was fascinated by it, by the transition I witnessed in my boyfriend of two years. It was a transition I never made.

And now. He's continued to change. Never just doing one thing. Going in-house at the charity. Bringing boys home, against the rules, who sleep in our spare room. He took one boy, Ozzie, all the way to Bristol, to show him he could use the train again, after a stabbing on it. Beyond the call. And then the work with our MP. It's so recent, attending her clinics. If he knew . . . if everybody knew, it would surely stop.

Suddenly, the burden of him is too much to bear. The burden of his *goodness*. It is impossible to live with somebody who is never tempted into jealousy or greed or rash decisions. He is never prone to egotism or material-ism or miserliness.

'No,' I say. 'I slept downstairs. Re-watched *The God-father*,' I add, although I didn't.

I don't know why I say it. I want, I suppose, to discuss it. Michael Corleone's transformation from good to evil. I am always looking for an outlet; a way to discuss the themes of my crime without talking about them directly. To discuss it and to not discuss it, all at once. As though, somehow, I might find a way of telling Reuben without really telling him.

'Oh, I thought we'd watch part two tonight,' Reuben says. 'It's number fifty-three, anyway. *Godfather Two*.' He finishes drying the mug and places it neatly in the cup-board, then turns back to look at me. I have never once slept on the sofa before, away from his warm body.

'Well, I'm sick of it now,' I snap.

'What's next – number fifty-nine?' he says. He runs a finger down the blackboard.

'I don't want to watch any,' I say, looking up at him, across the room from me, thinking, *Why can't you just be bad, like me?*

'There's something weird about you lately,' Reuben says. His tone is soft. Almost wheedling. I look over, and his jaw's clenched. 'You don't want to do anything.'

I say nothing, staring at him.

'No,' he continues, 'not like you don't want to do any-thing. Like you don't want to do anything *with me*.'

'Well, I do,' I say. 'I just . . .'

'You're never moody,' he says to me.

Tears fill my eyes as I stare down at my phone. I

open Facebook. Close it. Open Instagram. Looking for likes.

He's right. Before all this, I was happy-go-lucky, *too* happy, if anything; busy ignoring my problems, prioritizing ASOS orders and having just the right amount of tea, and three square meals, and being in *just the right mood*, before doing anything important.

'But you're moody. At the moment,' he adds.

'I'm not,' I say quietly, wanting him to stop talking, and wanting to tell him, all at once.

'Seriously. You've been in a mood for ages,' he says. He shuts the cupboard, irritated.

I commend his patience. Reuben would only have to be grumpy with me for an evening before I would say something.

'Stop being mad,' I say. It pains me to accuse him, but it's necessary. He can't think it's me. He must think it's him.

'I'm not being *mad*. Has something happened to you?' he says. His gaze is steady, his voice soft. 'Has somebody upset you?' he adds.

And I almost laugh. He's so sure of his own reliability, his niceness, that he would never presume it is him, or even to do with him. There's a kind of beauty in the logic of it.

He sees my hesitation, and says, 'What's happened?'

He's looking at me so gently, so convinced that something might have *happened* to me, rather than the truth: that I might have done something to somebody else. He is so convinced of my innocence. It might be partly about Reuben, but it is mostly about me. And yet it feels like it's about him, and only him. That I am existing – embodied – in his love for me. That, if he disappears, I might, too.

'I'm being normal. You were weird about my coat, too,' I say.

'The present that you lost,' he says. 'Carelessly.'

'You know me. I'm careless.'

'Not with things like that,' he shoots back, before speaking more quietly. 'Our things.'

And then he makes a funny kind of gesture. His arm briefly extends towards me but, when I do nothing – only stare at him – it flops uselessly by his side, as though he knew it would be futile.

'Forget it,' he says, with a sigh that breaks my heart.

After he leaves, I look out of the window at the relentless February snow that's covering, and slowly killing, our dying plants.

When I arrive home from work, Ed texts me.

Have you seen a set of keys? he has written. *Missing one.*

I stop dead, in the kitchen, with my coat still on, staring at my phone in horror.

He texts again, immediately following the first. *We think someone's been in*, he says.

Fuck.

Who's we? Who's discussed it? And why is he telling me? Is he telling me because he trusts me – or because he doesn't?

I can't risk this escalating, so I dial his number immediately.

'No,' I say as he answers. 'Why?'

'Oh, we can't find a set of keys and last week only one of the locks was done up. Not both,' he says.

'Well, I don't know,' I say, exhaling through my nose.

'Don't worry,' Ed says blandly. 'We'll change the locks. And check the CCTV.'

'CCTV?'

'Yes, there's some inside the offices.'

'Oh,' I say, speechless.

How could I have been so stupid? CCTV is both inside and out. How could I not have checked? Not have thought? Not have looked up even once in my six years of working at the library?

I hang up shortly afterwards, and gaze in thought at the blackboard, then blink in surprise.

Reuben has written to me on it, next to the list of films he has optimistically left up:

Hi,

I don't know how to ask you face-to-face and, anyway, you just deflect and it upsets me. I am wondering if there's something I need to know. If something's happened. Or changed. If you feel differently about me, just say and I will be nice, Jo. Reply here, if you want. And, if you don't, just rub it away, and it'll be like it never happened.

I will always love you.

x x x x x

I am keening by the time I reach the end, my mouth open in a cry that's almost animalistic, silent, hollow.

It is revealing myself to myself, facing that blackboard message. Self-preservation is more important to me than

Reuben. What an awful truth. I would rather live without him than face prison for life.

But the truth is more complicated than that: it would be worse than imprisonment, if he knew what I had done. His thoughts about me matter more than the entire world's.

I am crying as I erase it, the dust blooming around me. He's used the same chalk as for our film list, and the dust settles, red, on my hands.

24

Reveal

My doorbell goes on a random Tuesday afternoon. As soon as I see it is the police I feel white with fear, wishing I hadn't answered. My trial is not yet in sight, but here they are, still surprising me.

'Joanna Oliva,' one of them says. 'I am arresting you on suspicion of attempted murder contrary to . . .'

I don't hear the rest. It cannot be getting worse, I am thinking. It simply cannot be true.

Sarah arrives ten minutes after I do.

'They've re-charged you with attempt,' she says, when we're in a meeting room. 'Because of new evidence.'

'What new evidence?' I say. My fingers are trembling so much I have to lay my hands completely flat on the table.

'The experts have filed their statements,' she says.

'Our expert?' I say. 'Or theirs?'

She pushes two small piles of paper towards me. She points to the one on the right. 'This is our expert's report. You saw it in Costa. Briefly.'

'Yes,' I say.

It's chilly today and I draw my jumper around myself. Good. I'm glad it's cold. I can pretend it's still winter.

That this is not rushing towards me like an out-of-control freight train. Spring is far away. My internment is far away.

'He supports your version of events. Listen carefully,' she says, her elbows resting on the table as she reads the statement. 'The forceful push of the victim caused an injury known as a *coup*. The brain moved forward in his skull, propelled by the forward velocity.'

'It was his running, too,' I say weakly. 'He was running with momentum.'

'Yes,' Sarah says nicely.

She sips the tea we have been given. I notice her lipstick has left a hot pink imprint on the side of the cup.

'Coup,' I say. 'Right.'

'So, the brain moves forward in the skull. And then, because it was forcefully moved forward, it rushes back.' She's still reading from the statement but paraphrasing now, translating it into more understandable language. 'The second injury, as the brain impacts the back of the skull, is called the *contrecoup*. The brain swelled up as a result of both traumas, causing oedema and hypoxia. Okay? Swelling and lack of oxygen.'

'Yes.'

'You wouldn't have needed to know this if they hadn't done *this*,' she says, pointing to the expert report on the left. It's sitting on the table, too, its pages curled up against the cardboard cup, like fingers.

'What does it say?'

'The prosecution's report says that the hypoxia was caused by something else.'

'What's hypoxia?'

'Lack of oxygen,' she says.

I realize she only told me twenty seconds previously. 'Oh,' I say, and I feel my face begin to redden. Not out of embarrassment; I hardly care what Sarah thinks. But out of . . . panic.

Fear. Little beads of sweat bud on my upper lip and I wipe them away, irritated. I know what she's going to say.

'Their expert thinks that the victim – Imran – was in the puddle for too long. There were a couple of bits of evidence that he was in the water –'

'Yes, he was in the water. I never said he wasn't.'

'For longer than you said. Their expert says that parts of his brain began to die. His heartbeat was slower on admission than they'd expect. He was colder. His mammalian diving reflex had kicked in,' she says.

'What . . . I . . .' The words may be incomprehensible to me, but I understand what sits behind their meaning immediately: they know.

'They say his hypoxia is from – the drowning,' she summarizes.

'Right.'

'And we say it's from the fall.'

I must almost be believing my own lies, because I splutter, feeling angry. 'Can't you *tell*?' I say eventually, tapping my fingers on the prosecution's report. 'Can't you tell what sort of hypoxia it is? Can't we prove it's from the fall?'

She shakes her head. 'No.'

I think of all the medical things we can do. Laser eye surgery. Heart transplants. How can we not know this? But then, I think darkly: I am glad. I am glad they can't tell. Because they might be right.

'So we need to refute it. Cross-examine him,' she says.

'There's no evidence for this. It could easily be from trauma and swelling. Unless . . .' She darts a glance at me.

I see why she's really here: to check. To check and double-check, as lawyers do.

'Yeah,' I say. 'There's nothing to tell you. I got him out. Straight away.'

'Good.' She nods once, decisively, then sips her tea again. 'So, attempt.'

'Yes,' I say.

It's been hovering in the background, in the doorway, for the whole meeting. Waiting to be asked. Hoping it was a mistake.

'What's the sentence?' I say. 'For attempted murder?'

She looks at me and blinks, twice, in quick succession. She's surprised. 'Jo. They essentially sentence you as though it's the complete offence.'

'What complete offence?'

'Murder.'

I can't say anything.

She must realize, because she speaks again. 'With Imran's injuries . . . it would be twelve to twenty.'

'Twelve to twenty what?' I say, thinking she means odds. Short odds.

'Years.'

'Years,' I repeat.

Neither of us says anything for a few minutes.

'How can they do this?' I say. 'The hypoxia is . . . so his injuries are worse?'

'They have taken their expert's report and used it to infer something needed in an attempted murder charge,' she says, her eyes on me, looking at me carefully. 'They've presumed you didn't get Imran out of the puddle . . . that you waited. Deliberately. Looking at him.'

'What's that?' I say naively, not wanting to know, bracing myself for what's to come. 'What've they inferred?'

'Intent,' she says softly. 'Intent to kill.'

They interview me again, afterwards, on only the new evidence.

'When did you get Imran out of the puddle, Joanna?'

'Immediately,' I say.

'So how come he has got all of the injuries a drowning person might have? Why was he so cold? Joanna?'

'I don't know,' I say quietly.

Sarah sits next to me, impassive.

'I don't know.'

'They have upgraded the charge,' I say to Reuben as we are undressing.

He's been home for three hours, and I've said nothing.

His eyes widen, aghast. 'What to?' he says.

'Attempt,' I say, my voice strangling. 'Attempted murder.'

But how could I have been attempting to kill somebody I also rescued?

I know the answer, of course. You only need to momentarily attempt to kill somebody. It only has to happen once. No matter how much time you spend undoing it afterwards.

Reuben crosses the room and gathers me up in his arms. 'Why?' he says softly to me.

'The puddle,' I say to him. 'The stupid puddle.'

If he requires more information, he doesn't say so. He merely stands there, holding me.

25

Conceal

We meet Wilf for a drink after work. It's the first evening where the sun has some warmth to it, even though the air is still cold. *Apricity*. That's what it's called. A word Reuben taught me: the warmth of the sun in winter.

'How's things?' Wilf says levelly.

He looks guarded, standing in his suit, while Reuben and I are casual. I'm too casual; my clothes swamp me. The splint is off but my wrist is no better. Wilf leans over, takes a careful sip from his beer, which is almost over-flowing, then looks at me.

'Alright,' I say. I consider my brother, the boy who used to stamp his feet with excitement whenever we played together. 'How's work?' I add, because it's what I suspect he wants to be asked about.

He's standing oddly, his feet turned almost inwards, self-consciously, and I wonder why. Reuben shifts next to me. He'll be hating this. Usually I would throw him a sympathetic smile, a grateful smile. Promise him some quiet time later. A movie and some introversion. But I don't. He has hardly looked at me lately. His gaze has stopped landing on me. I don't know what to say to him, so I say nothing at all. Our life used to be so full, I find myself thinking.

Wilf hasn't answered, is looking vaguely behind me, so I say, 'How's your list?'

He told me about the list in the autumn. He was going to do ten big things a year. I wouldn't be surprised to discover I am a different species from him, from people like him. People who go to Indonesia to build an orphanage or who start up their own newspaper when they're twenty-five or join the UN.

'Alright – Stonehenge is all booked,' he says.

'You're going alone?'

He nods. 'Why not?' he adds after a moment. 'It's on my doorstep and I've never been.'

'I didn't think you'd be interested in Stonehenge,' I say, thinking that perhaps I would like to go.

'More up your street than mine,' Wilf says with a ghost of a smile.

Mysticism was one of my very first fads (I bought twelve quartz crystals), and it's been subsumed into the narrative of our family.

'What's after that, on your list?' Reuben says. 'You put us to shame. We've got no plans except a party, in July.'

And it's just that sentence which starts it all. As though it's an ignition, a catalyst.

'Laura's boat thing?' I say. 'I haven't been invited.' I remember last year, and the year before – always this time of year. They'll come over and invite us, in person.

But he had been invited already. And he didn't tell me.

'They texted me. I said we were both going,' Reuben says quickly, but his tone is off.

His eyes meet mine, for the first time in weeks and

weeks, and I see clearly what he's thinking; the error he's made in speaking without thinking. His brow wrinkles.

He doesn't know where we'll be in a few months' time, even though we are married, even though we promised to stay together forever. He's not sure.

Wilf turns and orders another drink, moving a few feet down the bar. He always drinks quickly. He does everything quickly. It leaves me alone with Reuben.

Perhaps he feels more able to confront me in a bar, because he says, 'Did you see my message? On the blackboard.'

'Yes,' I say, 'but it said . . . if I rubbed it off that would be that.'

'So you rubbed it off,' he says, looking across the crowds of people clustered near a set of high tables.

Two of them are holding hands, tightly, under the table, and I gaze at them wistfully.

I nod, though he's not looking, and when he turns his gaze back to me it is imploring.

'What's going on with you?' he says, and the sentence, and the context – when Wilf is only a few feet away, due to turn back any second – is so not like the considered Reuben I know that I overreact.

'Nothing's going on with me,' I say.

I intended my tone to be final, as though the conversation is closed, but it comes out hysterically. I thought I was putting on a better front of remaining the same. Just the other week I went out for coffee with Reuben's father – he brought me some political history tome to lend to Reuben – and he couldn't seem to tell. I thought I was holding up okay.

'You've changed – overnight,' he says. 'I know I said . . . I know I said you could just rub it off.' He looks at me. 'But I didn't think you would.'

'I haven't changed.'

'You're totally different. You used to be . . . affectionate and happy and . . . cool. You're so thin now. Skeletal.'

'*Cool?*' I say, my tone imbued with distaste.

Reuben considers me. The hand he's holding his red wine in is shaking ever so slightly, the liquid rippling. 'Yeah – cool,' he says. 'Happy with life. Not uptight and secretive.'

'I'm not secretive,' I say, though the animal on my chest is shifting again.

It disappears, for a while, when I am with people, when I am distracted. But it's back now. It comes back every night, like a domestic pet with a bedtime, a curfew.

And then Reuben says it: the sentence I have been waiting for, second only to 'Joanna Oliva, you do not have to say anything . . . but anything you do say may be given in evidence . . .'

He says, 'Is there someone?'

He says it quietly, his eyes on me. He isn't looking for Wilf. He isn't sipping his wine. He's looking straight at me, the lights of the bar reflected like candlelight in his eyes.

'Someone?' I say, embarrassed by his directness, and by my lies, my deceit.

They are exponential, my lies. They began with a single breath, the deep breath I took before I walked away. And with that puff, like a dandelion's seeds, my lies scattered everywhere that December night, even though I thought it would be too cold for them to grow. But here we are, in the almost-spring, and they are popping up everywhere. I am lying to Ed. To Laura. And to Reuben.

Two policemen walk by the window, uniformed, wearing fluorescent jackets that shine eerily in the night like bioluminescence. I cannot help but flinch. As if they might be about to point at me, through the window. They have visited me twice. The third time will surely be soon. I am done for. I am *wanted*.

One of them pushes open the door, and my bowels turn to liquid. I dart a glance at Reuben, who hasn't noticed them. At least he will know now. Why I am the way I am. Once again, I find myself thinking how amazing it is that he doesn't know, that he doesn't notice my gaze on the police officers, unable to look away. That he can't tell that every thought is taken up with the crime; the memories of it, burying the evidence, breaking into the library's offices. I feel as though I have been branded, right across my skin, like a farm animal, but nobody knows. Nobody in the world.

They walk to the bar. One meets my eyes momentarily. They speak to the man at the bar, then leave again. They are talking about me. I am sure of it.

'You know what I mean,' Reuben says quietly.

I don't answer him. Can't answer him. I'm staring at the police as they leave, thinking, *I have been so foolish with those stupid clothes*. It's too late to go and get them. But of course my colleagues will recognize my coat and scarf. I should have been brave enough to hide them somewhere else. Somewhere far away. Buried. I wanted them close, but the sense of security it gave me was false. And of course they will see me, imminently, on the CCTV. I haven't heard anything further from Ed, but surely it's only a matter of time.

And then Wilf is back, and Reuben looks away, but under the lights, his eyes look glassy.

26

Reveal

Reuben is unbuttoning his shirt. He's been in court. I don't know why – he observes client confidentiality fastidiously, so I would never ask. I am wearing jeans and a jumper and wondering whether this will be the last time I wear this particular combination. I am forever doing things like this, these days.

I am counting down the weeks to my trial.

The light from the hallway illuminates a slice of the bedroom where he stands, as if he is an actor about to give a soliloquy on a stage. The rest is in darkness.

It's been weeks since I have looked properly at his body, but something makes me look now, my eyes roving over him. I sometimes used to pretend Reuben and I were just friends, or new colleagues, or on our first date, and try to see him through fresh eyes. I do it now. Perhaps he's somebody who I can see through an open window on a summer night, undressing. I feel a bloom in my chest, as though I've been struck by Cupid's arrow, as I look.

He catches me staring; his green eyes are raised to me. 'You alright?' he says softly.

I nod, saying nothing. I close the bedroom door softly. The light from the hallway is shut off, extinguished, and we are in darkness. Reuben discards his shirt like it is a sheet blowing in a summer wind.

'I've seen the stuff online,' I say.

'Yes,' he says, his voice short. He continues to undo his trousers, sliding them off and standing in front of me in his boxers in the darkness. I can only make his legs out because they're so pale. He says nothing more.

'What do *you* think?' I say.

'About . . .'

'About us advancing the defence of mistake. The feminism.'

'It *was* a mistake,' he says, his tone perfectly walking a tightrope between a question and a statement.

'*Yes*,' I say. 'Of course it was.'

'Well,' he says, reaching behind me for a T-shirt.

I catch his scent. It's changed, but my brain, my body, they remember how it used to be, as if I have been prescribed nostalgia. Tobacco, from when he used to smoke. His deodorant. Mints. He brushes past me, grabbing a pair of loose-fitting jeans, and pulls the flies up, his back to me. He smells of different deodorant now. No cigarettes.

I wait.

He speaks, eventually. 'Isn't that kind of worse?' he says.

The long-sleeved T-shirt doesn't sit well on his frame. It hangs, looking skewed. I have always loved that about Reuben – that he looks scruffy even when he's dressed up; that he will often leave his shirt untucked; that as soon as he forgets to shave he looks like a hippy. But tonight he looks strange.

'What?'

'That it was a mistake.'

I frown, confused. 'Worse than what?'

'You mixed them up.'

'Yes.'

'You know what?' Reuben says. 'Actually, forget it.'

'What?'

'Nothing.'

'No, what?' I say.

Everything since that night is bubbling away, heating up to a high broil. That I was harassed, in a bar, by a man who felt like I was his property. That I wasn't merely acting on one night's vulnerability, but against the background of every walk home alone I've ever taken, every time a builder has yelled something profane at me, every time a man has stood too close to me on the tube.

'Well,' he says, and then, to my astonishment, he turns around and points at me. 'Why did you think they were the same?' he says.

'I . . .' I say.

What was it, exactly? The fear. The assumption. The assumption that came from a stupid pair of identical red trainers. Seeing a shadow leaving the bar, as I did, and panicking. That's all. That's all it was.

'They were. I don't know. Alike.'

'I work for an Islamic charity,' he says simply.

I have no idea what he means, until I do. I feel my body curl inwards, in shame, as though his words are things he's throwing at me, and I can keep them out by shrinking. And then I feel it. The first real spark of anger at my husband. Not because of his accusation, but because of how he's doing it. The indirectness. The passive aggression. I have no right of reply, because he hasn't said what he means. He's never usually like this. It is one of the many reasons I chose him: because I'd never have to guess how things were between us. Reuben has never not let me know where we stand.

'No . . . no,' I say, instead of saying all of the above. I can't stand up for myself. I don't deserve it.

If I were more like Reuben, I would be indignant. *Don't be ridiculous*, he can say of people who hold negative opinions of him. He will shrug them off, like a rain-soaked coat, and get on with his day. And, likewise, he will blink mildly at praise, but not let it go to his ego. For me, it is as though he has taken my very sense of self and poked his pointing finger right through it.

'Do you actually even know how it's been for me?' he says, wrenching open the door to our bedroom so hard that it swings wide and hits the wall.

I blink as the light floods in. We bought the copper lamp that's dangling above him in IKEA, thinking ourselves very trendy. Only, it hangs too low, and swings dangerously. *Shabby chic just looks shabby when you live in a shithole*, Reuben said sadly the day we hung it up.

Yep, I had said, and I'd loved to walk past it, would smile at it looking huge and orange and tacky. Now, I want him to look at me, to look at it, the way we always do when we're both in the hallway together. One of us would say, *Does it seem bright in here to you?* Or, *Is it me or does it feel a bit industrial-chic in here?* But he doesn't; he avoids my eyes.

'What?' I say, my heart jolting just like it did when Sadiq grabbed my hand in the club.

'It's been a fucking nightmare. And I know, I know, *I know* that it's worse for you . . .' he says, as though reading my mind, 'but it's shit. It's shit for me. And you've not asked.'

I say nothing, shocked at his upright body language, the door still vibrating after it banged against the wall, his accusatory, wide stare.

'You haven't even asked,' he adds sadly.

It's true, I think, swallowing hard, the hole in my chest opening up as though it is a cavity. In my own trauma, I have ignored Reuben's.

'Tell me . . .' I say.

'I'll tell you. I'm ridiculed at work. Or people ignore it entirely. They're embarrassed for me. Because of what you've done . . .'

I hear the ellipsis. His tone isn't harsh. It's sad, drawn-out. The drawl I used to love so much. No. Not used to: still do.

'I . . .' I say, gesturing stupidly, my hands flapping by my sides like a child's. 'I don't know what to say,' I add. 'It's hard for me. It's hard for everyone. I know.' I raise my eyes to meet his, even though it embarrasses me. 'I'm sorry. It's shit luck, and I'm sorry.'

His jaw is clenched, the way it is when he's building flat-pack furniture and doesn't understand the instruction manuals.

'I work for the muslim community,' he repeats.

'You said that.'

He looks away, towards the door, running a hand through his spiked-up hair. I should have said, *I knew what you meant by that*, but I don't. I'm not ready. I'm not ready for the man whose gaze didn't leave mine as he slid my wedding bracelet on to my wrist to accuse me of being a racist.

'It's not just that,' he says, sidestepping it too. 'I feel . . .'

'What?'

'I feel irrelevant,' he says simply.

The hollow feeling is back in my chest.

'Reuben will be fine. Reuben's always fine,' he says.

'I'm sorry,' I say, feeling like his problems are heaping on top of mine, like a teetering tower.

'I can't cope with this,' he says simply.

I blink, stunned. It's not a sentence I've ever known him utter. He can cope with anything. Is always calm, measured, capable. I've never known him become incensed by life; only by injustice.

'Do you think about him?' he says, shooting me a look.

'Yes. He's got a bloody brain injury. He doesn't know what drinks he likes,' I say. It was the most important detail to me and yet here, under the beam of my husband's inexplicable criticism, it sounds trite. Like I don't care, like I am trivializing his problems.

'Because of you,' Reuben adds.

'Yes, because of me.'

'Did he bleed?'

'No.'

'How hard did you push him?'

'Hard enough, Reuben,' I say softly.

'I could cope with it, you know. When you would hide congestion charges and overdue bills.'

'Could cope with what?' I say.

'You. And your avoidance.' He spreads his arms wide

in the bedroom, like an eagle squaring up to its prey. 'But now it's — don't you see? You won't let me discuss it.'

'Then discuss it.'

'How did it make you feel?' he asks.

'Horrendous. I regret it every day,' I say. I sound crackly, like my voice is being played on a gramophone.

'You've never said.' He looks at me through narrowed green eyes, like I am a curious specimen to him; a mystery. Like meeting someone with whom you get along well and then find out that they believe in the death penalty, or live in a yurt. 'Throughout all of this . . . you've never, ever said.'

'Well, I do think about him. All the time. I regret it. All the time. But I'm — I'm being charged. So my focus is . . . in defence of myself.'

I don't add that I didn't want to worry him; that I didn't want to moan all the time or make our entire life together about my trial. My crime. I should add it, but I don't. He should know, I find myself thinking. Doesn't he know me to be good? Why is he presuming my silence is to do with a lack of remorse, and not the landmine that's been detonated in the middle of my life?

'You had so much going for you, Jo,' he says, sounding sad, mournful. His voice is full of broken glass and he's not looking at me. His wedding bracelet slides down his arm. The red hairs have tangled around it and they catch the hall light, shining a strawberry blond.

'I didn't have anything going for me,' I say. 'A third-class degree. No career. All I had was you.'

He doesn't dispute the past tense.

'You need to bloody well get over that,' he says. 'So

what if you got a third? You were twenty-one. Plenty of people stuff up their life at twenty-one. Look at my young people.'

I swallow. I can still remember the moment when I found out my grade. There seemed to me to be an ocean of difference between a 2:2 and a third. A whole universe. Nobody got thirds. Plenty of people got 2:2s; laughingly called them Desmonds. A third was a joke. I went out, told Wilf and my parents the next day, when my hair smelt of smoke and my breath of wine. None of them said the kind thing; that it was still a degree, and a degree from Oxford. That I still mattered to them.

Nobody, that is, until Reuben.

'I know,' I say quietly. He's said this to me a hundred times before. 'But it was all that . . . potential.'

'Yeah, yeah, I know,' he says, waving the arm with the bracelet on again. 'Your school plays and your A-stars and your prizes for the best maths score.'

'Yeah, those,' I say, moving backwards, hurt by his words, his dismissive tone. As though my achievements are nothing at all. And, anyway, aren't they? They're relics. They could be uncovered by archaeologists, they're so irrelevant. Literally covered in dust in my parents' attic: the A-level results transcript I was so proud of; the reams of *naturally gifted* written on my school reports. They all turned to nothing. They didn't materialize, like hundreds of seeds that failed to sprout, to grow.

'What about the Jo of now?' he says. 'The one who can finish any crossword, even the cryptic one, before anyone else in the room? The one who remembers verbatim every single conversation she has?'

As he lists my attributes, I dismiss them in my mind, like pop-ups that need to be closed. Crosswords aren't a talent. Wouldn't it be better if I had one interest? I'm just a hobbyist. I'm a hobbyist at life. And as for my memory; a good memory isn't intellect. It's innate, like having a big nose or long eyelashes.

I think about what I actually do enjoy.

I love waking up on a Saturday morning when I have nothing – at all – to do, and making a coffee with whole milk and brown sugar, and taking it back to bed. I liked, at university, the feeling of leaving a lecture or seminar as it was just getting dark, and I would skip the library and go home and cook and have a bath and do *nothing*. I liked the first change of song as I stood in Oxford's dingy clubs, hearing the new beat and feeling like the night could go on forever. I liked the first smell of the cut grass during schooldays because it signalled that summer was coming. I like the first sip of a white-wine spritzer in early May. I like the feeling of leaving a shop with a posh bag full of lovely shopping, the string handle cutting into my hand.

I grimace, now; but what do all of these things have in common? It's that they are nothing. I like doing *nothing*. I am a loser. A woman without a *Thing* by which to define herself. A woman who, when faced with a dissertation due in at nine o'clock the next morning, simply turned her computer off at midnight, had ten hours' sleep, and conceded a fail. And now, here I am, my trial upon us – mere weeks away – and I'm doing the same thing. Avoiding. Ignoring. Wishing it wasn't happening.

'Or the way you add up everything as we go around Sainsbury's. No calculator needed. Or the way you understand everybody's motivation, just like that. You've got them worked out in a sentence because of their shoes or their facial expression. You could do anything.'

His words lift me, as though I am rising steadily up in a hot-air balloon. Maybe he's right. Maybe I still can do anything. Maybe this crime wasn't inevitable because I'm a shitty, flawed person. Maybe, maybe, maybe.

'But you chose to do this, instead,' he says, cutting the strings of my balloon.

It's not the word I notice – *chose* – though I note it. No. It's this casual gesture he makes. He gestures at me, palm up, like a parent might to a child's messy room, or an angry road user might to another driver. He thinks it is *something I have done* rather than *something that happened to me*. To him, I am not unlucky.

I don't say anything more. It's better not to. To distract, to avoid, to suppress. I don't want to know what he thinks. Not really.

He looks as though he's going to speak again. I can tell only because of how well I know him. He stops, opens his mouth, extends a hand to me. He has something to tell me.

His eyes meet mine.

But then he pauses, and it's as though I'm watching him rewind. He turns away from me. Whatever it was, he's kept it inside.

27

Conceal

Reuben persuades me out on the first day of spring. That's the line he used. The first day of spring. 'It's good to go out and enjoy ourselves,' he added, looking self-conscious as he peeled a potato. He passed one to me to do, but I declined; my hand still doesn't work.

I haven't been back to the library's offices at night. I've decided to wait it out. It's too dangerous. I can't break in again. It was illegal, what I did. I'm permitted into the library by day, as an employee. But stealing keys and going in at night – even though it's the same building; the one I'm paid to go in – is a crime. No. I can't do it again. The wavering is endless. My dithering over the right things to do. But I have to wait it out.

We go to a pub one street across from ours, called The Lemon Grove. The walk there is paved with nostalgia from when we first moved into our Hammersmith flat, not long after we married, and went through a phase of going out every evening for a nightcap. We'd take cards and play Newmarket. The barman would shush us, sometimes, when we laughed too loudly and too long.

The pub is old, with a TV in the corner. It's very Reuben. The opposite to the kind of place Wilf would take me – the wine bars with modern art and stags mounted on the walls. This is simple: warm and cosy, lit with candles in the windows. The windows overlook a courtyard, not the street, and so I can't look for the police. The relief is immediate. Nobody can see me in here. Lawson can't see me in here.

'Gin?' Reuben says to me, one elbow resting on the bar. He's taken his coat off already. His cheeks are flushed – even though it's neither warm nor cold outside – and the sleeves of his white shirt are rolled up. 'You could do with the calories,' he murmurs.

'No,' I say immediately. I haven't drunk once, since. But then, something changes my mind. His expression, maybe. Or perhaps it's just the thought of the enticingly sharp cut of the lemon, the piney tang of the gin. 'Oh – yes. Forget it,' I say. 'Yes.'

He raises his eyebrows, but doesn't say anything, and I wonder what he thinks of this; this strange date night that feels to me like a sort of swan song. He orders a red wine, and we stand awkwardly at the bar.

It's late. Just after ten. That's why I agreed, I suppose. The romance of popping out to the pub, just like we used to. It felt safe. In half an hour, or maybe an hour, from ten o'clock until last orders, with Reuben, I can't confess. I can't get drunk enough to confess. And so I agreed. And here we are.

I take a sip of gin just as Reuben murmurs, 'Table,' and steers me towards it.

My drink tastes so sweet and mellow. There's nothing like it. Like spring in a glass. 'Ah,' I say, a tiny, tiny dart of happiness firing my heart as I sip the G&T and look across at my husband. It's the first spark of pleasure in my

Afterworld. I try to dampen it down, like an ember just beginning to burn. I can't feel it. I can't let myself feel it. I don't deserve it.

Reuben sits down opposite me in a booth. The leather underneath us is red, faded and cracked. The table is sticky on top, with a huge pillar candle between us. Reuben moves it so he can look properly at me. I had forgotten he always used to do that. He leans forward, those freckled elbows on the table, and looks at me intently. He can make my insides feel molten when he holds my gaze in this way.

'What's new?' he says.

'Been texting your dad,' I say, trying to make conversation. 'He sent me a BuzzFeed link to twelve joyful dogs. I think he's learning. What I like.'

Reuben laughs softly. 'No more asking you your thoughts on the break-up of the Soviet Union,' he says.

'Life's too short for that.'

I remember when I first met Reuben's parents. I was trying to hold my own during a conversation about Assad, and Reuben texted me from across the room: *A commendable performance.*

'So, Oliva,' he says now, holding my gaze. 'It's been ages.'

I stare back at him, the gin working its way around my bloodstream, the pub narrowing to just me and him, the way it's always been, the way it always was. I know exactly what he means. And it's fair enough. I almost groan with it. Imagining taking his clothes off. Feeling that hot, strong body against mine. But then . . . I'd tell him. Post-coitally, when I would always cry. I'd tell him.

I stare back at him, wanting to stay there forever,

crucified by those eyes of his. They have me impaled, right on the booth in front of him.

But then, a flicker on the television behind him, and I can't help but break his gaze and look. Something compels me to.

It's on mute, but the ticker headline is running.

Canal death inquest to commence tomorrow

It scrolls along the screen, white against red. Bandages against blood. The inquest. I didn't even know there was to be one. I haven't been able to google it. Haven't felt able to buy the newspapers. I didn't know. I didn't know it was tomorrow.

Reuben is still staring at me but I can't look at him again. I can't let him know I've seen the screen. I need to cover it up, like somebody under-confident covering their entire body, their worst bits, in loose, draped clothing. He can't know.

They could conclude anything tomorrow. What are the verdicts? I can't remember. Accidental death? Unlawful killing? Or are those crimes, instead? I don't know. I don't know. But, tomorrow, it seems I might. And then, they will come for me. Again.

I sip my gin and look at the tiny picture of Imran's face on the bottom of the news programme. Imran whose face will no longer age. Imran who is buried in the cemetery opposite the mosque.

I haven't spoken since Reuben did, and when I look back at him I see that he's gazing down into his lap, shaking his head in something resembling disbelief.

But I can't deal with him now. I can't give him anything of myself. Right now, with the inquest verdict on my mind, I want to be alone, at home, to think it through. To say my sorries, offer them up to Imran. To commemorate. To digest it all.

I down my drink, start to fiddle with my phone, ignoring Reuben.

'Let's go, then,' he says after a few moments.

He shoots me a sorrowful look as we weave our way through the pub and I catch a gulp of tears in my throat. I cannot even give him one evening. Not one evening without something happening, something related to what I did. It is like a voracious weed, spreading into and invading every part of my life.

He doesn't reach for my hand. Doesn't look at me. We pass underneath another television, right next to the exit, and he stops and looks at it, pausing just infinitesimally. 'Oh, there'll be hell,' he says, looking up at it, then back down at me.

'What?' I say, my voice barely a whisper.

He looks at my stricken expression and must read something else into it, because he shakes his head, his mouth tight, and says, 'Forget it.'

We walk home in the cold, in silence. As we reach our door, a siren sounds in the distance. I hear footsteps along the road. I fling the door open and lock it behind us, peering out. There's nothing. The siren has passed. The footsteps were Edith's daughter.

28

Reveal

On the morning of my trial, my phone springs to life, as if woken from a slumber.

'Hi,' I say to Sarah.

'Joanna?' she says.

I look at the clock in the bedroom, glowing green across the room at me.

'It's six o'clock,' I say. My body is trembling with anticipation. Maybe they're calling it off. Maybe they've realized it's all a mistake.

'Just checking you're ready,' she says. 'Got the suit?'

'Got it,' I say.

We said I'd buy a new one. A nice one, from Hobbs. Reuben paid. I haven't earned any money for six months.

The kitchen is cool and quiet. It used to get slugs in overnight, coming down the steps, we presumed, until I laughingly suggested we plug the holes with Blutack. Reuben was amazed when it worked, called me a genius.

But it still has a smell. Chilly, wet. Like cold stone buildings. I didn't think it was possible to smell your house's smells unless you'd been away. But maybe my body and mind are preparing me. Maybe I am already in prison.

Or may as well be.

'I want to go to Little Venice,' I say to Reuben.

I'm sitting on the end of the bed. He was like a wooden board beside me all night. It occurs to me, in the back of my mind, that I'm not sure where I will sleep tonight. It might be here.

It must be here.

The alternative isn't possible, though I'm aware of it, like the Syrian war on the television, like the Boxing Day tsunami. It plays out, in my blind spot, looking too horrendous to be real.

Somehow, I know that, whatever happens later on today, nothing will be the same, even if my head does hit this pillow tonight. I won't seriously come home and resume my life. How could I? What life is left?

'Okay,' Reuben says. He doesn't question me.

I am like a person granted their dying wishes. Whatever I say goes.

He doesn't check that we have time. He takes the back seat, again and again. He puts his clothes on, his limbs moving automatically.

I avert my gaze.

This station is Warwick Avenue, the tube announcement states dispassionately. My hand slides on the red pole I'm standing next to.

The doors open and we get out and follow the journey I made that night. I got the tube here, met Laura, injured

248

a man, and never came home again. Not really. Reuben reaches for my hand and I stop in surprise. It's warm, and he squeezes mine. It's less of a lover's gesture and more of a carer's. He is showing solidarity. I appreciate it nevertheless.

I ascend the tube escalator and emerge, walking for a few minutes in silence until I see the Little Venice bridges.

'It's over there,' I say.

Reuben nods, although he must surely know.

The dregs of the May blossom hang on the trees, a mouldy pinkish colour, and it's a glorious day. The trees have hit their stride; verdant, overgrown, approaching midsummer. A couple are embracing at the other end of the bridge. I can't look at them. I, a wife in the last chapters of her story, compared to them, at the very beginning. I may as well be old; a haggard, homeless nomad.

It is too painful to be here, in beautiful London in the springtime, like looking at glass reflecting the sun too sharply. Little Venice is just waking up. It looks to be a perfect June day.

I walk across the road and stare at the spot. The spot where it happened. You would never know. There is no crime-scene barrier up. No white chalk outline. No bloodstains. Nothing. Just a normal spot in the heart of London, some brick steps. Some shrubs. A tree. The place where my life changed forever. The grass just over there has recently been cut, too close, like a newly shorn animal.

I look at Reuben. He's staring down at the flight of stairs.

I take a step forward and sit down on one of the stairs. The concrete is already sun-warmed.

I'll see him today for the first time. I've seen snatches of him on the news as my trial approached, one video on the BBC website which I watched over and over, covertly, like an ashamed teenage boy with an obsession, but I've not seen him in the flesh, not since that night. Sometimes, when I'm reliving it, I still picture his face as Sadiq's, and have to correct myself. I'll see Sadiq, too, of course; a traitorous witness for the prosecution. All three of us, connected together, through my actions.

I keep thinking of the doctor's witness statement. I can't stop.

He's forgetful. Demotivated. Anxious. Depressed. He has to *outsource his memory*. That's the phrase they used. He relies on Post-it notes and calendars. Otherwise he won't know what he's doing that day.

Because of me. Because of my mind. Because of my body. Its reflexes. A rush of chemicals released.

It's like a kind of telepathy. Imran and I were at the centre of an event that's changed our lives forever, but we can't see each other.

And it's funny, but it's not in the courtroom that I realize. No. I'm not in the dock, looking at the victim slowly, painfully, arthritically making his way into the courtroom. And it's not when I'm cross-examined, re-examined. And it's not when I'm faced with a judge telling me how wrong I was, or with Imran's sister, or his cousin, or his parents.

No. It's here, sitting on these steps, my husband standing up next to me, a hand extended so I know he's there. I realize when I look down at these steps, which bear no scars from what happened that night six months ago.

It was wrong. I ruined somebody's life, for no good reason. I have no justification. No excuse.

I deserve everything I get.

Reuben gives me a small, sad smile as we leave, doleful and strange.

'What?' I say softly.

'Nothing . . . just.'

'What?'

'Nothing,' he says again, even more sadly this time.

'You look sad,' I say bluntly.

He squeezes my hand. I like the squeeze, at first, until I realize it's part of his removal. He withdraws, and places his hand back in his pocket, even though it's too warm.

'I am sad,' he says. 'I'm sad about Imran. And I'm sad about you.'

'Me, too,' I say, looking at him as we walk towards the tube.

The sun is already warm over London. It will be a beautiful Monday, for most.

My whole life I've ignored the people who don't get to experience those beautiful Mondays. The homeless and the people looking for drugs. The people who want jobs and can't get them. The people checking in for bail every day. The people attending at contact centres. The people in care homes, no visitors. The chronically sick. The forgotten; the people in the justice system who were invisible to me. And now, here I am. It's only right. I deserve it. I had thirty years of a middle-class existence, only worrying about needing a *vocation* and when I'd ever find the time to have a baby.

But now everything's changed, and I am other.

'Really sad for Imran,' Reuben says.

His words irritate me, and I can't work out why for a moment. I walk along the street lined with white mansions, to Warwick Avenue, confused at my own emotions, wondering what it is. The thing I'm trying to hide from.

And then it reveals itself to me. It's my expectations: I expected more. Of my husband. I expected him to feel sorrier for me. To want to tell everyone my side of it. Instead, he's being fair. Reasonable. Rational. Isn't he?

But maybe not to me.

I look at him. He's squinting into the sun and I can't see his eyes.

29

Conceal

We are in the offices, today. The backrooms, inputting data from our stocktake. I like these days. These unusual days, away from the mobile library where I look for Ayesha at every turn. I like to be here, static. I hear the sirens too much out on the road. End up hiding in the bus from innocuous Police Community Support Officers. My anxiety is getting worse, not better. I see things, sometimes. Things I'm not really sure are there. Flashes of blue lights coming for me. I look constantly, shiftily, at the CCTV, which now stares back at me, unblinkingly, from the suspended ceiling.

I haven't been able to find out the inquest verdict, despite trying to catch the news every night for weeks without attracting Reuben's attention. Who knows what it said? Unlawful killing, I bet. Unlawful killing by Joanna Oliva.

Nothing more has happened about the keys. But it's just a matter of time. I know it. They're still in my hand-bag. Anybody could find them at any time. I'm too scared to put them back. Frozen in procrastination, as ever. The police haven't been again, either. But they will. I am sure of it.

'Adult fiction?' Ed says, typing into the computer.

'Five hundred and two,' I say. My hand aches after moving the books around so much.

'Ah,' Ed says, and something in his tone of voice makes me look up.

And there he is. Reuben. At the door, holding a bunch of spring tulips. They're yellow, incongruous against the tired, shabby surroundings.

'What're you . . .?' I say.

He shrugs, a small, self-conscious shrug. He's wearing a T-shirt, his freckled arms out, and I see his stomach muscles tense under the material, the way they do when he is shy, feeling exposed, and my heart twangs for him.

He gestures uselessly with the flowers. 'I bought you these,' he says quietly. 'I thought we could . . . go somewhere. In the weather.'

It's been six months since that night. The world's turned from long nights to long days, sailed around the sun half an orbit, and yet hardly anything at all has changed. I look at the flowers, and that's the part that breaks my heart. Reuben has never once bought me flowers. And here he is, with a bunch of them, forced to act so utterly out of character to try and bridge the gap I've formed, to try and journey back to me. I imagine him picking them out. He'd have chosen carefully, slowly. His palm out as he thought, scanning over the flowers. Perhaps he picked the most expensive bunch, or the prettiest. He'd bring them to my work, he thought. Surely he would be able to find a way back to me, with flowers? A few tears leak out of the corners of my eyes and I shake my head again and try to stop them, even though tears are nothing to me now.

'Oh, I . . .' I say.

'Anyway, here they are,' Reuben says awkwardly. And then he speaks again. And maybe it's because he's trying to cover up the tense silence. Or maybe he welcomes the change of subject. 'Hey, maybe your coat's here? Have you seen Jo's coat?' and he turns to Ed. 'She lost it in the winter . . .'

Of course he'd ask, I find myself thinking. He hasn't seen Ed for ages, but of course he'd remember to ask. He probably noted it somewhere, for the next time he came.

I feel my face heat up. Oh, no. This isn't happening. My coat is just over there. Reuben will recognize it immediately. I have been so concerned about the CCTV, and the stupid keys, I forgot the main thing: that hiding my own evidence in my place of work was unbelievably, unspeakably stupid.

'Jo's coat?' Ed says. 'No?'

'She lost it.'

'Oh, let me check the cupboard,' Ed is saying.

The world is becoming quiet and dim around me. I need to disappear inside my mind, somehow. I cannot witness this fallout.

'It won't be here,' I croak.

'You don't know where you lost it,' Reuben says. 'That's the point.'

'I wouldn't have left anywhere without it in winter,' I snap.

'Well, it's not at home.'

Ed holds a hand up, like we are bickering children, and locates his key on his belt.

It's okay, I tell myself. *It's okay*. I can pretend not to know why it's in there.

But the shoes.

Reuben will recognize the shoes. No work colleague would have, but Reuben will. They are completely distinctive. Worn once. He will not hesitate to exclaim that they are all mine.

And Ed knows about the keys. That time some careless burglar left one lock undone. Me.

And Ed, I realize, with a painful swallow, knows, too, about the police. That they asked me about that night. That I have questioned Ayesha on the bus.

It will all unravel. Right here. Right here, in front of me. There is no way around it.

And, finally, it is no longer panic I feel. It is something else. Something worse. A spidery, shivery, certain dread, like seeing a knife swing towards me, like watching somebody cock a gun, and aim it at me.

I strong-arm in, trying to steer the conversation away. I point at the flowers, gesturing to Reuben's general presence in our office. 'I thought we were seeing Wilf,' I say weakly. A pathetic attempt at distraction. We were supposed to be meeting him at the opening of some bar he'd invited us to.

'I've cancelled,' Reuben says.

Another un-Reuben thing to do. He would never usually take control of me in this way. He must be serious.

'Oh – but how is Wilf?' Ed says, stopping, the key in his hand.

I blink, wondering, for just a second, why he is asking. He never usually enquires about Wilf. And then I see his expression. Clear concern, the eyebrows knitted, behind his thick glasses.

The blood runs from my face. I'm surprised nobody else can see it; that it's not cascading right down my neck in red rivulets. Wilf. That lie I told.

Ed's still holding the key, standing by the cupboard. He is going to go into the cupboard, and find my things. And then he is going to tell Reuben that Wilf's girlfriend is dead; that I told a stranger this. And either one of these facts, or maybe both of them, will hand me over. It will expose me. They will figure it out.

It's strange how wide the range of bad emotions is.

Happiness seems somehow saturated. The feeling of stepping off a plane in a foreign country is the same as leaving work on a Friday and waiting for a takeaway. The feeling of getting into Oxford is the same as taking a bite of a fresh mango on a summer morning. Marrying Reuben was the same as curling up with a great book on a wintry Sunday. Happiness, it seems to me, is either *on* or *off*.

And yet, the bad emotions. Their wingspan seems enormous, like an albatross's. The wretched, stomach-churning ache of guilt. The thud of shame. The slow, hot, wet-eyed creep of disappointment. A deep, throbbing sadness. Missing somebody so much that the world feels utterly altered. The empty, dreadful feeling of loneliness. I'm so alone with it; with it all. I fantasize in the shower about telling somebody. It's the only time I let myself dream about doing it. Laura. Reuben. Ed. Wilf. Even my parents.

And now this: back to panic. Wanting – above all else – to be able to keep my terrible secret. The contradictions of it don't make any sense to me.

'He's fine,' Reuben says, a frown casting a sheen across

his features like a lamp switched on in the next room; the effect is subtle.

'Is he really?' Ed says.

And all the while, I'm watching it, like a natural disaster unfolding in front of me. Oh, that lie. How stupid it was. How needless. I could have said anything. That I was visiting a long-dead relative at the mosque. That I was seeking spirituality. Why did I have to mention my brother?

Ed looks from Reuben to me. It's a casual look, but it's significant to me. He puts the key into the lock of the cupboard and turns it.

I've been so careful around other people. Reuben. Laura. But not Ed. His presence is so benign, almost like a priest or a therapist. Impartial. But work is where we reveal ourselves. Our day-to-day selves. You can't hide things from your colleagues.

I think of all the things he's seen. Me asking Ayesha about the investigation. The police. Oh God, the police. The lie about Wilf. The change in me. Surely, he's noticed.

'Yes – he's fine? I think?' Reuben says, looking at me. He's still clutching the flowers, but his arm has dropped down to his side, defeated. The tulips hang upside down.

'When did it happen – again?' Ed says. 'December? January?'

'When did what happen?' Reuben says. His gaze swivels to me. It's open, expectant; only slightly questioning.

'Let's see in here,' Ed says, pulling the door to him. He looks at Reuben, pausing again. 'His girlfriend?' Ed queries, a flash of teeth showing as he smiles and frowns, simultaneously, in disbelief.

'What girlfriend?' Reuben says.

Ed grabs the basket at the bottom of the cupboard and begins to rifle through it.

It's playing out in front of me like a horror film, and there's nothing I can do to stop it.

'His girlfriend who died.'

'*Who* died?' Reuben says, looking at Ed. 'Jo?' Reuben says to me.

I glance up, and Ed is staring at me, his eyes narrowed thoughtfully. Those dark, calm eyes. As I meet his gaze, for a moment everything stops.

His hand grasps my coat and begins to pull it out.

Reuben says, 'That's it, and those are your shoes!' and stares at me.

And then Ed raises his eyebrows, just enough. He is telling me something. He is telling me that he knows. No. Not quite that. He is telling me that *perhaps* he could know. He suspects. He might not know what yet – it is the same as the imagined sirens, the hundreds of times I have lain awake in bed, *certain* a policeman is raising his hand to ring the doorbell – but he suspects *something*.

Adrenaline zaps up my arms and down.

Without thinking, I open the door to the office and walk out into the night.

I don't look behind me.

I don't turn around.

I've got to leave. That's all I'm thinking. Somebody knows, and I have to leave.

30

Reveal

We have to go in the front door of the Old Bailey, on Old Bailey Street. There's no other way, Sarah tells me, not unless I'm vulnerable or must remain anonymous. The doors, compared to the building, are surprisingly un-grand, and we push through a dark turnstile and into the foyer.

It's still early, and it's quiet around us. Reuben hovers by my side. He looks how I think I should feel; he has trembling hands, a sweaty forehead. His stomach is prob-ably churning. I am nothing, here next to Sarah. I am so at the centre of things that I have become the eye of the storm, sitting calmly in the nucleus. As though, if I don't think about it, if I disassociate myself enough, whatever happens in that courtroom won't actually be happening to me.

I have unthinkingly felt the weight of the justice system everywhere since that night: in my daily reports to the police station; in the smell of the prison-issue T-shirt because my chiffon top was taken to forensics; in the law-yer's office with her Latin phrases. But, here, I feel it more than ever. In the grand, marble architecture, in the sweep of the robes across the courtroom, like something out of *Harry Potter*; the wigs and the crests and the security guards and the reporters hanging around, trying to get a story.

'There aren't any rooms here,' Sarah says. She raises an eyebrow.

We sit down at a marble table and chairs, right in the centre of the foyer, outside Courtroom Two, and wait.

A man approaches us. He has rimless glasses on, brown eyes, bushy eyebrows, a mop of curls poking out from under his wig, a five o'clock shadow – even though it's before eight in the morning.

'I'm Duncan,' he says, extending a hand to shake mine. It protrudes unexpectedly from his robes. 'Your barrister.'

It seems absurd to me that I'm only just meeting him, but I'm assured this is how it works.

Reuben is drumming his fingers on the table. It makes a deadened, muffled sound on the marble. They're like a relic from the past, those hands, even though I've been living with them, even though nothing has ostensibly changed between us. But I remember them how they used to be. Before everything changed. The way they played the piano to soothe me, reluctantly; he never liked being talented. The way they would reach, extending towards me, at night. Nostalgia; the worst emotion to feel about a husband.

'Can I have a word – about the scans?' the barrister says to Sarah.

She nods, not saying anything. She's in control, feeling no need to appease him.

He's brought a case of documents with him. I am not surprised that they are evidently going to discuss my case away from me. It's the way of it. The whole thing is much bigger than me now. They're only a few feet away, outside the courtroom door, their heads bent together. He crosses his feet at the ankles and I see a flash of lime-green socks as he scratches one ankle with the toe of the other shoe.

'I'll get us some coffees,' Reuben says.

That doesn't surprise me, either. He's bought a thousand coffees during the run-up to this trial. Both when he was involved, and Sarah was questioning him in advance of him being cross-examined, and when he wasn't. It seems to be something of a role he's taken on.

The lawyers arrive back, their faces expressionless, and I look up at them like a child.

'Oh, yes, be good if we could have five minutes, too,' Duncan says to Reuben as he returns with drinks. His voice is so posh that the words run on together. 'Take a proof.'

It's so strange to me that my life has become textualized in this way. The inconsequential phone call I made that night saying I was frightened, that maybe I was being followed. The receiver of that call has become a witness. The events turned into language to be argued over in court, broken down into witness statements and statements of fact and key bits of evidence; the call logs, the corroboration from Laura that Sadiq was in the bar, harassing us. She's not needed until later in the week. Reuben's not, either. But perhaps this is the best time to go through things with him; while we are calm, not mid-trial.

Reuben is nodding eagerly at the barrister. He thinks he can sort it. If he testifies well enough, he can change things for the better. As ever. 'You alright? On your own?' he says to me over his shoulder.

They walk, only a few feet away again, and I'm left looking at the surroundings. The staircase is made of mock swords instead of balusters. Every other railing points downwards, ending in a sharp tip.

'Yeah,' I say, glad of the alone-time.

When you're in a process as big as this, hardly anybody ever leaves you alone. I'm glad of it, stepping down from main actor to understudy, alone offstage, in the wings. I close my eyes, pretending the foyer is less shabby. It's an anteroom, perhaps. In the White House. I've done something with my life, and I'm waiting for the President. Yes. Perhaps I am his trusted adviser. We'll eat risotto, the President and I.

I keep my eyes closed, a small smile on my face as I imagine.

31

Conceal

When I eventually arrive home, Reuben is watering the plants on our steps. He uses a watering can, carefully pouring just the right amount into each pot. I should be explaining myself to him, but I'm not. I've practically run here, after walking around for hours. Running from Ed. From the police who are surely coming.

'Where have you been?' he says, though it doesn't sound like a question. 'What was all that? Ed told me when you left . . . about Wilf.'

'What did you say?'

'I said it wasn't true.'

Oh shit. If Ed didn't know before . . .

'It was a stupid lie,' I mutter, my face flaming.

Reuben's green eyes widen in shock. 'Why would you say that?' he says, and, to my horror, he sounds sympathetic.

He loves me so very much that he's willing to hear me out about such a fucked-up, dysfunctional lie.

I look through the kitchen window. The tulips are in a vase on the windowsill.

I watch him for a moment. He stops looking at me and waters another plant. Some of the water comes out of the head of the can unevenly and sprinkles on to the concrete steps.

Unlike the plants that Reuben tends to, which are just budding in the summertime, we are dying, Reuben and I. The symptoms of our demise are everywhere: that we haven't crossed a single film off the blackboard for months. That we used to sleep naked, but now I sleep in a T-shirt and pants, unable to cross the line in the middle of the bed, physically or emotionally. That I answer Reuben in one-word sentences, so much so that he no longer bothers asking me any questions.

And so here we are. I'm on the steps, my jacket slung over my arm. He's just straightening up.

Unbidden, an image of the police pops into my head. Ed will have called them. Won't he? It seems certain, inevitable, to me, but paranoia has obscured my vision, like the dye they used to put in my eyes at the optician's when I was younger. That blond policeman, and his smaller, dark friend. Their tread along Hammersmith Broadway. Turning right at Byron Burger. Then left. On to my street. I've got to get away. I can't be here to see Reuben's face transform the moment he realizes what I have done.

But before that, I think sadly, looking at Reuben, I need to offer something up. A sacrifice. A ritual. A last-ditch attempt.

And this isn't fair, anyway. This pseudo-relationship that confuses and irritates Reuben. He should be free to find somebody else. He shouldn't be burdened, either, by a confession, by having to cover up my crime with me.

'Why'd you throw your stuff away?' he says, as if reading my mind.

He doesn't look suspicious. He just looks sad. Reuben may not know, but Ed must.

'I didn't want your coat any more,' I say, swallowing back my tears as I lie to my husband.

I look down. He's got no socks on. The air is warm and soft. He winces as my words hit him.

I will miss those feet. And those freckled hands. That brow.

'I can't live like this,' I say to him. 'I'm sorry but I'm not happy. I'm just not happy with you – any more. I haven't been for ages.'

It's a commendable performance, I think. The words are false but my tone rings true. I sound distressed, resigned, but honest.

Reuben's head snaps up and he sets the watering can down on the step. It teeters for just a second, then stills, the sound echoing out in the quiet around us. His mouth has fallen open in shock. Disbelief is etched in lines across his forehead. And, worse than that, there's judgement, too. A kind of *I knew you'd do this.*

He puts his hands on his hips, his weight set back, looks at me, and says, 'Do you mean that?'

I look him directly in those forest-green eyes. 'Yes,' I say.

And there it is. Us. Severed. Killed. One marriage, shot dead.

He stares at me for just a moment longer. I expect he thinks it something banal; quotidian. That I have tired of him. That there is another man. That my low self-esteem has pushed him away. He would never guess it's this: murder. In cold blood. And it's better that way. For him.

'I see,' he says softly.

He is, in our relationship's death as well as in its life,

266

true to himself. He doesn't bargain with me, pressurize me, demand answers.

After holding my gaze for a second more, he simply turns and walks inside, without me.

32

Reveal

I see Reuben and the barrister speaking and, only a few feet away from them, Sarah speaking to another, different barrister. The prosecution, maybe? That barrister is tall and blonde, wearing kitten heels. Her nails are painted nude, her foundation elegantly blended, her cheeks highlighted as though she's been caught in a slice of moonlight. In another time, I'd have wanted to ask her what product she used, and then I would have bought it, smearing it ineffectually over my cheeks, looking like white stage make-up.

Reuben and Duncan are by the door. The barrister is gesturing, and Reuben is following his hands, his eyes watchful. They bend their heads even closer together. Duncan covers his mouth with a hand.

After a few minutes, Sarah arrives back, and I raise my eyebrows at her.

She says, 'Not the prosecution. I know her. A friend.'

I blink, trying to calm myself.

Duncan returns, and his posture is strange, his shoulders rounded, as though he has just been told off. He runs a hand across his forehead. Reuben hands me a cup of coffee – my last, in the outside world? – and I take it, thanking him with my eyes. I should be making the most of this. Duncan smiles reassuringly at me, and I chastise myself. I'm imagining everything; inventing their back-stories and lives again. Reading the worst into my barrister's body language, worrying he is incapable of defending me, does not believe in my case.

'I need the toilet,' I mutter, wanting to be, just for a moment – for the last moment before my trial begins – alone.

'I have to come with you,' Sarah says. She smiles apologetically. 'They want to keep you apart from the witnesses. And your jury.'

'My jury,' I echo. I hadn't thought of it. But – of course. They must be here. As I gaze around, I see the signs up. White laminated signs, with a red arrow on. 'First day jurors, this way,' they say. Twelve men and women. Here to judge me on what I did. I can hardly comprehend it.

'Look,' Sarah says, stopping my thoughts. She points up high above the doors to the courtroom, to what – at first – looks like a mark on the wall. 'It's a shard of glass,' she says. 'From an IRA bomb.' She points behind her, to the doors, to the road outside. 'It got embedded. And they left it. Two hundred people were injured, and the only person who died – they died of a heart attack.'

I stare at it.

If that could survive – that dysfunctional, flawed emblem – I find myself thinking, then so can I.

Sarah takes my arm, leading me to the toilet. The cuffs of my white shirt are stiff and starched against my wrists.

It happens in a moment. We could be two people crossing paths at the concourse of a busy train station or airport. She's dressed in a long grey cardigan that she's dragged over her hands like a child might, in comfort, maybe. Her hair is long and sleek, her eyes lined like Cleopatra's. She looks just like him. Like Imran.

She doesn't see me; doesn't recognize me. I can't speak to her, and so I duck my head, but I can't help looking at her as she retreats. I'm sorry, I think. I'm so sorry.

Sarah checks the toilets are empty then waits outside for me. I stare at myself in the mirror. I look older. I wonder if there are mirrors in prison. Perhaps they would be too dangerous, too easily broken. Perhaps I won't look into my own eyes for years to come. I take ages in there. Sarah probably wonders what I'm doing, but I don't care. I use the soap, pretending it's fancy hotel stuff, look into every stall, steady myself, looking in the mirror. I'm at least ten minutes.

When I'm out, something is different. Sarah's body language is rigid. She leads me to a table; a different one. I can see Reuben and my barrister sitting opposite us, at our old table.

'Joanna,' Sarah says. 'I want you to listen carefully.' She takes a shuddery breath, and my body seems to know what she'll say before my mind does. 'The prosecution has offered a plea bargain.'

I'm not surprised. I knew they would; she said they would, after they upgraded my charge.

'And I think you should plead,' she says.

She looks as though she has thrown a grenade. I slam my hands down on the marble, shocked and terrified. And then, as though he knows, Reuben appears by my side. He makes a noise like an irritated horse.

'Plead?' I say.

'They've offered a better plea than I thought they would,'

she says. 'They initially went back to a section eighteen offence but I was very robust with them. I indicated you'd be interested, and they've just offered a section twenty.'

'Section twenty? Why did you say I'd be interested?' I say. 'I want my trial – my say.'

'To see what they'd offer. The lesser offence. Remember? On the ladder I showed you? Section twenty is GBH, Jo.'

'GBH,' I say. 'Right.'

'I think you ought to plead guilty,' she says, and she gives me a look.

I'll never forget that look. Pity and sadness and guilt all at once. Like somebody seeing the saddest thing they can imagine. A homeless person stealing bread. A toddler in Aleppo. There's that pity, but something else, too. Something in the slant of her eyes and the tensing of the muscles either side of her mouth; she's relieved. Relieved this is me and not her life. That this didn't happen to her. She is glad of it.

'Plead guilty – now?' I say. 'We're about to go in. All that – all that work,' I say pathetically, thinking of her reams of notes on the doctrine of mistake, her arguments about how unsafe women always feel when walking alone at night, how they're inclined to overreact. *They're not legal*, she told me, *but they are arguments*. I think of all the experts' statements and the bundles of papers brought here today in suitcases. All for this? It seems strange to focus on all of the hard work, and not that I might be about to be sent to prison. But I do. I can't help it.

'Your sentence will be reduced by one tenth for a guilty plea at the courtroom door,' she says. 'And I didn't ever think they'd offer a section twenty up.'

'What would the sentence be?'

'The range is a suspended sentence – which is unlikely – to five years.'

'What will it be for attempted murder?'

'Six years is the very minimum. But in your case, ten years to life.'

I close my eyes. I wish I had asked months ago. Armed myself, not ignored it.

'This is why they changed your charge,' she says. 'So you'd be more likely to take a plea. And it's such a good one. Not just a section eighteen. A section twenty. They've come down a lot, Jo.'

I freeze up. She takes it as a lack of understanding, and moves her hand over the table towards me, like a mother making a conciliatory gesture to her child over dinner. Her palm squeaks against the marble. Next to me, Reuben is motionless. His neck has turned blotchy, uneven, the way it does when he's approached in the street for directions or spoken to directly at dinner parties. The heightened colour creeps up behind his ears. He's panicking. We all are. He thinks I am going to go to prison.

I meet her eyes. It's time to ask the question I should have asked months ago. 'What would you do?' I say.

'The thing is, Jo,' Sarah says, and then, like a doctor breaking bad news, she reaches properly across the table for both of my hands.

Reuben shifts out of the way, probably embarrassed. Duncan appears behind us and clears his throat, a soft *uh-ah*. And then, in my mind, it's just Sarah and me, looking at each other.

'Here's the next three years – say.' She holds a fist out,

272

like she might be holding a spider enclosed in it. 'And here's the next twenty. Pick one.'

'I see,' I say.

'You'd be gambling.'

'Do you think I can get off?'

She looks me dead in the eye. 'I think you should take the plea.'

'Is there any chance they'll – suspend it?' I say, the lingo becoming familiar to me.

'No,' she says.

The hopeful fire inside me goes out.

'Unlikely. The guidelines say you'd get some time . . . but they might be lenient. In sentencing. You never know. They take all sorts into account. And you'd get a bit of a reduction for pleading guilty. And a section twenty is much less serious. There's no risk of you getting a huge term.'

'Maybe they're not confident in their case?' I say hopefully. 'Maybe that's why they've offered it.'

'You don't want to play that game. I think you should take it, Jo.'

'What'll I get?' I say, my mouth and my throat and my eyes and my chest full of tears. The hollow feeling's finally gone, but it's been replaced by something else. Shock, maybe? I don't know. I never thought this would happen. I've got all my things with me. My handbag. My iPhone. I thought I might go to prison, but not today. I thought it would happen after the trial. 'What do you think? Really?'

'Five years. You'd be out in two and a half. You'd do the rest on licence.'

Two Christmases.

Two summers.

Almost a thousand days.

If I'd seen my own case on the news a few months ago I might've raised my eyebrows. Said the woman deserved more. She seriously injured someone. *His life will never be the same*, I would've said. How on earth could I have been so sure of everything? Did I think years were something other than the earth orbiting the sun, then? Did I think years in penance went faster, that people ceased being human after they made a mistake? I don't know. I don't know. It turns out, when you're facing them, years are years. Two and a half years. A huge amount of time. And yet I know logically that it is better than ten years. The stakes are too high to take the risk.

'The hypoxia,' Sarah says. 'That's a strong point. And the coup and contrecoup injuries. They will argue that you left him there for too long, in the water, and their expert will back that up. They'll say you ought to have foreseen the sharp steps. The puddle. They'll ask you if you know what happens if you land, face down, unconscious, in a puddle. They'll ask you if you knew it was raining and, when you say yes, they'll ask you whether rain causes puddles. And then they'll have you. Even if you say you got him out immediately. They'll say it takes one breath to drown. They'll say you should have known – you would have been able to see him gasping for breath, because his chest would have been rising and falling violently. Or they'll say that you're lying, and you stood there for ages, watching him almost die. And you'll have no answer. No matter what the experts say. They'll say you intended to kill. And it's a – it's a strong argument.'

'I never meant any of this,' I say.

He gets up, his body language defensive. He waves a hand.

'Don't apologize to me,' he says, and I'm surprised to hear his voice is husky. 'But the babies,' he says, looking at me. 'What about the ginger babies?'

'We'll have to wait,' I say.

His tears fall anew, at that.

And then I'm being led away and my entire body is trembling and I'm being taken into the courtroom and it occurs to me that this is the last time I'll breathe true, free air for a while and these are the last windows I'll see and it's the last time for a while that I'll feel my own bag in my hand, my own shoes on my feet, my husband's grip in mine, and I try to take it all in but it's impossible to enjoy them, these dying moments, these dog days. I think maybe we can adjourn it, over and over, like people on death row, just about managing to stay in the sun by running as the globe turns, but it's just impossible. It's impossible.

I get four years, only reduced by just a fraction for a guilty plea. I'll serve almost two years. But that's all. They're all my reductions. No more for me.

Two years.

Two Christmases.

Almost seven hundred sunrises, all missed, unless my cell has a window. Maybe it will have a window with bars. A slat that I can dangle my hand out of.

Ninety-three Sunday nights, none spent with the luxury of worrying about work.

Two years.

Twice around the sun.

'I know,' Sarah says kindly.

I glance left at Reuben. Tears are coursing down his cheeks.

'Take the plea, Jo,' she says. Still patient, her cool hands still around mine. 'Take it. Bite their hand off. Serve the sentence. Get on with your life.'

'Is this . . .' I look wildly around me, feeling like an orphan about to be transported; like an evacuee. A detainee. Somebody being deported. All those gruesome, human things I'd avoided. Everything Reuben tirelessly campaigned about. Always at protests. Always at the House of Commons. The refugee crisis. The legal aid reforms. The social services cuts. I ignored them. These issues that didn't affect me. Until they did.

I think, too, of my revelation in Little Venice. It's not just the right thing *for me* to accept the plea, but for Imran, and his family, too. They won't have to face a trial. They won't have to see me deny it. And I will serve time. Serve time for what I did.

I'm ready, I think, raising my head and looking first at Sarah's blue eyes, and then at Reuben. It's time. It's time to do the right thing.

'I'll plead,' I say.

Reuben's head drops forward, his chin thudding on to his chest. I hope, one day, when I'm out, or when he's come to terms with it, that he'll be proud of me, somehow, in amongst this mess. That he might find something to love, something to be proud of, amongst the shite, like finding glistening raindrops inside a spider's web. I was brave, he might think one day. I faced up to what I had done.

'I'm sorry,' I say to him.

33

Conceal

It should be the break-up of my marriage that thrums in my mind as I get into my car, but it's not. It's Ed. He knows. He knows, he knows, he knows. I have been so reckless. I add up all the instances where he has seen me. The police outside our house. Cornering Ayesha in the back of the bus. And then the lie about Wilf, uncovered in front of Reuben, along with the clothes.

I get in my car, headed nowhere. Away.

This is the thing with being a criminal. There's no way further down I can go. I am at the bottom of the well. I've already killed someone. I've already covered it up, hidden the evidence. Running away won't make it any worse, and I might just get away with it. I am lawless.

I take a left down our street, then a right and turn on to the Hammersmith flyover. It's busy. I don't know why. I don't know what day it is. Maybe it's a Monday morning — rush hour. Who knows?

I don't signal. I pull on to the roundabout at full speed, my bad hand stiff and painful around the steering wheel. I don't know if I don't see him coming, or if I don't care.

And then his headlights are flashing, like eyes lighting up in surprise, and I am hearing and feeling all the

277

evidence that I've crashed – the metallic sound, the crunch, the sensation of being thrown forward. But I'm sure I haven't – positive, actually – because I am still thinking these thoughts and the elephant is still on my chest.

And then, of course, there is nothing, until I wake up.

One year and ten months later

34

Reveal

The final key opens the final lock and I am released without ceremony. Nobody can see and sense the things I can; it feels like the bones in my neck are extending as I look left, then right, seeing both horizons for the first time in nearly two years. How strange it feels to smell a woman's perfume as she drifts by me, walking into the main visitors' reception. I try to discern the notes. Something woody. My nose is out of practice. I have only smelt cigarettes on the yard and stale dinners and sweat for two years. These other scents – these outside scents – feel strange and uncertain.

There's a bus at the end of the road. The timetable has become electronic. A computer has been installed, orange font on black. Like the tube. Suddenly, as I'm walking – the furthest I've walked in years – I'm gripped by a feeling that, although the sky is the same, the sun is the same, the grass over there rippling in the April wind is the same, perhaps everything is different. Alien. I feel a prickling kind of anxiety, but I rehearse the self-talk the counsellor recommended. *I'm safe. I'm a valid person. Those thoughts aren't true.*

Feeling calmed, I round the corner to the car park.

And there he is.

Reuben, in our car, the engine idling.

'Where do you want to go?' he says softly, the engine still running. He hasn't turned to face me fully, and he hasn't yet kissed me hello. The counsellor said he might not. The probation officer didn't want to discuss it, but the counsellor did.

The counsellor – Alan – said it might not be like coming home from a holiday. It might not be like slipping into an old pair of worn jeans.

I'd argued with him, at first. Two years was nothing, I said. I'd had jobs for longer. Dresses from H&M that cost £12.99 and I didn't expect to last but did. Hardly anything could change in two years. Everybody was still on Facebook and sharing cat photo memes, I had said.

He had looked at me sympathetically then. Almost pityingly. He had a birthmark on his cheek that I always wanted to ask him about, but never did. He changed the subject, asked me about where I'd go home to.

'The same flat. The same basement flat,' I had said triumphantly, as if I had won that argument.

And he'd asked me how I felt about that. I hadn't answered. It seemed so theoretical. That flat in Hammersmith. Like a relic from an old life.

For two years, I've had all my meals made for me. My laundry washed for me. My days metered out. Yard time at four o'clock. Association – time outside my cell – at six. Lights out at ten.

'Home?' I say, remembering the first time we went home after our honeymoon.

There was no carrying over the threshold – of course not. Reuben said bluntly, 'I'm not going to carry you.' We went inside, and I ripped too enthusiastically (with a knife) into a packaged set of feather pillows, and made the worst mess I've ever seen. Reuben merely looked at me, and said, 'So this is married life with Joanna.'

Reuben leans forward now, starts the engine, and then programmes the sat nav as we're moving. We're far from home, out here in Surrey.

'I'll do it,' I say, leaning forward and reaching for the sat nav.

He shoots me a strange look.

Perhaps, years ago, I might've sat and daydreamed. But it's different now. I have a plan, and getting home is just the beginning.

'It's fine, really,' Reuben says.

During every visiting hour, on reading every letter, I thought he wanted to touch me, but couldn't. But now, here we are in the car with – remarkably – nobody looking, and he doesn't seem to want to. I shift on the car seat. I'm used to hard benches. It feels cloying, like I can't get out of it when I want to.

Reuben brings the car to a stop at the barrier, his foot just bouncing on the accelerator. I wonder if I'll be able to drive; if it will be like riding a bike, or if I'll need top-up lessons. I imagine it in my mind. Swinging up through the gears. Taking a roundabout. No, I remember. I remember.

'Oh, before I forget,' Reuben says. He opens the glove box, handing me an iPhone.

'Where's mine gone?' I say.

I missed that old iPhone with its curved edges. This one in my palm feels huge. I can't find the power button, like a technophobe, and Reuben presses it for me.

'I got your number ported over. Yours wasn't compatible with anything,' he says, looking mildly incredulous that he's having to tell me. Somehow the expression is very Reuben. The quiet helpfulness, but also the disbelief. That judgemental edge. The way he makes his opinion known.

For the first time, it irritates me. He was the same in visiting hours. The glances up beyond me. It was a very specific emotion that flitted across his face. It was shame, but by proxy. Shame for me. Whatever that is. Embarrassment? I saw it all the time; as he brought my clothes in to me in a bag that had to be scanned. As he saw me interact with other prisoners who had become my friends.

And the rest. The stuff a past me would have avoided thinking about. That, sometimes, I was actually happy, in there; that you have to be. You can't stay miserable for two years, not really. Not all the time. And Reuben saw that, and he wondered about me. I know he did. I need to ask him about it. Soon. There's lots I need to ask him, but I consider what the counsellor said: that I cared so much about other people's opinions that they came to construct me. And, when I removed them all – at my sentencing hearing, when I was metaphorically stripped down – there was nothing left. We found my sense of self together, me and Alan, in that prison.

There was a lot of truth in what he said. And so I take a deep breath and blow it out slowly as Reuben takes the roundabout. Second gear, to third, signals left to leave the roundabout. I will talk to him soon.

I get the Post-it note out of the pocket of my jogging bottoms and open it. On it are three numbers, collected over the last few months as the girls left before me. I key them into the phone, laboriously. It takes ages.

Reuben's eyes land on my hands a few times but he says nothing.

I text the first number, Elle's. Almost immediately, I am added to their WhatsApp group. It's called 'Outsiders'. I'm the last one out.

I tap out a reply. When I look up, I realize Reuben has been watching, but he turns his head away as if he hasn't.

The plants have gone. That's the first thing I notice. The flat looks smaller and shabbier than I remember, which doesn't make any sense, because surely everything is salubrious compared to Her Majesty's pleasure.

I look around. There's the living room. The lights are off, of course, but I can still just about make out the glossy wooden floor, the neutral-coloured rug.

'Alright?' Reuben says, smiling politely like he's a bell-boy showing me to my room.

I nod quickly. My phone is vibrating nearly constantly in my pocket. I wish I had a room to escape to, to look at it in private.

We descend the steps and, as we do so, a neighbour pops out. I'm delighted to see it is Edith. I had thought of her, randomly, about a month into my sentence, considering that I would likely never see her again. But here she is, one hundred and four years old. She waves, as if nothing has happened.

Reuben looks at me. 'The dogs died,' he says, and I feel like I've been punched in the stomach.

The flat is immaculate. That's the first thing I notice. I wonder how he's been affording the rent by himself. I don't know, of course. This kind of intimacy, this every-day mundanity, is impossible in prison.

The sofa is different. Black leather. I don't like leather sofas; I find it sticks to my skin, cold in winter and slimy in summer. He didn't tell me about it. Why not? It looks masculine, oppressive in the living room.

'Oh,' I say, speaking before taking it properly in.

On the side of the cupboard is our blackboard. We were halfway through the list of films. They're still there, all listed. I reach over and touch the chalk with my finger-tip. He's gone over the titles; their edges are blurred in places, as though I have double vision. They must have faded repeatedly, and he's re-traced them.

'Wow.'

Reuben nods. 'I thought you'd want to resume. I've not watched any of them,' he says.

I turn and look at him. I haven't been able to see him properly in the visitors' centre. The fluorescent lights made everybody look weird, their eye sockets in shadow. He didn't look like himself, anyway. He dressed more smartly than usual, and his body language was directed even more inwards, like a turtle. I wonder what he's been doing. He hasn't really said, except 'the usual', with a wave of his hand. He hasn't wanted, I suppose, to eclipse my problems with his. Typical. Has he been seeing friends? Has he been lonely?

It's as good a time as any to try to open the conversation up. The counsellor said to do it as soon as possible.

'So this is your life. This has been your life,' I say, turning away from the board where I've accidentally rubbed away the stem of the *f* on *The Godfather*.

'Yes,' Reuben says, flapping his arms at his sides, slightly self-consciously.

'Hard to just – fit back in,' I say, with a small laugh. I look at the cupboards. I open the mugs cupboard and find plates inside. I can't see the kettle. It's not out on the work surface. The kitchen is fastidiously neat, more so than when we lived together. Not a thing out. Scrubbed clean.

'Where's the kettle?' I say, without thinking.

'Oh,' Reuben says, and then, to my astonishment, he pulls it down from a cupboard. 'I got a wireless one. Less clutter,' he says, filling it at the sink and flicking it on.

'Doesn't it wreck the cupboard when you put it away?' I say, instead of saying the things I want to say.

Reuben stops, then looks at me. 'It's fine,' he says stiffly, like he is my landlord and I am his lodger.

I scrutinize the cupboard. Bloody hell. Imagine putting it away *every time*. This is what happens when a neat freak lives on their own for two years.

'We're not seriously going to just resume the greatest movies of all time, are we?' I say.

He turns to me in surprise. Perhaps my tone – it's more direct, these days – sounds too harsh. 'Why not?' he asks.

And I think of what Alan says: *Is Reuben really always right? Is anyone? He sounds like he can be a little immature to me; he sees things in black and white, maybe? And Laura, too?*

I walk out of the living room and into our bedroom. The bed's the same. The duvet has the same blue and white checks that I chose once in Next.

The bedroom has been kept clean. So clean that as I look out on to the shabby garden above, running my finger along the window ledge, it doesn't catch any dust. It's pristine as I withdraw it. Already, I can feel the adjustment. I should be pleased I have a bedroom, privacy, freedom, a smartphone in my hand again, a clean, private shower in the room next door but one. The ability to do *whatever I like*. The pub or the cinema or anything, really. But I don't. I feel sad for the lack of my cell, even though I had to use a chair to climb up on to my bunk. I am uneasy, a small ball of snakes in my stomach, not doing anything, but just wanting me to know that they're there. And I feel curious. No, more than curious. Suspicious. Of myself.

Finally, the nightmare is over. As over as it ever will be, anyway. It'll always be on some record, somewhere. It may be considered spent one day, but it is too violent for me never to disclose. And yet. I'm not relaxed, happy. I'm . . . what? Homesick? Could it be? Maybe I will be better when I am no longer out on licence.

'It's Friday,' Reuben says, walking into the bedroom. 'Friday night tonight.'

Friday night was always film and takeaway night. But Fridays in HMP Bronzefield were the only day on which we weren't allowed visitors. Ninety-three Fridays later and I hate them. I shudder.

'Is it?' I say, hoping I sound convincing.

It's impossible to mark time without the beat of the Monday to Friday, without the seasons. We were allowed in the yard for an hour a day but it was impossible to really feel the weather without the punctuation of daily life.

What is a blue sky, or rain, or high or low temperatures without the other things from those seasons? A first barbecue, or an office disgruntled by snow at the end of March, or the light traffic during the school holidays, or an ice lolly on my lunch hour? They were context-less, my seasons.

Reuben leaves me to it and I get out my phone and see he has organized it so that my contacts are already in there. I find Wilf's name and press *dial*.

He answers on the first ring, and I smile. It wasn't always this way, after all. Some good things have happened.

'Why, is that Joanna Oliva – a free woman?' he says.

'Yes,' I say, my voice imbued with something I don't feel when talking to anybody else. Lightness, maybe.

He visited every Tuesday and Thursday afternoon, once I'd accrued enough good behaviour to allow as many visitors as I wanted. It was more than anyone, except Reuben. But Wilf's were the visits I looked forward to the most, in the end.

'How is it?' he says.

I sit on the bed. Is it a different bed? It bounces softly underneath me. No; I'm just used to the harder prison-issue beds. I can't imagine having a weighty feather duvet against my skin. I stand up again.

'Weird,' I say. 'Indescribably odd.'

'I bet,' he says softly.

We talked about all sorts during those visits. Mum and Dad. The way I always used to know where Wilf was during childhood games of hide and seek because I knew him so well. We talked about our first holidays abroad and how we used to close our eyes as the aeroplane took off and pretend we were flying through the sky like birds. Wilf once told me he slept without a duvet over him for three nights running, after he watched Mary Poppins tuck Jane into bed and wanted Mum to do the same thing for him. She never did, he told me wryly.

We talked about what I'd do. Afterwards.

'You're so great with people,' he said to me, one Thursday. 'Do something with people. *You* understand them.' His eyes squinted as he said it. Envy, I guessed. It was the first time he'd expressed such a thing.

On a Tuesday, one and a half years in, he came in looking different. His face was still the same, with the dark beard, and he had his usual purposeful walk. But there was something about his features that was different. His lips curved in a private smile, the kind I used to see on Reuben's face when I was texting him at boring parties from across the room.

'What's going on?' I said, inching eagerly across to Wilf.

'It's dumb,' he said.

I gestured with a single hand, palm upturned, to the scene around me. 'You want to see dumb?'

No doubt he could see the carnage of visiting times unfolding behind me. Men and women squabbling and guards hovering nearby, ready to break up any fights. Women saying things like *I can't fucking stand any more of your fucking shite*, and men leaving early.

'Good point,' he said.

We were just starting to joke about it. Just tentatively, like two children dipping a toe in the freezing cold ocean for the first time before splashing fully in.

'Well, this wasn't on my list,' Wilf admitted. He had become self-deprecating. Another change. 'Today I was supposed to go to work, see you, then go to my Spanish class.'

A-level Spanish was one of the items on Wilf's list that year.

'You can do things not on your list,' I said. 'Amazingly, some of us don't even have lists.'

He looked up then, his eyes catching mine. We both had brown eyes, the exact same shade, but his were big and round, and close together. When we were little, we used to study our eyes, in the bathroom mirror, standing together, jostling, on the lid of the toilet.

'There was a woman on the train here . . . I never would have met her, normally,' he said. 'A Tuesday afternoon train.'

'No way,' I joked. 'Who is she?'

'She asked to use my phone. She was . . .' He whirled his finger around, giving me the impression of wavy hair. 'I don't know – nice. Pretty.'

'And did she use it?'

'Yep,' he said, going to pat his pocket, before remembering he'd had to surrender his phone on the way in, like airport security. 'Oh,' he said. 'Yeah – she did. She didn't call anyone. She sent a text.'

'Right.'

'I looked. At what she sent.'

'Stalker,' I said, and it was like the sun had come out on my life again, however briefly. I tilted my head up to it.

I had missed that sibling banter. The inmates didn't do it, not this sort of thing. And maybe, I thought, as I tasted it in my mind, maybe I had missed it for longer than my prison stay. Maybe I had missed him, my brother Wilf, for years.

'True,' he said. He rubbed his beard, looking wolfish. 'The thing is . . .'

'What?' I wanted to hurry him up. Visiting hours were so short, like tiny pockets of air in the vacuum of my week, and he was spending them umming and ahhing.

'I don't know. She handed it back and then she just gave me this really smiley look. She got off at Charing Cross and I watched her go. She was dressed in a big coat and purple hat, even though it's . . .' He gestured out of the window of the visitors' centre.

I couldn't really tell. It looked the same as ever. The sky was a flat, blank white. The only trees were evergreen trees, anyway, and I couldn't really see them properly.

'It's a really mild winter,' he added.

I liked that he told me. Reuben didn't tell me; he was embarrassed I didn't know.

'And then what?' I said.

'She had signed it with her full name – she was late to give a presentation.'

'What's her name?'

'Minnie.'

'And have you googled her?'

'*Maybe.* I thought that was – that was odd.'

'You think she likes you?'

I was feeling desperate not only for the contact with my brother but for other things, too. A story that wasn't only on the television or in books. Gossip. A titbit. And, maybe most tellingly of all, intimacy. It wasn't possible during visiting hours, during letters. It was impossible to have all of the things that need to line up to form a relationship. The flash of an eye-roll when crumbs are left on the work surface. The movement of a foot next to another in bed on a Sunday morning. Even a text. Not a formal letter already opened and read by prison staff, but just a missive: a *saw this and thought of you*. The kind of communication we took for granted. I was craving it. Prison ticked the main boxes; I got the socialization and the hour's yard time and fresh air every day. I had counselling if I wanted, and I took courses. But ... nothing else. There were no impromptu snacks. No giggles over a midnight film with a friend. No break-ups. No train rides with a latte. No impulse pairs of shoes bought during lunch hours. And didn't I deserve it, that deprivation? Of course I did.

'Well, I was wondering whether you think I should – say hi?' Wilf said, and I flushed with pleasure. He leaned forward, his expensive cufflinks hitting the plastic table, and added, 'You just always know about people. I never know. It's like people are French and I'm English.'

'How?' I said.

'You know,' he said quietly.

He didn't elaborate on it then, but later he told me: he'd always been jealous of me. How naturally things came to me. Not just my perceptiveness, he said, but my intellect, too. He was always working so hard behind the scenes, and there I was, finding it effortless. I was gobsmacked. Had never thought he might be jealous of me. He was amused, too, when I said the same back.

'Anyway. Her surname's Tarling. Pretty unusual name. I've googled her.'

'*And?*'

'And she's . . . she's nice. She was going to present on law reform. To do with the NHS. How it runs. Lefty stuff,' he said with a twisted smile, a nod to when he once called Reuben's job *lefty stuff* and Reuben's nostrils flared like a horse's.

I stared at the ceiling, enjoying the slow, unravelling feeling of my brain waking up again. Not intellectually but – something else. Interpersonally. Not just making friends for self-preservation.

'As long as you seem normal, I'd be flattered that you were checking me out,' I said. 'Most women would be flattered, I think.' I went to add something self-deprecating like, 'But then, what would I know?' but stopped myself.

Alan would say I was good enough. Even with a third-class degree. Even while imprisoned.

My entire life I'd been so bloody frightened of what everybody thought of me and my failed existence and yet, when I failed spectacularly – sank so much lower, so much worse than failing a degree – I realized the truth of it: nobody cares what you think as much as you do. Not even close.

'What're you gonna do?' I asked Wilf.

'I thought – well, I thought I might Facebook her? If you don't think that's nuts?'

'Tell me about the smile,' I said.

'She was waiting – I think. Just looking at me and smiling widely, her eyes all lit up. Like she was coaxing me to do something.'

'Yeah – Facebook her.'

Wilf's persistence was nothing like Sadiq's. Here was true, happy chivalry.

'Consider it done,' he said.

We talked of other stuff then. Of the counselling diploma I was doing. Who my friends were. How Reuben and I were managing. I didn't get to find out what happened until the next visit. Prison was a serialization of my social life.

Now, at home again – wherever that is – I tell Wilf I'll see him as soon as I can, and hang up. I can no longer avoid thinking about the difference between Wilf's and Reuben's visits. Wilf's eyes had always been squarely on mine, as though I was a person who had lost a leg and it was his job not to look at the stump, to make me feel as normal as possible. Reuben's eyes had drifted around. To other prisoners. To the guards. Lingering on the multiple locks, the procedures they went through in a closed prison to ensure the dangerous prisoners – me – did not get out.

I wander down the hallway and into the bathroom. I could run a steaming bath, my first in years. Grab a book. The freedom doesn't feel glorious; it feels frightening. How does anybody ever decide what to do?

I wander further inside. It smells of bleach, which tangs my nostrils.

There's a tiled windowsill that is empty apart from one shower gel and what looks like a flyer, folded in four. It must have come out of Reuben's pocket. Tentatively, wanting to know more about this man I'm living with after two years, I unfold it.

I'm surprised to see his name in the upper-left quadrant. *Reuben Oliva. Jazz pianist.* There's a photo of him. He's silhouetted, but I can tell it's him. That head-bent pose. That theatre. It used to be just for me. It used to be classical music, not jazz. He hated jazz, said it was pretentious. And now . . . I blink, reading the rest of it. He plays at a jazz club. Every third Thursday of the month.

I discard the flyer. It's not a big deal. I'll ask him about it. Later.

Standing in the bathroom, I strip my clothes off, but stop, naked, pick my white T-shirt up, and clutch it in my hands. I bring it to my nose. It smells of nothing. Not the grimy prison smell I used to be able to detect, in those awful early days. Not the dust and the stale food and the cheap detergent. It smells – I realize, as I hold it to my mouth – of home. I can't take it off. I can't wash it. I slip it back over my head. I'll take it off soon.

I reach my hands down underneath the T-shirt to skim my stomach. Thirty-two. I feel the skin move underneath my fingertips. Thirty-two and I've not got much time left to have that auburn-haired baby.

I need to start trying now. Now or never. I'll ask Reuben that, too. Somehow.

35

Conceal

It's time for the hospital again, I hope for the last time.
I'm sitting in the waiting room. I always shake when I'm
here, at my consultant's office, though I don't know why.
There is nothing scary here. I did an online CBT course,
and I try to put it into practice now. One by one, I look at
the objects around the room, listing any ways in which
they could harm me. The wooden desk in the corner? No.
Not scary. The wastepaper bin, full of sheets of paper
and one green prescription? No. The photocopier behind
the desk? No. I am safe. I am okay.

It is a hospital in the suburbs of Birmingham. A large,
white building set back from the street. As I sit in the
makeshift waiting room with its high ceilings and dado
rails, it is bright, hot sunshine outside. Almost summer.
The pavement moves in and out of shadow as a tree blows
its leaves around. There's never a receptionist here. My
consultant calls patients himself.

'Joanna.' Mr Dingles appears in the door of his
office.

I cross the foyer, my shoes squeaking on the linoleum,
and follow him.

A total hysterectomy due to the severity of the pelvic
trauma. It was the gearstick that did it. I often wonder if it

was so severe because I was so slim, without padding, but the medics tell me not.

A punctured lung. I still can't walk far. I need to sit down on benches in shopping centres and pause for breath at bus stops.

An old tendon injury my hand will never recover from, improperly looked after, and made worse in the crash.

That's what I did.

That's what I did to myself.

'Our last appointment,' he says kindly. 'How have you been?'

Mr Dingles is polite to a fault, always enquiring after me, right from my first outpatient visit when I could barely get out of the taxi. He always asked me how I was, as though I wasn't a patient; enquired as to my weekend plans.

'Okay,' I say.

I don't avoid the hospital appointments, evading treatment, as I might once have done. I turn up, every single time, and battle through. Learning to live with it. My injuries, and the rest.

He gets out his checklist. We use the same one every time I see him, though he is more relaxed about it now.

'Hot flushes?' he says.

'Calming down.'

'Leg pain?'

'Still there.'

'Hand pain from your old injury?'

'Better.'

'Breathing.'

'Shot,' I say, with a rueful smile.

'It'll get there,' he says, then puts his glasses back on and regards me. 'Paranoia?' he says.

I shrug. 'It's gone now,' I say.

I've said that in every appointment for the last year, but he still asks.

'I don't understand it,' he said once. 'Where would paranoia have come from? It doesn't fit with your other symptoms.'

It had been on my notes, from A&E and intensive care. I had tried to play it down, because it certainly wasn't medical. But now, two years on, and looking back, I wonder if maybe it was. The ongoing strain of the guilt. The stress hormones in my system. They clouded things over in my mind until I became sure that people were *after* me. But then I see Ed's eyes in my mind and still feel sure that he knows.

I don't know what's true. I don't know what's real.

'You're doing well,' Mr Dingles says.

I nod, quickly. He doesn't know, of course. He thinks me incredibly unlucky, is all. A woman who forgot to look right, once, as she approached a roundabout. A woman who lives alone in Birmingham. Who is never accompanied by family.

Reuben came to see me in the hospital, and I reiterated our break-up, there and then. Told him I was moving away, to Birmingham. Told him to tell Ed. That I would tell everybody else myself. Reuben argued, until I said I really didn't love him any more, and then he dropped it. Conceded obediently, like a dog who'd been abused in the past.

Mr Dingles runs his usual batch of tests on me. Scraping things along the soles of my feet. Asking me to spell words backwards. Assessing my gait. Giving me puzzles, which I ace, of course.

He performs a final test on me – making me touch my fingers to my nose – and then we are done. Over a year after. Almost two. We are done.

'Well,' he says, 'I've never met someone quite so . . . who faces up to things so well,' he says, nodding twice, little head bows as he looks at me. 'Head on,' he adds.

I very nearly laugh. *Me* facing things head on. But he's right. I read about avoidant personalities on the Internet. It was like I had found a definition of myself in a dictionary. I turned the words over in my mind, and then I changed.

I shake my head quickly, and say goodbye to him.

He lingers in the reception area. 'Jo,' he says to me as I turn to leave, extending a hand towards me. Evidently he's not ready for this to be my last visit, either.

'Yes?'

'It will get better,' he says, holding his hands out, palms up. 'This isn't . . . the end of your improvement.'

I flush with pleasure. I want him to like me. Of course. I'm *glad* he likes me. I wonder if I am his best patient.

I look around the empty foyer and he stills, looking at me carefully. 'Take care,' he says. 'And give less of a shit.'

'What?' I say, a tiny giggle escaping.

'You care so much. About everything.'

'My recovery,' I say, unsure of myself. I'm glad there are no other patients here to hear.

He leans against the reception desk. His clinic is almost always empty. The rows of chairs give it an abandoned feel. It's not private, but it feels it.

He shrugs then, still looking at me, but saying nothing for a moment. 'Yes. It'll come. That'll come,' he says.

I nod.

He opens his mouth, hesitates, then says it anyway. 'I mean about life, Jo,' he says. 'That would be my number-one tip for . . . recovery. Try to care less. You're obviously a striver.'

I smile, a twisted, ironic smile. It's not actually very funny.

'So just . . . relax more,' he says.

He doesn't know. Of course he doesn't. He has never asked why I am cagey. Why I left London, why I am unmarried – now – or about what preceded the accident. He probably knows there is something. But he's never asked what.

I look across the foyer and out of the window. A couple of cyclists ride past, their wheels spinning like speeded-up second hands on a clock.

'I promise – you will get better,' Mr Dingles says to me.

For a moment I wonder if he means something more than my medical recovery. I wonder what he'd do if I told him. If I told him everything from the beginning.

'Be less serious,' he advises me.

I let out a tiny laugh. My first in months. 'How?' I say.

'Try it,' he says again, before disappearing back into his room.

I look sadly at the spot where he was standing, my doctor, before he discharged me. It would work, his advice, for almost anything – *anyone* – else. But it is not really for people like me. He doesn't know. He doesn't know who I am. What kind of person I am. That advice is not sound for bad people who've done bad things. Who need punishing. It is for good people. Good people who can't say no. Who put themselves down. Who flagellate themselves over their degree result for ten years. Who don't do enough ironing or who feel guilty for not going to the gym. People like the Joanna Before. Not the Joanna After.

I step outside. I don't feel the cold like I used to. I'm fatter again. Not at my old weight, but almost. It's true what they say – well, sort of. Time doesn't heal, but it does help.

Birmingham is leafy. Run-down, in places. Upmarket in others. It is nothing – absolutely nothing – like London. Real London. Reuben's London, with its ancient corner pubs. The cobbled streets. The blue Bloomsbury signs on buildings. Our London.

And so, exactly contrary to Mr Dingles' advice – but perhaps being discharged has been a catalyst – I suddenly know what to do.

It is time to stop avoiding everything. It is time to face it.

36

Reveal

I can't remember how to top up my Oyster card. The wallet I kept it in – a Cath Kidston one – is faded, looking dated and tattered around its sides. The machine seems incomprehensible. Was it always touch-screen? I try again.

I use my bank card; a new one arrived halfway through my sentence, after the old one had expired. I hope it's got the same pin.

After a few seconds, I see there's no slot for the chip and pin. I scan the machine, feeling like a tearful alien.

'You just need to put the card there,' a Scottish man using the machine along from me says. 'There,' he says again, indicating a panel on the front of the machine that I hadn't noticed. It's yellow and has three curvy lines on it, like a Wi-Fi sign, and as I press the card to it, it beeps. I look to him, hoping he'll explain, but he doesn't. He merely does the same on his machine, then turns away from me to the station.

I'm almost afraid to try getting through the barrier in case that's changed, too. I wonder if everybody can tell? My lack of knowledge of how the world works. My prisoner's pallor. Perhaps I am unknowingly branded, somewhere.

But then I think about what the counsellor said, and tilt my chin up. It doesn't matter what they think of me. And, besides, nobody cares. I wrote to Imran, while I was in prison. Alan told me he wouldn't write back, but he did, just once. The writing was shaky and all over the place. I traced those letters as I cried. *I am getting a little better every day*, he wrote at the end, the letters huge and sloping down the page. And it was that childish sentence that did it. As though he needed to apologize to me for his condition. I cried for the rest of the night in my cell, too.

I walk through the barrier – that hasn't changed – and board the tube to Laura's.

She still lives on the barge, and it's like a step back. There are things on it that I didn't know I'd remembered. The Rosie and Jim dolls in the window. The way they have all sorts littered on the roof. Plates and cups and cutlery.

There's a cat, a long-haired black and white cat on the roof, I know to be called Sampson, who I've never met. I heard about him during Laura's sporadic visits.

Laura dashes out, her arms outstretched, before I can finish truly looking and reacquainting myself.

'You're back, you're out,' she says. She tilts her head, looking at me.

'I'm out,' I say, and her scream of pleasure, the way she embraces me, quickens my heart. I forget her infrequent visits. The way she started speaking to me like I was a distant acquaintance.

Jonty emerges from the boat, waves briefly, and we follow him in.

And although I recognize the objects – the teal mugs,

the patterned cushions – it's the smell that does it. That old-fashioned, dusty, tannin smell. Like the bottom of a teapot. A caravan smell. I breathe in deeply.

But that's when I see the boxes. They're everywhere. Ten or fifteen of them.

'Been on Amazon sprees?' I say.

'I said – we're moving.' She's lighting the gas underneath a hob kettle, her back to me as she says it. 'I meant to say, when I came, that we'd found a buyer, but it didn't seem –'

'Oh,' I say quickly, nodding.

People never feel they can tell you anything when they come to visit you in prison. Or their news will be caveated. *It's nothing compared to what you're going through, but . . .* they will say, or, *No, no, enough about me, I'm here to see how you* are. It was well-meaning, but not what I wanted.

'Where to?' I say, trying to keep my tone casual.

Jonty is sitting at the very end of the barge, outside in the sunshine. His tanned skin is illuminated. He looks older. Everybody looks older. I saw them ageing, in weekly or bi-weekly snapshots, but everybody's skin looked old under those fluorescent lights.

Laura's hands are veiny. Her crow's feet obvious even when she's not smiling. Two deep lines either side of her nose. Jonty is fuller in the waist. He still has his boyish body language, but, a few years ago, he'd have been over here, showing me something, talking to me about his jobs. And now, he's over there. Maturely giving us our space. But then, I think, frowning, I forced us all to grow up. Of course he's giving us space. I have just been released from prison. I made this maturation happen.

When Wilf came back to visit me, two days later – the Thursday after he first saw Minnie on the train – he, too, looked older. He had greying hair at his temples. My brother, I found myself thinking. The boy I used to play in rock pools with, pointing out darting crabs and tiny fish.

'Okay, so,' he said, sitting down opposite me again. He kept his eyes trained on me.

'Yes,' I said, sitting forward.

It seemed easy. There were none of the barbed comments, no competing. No gloating about his houses. He had done that, hadn't he? Or had I just read that into what he'd been saying? I couldn't tell, but I wanted to ignore it. Just concentrate on him.

'Your beard's greying like Monty's,' I said, with a laugh. Monty was Mum and Dad's old tomcat.

'Is it?' Wilf said, laughing self-consciously as he reached to touch it.

Where previously he'd been swarthy – we both always tanned easily, but he had golden-brown hair, too, which lent him the look of somebody who spent all his time outside – his palette now had silver in it, and it made him look completely different, somehow.

'Yep,' I said.

He reached to touch my hand, then, even though it was banned. The pleasure of it. Of another warm hand upon mine, so delicately it may as well have been an insect landing on my bare skin in the summer. It was exquisite, that pleasure, but I didn't tell him so.

'I Facebooked her.'

'*Oh*,' I said. I could feel myself smiling widely. I had

306

known that prison would be upsetting. That I would be lonely. But I hadn't anticipated how often I would be bored. It was all the time: relentless boredom, time moving as slowly as honey off a spoon.

'Is that weird? I haven't told anyone but you.'

'Your secret's safe with me,' I said wryly, and he laughed. 'What did you say?'

He cleared his throat. 'Just that I thought she seemed really nice, and that I wasn't a stalker, and if she wanted to get a cup of coffee I'd be up for that.'

'And?'

'We're going out tomorrow.'

'Oh no – I won't hear until Tuesday,' I said. That's what the counsellor and I had been talking about. The losses. These pangs – these small hurts – I had to endure them. For justice.

Wilf sat back, his mouth turned down. He was drumming his hands on the desk just like he had done at the dinner table for my entire childhood. He was a fidgeter. That energy had transformed into something else when he reached adulthood – into climbing Mount Kilimanjaro and dealing with a property portfolio – but, right there in the prison, it was like he was eight again, brought in from the summer evening for dinner against his will.

'Yeah,' he said sadly after a few seconds. 'Something to look forward to, though?'

He was always like that. Perhaps it's why he got so far ahead. He was always so positive. A born optimist. *It'll be Friday again in a few days*, he would say breezily when we were working awful factory summer jobs during our university years.

'What did she say?'

'Just that she felt the same. A connection – she said. She felt a connection, too. We're going to Hawksmoor at Spitalfields.'

'Serious,' I said, trying to ignore the hollow sensation in my chest.

The feeling got less and less as my sentence ticked by. It had been eighteen months. But, sometimes, it came back. Would I look forward to a glass of wine in a bar on a Friday night in such an innocent way ever again? Probably not, I thought. I couldn't imagine life beyond HMP Bronzefield, and I certainly couldn't imagine going out on a Friday ever again. I nodded to that past Joanna, with her carefree nature and her naivety, just like the counsellor told me to do, and tried to make the best of what I had. It would be Friday soon, as Wilf would say.

On the barge, Wilf fades from my mind as I turn now to Laura.

'Canary Wharf,' she says, the gas lit. It smells of bonfires and holidays and my childhood, that extinguished match. The nostalgia of the smell masks my shock.

'Canary *Wharf*?' I say. I cannot imagine a place less like Laura.

'We have grown up,' she says, sitting down heavily on the sofa.

The sofa that turns into my bed when I stay. When I stayed. I look sadly around the boat. Soon it'll be sold.

'The agency . . .' she says.

I remember she finished her graduate scheme and got a job in advertising. Switched from marketing. From the woman who used to read her tarot cards every night.

'It's in the City,' she says. 'Jonty's in at *The Times*. He knows someone . . .'

'Right,' I say faintly.

And suddenly, being in the spring sunshine and visiting my best friend's boat and being free to grab a cup of coffee on the way and faff about with my Oyster card in the tube station seems to mean absolutely nothing. I don't have a job. I have a criminal record for serious assault. I don't know where the plates are kept in my own house, would have to think twice about what my postcode is.

'I can't imagine you in Canary Wharf,' I say, all the while thinking, *I have no right to comment at all*. I'm like an imposter. I don't know these people.

I feel a familiar sort of panic rising. I used to feel it late at night in my cell, when I knew nobody would come for me. And now, here, *free*, surrounded by people I love, I feel it again. The sun outside seems to fade and the freedom feels like an illusion. What if I . . . what if it happens again? I find myself thinking. What if I reoffend? The statistics are against me. I know it's irrational – Alan would tell me it's just the primitive part of my brain, trying to protect me from every eventual outcome – but it feels real, to me.

'Which agency?' I say, trying to distract myself.

'In business development,' she says, instead of answering me. 'Suits and boots for us. Canary Wharf flat. Then suburbs. Babies.' She lifts her phone up and responds to a text.

'God,' I say, looking away from her. 'Are you still . . .'

'Painting?' she says.

Her paintings were always so beautiful. She had such

flair. Was a true artist; would go into a painting hole sometimes, for weeks at a time. I left her to it, going for drinks with her when she emerged.

'Yeah.'

'Not really,' she says. 'It wasn't . . . I don't know. It wasn't making me happy. I was just trying to get somewhere with it. I read something which says you should give up gracefully things not meant for you, and I thought . . . I don't know. With everything that happened to you,' she says, as the kettle starts whistling, 'I just thought . . . I should stop messing around. You know? You had two years taken away and I want to just – get going. With life.'

'Sure,' I say easily, while reeling.

She picks up her beeping phone again. Her body language is cagey, which makes me look even more closely. Eventually, I stop and just ask her.

'Who's the texter?' I say.

'Tab.'

'Tab?'

'Tabitha. She's one of Jonty's friends. We met on the boat, last summer.'

'Your boat party,' I say.

'Yep. She's nice. You'd like her. She's a teacher.'

'Where does she live?'

'Kent. Commutes in.'

'A commuter,' I say. 'I guess you don't do many Friday drinks with her.'

'We do different stuff.'

'Like what?' I ask, telling myself that it's okay. It's been two years. Of course she's found other friends.

'We sit in her garden,' she says. 'It's massive. Suburbia's kind of appealing, actually.'

'You're moving to Canary Wharf.'

'Yeah. We probably will move out, one day. It just makes sense, doesn't it? That's why everyone does these things. Because they make sense.'

I scrutinize her face. She still has the same squinty eyes, attractive colour in her cheeks requiring no blusher. But inside is different. It must be, for her to say those things. We once sat on the steps on the way down to Gordon's bar, drinking red wine and looking down into the crammed, candlelit cellar below. 'London's oldest bar,' Laura had said, and we had agreed then never to leave, never to be *miserable on the 07.04 to Paddington* like everybody else. 'Why would I move away from all this?' I had said, gesturing down into the bar and behind us, at the buzz of London on a warm Friday night.

'Well, I won't,' I say now.

Laura shrugs, grabs a storage box and passes it to Jonty, who disappears off the boat. Her phone goes again, and she taps out a response.

'We should go out. Together,' I say, gesturing to her phone. 'I'd love to meet her.'

Laura hesitates, just barely, then continues texting. 'She doesn't know you,' she says after a few seconds, still looking down.

I see, I am thinking. *This is why you didn't visit much*. I had thought our friendship was merely on hold; nothing worse. But I see now.

I swallow hard, not looking at her. It will be natural, Alan told me, for people to have moved on. I look at

Laura, and try to be compassionate. I couldn't be a friend to her, not while I was inside. And so she's found another. Someone else she will text all day long, like she used to do with me, even though I am back. I close my eyes and turn my face to the sun, trying to enjoy the feel of it, of the London air around me. I'm no longer in my own dead suburbia at Bronzefield, and I should appreciate that.

'What does she teach, anyway?'

'Tab?'

'Yes.'

'Law,' Laura says quietly.

My head snaps up and I see it now. Her avoidant gaze. The wrinkled brow. She is embarrassed for me, and ashamed of me, all at once.

I go and sit down in a shadowy corner of the boat, behind a stack of three unmarked boxes, and think. I'm responsible for my friend giving up her art and joining the rat race. I'm responsible for my friend finding a new friend. A replacement. I look up at the wooden ceiling of the boat, smelling the matches and the tea and the wood, and wonder if the effects of my mistake will ever wear off. They might never stop spreading, like a drop of contaminated water that poisons people for miles around.

I deactivated my Facebook account in the run-up to the trial. I didn't want the press looking at it, going through my photos, my updates. The privacy settings were a quagmire, too confusing to navigate, and so it went. Giving up Facebook would have been a real punishment, at one point in my life, but it was just collateral damage at that time.

I log on again, now, and reactivate it. Facebook lets me

straight away. It seems it lives forever, waiting for you to log back in like a faithful guard dog.

I've not had access for two years, and have forgotten how to use it. Either that, or it has changed. My wall has gone, replaced by a strange timeline. I try to locate the things I want to look at. My relationship status. Married to Reuben Oliva, who still looks like a greyed-out ghost. I hide a smile. Some things don't change.

I look for Laura's profile, and see she's changed it from the intermittent photos of her art, her projects, funny, arty, angular shots of her and Jonty, or a zoomed-in photograph of her blunt fringe, to something more benign, more corporate. Just her, standing on her own at – a wedding, perhaps? I dig deeper into the photographs. Yes. It was a friend's wedding. She'd been terminally single at university, always clinging too tightly to boy-friends, forever having a 'life-changing weekend' with a new man who never stuck around. And now, here she is, on my Facebook newsfeed looking stunning and grown-up, with a jowly, handsome man at her side.

Facebook is no longer just my friends' updates. People now seem to *like* loads of brands, which in turn post witty updates. It's different to how it was. It's in one of these updates that I see a pub in Dalston is doing a tarot night. It is exactly up Laura's street, and so I tag her, in the way I have seen people starting to do. I can see she's online – a little green blob next to her name – but she doesn't reply. After a few minutes, she logs off.

Just as I'm about to log off and close the laptop, I see my own relationship change. In one blink, it goes from *married to Reuben Oliva* to *married*. Confused, I click

Reuben's name. He's still there. I don't understand this new Facebook. I will have to ask him later.

I close the laptop. It's too much. Like I have missed the middle three series of *Lost*, or something. Only it's not *Lost*. It's my life.

I go and find the white T-shirt, taking it out of the washing basket. Already it smells musty and damp, but I can still smell the prison smell on it. I breathe deeply, trying to ignore myself, my thoughts. The realization that – maybe just a little bit – I miss it.

'I haven't told anybody this,' Wilf says, speaking quietly.

We're in a Bill's, off Covent Garden. He's fiddling with the cap of his beer. We've just ordered burgers. Minnie is joining us for afters. *Maybe pudding*, she texted Wilf. It'll be strange to meet her, finally.

'What?' I say.

The restaurant is bizarre. It's so loud. So jovial. I was overwhelmed by the menu, that I could order anything I liked whatsoever, and so Wilf helped me choose. My phone has been beeping constantly, with updates from my friends from Bronzefield. Wilf's eyebrows rise in curiosity until I turn it on to its front.

'No . . . let me see,' he says.

I extend my hand towards him, embarrassed, passing him the phone. It's lit up with about forty messages.

'Rose, Fi, Yosh and me,' I say.

'Yosh?' Wilf says, and he laughs.

I like that sound. He looks at me. His eyes look bulbous. They always did. I used to call him Goggle-eyes. He'd laugh, and call me Jojo.

He's still staring at me, and I say, 'You want to know what they did, don't you?'

His face creases into a smile. 'Yes,' he says.

I show him the group. Fi is talking about recruitment consultants needing paperwork she doesn't have. Yosh has told her to ask her probation officer. I see Wilf trying to hide his surprise that I'm now part of this world.

I shrug. 'They were nice to me,' I say.

'I see.'

'It was a category A, so brace yourself.'

'I know,' Wilf says. 'I had to take my shoes off in case I was carrying anything in for you. So what did they do?'

'Fi killed her boyfriend. In a road traffic accident. First offence. She was – only just – over the limit. He died, she survived, she got done for dangerous driving. Two years. She's totally and utterly fucked up by it.'

'Two years. Jesus,' Wilf says.

I'm surprised by his surprise.

'What use is that?' he says.

'She'll never do it again. That's for sure. Whether or not she went to prison,' I say.

'How far over the limit?'

'She'd had two glasses of wine. She's – she's small. And she just . . .' I stop before I say it, then say it anyway. 'She's just not a very good driver. That's the heart of it. It was raining. Bloody rain,' I add with a faint smile, 'and she just lost control. So. There you are.'

'Jesus,' Wilf says again.

He's waiting for the others. I can see it. I don't begrudge him. It's normal. Everyone does it. They might ask you about your day, what your weekend plans are, but as soon as they know you've been in prison, it's all they want to know. You are reduced to a crime. In my case, a most violent one.

'Rose glassed someone – another woman. Yosh – she's Japanese – stole money from HSBC, in her job. Her husband had been made redundant, so she hacked in . . .'

Wilf blinks. He's wearing a green T-shirt that makes his eyes look browner. As he reaches to sip his beer the sleeves ride up his biceps and I see a faint tan.

My phone lights up on the table again. *It will get better,* Yosh says, then sends a row of kisses. Wilf's eyes stray to the message, then back to mine again. These are my new friends. They are more like me now – on the inside – than Laura and Jonty. Perhaps they're more like me than Laura and Jonty ever were.

We lapse into silence. Our burgers arrive. I think of Imran, as I do often. I wonder what he's doing. I remember the carers and the memory loss and the personality changes. I shouldn't be here, sitting in Bill's, feeling fine, I think. I raise my drink to my lips, but on the way, I say a toast to him. To Imran. *I'm sorry.*

It's a few minutes before Wilf speaks.

'When I was at uni,' he says, speaking in an even lower tone, blotting the droplets of water that have come off the bottom of his beer bottle with a napkin, 'I had a girlfriend.'

I think back. We overlapped by a year. His final year of Cambridge was my first year at Oxford. I went to see him, five or six times, maybe, at Cambridge. Mum and Dad wanted me to get used to 'that sort of environment'. And, besides, I wanted to see. I meet his eyes and feel

316

something. Wistfulness, maybe. Nostalgia. That was right before he changed, that final visit, at Christmastime. After that, he began setting up businesses, selling on products for friends. Tuition. The work – the homework – came easily to him. He ran the London marathon right before his finals began. Started sneering at how passive I was, letting life fall into my lap rather than going out and grasping it.

But there was never a girlfriend. Not even a sniff of one, a shared smile, a woman slipping out of his room before I got there. I had often wondered why. He'd had one two-week relationship, in the final year of his A-levels, with a geeky woman who liked role-playing games. She was a slightly dowdy woman who had turned out to be sexually adventurous, and he'd made me laugh about it over Christmas dinner.

'Did you?' I say, thinking hard. Perhaps he did. I didn't know everything about his life while he was at Cambridge.

'Yeah. Beth,' he says. His face clouds as he says it, his golden eyebrows drawing together. He pulls his lips inwards, creating dimples either side of his mouth.

'What happened?'

He inhales deeply then blows the air out through his nose, like a smoker. 'She died,' he says. 'She died,' he says again.

'What? When?'

'We'd been together two months. Stupid, really. I'm not anything. Not a widower. There's no word for it. But it wasn't . . . a fling. I loved her,' he says.

'We never knew,' I say softly, wondering if he suffered

as I did, with loneliness, with guilt, with that hollow feeling. Different but the same.

'I was . . . I don't know. It didn't feel legitimate, somehow,' he says. 'I was there. She had sudden adult death syndrome. Died in her sleep. I woke up spooning her. Spooning her body.' He gulps.

I nod, quickly, my eyes wet. My poor brother, alone at university, barely an adult. No wonder he changed. No wonder he changed so much, so quickly.

He meets my eyes. 'It didn't feel legitimate,' he says, 'to mourn. So I did other stuff. Lists. Felt insanely jealous of you when you met Reuben. That you had all those friends. I was always rubbish with people, and the one person who had loved me was taken.'

It wasn't just that we had both suffered. The grief we'd both felt, me causing it and him suffering from it. It was something else, too: it was his comment on legitimacy that had me nodding. For the court proceedings, and for the entire time in prison, I hadn't felt that Sadiq had been a *legitimate* threat. That, somehow, it was my fault. And much of it was: my overreaction, my recklessness, my failure to check that it was him. My *unreasonable force*. But there was something in that illegitimacy. I understood it. Feeling like I wasn't a real victim, even though, until the point where I overreacted, I had been. Real life was complicated.

'It was legitimate,' I say simply, reaching to take my brother's hand across the table, no prison guards watching.

He grasps it gratefully. 'It didn't feel it,' he says. 'I'd known her for less than sixty days. We met on a night out – she was brand new to me. I didn't know of her at all until that night – and then we were an item, but I didn't tell anyone. It was the end of winter when we first met. Just after you visited.' He gestures out of the plate-glass window, down to Covent Garden below, then sips his beer. 'She died after Easter. Do you remember? The one where I didn't come home?'

I nod again. 'Yeah.'

We'd wondered what he was doing, the Easter of his second year. He didn't come home, said he was working in a bar in Cambridge. But then, that summer, he arrived home as usual, as though he'd never left.

'She died on the Easter Monday.'

'I'm so sorry,' I say. 'That that happened to you.'

I meet his eyes and he nods, once.

'You can buy a sack of organic potatoes from here and take them home,' Wilf says, reaching across and pointing to an item in a side box on the menu.

'No thanks,' I say, with a faint smile.

He smiles too. 'I wanted to tell you,' he says, 'but instead I was . . . I don't know. Barbed. With you.'

'We were jealous of each other.'

'I was certainly jealous of you,' he says. 'You seemed to have it all.'

'What? *You* have – you got a first. From Cambridge. And you have four *London* properties. And your job . . .'

He looks at me, not saying anything, his round eyes just staring. Suddenly, I can hear myself. What would I rather have? Reuben and the people in my life – or money and a degree? It's easy. I've never looked at it that way before.

'God,' I say. 'I had no idea.'

'I know. Why would you?' he says. 'But it well and truly

319

messed me up. And Minnie is now . . . the first woman, since.'

'At all?'

'No,' he says, making a sort of equivocal gesture. 'There have been girls. But they never stayed over. I just – I don't know. I just thought . . . I just thought they'd die, I suppose. How messed up is that? If they stayed with me. It's like an incorrect thought went into my mind – that I caused it, somehow. And even though I know it's not true, I couldn't . . . I couldn't get it out of my head.'

I am nodding vigorously again. Everything he's saying is true.

It's so easy for false thoughts to pass through the net of your mind, not being caught, and to become truths.

'Notwithstanding your crime, don't you think that's . . . a harsh assessment of yourself?' Alan had said once, when I told him I had never studied enough, always procrastinated, was stupid, career-less. And look what had happened: that crime. I'd blinked as he said it. Harsh? No. The Old Bailey had sentenced me to two years in prison. What could be harsher than that?

'But what is the benefit, Joanna,' he had said, 'of beating yourself up, now, about it? Who wins?'

I had answered, simply, 'Atonement.'

Alan had shrugged, as if to say, *Who cares about that?*

I keep thinking about that conversation, now. It's strange to realize you might have been wrong for your entire life.

'Seen Mum and Dad?' Wilf asks, spearing an onion ring.

I shake my head.

He gives me a curved half-smile, at that.

But he doesn't know. They came separately, Mum and Dad. Every single week, just like Wilf. It was better that they were separate. Like I'd split up a tribe, or something. It was healthier. After a few months, Dad reached over the table, and tentatively touched my hands, even though we weren't supposed to. 'It doesn't matter, you know, Jo,' he had said. I had nodded tearfully, wishing the moment could be extended forever, that I didn't have to return to my cell, alone again until the next visiting slot. 'We don't care.' That was the closest either of them came to apologizing.

But it didn't matter. I am a valid person, whether or not I got a degree. Whether or not my parents are proud of me. Whether or not my brother likes me. I tilt my chin up, by myself, now.

Wilf nods, picking up his beer again and ripping the label off. Then he puts it down and reaches for me, and grips my hand with his. His hand is cold and wet from the condensation. 'I'm glad you're meeting Minnie,' he says. 'Before anyone.'

'Me, too,' I say. 'Me, too.'

37

Conceal

I write the final line of the final scene and break for coffee. It's funny, but despite everything, my mind has
become strangely quiet, stilled. I have no smartphone.
No Instagram, any more. No posts on Facebook. People
know where I am, of course. I'm not hiding. I am
merely . . . sequestered away.

I sit back and look at the final line. I change one word,
then sit back again. That's it.

It's done. One hundred thousand words. I would never
have thought I was capable of it. But I've done one thousand words per day, every day, after work. No matter the
time. No matter my plans (which aren't many). It was
never easy, exactly. But I didn't give up. I just kept building the bricks, one by one.

I wrote a book called *Deep Down in the Dennys* when I
was eight. Wilf proofread it, and then we 'published' it,
running ten copies off on our new home laser printer and
selling them at the school for five pence each. I wonder if
he remembers.

On impulse, I navigate to Facebook and type his name
in. It was a name as familiar to me as my own, one I have
surely seen written almost as often. Wilfred. He used to
hate it.

He's changed his profile picture. I open that and stare at it. His long nose. He's wearing Aviators, and in them I can see his arm reflected. It's a selfie. All of his other pictures are just him, too. At the top of mountains. Running marathons. On a boat on the high seas. All selfies.

He hasn't met anybody, then. I wouldn't expect him to. He's too cagey, remote.

There's nothing else to see, so I click off the page, feeling alone, suddenly, in my bedroom. It feels like a past life.

The novel's stored safely on my laptop. I'll give it a read over, then send it off soon. I have a list of agents Blu-tacked to the wall and I take it off, now. Now that I'm ready.

A small suitcase is packed, and the laptop goes in first. I'm thankful, in a funny sort of way, for these two years of freedom. It's been a completely pure, undiluted form of freedom. I've been able to do absolutely whatever I wanted. I've got the book down. I've watched whatever I've wanted. I've worked where I wanted to, in mobile libraries, of course, surrounded by books and their musty scents and the gentle rocking of the bus when there are too many people on board. It might not be what I want to do with my life, but it has been good.

And now it's time.

Before I leave, I get the shoebox out. I allowed myself one box.

I sort through it, pulling out the items like they are relics. And I suppose they are: artefacts of my previous life. They're preserved, not even dusty, as I hold them in my hands. The wedding bracelet. The list I wrote the day I got here. It contains everything I could ever remember Reuben and I saying we loved about the other. There are only twenty or so items on it. It was the best I could do, after the accident. I wrote it before they faded even further from my memory. Reading it now produces a warm feeling in the depths of my stomach, like having a hot chocolate with brandy in, at Christmastime.

I close my eyes, trying to taste the tang of Before. That lovely life with that lovely man. That carefree life. It never felt carefree. But, of course, it was.

There are other things in the box, too. A newspaper clipping about a protest against the closure of the library, with Reuben front and centre holding a placard saying *Knowledge is power.* I loved him for that protest. That protest meant he understood my job, as well as the wider politics. But it frustrated me, too. I didn't want to go. Usually he'd leave it, but he just couldn't understand why it wasn't top of my list, standing in the cold with a placard. That clipping – it stands for all of it. That belligerent side of him. The one I loved, too. His flaws. I loved both sides of him like a mother should love her children: equally.

Absent from the box are the things that are impossible to capture. The way he looked at me across rooms. The dirty texts he'd occasionally send, which shocked and titillated me. The way he'd organize himself around me, tolerating my chaos, amused by it, even.

There's a skylight, in my loft room, and I open it and peer out, looking at the tops of the buildings, taking in some summer air. There's been a heatwave for the last few weeks, and it's sticky and airless up here. I like to look at the rooftops in Birmingham. I never could in London. I was isolated, tucked away into a flat right in the bowels of the city. Reuben would hate it here. Would hate the things I like: the proper recycling bins. The driveway. That my neighbour occasionally invites me to her barbecues, even though she knows I am a recluse. That I can hang my washing outside. Reuben would be appalled by this banal suburbia, away from the city lights and twenty-four-hour shops. I almost smile to think about it.

As I look out at the darkening air above the rooftops, I wonder if he's still in Zone Two. Still living in rented accommodation, still within walking distance of a hundred pubs, a thousand exhibitions, the river. Our river. No. Let's not think of him.

My hand is on a clutch of papers from the box. It aches less today, my bad hand.

The name of my lawyer – Weston Michaels – is franked across the back of the letter. It was painless. I thought it would be. Not that I had ever given divorcing Reuben any thought, of course, but it was. He was his reasonable, dispassionate self. As consistent as a stick of fairground rock with his traits running evenly all the way through him.

I enclose your decree absolute, the letter says. No mention of 'I am pleased to'. I liked that about my lawyer. He knew there was nothing pleasing about any of it.

I separate out the pieces of paper, and there it is. I haven't looked at it for months, but there it is. Stamped with a County Court logo, in blood red.

I trace a fingertip over the names. Joanna Oliva, the Petitioner. Reuben Oliva, the Respondent.

I could change my name now. Meet someone new. I try to imagine Reuben's antithesis. What kind of man would that be? He wouldn't vote. Wouldn't read books. He'd like the simple things in life. Two weeks in the Costa del Sol every August. He'd not worry about the treatment the cheap beef in his McDonald's had been subjected to. He'd be sunny, warm. He'd like Saturday morning sex and football matches. Maybe he'd gamble, or download movies, or do something else mildly illegal, such as putting in a whiplash claim when he didn't have any injuries. I shudder. He's not for me, that man.

I wonder if Reuben received exactly the same document. Probably. He never said. Not a word of contact after I said I wanted a divorce. Classic, dignified Reuben.

I trace his name. That beautiful name. Reuben Oliva. It tripped off my tongue. I was so happy to take it.

I can't help but wonder what he's doing now. Worst of all, maybe, I wonder what might've been. If he knew. If he might have accepted it. Protected me. Forgiven me.

No. The reasons I love him are the reasons I could never have told him.

Loved.

Love.

I dream of Reuben, and, in the middle of the night, I get up and go into my tiny garden and look up at the sky and the stars and the moon. They're so clear here. It would be nice, relaxing in the warm night air, if I wasn't breathless and tired. My body slows down more at night than it used to. It takes me an age to wake properly in the mornings.

What's he doing? I wonder. How is he? I wonder if he

dreams of me, if he's thinking of me right now, wherever he is, whatever he's doing. Maybe he's reading something heavy. Something meaningful. Something good. Watching BBC News, unable to sleep in the heat. Playing the piano. Slagging off politicians on the Internet. Something like that. Something good.

38

Reveal

Laura and Jonty are having a party on their boat. A farewell party, she called it in the text. As Reuben and I arrive, the side is strung with fairy lights. The boxes have gone. The random items from the top have gone, too. It's a shell. A husk. It has lost its smell, I realize, as we step inside. Everyone is gathered at the other end, and Reuben and I are alone in the last of the sunlight for a moment. He pours a plastic cup of red wine for himself, then looks at me, his eyebrows raised.

I nod. He pours the wine and I sip it. I find I like the taste of the heavy red. I never used to.

Laura arrives at my elbow. She's wearing different clothes. Almost office wear. Cropped, patterned trousers. A black vest top. Her hair's been straightened.

'Your second outing,' Laura says. 'How does it feel?'

It occurs to me, as she asks, that Reuben hasn't, and I dart an uncomfortable glance at him, as though I shouldn't be discussing it.

'Weird,' I say.

She doesn't laugh, though Reuben does, a small exhale of air through his nose. She merely appraises me, her head tilted to one side.

The spring heatwave continues, and outside the air is

warm and sticky. Reuben sips his wine, looking up at me. His eyes are squinting at the last rays of the sun. His eyelashes ginger. I used to love looking at those eyelashes in the early days, when we'd spend entire days in bed together. I used to stare at them while he slept, terrified he'd wake up and think me a psychopath.

'She's catching up, aren't you?' Reuben says.

I nod. He's told me all about what I've missed. A referendum. Three plane crashes. Two local council elections. A vote for air strikes on Syria. Two Beyoncé albums. Reuben was the best person to tell me – but it's like being given a synopsis of a movie. I don't know. I wasn't there.

'So what's changed?' Laura says. 'I'm interested in an alien's perspective,' she adds, with a grin.

The joke's not funny, though. *I wouldn't be so alienated if you had visited*, I think.

Jonty joins us, holding a glass up to me.

'Nothing and everything,' I say.

Reuben has stepped a few feet away from me, just outside of the circle. He's looking over the side of the boat, at something down in the canal.

I look up, at the pale moon and the first stars.

Laura's gaze strays to him momentarily. She's wearing a choker, terracotta lipstick.

'Are chokers in fashion now?' I say, trying to keep my tone light.

Laura laughs. 'Yep,' she says. 'They are.'

One of Jonty's friends is standing nearby, holding a beer in a Mason jar. He's got a beard and is wearing braces. 'Be sad to see you leave the boat,' he says.

'Corporate life beckons,' says Jonty.

'I think I should get a job,' I say to Laura.

She beckons me over, frowning, and we sit together on the edge of the boat. It's bobbing gently. It feels like me, that boat. Untethered.

'What're you going to do?' she says.

'All recruiters want references. And – bloody hell. I have a *record*. I'm out on licence.' It still sounds distasteful as I say it, even though I'm used to it, have had enough therapy to accept it.

'Don't they – help?' she says.

'Yeah, my probation offic–'

'*God.*'

It's the tone that gets me. The harsh cut-off, my sentence sliced cleanly as if by a guillotine. She doesn't want me to discuss it. I am a pariah, like somebody who insists on discussing the death penalty or their sex life at a party.

'I want to be a counsellor – I think,' I say. Move on, Joanna. Just move the conversation on. 'I think I'd be good at it. I don't know.'

I say it quietly to her, while Reuben, Jonty and the stranger stand a few feet away from us. She's the first person I've told, other than my own counsellor. I shrug awkwardly. I look down to the end of the boat again and out at the canal. 'It's boiling,' I say. 'Is this global warming?'

Laura smiles, shifting closer to me, bumping her knee against mine. 'I think you'll be a great counsellor,' she says. 'You're – you know. Sympathetic, but not off the wall like me.'

'Do you still do your hippy stuff, even though you're a corporate suit now?' I say.

'Yeah – of course. I read your cards the night before your trial. I never told you.' She brushes her hair off her shoulders.

And I see that she's not changed. She's just . . . grown up. We've all had to. Whether we liked it or not. Because of me. Because of lots of things.

'It said you'd be betrayed,' she says. 'I got the ten of swords.'

'Betrayed,' I say. 'Huh. The State betrayed me – maybe.'

'Maybe,' she says, though she looks as though she knows something else.

I want to press her on it, but don't. I'm too afraid to.

'It's all totally messed up,' I say. 'Every night, while I was inside, I ticked off another day. But now it feels . . . well, it doesn't go away. I was a criminal. Now I'm an ex-criminal. Nothing's changed, really. I'm free but . . . not.'

'You *are* free,' she says emphatically.

'Not from the past, though. My record. I don't even know where to start. It's – I can't describe it to you,' I say. 'Once you leave society you're sort of – rudderless. It's not a case of just walking to the nearest recruitment office. They're not interested in me. I've committed one of the worst violent offences. Every criminal's got an answer. I'd just sound like the rest of them if I said I wasn't really violent.' I stop speaking, then try to start again. *Even you*, I want to add. *Even you lost interest.*

'But you're *not*,' she says.

She is being so nice. I can't say it. I can't accuse her.

I shrug. 'I was convicted.'

'Yeah, but –'

I hold up a hand and she goes silent. I've worked hard

331

at accepting what I did. How wrong it was; my remorse is now a part of me, too.

'It's just hard, is all,' I say after a few minutes. The sun's set, and the outside of the boat is lit by the fairy lights alone. 'It's not how I expected. I can't just . . . slot back in. Everything's changed. I've changed. I've got to – start again.'

'Why?' Her face is knitted with concern.

'I'm thirty-two. I mean – I want a baby. But we need to . . . we need to get used to each other again. Living together.'

'Just tell him,' she says in a low voice. 'He should know that sort of thing.'

'It's . . . I don't know. I don't have any right to complain,' I say. 'I committed a crime. But it's so *knotty*. I've been robbed of time, and now I feel like I can't just try to catch up with life, because everything's different. But I'm thirty-two and if we wait another year . . .'

'Well. You'll be a better mum now – after. After this,' she says.

I turn and look at her. A thin layer of sweat sits on her upper lip.

'You think so?' I say.

'Yeah. Totally. You have a plan. You're – I dunno. Different. You'll be a good mum,' she says. 'You seem . . . you seem different. More yourself. Less timid.'

'I wasn't timid.'

'I don't know. Not timid. But you seemed to be apologizing for yourself. Now you sit up straight. Properly.'

'Excuse me,' the man with the braces says. He's turned away from Reuben and Jonty and is looking down at us, his hands on his hips. 'I *do* know who you are,' he says. He's just remembered something, his gaze on me.

I feel my cheeks heat up, as though someone's pressed two hot pads to them, like Wilf used to do with the oven gloves when we were baking. I would shriek with joy in our kitchen while Mum and Dad tried to shush us.

'Sorry?' Laura says to him.

'I *do* know who you are, and I don't mind you being here . . . but it makes me –' He stops, looking thoughtfully up at the scenery beyond us, then down again.

Laura and I stand up. Reuben and Jonty are looking on, confused.

'It makes me uncomfortable to hear you discussing *what you did*,' he says, fixing me with his gaze. 'When we're all out trying to enjoy ourselves.'

'You mean our private conversation about her life?' Laura says.

'Leave it,' I mutter. 'I'll just – I'll just go.'

'Mate,' Jonty says. Calm, happy, mild Jonty's face has gone ashen, his brow pulled downwards. 'Mate, I think it's about time you took your uncomfortable feelings at my very good friend's suffering, and got the fuck off my boat,' he says.

Reuben gets his phone out and looks down at it, ignoring us.

Jonty's walking the man over to the edge of the boat. Laura grabs my arm. Her hand's warm and damp, and she says, 'I'm *so* sorry, Jo. I had no idea he was . . . I had no idea he would be so rude. So judgemental.'

My face is burning. *But you are, too. Only internally*, I think.

'We're all here,' Laura says.

Reuben's still looking at his phone, and we both glance at him. And suddenly, I realize. Jonty marched the guy off. Laura consoled me. But what did Reuben do? He turned away when I was discussing prison, and he stood by and said absolutely nothing when I was being harangued. How can he justify that? How can he say nothing?

I look at him, but he's not looking at me. He's looking down. At BBC News, probably. Some war. Some tragedy. He'll care about that. But what about here? What about events in his own life? Me?

We leave shortly afterwards. The evening isn't salvageable. We can't get it back. The boat is still lit up behind us as we walk along the canal towpath. Reuben reaches for my hand and I feel like there are a hundred Joannas walking along here next to me. The Joanna who hurt Imran and called 999. The Joanna who visited the canal the day she went to prison. It's not the same canal, but it may as well be. I take a deep breath, smelling the air. London smells the same as it always did in the early summer: musky, congested. But, just like after a particularly long holiday, I can truly smell it again.

I take another deep breath, and then I ask him. Dispassionately, directly, in an adult way, as I've been told.

'You didn't defend me,' I say quietly.

Reuben's hand is still around mine. 'What?'

'To that man. That man who said I was making him uncomfortable.'

'No,' Reuben says.

'Why not?'

'Jonty defended you.'

'Well, yes,' I say.

We negotiate the pathway as it narrows. Even though we go in single file, Reuben still has my hand in his. It starts to feel strange, that hand in mine. Like we are clinging on to a useless life raft.

He's saying nothing as the path widens again. The air is soupy and warm. A fine layer of sweat covers my skin. The air was always so controlled in prisons. I haven't sweated for months. It feels nice as it evaporates, like fine, soft cold needles prickling my skin.

'But why didn't you?' I say.

Reuben drops my hand. We are separate now, on the towpath. It looks perfect, this night, walking along with my husband. It's what I've counted down to for two years. And yet it's not perfect. The lights of the boats glow strangely and the world feels too big and I am utterly alone, it seems to me, with no idea of my next steps.

'I . . .' Reuben says.

And then I see it: a brief closing of his eyes, a straightening of his posture.

'I was embarrassed,' he says simply. 'I didn't know how to handle it.'

'Right. So you . . . didn't,' I say.

'No.'

'Why not?'

'What is all this – all this navel gazing?' Reuben says. 'I lost you for two years. I watched all the fucking TV shows you could ever imagine in those seven hundred nights. You know? Why do we have to fuck it all up with this analysis?' He grabs my hand again and squeezes it slightly too tightly.

'But you're so – you're so liberal,' I say, spitting it out like an accusation, as though I have always resented his liberalism, which isn't true. 'You're all for rehabilitation. And innocent until proven guilty. And making mistakes. That's your whole,' my hand is moving in circles in front of us, like a Catherine wheel, '*ethos*.'

'Yes,' Reuben says.

'Seems like you're not liberal when it's on your own doorstep. When *I'm* on your doorstep.'

His jaw clenches at that, but he says nothing further. The conversation is closed, banging like a prison door in the night.

It's time. We both know it. Our only intimacy for over two years has been across a table. Limited touching. Eye contact only. I've showered communally with other women, slept under the sometimes watchful gaze of security guards, but now here I am, with my husband, in this most usual and intimate arena: our dim bedroom. He takes his shirt off and I see the body I haven't seen for years, not properly, not like this, lit up by the lamp, reflected again in the window.

He looks at me, a serious, suggestive look, then walks over, brushing my hair back from my face. I shiver at that touch, that sensual, sad touch. There were a thousand Joannas out tonight, and now a thousand Reubens are touching me. The Reuben who sat on the stairs with me at an Oxford party almost a decade ago. The Reuben who proposed to me, who married me, who stayed with me during my incarceration. And here he remains, still wanting to skim those elegant fingertips over my forehead.

'Number three thousand-odd, I reckon,' he says softly, his breath tickling my nose.

'Are we?' I say. 'We missed a few.'

'I kept track. I made a list,' he says, gesturing behind him, but not moving. I've no doubt there is a list, somewhere. He wouldn't lie to me.

'Can I see it?' I say back.

'Later,' he says pointedly.

And then we are kissing, and then he is inside me, on the bed, the same old way we used to do it: seamlessly, as though we were meant to.

And then, as he comes, he says it. 'I'm sorry.'

I think I mishear, at first, but I haven't; I know I haven't.

Afterwards, lying on his side, facing me, stroking my hip, he doesn't acknowledge it, and so neither do I.

He stands and flicks the lamp off. We always used to sleep, right away, after sex, neither of us needing to read.

But as he's standing there, in total darkness, his body ghoulishly lit from the street lamp outside, I look at him. He seems to be hesitating, wanting to say something to me, but then stops himself. I sit and look properly at him. There's an expression on his face, for just a moment. Agony, I would have said, if I didn't know better. He looks agonized. After a moment, it is gone.

He turns and leaves the bedroom. He goes and washes. I hear the tap running. He is washing me off himself.

I'm watching Reuben play, for the first time, at a jazz club nearby. He wears a suit, to play in, with trainers, and everyone seems to know him. They don't seem to know who I am, and I wonder what he's told them.

337

We have descended some wooden stairs into the basement where the lights are low and purplish. It smells of stale alcohol and sweat. I miss the cigarette smells. Not only from when they used to be allowed in public buildings, but also from the prison. Everyone smoked in the yard where our clothes were hung out and blew in the wind, and so everyone's clothes smelt faintly of cigarettes. I got used to it. It's one of the many smells that mingle to form home for me.

Reuben's playing style has totally changed. It's become more theatrical. He bends backwards, his back arching, and then he almost falls over the keys, his head bent low.

I half watch him, wondering who he is. I've had a total of six hours a week with him for two years, at communal tables pushed so close together they might as well have been linked, like at a bingo hall or at Wagamama's. The chairs in the visitors' centre were hard, folded metal. They made Reuben uncomfortable as he sat there for the duration of his visit. We often made small talk. He was never a great talker, and he couldn't easily touch me. And so we talked of stupid things, things neither of us cared about. The weather. How I was finally learning to cook – his mouth twisted into an indulgent smile, at that. I couldn't get him talking, not the way I used to. He was too shy. And we couldn't just *be* with each other, the way our relationship demanded. Just sitting together in the living room, occasionally remarking on the news. Taking a lasagne out of the oven, the steam misting up the room as Reuben got a plate out and asked me how my meeting had been. We had none of that. Our relationship had been strip-searched, like me, and I didn't know whether or not it had survived.

As I watch him now, I wonder if Imran ever does things like this. Goes out to see jazz. Exists in the world. Enjoys things. I think of him often. I wrote to him, again and again, after his first letter, but he never responded.

Reuben joins me after his set piece. He weaves his way across the room. I can see him easily – he's so tall – but he moves differently than Before, as though he is some sort of celebrity now.

He's holding a glass of something dark to his chest. It's barely more than a shot. He's leaning over me strangely and I realize with a start that he's drunk. He's never usually drunk, can drink a bottle of red and be seemingly unaffected.

'The thing is,' he says, slurring strangely, not looking at me, his hair dark in the dim lighting, 'I don't even know why you're here.'

'I wanted to see you play,' I say, twisting my wedding bracelet around my wrist.

They wouldn't let me wear it in prison. A gem-less ring or nothing, they said. It lived in a locker for two years. It came out as shiny as it went in. It had nothing to dull it; no life.

'Oh, did you?' Reuben says, with a faint smile. There is something dangerous about his tone. Mocking.

'Yeah,' I say, looking up at him.

His eyes finally meet mine. They're black.

'I don't know why you'd want to hang around with me at all,' he says.

339

At first I think he's talking about the constant Whats-App notifications I receive. He always frowns when I receive them, until I feel like a naughty child, reduced to tapping out replies to people in the toilet.

'What?' I say.

'I don't know why you'd want to hang around with me at all,' he says, louder this time, right in my ear.

When I pull my head back, I see there are tears in his eyes.

'I might preach about doing the right thing, but do I?' he says.

'I don't know . . . I don't understand what you mean.'

He leans close to me, so our faces are level. His breath smells sweetly, of alcohol, just like Sadiq's did. I jerk my head back.

'It's all my fault,' Reuben says. 'That's why I hid our relationship on Facebook.'

'What? What is?'

'Your *incarceration*.'

'No, it's not,' I say.

I go to turn away, ready to leave, but he pulls gently on my wrist.

'I told the barrister,' he says.

And it's those four words that change everything.

'You told the barrister *what*?'

'When your barrister took my proof. He asked me about the call records. How long Imran lay in the puddle for. And I crumbled – stammered, Jo,' he says softly. 'And then, after I'd crumbled, I told him everything. Your lie.'

He's speaking so softly I can only just hear him.

Somebody else has taken the stage, is playing a moody tune. It's a woman and her voice fills the club.

'What? Why?' I say.

I look at him, remembering that morning. The air was chilled in the courthouse and my limbs felt as though they were full of ants. I remember that. I remember it all. Reuben going to chat to the barrister, Duncan. Both of them coming back, faces sombre. I thought myself merely paranoid. Shortly after that, I was offered a plea bargain, and I took it.

'I took a plea,' I say.

'Because of me.'

'Was it?'

'They offered a plea. But Sarah advised taking it . . . because of me. Because I made your risk too high. I was your only witness and I just – I couldn't lie to your barrister. Not *wouldn't*. *Couldn't*. I was . . . he asked me directly. And I tried to lie. But it was obvious. He said I'd be cross-examined on it. Because of the medical experts fighting over whether there was hypoxia. So, I told the truth. That you lied. It was me,' he says. 'I shopped you.'

His voice breaks on the last line, and then he's crying, standing alone. My husband. My betrayer. He has held my hand and stabbed me in the back, all at once.

I stare at him, too shocked to say anything.

That first night, in the designated First Night Cell, where I was put on suicide watch because I was so shocked and alone. The fleece pillow I cried into that dried unnaturally quickly. The nights I counted down. Each strip search. Each random drugs test when I had to wee in a pot. Looking forward to being on cooking duty because it would earn me money to watch the television and give me something to do. Feeling complete and utter panic the first day in the yard as I knew nobody, like we were in Azkaban and they'd had their souls sucked out of them. The two years. Experiencing time stretched thin like wire. Having nothing at all to look forward to. Out, now, my life in tatters.

And it could have been avoided. Perhaps. In part. Not made worse. If the barrister hadn't known about my lie . . . if Reuben hadn't told him. We might have gone to trial. I might have got away with it.

I stare at him, still shocked. He's leering strangely at me.

'Why didn't they tell the prosecution?' I ask.

'They don't have to. But they got you to take a plea. They wouldn't put a liar on trial. Either of us,' he says.

'Why didn't they tell *me*?'

He shrugs, just looking at me. 'Why would they?'

'I don't know.'

'So it's fair to say I caused all this,' he says, gesturing at me.

'All what?' I say, my voice only just above a whisper.

'This detritus,' he says, his voice going back to his London roots, the way it does when he lobbies, when he gives soundbites to the news or speeches about Islamic prejudice.

'Detritus.'

'The detritus of our marriage.' His eyes are still on me, the drink still held to him, curled up against his chest. 'After I poisoned it.'

'You didn't poison it,' I say automatically.

'We both did.'

'What are you saying?'

Reuben leans against the wall in that way that he some-times does, resting his weight against it, his head tilted. 'I can't bloody do this any more, Jo.'

'Can't do what?'

'I just . . . I waited, and waited, and waited for you.'

'I know, I . . .'

'*House of Cards. Game of Thrones* twice. *Homeland,*' he says, talking over me.

I frown up at him, baffled.

'*The Good Wife. Breaking Bad. Sherlock. Mad Men.*'

'I . . .' I stammer. I don't know what to say to this rant-ing man in front of me.

'All these things watched in the hours and hours with-out you. I'm so fucking tired of watching television on my own.'

'But I'm back now,' I say, spreading my arms wide.

My drink sloshes. It's just a Coke. My hand's wet from the spillage and I glance at it, breaking Reuben's gaze. I feel my skin getting sticky as it begins to dry.

'You're back, yeah,' he says, looking down at me, his expression suddenly tender.

No, not tender. Something else. I step closer to him, and his body accommodates mine, as it always has. And then I'm in his embrace and his breath is alcoholic as he ducks his head to mine, and his body is warm and solid.

'You're back, Jo, but I grieved for you. I miss you.'

'You miss me?' I say. 'But I'm here.'

'I still feel like I miss you. Or that you're gone.'

I look away.

'I grieved for you. Yeah,' he says.

He's talking the most I've known him talk in recent

343

times. His words are tripping over each other like clumsy children marching in line on a school trip.

'I watched all those TV shows on my own and I got over you.'

'You got *over* me?'

His truth is so painful that I close my eyes against it. If I could go back, and not call 999, and walk away instead, I would. Oh, in this moment, I would.

'I mourned you. I didn't do anything. I stayed inside all the time. Work put me on . . . you know. Back office duties. I had nowhere to go and I didn't want to see anybody.' He shifts out of the way as another couple moves past us. His body jostles mine. 'I wasn't wearing black. There wasn't a funeral. But there was grief.'

'Well, now I'm back – from the dead. And aren't you pleased?'

'No, Jo,' he says, shaking his head sadly.

And then I realize what his expression is. It's pity. He pities me.

'No,' he says again.

The woman is still singing loudly on the makeshift stage, a blues number, but we don't have to shout now. Over here, as our marriage ends, the volume's on low.

'They don't tell you, but grief has a lot of anger. Sometimes people are angry that people die . . . that they left them.'

'You're angry.'

'Oh, yes,' Reuben says softly. 'I'm so, so fucking angry with you, Jo.'

My head snaps back, reeling, as though I've been slapped. And haven't I? No, worse than slapped. Diced

344

up. Skinned. The top of my head sliced open and my insides taken out.

'You were so stupid,' he says. As I begin to protest, he holds a hand up. 'I think of that night sometimes. If you hadn't made that mistake. How different things would be. We'd probably have babies. Different house. We were so happy, Jo. Even that night – just an ordinary Friday – I was looking forward to you coming home. I always did. With your daft schemes to *buy a smallholding* or *open a juice bar*. And now it's . . . it's all wrong. It feels wrong. You being home. It's too . . .'

'But you'll get used to me again,' I say. 'I'll get used to it all again. I'll still come up with stupid schemes, if you want.'

'But you're different now.'

'No.'

'And you . . . you seriously injured someone. You went to trial.'

'Yes. You can't forgive that? A mistake? Is being *right* and *good* so much more important than me? And loving me?' The anger comes as his betrayal really hits me. How could he? How could he? I would have told the police absolutely anything for Reuben. Anything at all. I would have lied for him. I would have buried a body with him. I would have given him an alibi.

I realize as I stand and stare at my husband that I hardly know him at all. His honesty – his goodness – trumps everything. Even me.

Reuben shrugs then. And for all his words and all his judgement and all those nights he spent alone, peeling – emotionally – away from me as I counted down the days in prison, it seems shocking it ends like this. With a shrug. A lazy, contemptuous shrug. As though he doesn't know, doesn't care to find out.

He moves out two days later.

Two days after that, his father dies.

39

Conceal

There is only one eventual destination on my list as my train pulls into London Marylebone but I put it off. I guess some of my habits might subsist for longer than they should. Procrastinating. Faffing around. Stopping to take a photograph of the light that streams in through the entrance of Marylebone, even though nobody will ever see it. I have always loved that view. The trees. The openness. Almost like it's the edge of London, and London truly begins just beyond it. *Come in*, that square of light beckons.

I take a walk along the river on my way to the exhibition, even though it leaves me breathless and tired. It's like coming home. I had forgotten how much I love London. I had forgotten its exact character, like being reunited with an old friend and seeing anew their mannerisms.

It's boiling and my skin prickles with the heat. We're four weeks into a heatwave and everybody is already bored of it, complaining about not being able to sleep and that hardly anywhere has air con. People have stopped Instagramming the sky and the trees, and have started taking photographs of the bad things instead. The parched grass by the sides of the roads. The dried-up canals, boats' bodies exposed like corpses. I don't like looking at them. It's like seeing somebody with their clothes off, seeing the bottom of the river bed.

I can't be in London and not think of Reuben. They are interrelated. I try to stop myself thinking of him so often, at the moment. Somebody cycles past. A father and daughter are finger-painting down at the river's edge together – there's a spare paintbrush in a jar of cloudy water on the ground by the steps up to Tower Bridge, its end hardened with blue paint. I can smell that chalky smell. I have always loved it.

First right. Second left, down a cool, dark alley. I don't think I will ever forget that night, two Decembers ago, when walking down an alleyway, but it doesn't chill me like it previously has. I stand still in the shade for a second and look. Nobody's coming. I know that now. But, somehow, it's no longer about that. The guilty don't only worry about getting found out. Here I am, two years on. I have almost certainly got away with it, and yet there is no relief. Because it was not really the paranoia that I was struggling with: it was the guilt. They were two sides of the same object, but they were different. And one was not chased away by evidence, by facts, by reassurance. It was there – my chest animal – because I have killed a man. And it will always be there, forever. I accept its weight, now, and don't fight it. It's here to stay.

Three people pass me on my way down the side street. The world is full of people. Everyone knows that. But this world I'm in has one fewer. Because of me.

I reach a door that has the laminated card on it, its green string yellowed at the edges, push it open, and go inside. Outside is so bright that my eyes take a few seconds to adjust to the blueish darkness.

The floor is unpolished wood and there are paintings hung around the walls. For a moment I think that I'm accidentally in somebody's house and I start, my whole body shaking – this bothers me more than most. I have invaded too much. I have taken something that wasn't mine, in Imran, already. But as my eyes adjust, I see the paintings and the little placards and know I'm in the right place.

I saw it on Facebook. It popped up, a mutual friend having liked the event in my newsfeed. Laura. Her paintings. Her first exhibition.

One of the paintings portrays a set of people going through the tube barriers. It's almost photographically real. The tube maps on the back wall, the man selling flowers just inside the station. The people's coats and umbrellas. There are autumn leaves and puddles at their feet, dashed white as they catch the overhead lights. It's clear they're supposed to be commuting. But all the people are in the same position, like zombies going through the barriers. Drones on a commute.

I can't resist reading the plaque. *By Laura Cohen*. My Laura. My eyes fill with tears. All those years of striving. All those tries and fails. Of all the people in the world who try to do something artistic, and all those people who never, ever get there; who never finish paintings, and who never get taken on. She made it.

I take in each one in turn now. They're a slant on corporate life, I see. They're almost funny. A woman at her desk with all of the Mondays to Fridays crossed out on a calendar. The clock a huge hourglass, suspended above her. A man, sitting in a kitchen with 'home' written above the door, saving up in a jar labelled *Deposit*. It's a satire on modern life. Her breakthrough work. It's not what I thought it would be, but isn't that always the way? I thought she'd sell her feminist paintings, the one where a woman walked down the street with forty pairs of eyes on her, the men looking away from what they were doing. All with the same photographic, portrait-like quality. I always thought she'd sell those. But this was it: the work that broke her through.

I linger there for an hour, looking and looking. Searching for hidden things in the paintings. A barge boat, or someone who has my lip-shape or body language or unruly hair. But there are none. There's no evidence of me, in the exhibition of the person who used to be my closest friend.

Of course not. I left her; I left all of them.

Just as I leave now, in an alcove on its own, there's a painting I didn't see before. I peer closely at it. The insert says it's the painting that captured the art dealer's attention.

And there they are. A woman, lying on her front in her bed, the green WhatsApp display clearly visible. Laura's caught the sheen of an iPhone just perfectly. I would have believed it was a phone, superimposed right there on to the portrait. The canvas is split, a bed in a different room set out in the other half of the frame. There is another iPhone, and another woman, but she is transparent. I look at it curiously, wanting to trace a finger over it but not daring to. I can see the pink bedsheets through her transparent body.

I stare at it for a few more moments, until I understand it.

It's ghosting.

I ghosted her.

She painted it.

And that's what got her her break.

There's a photograph of her, underneath the insert. I lean closer to it and squint.

Her short hair is decorated with a green, jewel-toned scarf, tied in a bow at her crown. She's wrinkling her nose as she grins widely at the camera, a glass of something in her hand. Her arms are almost completely covered with tattoos. She looks like an artist, but still Laura.

Next to her there's a selection of photos from the launch, arranged around a press cutting. They're recent, the glass frame they've been placed into shiny and new-looking.

There's Jonty, looking just the same, in braces and a trilby hat, looking twenty-one as he grins at the camera. There's Jonty's sister – God, what was her name again? Laura always said she was stuffy, conservative. Emma, maybe?

And there, in amongst the crowd, is a face I didn't expect to see: Reuben's.

He's there, in a shot of the room, but right next to Laura. My first response is flattered: that I meant so much to him that he maintained my friendships after I left him. The second is suspicion. Not of anything romantic, but imagining that the two of them might've met up, tried to figure out what really went wrong with me, presuming Ed didn't tell them. They'd hypothesize in our local pub, together, just the two of them.

I swallow. My throat feels heavy and full, like somebody has rolled a tennis ball down it.

I look again at the transparent woman. It's done in acrylics, I think, and so cleverly. The paint is there, but not there, all at the same time. I look at her transparent body, her half-there clothes. Her form that doesn't leave a dent on the bed, nor cast a shadow. The details. She's not me, and yet she represents me, see-through with guilt, all at once.

This was my price, I think. Reuben. Laura. Wilf. The accident. I've lost things. That is my atonement, I think naively. That was my prison sentence. I think of Ayesha and I think of Imran, dying alone, friendless, in that puddle.

Take them, I tell the universe. *Have them, and make me pay.*

It is a fair price.

It is a just price.

But it is not enough.

As the evening falls, I catch the DLR to the City. I am not ready to see the man I most want to. Not yet. The man who could always make me laugh with a mere shake of his head as I arrived home from Hobbycraft with an entire Make Your Own Wicker Furniture kit.

But for now I want to connect with Wilf. To see him. To see what he's up to.

I arrive in the City and go to his work first. It's a Friday night, but he's far more likely to be there than anywhere else. He works on the ninth floor, he once told me, and I've remembered. I stare up at it. I'm tired from all the walking. It's the most exercise I've done in years. My hand aches. It's dusk, still warm, and the street lights are popping on. The sky is fading to a blue so pale it almost stays white. The building's dark against the stark sky, except for one window. On the ninth floor. I stare up at it. Second from the left. Fourth from the right. Lit up, like a lighthouse in the spring sky. I stare and stare, hoping for a glimpse of him, wondering what we might do together if he looked down and saw me here, for the first time in two years.

'We lost our way a bit. Me and Wilf,' I told Reuben on the stairs at that party where we met, when I made him talk, when the words began flowing out of us like gently spooling yarn.

'Why?' Reuben had asked.

'There's no reason,' I said.

I think Reuben understood. Nothing serious happened with Wilf, and that made it worse. We were just too different for the flower bed we sprang from to bind us together.

What would we do if things had been different? If, maybe, I hadn't failed at university, or if we had, somehow, found our way back to one another? I could have turned up in his office, spun round on the chair, ordered takeaway for him, helped him with whatever it was he was doing. Or, maybe, we'd walk. Towards the river. In between two tower blocks, navigating their ground-floor car parks, lit up in the gloom, and down to the docks where it almost feels like the seaside, where it smells of fish and the river laps gently. We wouldn't be able to talk about the things we used to talk about. What if there was a Narnia entrance at the back of our huge airing cupboard? What if we could fly, and it was just that no human had yet found the magic combination of moves? But we could talk about our parents and the things they used to say to us. The way Dad had told me he expected eleven A-stars from me, seriously, over Christmas dinner, and Wilf had guffawed. 'I got one A, and I coped,' he had told me. I could have asked him if he felt it, too: the weight of their disappointment. Their neglect, even though we went to Cape Town for the summer, even though we went for walks in meadows and for meals by candlelight at castles in the winter. I could ask him if he felt it, too: the neglect that sat behind it all, like a disturbing backdrop. Or if it was just me.

We could do something, here in London, while we have that conversation as adults. Something as brother and sister. Something as allies. Something as free adults who can do whatever they like in the world – go and eat overpriced candyfloss by the river or go on the London Eye or do absolutely anything at all.

At my eighteenth birthday, it was Wilf who ensured I had a good time. Not with drink or friends, but taking me into the garden just after midnight on the anniversary of the day I was born, and releasing a pink balloon into the sky with me. I remember that more than anything, too. What changed between us? I'll never know. And so, because I've stopped avoiding things, started facing up to things, I sigh, then get out my mobile and call him. His phone rings, then, after four, goes straight to voicemail. It's not a natural cut-off. He's pressed the red button. I can tell. He must still have my number. It's been over two years since we last spoke, but he must still have it.

I try him again. For old time's sake. To give him the benefit of the doubt. Maybe, I think hopefully as it rings out, we could just do nothing. Nothing at all. Go to his.

Go to a bar. Eat chips by the river for the last time. Or share two beers, like we did the night before he went to university, in the old barn, sitting on the hay bales in the rafters.

The light in the window doesn't change. I stand, staring up at it for a few more minutes. I no longer avoid things, but I can't force them, either. I can't make him answer.

Never mind, I think to myself. The last time Wilf and I said anything meaningful to each other was when we were eighteen and twenty. It wasn't meant to be.

My eyes are damp from staring up at the window and I tell myself it's because of the hot breeze, because I am staring at the bright light shining in the darkness.

His phone cuts to voicemail again and I hang up. I walk away, looking backwards, once, twice, at the light still hanging, suspended, in a glass box in the dark. It stays on. I never see him emerge. And he doesn't call me back.

40

Reveal

'Well, you seem very together,' the trainer says to me.

He's called Simon, and he's of that benign posh look; curls on the top of his forehead like a toddler's, rosy cheeks. I am sure he likes fine wines and the races and doesn't worry too much.

'Really,' I say. 'I'm . . . I'm having a hard time adjusting after I'm out.'

I don't feel embarrassed, as I usually would. It's a centre for counsellors to train who have been somewhere tough themselves. I don't know what Simon's backstory is, but his colleague Emmett used to be homeless. There's an abstaining alcoholic and someone who was brought up in care following abuse. And then there's me. A woman who has to think very hard about how to operate the Oyster card top-up machines. I say as much to Simon.

'Yes,' he says, leaning forward, his tanned arms on his knees. 'But isn't that an example of being *totally* normal? Not adjusting after prison?'

'I . . . maybe,' I say, struggling to know.

'I think that's an example of being good. Not bad,' he says. 'You'd be mad if you could adjust to that.'

'I think of Imran, too. All the time. About his injuries, and how he is, these days.'

'Also normal. You care about him – because you're a human being,' he says, with a smile.

'I know he won't have *recovered*,' I say. 'But I hope he's . . . I don't know. I just hope.'

'I know . . .'

He pauses for a second, then runs down a tick sheet as we decide on the next steps.

'So you did the diploma in prison?' he says.

I nod.

It took a year to get them to offer it to me. The old Joanna – as I have come to think of her – would have done nothing about that. Would have watched box sets and read books and ignored it, then been periodically disappointed on birthdays and when ringing in the New Year that nothing had changed. But this Joanna is different. Somehow, when society had decided I was worthless, I decided quite the opposite, and went after what I wanted. It was only me and one other woman – Dani – in the workshop room getting that diploma in counselling. But it was worth it.

'Yes,' I say. 'Now I need a placement.'

'And how do you feel your crime . . . intersects with your position as a counsellor?'

I sit back, thinking. In every way. It impacts my life in every way. Shaping who I am around the edges and deep inside, as if I am woodwork, whittled away by the events of that night in December and since.

'I give less of a shit what people think of me,' I say, eventually. 'My parents. Anyone, really. I don't care any more. And . . .' I pause, thinking. 'I used to have this thing where I'd look at other people – Proper People, I

357

used to call them. And I'd compare their exterior with my interior. But I don't do that any more. I am . . . I am a Proper Person.'

Simon nods, once, then laughs. 'I think you're set,' he says.

Laura and I meet at the Gondola after her first day at work. Her hair has caught the sun during the heatwave. Her body, her face, they have the relics of the hippy she used to be – I can see it in her casual body language, in the earring I know to be hiding halfway up her ear, underneath her hair, but most of the traits have been bleached out, as if they've been left out in sunlight.

She knows about Reuben, and is stirring her drink thoughtfully. We're sitting outside, the air humid and thick-feeling, like a winter duvet over our shoulders.

'I've spent the day freezing,' she says. 'Offices overdo it in heatwaves.'

'Do they?' I say vaguely.

We pause. It's awkward. It has never been awkward.

'How's Tabitha?' I say, sounding spiteful.

Laura shrugs. 'She's well.' She looks at me. 'You're sad about it.'

'Oh, I'm not. I know,' I say. 'We couldn't be – we couldn't be friends. Not properly. While I was inside.'

'No.'

'But it seemed like you – well, maybe like you were a bit ashamed. Like you *wanted* to move on.'

Laura exhales through her nose. 'It was hard, Jo. You know? It was tough.'

'Yes.'

'I'm sorry that it was, but it was, for me. It felt like everything had changed.'

'It did.'

'I know. I'm sorry.' She holds her hands up, palms to me. She's still wearing all of her rings. 'There's no excuse. I wasn't good enough. I wasn't a good enough friend.'

'It is kind of unprecedented,' I say. 'Prison. In the – in the circles we move in.'

'You're telling me,' she says, with a little laugh. 'We all – I don't know. We all struggled. It was a big adjustment, for everyone.'

'I know,' I say quietly. I tilt my face to the sun again. 'I'm glad we're here and not there.'

'I'm sorry,' she says, holding my gaze, her expression sincere.

'Let's moan about Reuben, instead,' I say, thinking, *Come on, Joanna. Be an adult. Forgive.* Alan would say I ought to. And maybe I can. Reuben wasn't perfect. Laura wasn't perfect. And I certainly wasn't perfect.

Laura pauses for a moment. 'Reuben,' she says. 'Maybe you actually broke up two years ago.'

'What? What about what he did?'

She holds a hand up, and says, 'Did it feel like you were together? Last year?'

I think of Reuben's aged face as he shouted at me two nights previously. I think of the empty feeling I carried around with me in prison. I think of Reuben's serious expression, across the table in the visitors' centre. How he came at all the times he could, but never really said anything.

'Nothing in prison feels very real,' I say.

Nothing *could* be real. Those moments in the visitors' centre were so weak, as though real life had been distilled and distilled, over and over, ending up with a homeopathic remedy: take two drops for a relationship. One for a friendship. Three for a normal Christmas dinner. Everything was displaced from reality to such an extent that it was hard to remember if reality continued beyond the prison walls.

'The reason I ask,' Laura says, bobbing the straw up and down in her drink, just like she did that Friday night, 'is because I think maybe he's just reacting how he wanted to two years ago. Now.'

'He shopped me,' I say.

'He's a child,' she nods.

'I have *never* felt so betrayed. In all my life.'

'I think he's very angry with you. But he has been . . . contrite. You know? He missed you so badly. He sang this song, in the jazz club. He cried during it.'

'You went to see?'

She nods. 'He had – he had hardly anybody, Jo. Without you.'

'What was the song?'

'It was all about your life together, I think. There weren't many lyrics. But it was called "Our Blackboard".'

My eyes fill with tears. 'Well,' I say thickly. 'You can't always have what you want.'

She squints up at the sun. The canal is still in the heat, the flower-covered barges looking like ornaments. 'I miss my barge,' she says.

'You didn't have to give it all up. The whole hog.

Give up the art. Get the corporate job. The house in suburbia.'

'I did,' she says quickly. 'It . . . legitimized it. For me. I have to buy into it. It has to be so.'

'A house. A Volvo. Three kids.'

'Maybe,' she says, spreading her hands wide.

I feel a wave of jealousy. Reuben and I would have been brilliant parents. I know we would. I would have taught our kids about imagination, and people, and the power of dreaming. He would've taught them about politics and art and classics and economics. They would've been ours. Little socialists, no doubt.

'What I meant was that the way he reacted came from . . . who he was,' she says.

'Reuben?'

'Yeah. He's an idealist. Isn't he?'

'Of course.'

'But maybe he hasn't really grown up. We're all idealistic in our twenties.'

'He's the most mature person I know.'

'Is he, though?' She looks across at me, playing with a splinter in the wooden table. 'Is that true?'

The Gondola seems so completely different in the summer to how it was that winter, years ago. Almost like the peculiar displaced feeling you get when you go to view a house, and then you move in, and it seems utterly different in ways you can't describe or justify.

I didn't even know it had a beer garden. I can just about see inside, through an old-fashioned window, to the bar. It's smaller than I remember. Insignificant.

'Maturity is flexibility,' she says. 'Look at me. I wanted

to be an artist. It didn't work out. That's life. It's not perfect – and people aren't perfect. I think he's childishly angry with you.'

'Yeah,' I shrug. 'He probably is childish. He – he robbed me, Laura.'

'I know,' she says, nodding rapidly. 'I know. But, he did miss you.'

'I know that, too.'

It's true. I know both things, and both things are true. Reuben is good and bad, all at once. So is Laura. And so am I.

I look down into my lap, away from the window. 'Let's not talk about him,' I say, with a wan smile.

Her phone lights up. I can see it's Tabitha. She doesn't look. She places it in her handbag. Later on, she texts me. Just a funny meme. I send one back.

Wilf asks if I want to go and see Mum and Dad at the end of June. 'I'm going next week,' he says.

'Maybe,' I say.

The new relationship, forged in prison, feels too delicate to bring out into the open yet, like a loaf of bread only just beginning to slowly prove.

We're walking side by side to a restaurant in Covent Garden. It's almost empty, the cobbled streets speckled with puddles. Everyone's gone inside, the early summer already ended. A couple of smokers stand underneath a dripping awning. Wilf waves at one of them – a colleague, he tells me.

'Doesn't really matter either way,' Wilf says. 'You can do what you like.'

'I might come,' I say tentatively.

'Good,' Wilf says, linking his arm through mine as we walk. 'I've been meaning to show you something,' he says.

'What?'

He gets his phone out. 'You probably don't even want to know now,' he says. 'But I thought I would . . .'

I take the phone from him. They're texts. Texts between Reuben and him.

How was she today? Reuben has said. Wilf fills him in, and he asks again, two days later.

And then, one of the latest texts. They stopped when I got out. *It's too hard to go*, Reuben's written. *I miss her too much.*

Wilf shrugs. 'He did really miss you,' he says.

'I know.'

He puts an arm around me.

And it's not a fair trade-off, and it's not a consolation prize, and I may have lost Reuben, but if I hadn't handed myself in, I wouldn't have Wilf. And that seems, somehow, to be right. Just.

41

Conceal

It's time.

I remember his address. Of course I do. I've never been, but he spoke about it all the time. Ed was one of those people who would tell you all aspects of his life: his uncle who liked fishing; that he was struggling to find a table to fit in his round dining room; how well his garden plants were blooming. He used to refer to his house by name – Oakhalls – as though it was a person.

Oakhalls, Chiswick. It was easy to find. I'm surprised I've never been, when I come across it. It's a house to have gatherings in, with a trellis up one side, the wide, arched doorway framed with flowers. It's enormous. Somehow, in all his sharing, he had never quite conveyed to me how nice it was. Set back from the road, with a white frontage – in *Chiswick*. It must be worth more than a million pounds. They bought well, he would say – I can see it now – with a wave of his hand.

It's only just after eight o'clock in the evening but the street feels quiet and isolated, as though it will be antisocial to ring the bell. I do it, anyway, although my hands are shaking.

It's time. I'm ready. I take a deep breath as I see a shadowy form moving beyond the frosted glass, magnified and then re-magnified, refracted over and over.

A woman opens the door. His wife. I recognize her immediately from the hundreds of iPhone photographs Ed showed me every Monday. Of barbecues and days out ice-skating and visits to National Trust properties. She probably liked me, once, I think, as I study her face. There's recognition. A dawning, eyebrows up, an almost-smile.

'Is Ed around? Sorry to call so late,' I say.

I wonder at my own politeness, considering what I am about to do. I'm breathless. I'm always breathless, but it's particularly bad right now. The nerves, I suppose. It's as if my body slowly disintegrated, during the accident. And, even though I'm better now, the scans clear, all fixed, put together again, it's like I am cracked, fractured, less able than I was to sustain all the things a body should be able to rely on: nerves, a quick run for a bus, adrenaline.

'Yes,' she says.

She's wearing a skirt that touches the floor and a long necklace, which clunks like a wooden wind chime as she steps aside. I marvel at these people who do not wear pyjamas on Friday nights in their own homes. Perhaps they dress for dinner. Ed was always oddly formal, in some ways, eating leftover pasta salad with a knife and fork brought from home on the counter of the library bus every lunchtime, wearing beige pullovers and matching shirts underneath.

Ed appears behind her, and I'm shocked by how much he's aged. By how much everybody seems to have aged. He's much more tanned – a recent holiday? – and has lost absolutely all of his hair, his bald head covered in liver spots. He's more stooped, too; I notice a prominent hump, see the curvature of his spine. He is . . . he's old, I realize with a start. My Ed.

'Joanna,' he says. Or rather, he doesn't say it; he mouths it. Joanna. His lips form the 'O' and then the 'A' of my name.

'Ed,' I say simply.

His wife steps aside and – to my surprise – he comes out the front and shuts the door behind him, using a hand behind his back. He knows, and she knows, and they all know, I find myself thinking – the thought as automatic as my own heartbeat. But it doesn't matter now. It doesn't matter any more. I have to keep reminding myself.

I stand awkwardly outside his front door while he stares up at me. He's shorter than he was. It's something more than his hunched form. He has lessened, somehow.

'I . . .' I say.

He stares dispassionately at me, his eyes huge behind his glasses, saying nothing. He's making it hard for me. I contacted everybody except Ed, after I left. I didn't contact Ed once, not even when I needed a reference. Even though he had been a friendly colleague for six years. Even though he was Ed. I couldn't. I wasn't strong enough.

'Joanna,' he says again.

I scrutinize his face, trying to tell.

He shrugs helplessly, looking up at me. 'I . . .' He holds his hands out, then shrugs again. Smiling and looking sad. 'You left,' he says, eventually.

'Yes.'

He stares at me for a long time. Two, three minutes. His eyes are roving over my features. 'I never thought you'd leave,' he says softly.

His dark brown eyes are on mine and our gaze is speaking a thousand words that we can't verbalize.

'Did you . . .' I start to say, but the words dry up in my mouth, like an outgoing tide that cannot reach the same spot on the shore. I am reaching, and reaching, but after two years, three in December, countless losses, an accident, I cannot bring myself to say it. I can't articulate it. It is as if my crime has moved to a sad, unspeakable, black part of my soul. The shame and the noise and the panic would be too much.

He reaches for me, then, and I see, after the shock and the sadness my rejection must have caused him, underneath all of that is sympathy. Of course. Of course he's sympathetic. He's *Ed*. I was so certain I knew how the people in my life would react that I didn't bother even trying to tell them.

He meets my eyes now, and he knows. I grasp it so fully, it's as though the knowledge has materialized, fully formed, on his circular driveway in front of us. It's not the hazy paranoia of two years ago. It is knowledge. I think that perhaps he didn't know then, but he does now, somehow.

He steps towards me, and I back away, a horse about to bolt with fear. He reaches a hand out to touch my arm, then stops, his fingers steady in mid-air. He's wondering what to say, I see, as he scrutinizes me.

'You know,' I say.

He nods, once. Less a nod and more a certain, downward confirmation. I can't say another word.

'I figured it out,' he says. 'I asked some questions, after you left in haste. After you behaved so strangely, on that day in the office. I asked some questions and I pieced it all together. Nobody else knows,' he adds.

I'm grateful for that. It spreads through my bones like the sun on the first hot day of the year, warming me.

'The clothes.'

'I didn't tell Reuben anything. All he knows is that you dumped your clothes. And that you lied about Wilf, of course.'

'I can't . . . I've come back to do some things but I . . . I can't stay here,' I say, still reeling from the shock of his admission.

He nods again, not saying anything, just looking up at me, sadly. A letter's sticking out of the top of a wooden box fixed to the side of his house. The envelope looks dry, parched in the heat. I focus on it, not looking at him, not able to.

'Thank you,' I say to him.

He nods, once, in acknowledgement.

He kept my secret for me. How can I ever truly thank him?

'She stopped coming to the library,' he says softly.

His voice is huskier than it used to be. Or perhaps he is just upset, speaking quietly to me, outside his house, so his wife doesn't hear, so that she doesn't know our secret, too. Once again, I find myself wondering what happened that night I left him in our offices. I went home and dumped Reuben, as though he was a dress that had to be returned because I needed the money badly; looking for short-term solutions to my problems. But what did Ed do, that day? I wonder. And what did he do when he heard about me?

'Did she?' I say, ready to face things. To stop avoiding them. 'When did you last see her?'

'That time with you,' Ed says with his Ed-like laugh. He brings a hand self-consciously to his mouth and covers his lips, then exhales again, another little laugh. 'She never came back. And the police stopped investigating.'

'Oh,' I say quietly. 'I'm here to . . . that's why I'm back.'

Ed shrugs, not looking at me.

Nobody ever came for me. He never told anybody. I wonder how much of it he had to cover up? Did he ever look at the CCTV?

'Are you really?' he says. He places his hand on the doorknob, and I see it's my time to go. He may know, he may have kept my secret, but the friendship's over: of course it is. 'Does it matter? Now?' he says sadly.

'What do you mean?'

'It's over, Jo,' he says. 'You've . . . you have suffered. Haven't you?'

'Yes, but –'

'Who would it help?'

I look down at my feet. It's as though he knows about my novel. It's all ready. It's all ready to go. The book I have written about a woman who commits a crime but chooses to hand herself in, and all about the man she pushed and who he was and what he liked. It's all ready, so that I would be ready. But I'm not so sure I am now. The reasons for handing myself in that seemed so clear this morning are hazy now.

'I'm sorry,' he says to me. 'I'm sorry it's this way.'

He opens his door with a loud click.

I look at him for one last time. Of course it is this way.

I'm a killer. He is forced to live with my secret – I wonder if the animal's on his chest, too. And I left him with it as I bolted. Abandoned the scene.

'Me, too,' I say. I turn away from him, momentarily not feeling the guilt or the shame or the paranoia or the panic, but just the sadness. That I was there. That it happened. That I made it happen, and how I acted afterwards.

I hang my head, for a moment, and he reaches out again, and this time his fingers land on my arm as softly as the breeze itself. I feel the elephant shift its weight, just for a second. I bring my hand down on to his, and we clasp our fingers. And then, without another look at him, I turn and walk away.

The decree absolute listed our old flat as Reuben's current address, and so I go there. I don't know how he affords the rent alone. It is a strange thought, one I would only ever have in London, and it promotes a rush of nostalgia for those times; those funny, happy times watching the top one hundred movies of all time and hearing the woman in the flat above us arrive home in her heels at three o'clock in the morning, and walking to the underground station in the rain together.

Hammersmith is dusty and hot. It's late by the time I'm walking up our road. I train my brain not to think of all the places I was when I was panicking – that entrance to the tube station, the stretch of path outside our flat, the road where I fell – and instead look for the happy memories, too. There must be some. That Sunday when we got back from our honeymoon and I felt so pleased to be home again, with our English tea and our own bed and even our commutes: married. The first time Reuben took part in our local MP's surgery and he kissed me goodbye, that Saturday morning, the kiss quick with his excitement. How I would feel when I watched him playing the piano in the back bedroom. I loved the theatre of it. His body language changed; his body changed. He bent low, towards the keys, paying attention to the high notes as though they were plants he was nurturing. Nothing like his usual, dour, stooped form. The one I loved equally. The one I loved just as well, for its differences.

I am standing on the street outside now, looking down at our front door. He's probably out, on a Friday night, two years later, but I look in the window anyway.

There's evidence of him everywhere. The plants on our steps that the postman always had to gingerly inch past are still well cared for. An Islamic Relief sticker in our kitchen window. He's still here. I puff my breath out, into the hot, summer air, take a second, and ring the doorbell.

He opens the door, which surprises me. Not because he's in, but because he always used to ignore the doorbell. He wouldn't be at all intrigued by it.

And yet here he is, in front of me. In dark skinny jeans and a white top. He's barefoot. I didn't think he'd age badly, with his freckles and his ginger hair, but he has.

As he realizes it's me, his expression darkens. That's the only way I can describe it. His lips purse. His eyebrows come down. He tilts his head back in a reverse nod; how he conveys recognition. Even after two years, I recognize it all. The way his fingers linger on the door frame. The way he holds his weight on one foot, the other resting on his ankle. The way his green eyes are darting over my face, trying to glean something.

Eventually, he holds his hands up, palms to me. A gesture of defeat. And then he steps aside and lets me into the flat I lived in for years.

It's almost the same, but it's more sparse. That's my first impression. All the *stuff* was mine. Painted peg magnets I stuck to the front of the fridge. Stacks of magazines I subscribed to and never got around to reading. They're all gone. The surfaces are empty. It's strange to see how he would choose to live, without me. That I was clutter in his life.

He leans against one of the white bar stools. I can't sit on the one next to him – it's far too close – so instead I stand awkwardly.

'Long time no see,' he says.

'Yes.' I put my handbag down on the floor, as I have done a thousand times before. I wonder if Reuben is thinking the same thing, because his eyes stray to it, then back to mine, and for a moment I think they look glassy. If only.

Everything else is the same. The sky outside. The wooden flooring underneath my feet. The man in front of me. Why can't this be a few years ago? Before. Time stretches strangely in front of me, and for just a moment I let myself pretend.

I stop and pause. This is it. The moment. I will afford him the courtesy of telling him. And then . . .

'How are you?' he says, his gaze searching.

I remember the last time I saw him, in the hospital, where I reaffirmed that I didn't want to be with him.

'Fine, now,' I say.

We talk briefly of my injuries. He knew what they were – and he tried to visit multiple times, after the first time, but I wouldn't see him. But I tell him, fully, now. My pelvis. My hysterectomy. My rubbish breathing capacity. He doesn't seem fazed.

'Right,' he says.

'I had a reason. For leaving you,' I blurt out.

It comes back to me, interacting with him, as if I've never really stopped. It's like riding a bike or catching a ball. Our directness. The stuff I couldn't say to anybody else. No wonder I left. It was too hard in those early days.

'Did you?' he says. 'Other than not loving me any more?'

He says it so factually, it's as if he has opened me up, right there in the kitchen. I draw my arms around myself. I was away from the damage I caused everybody, with my guilt, and I never saw it materialize like this.

'I never stopped loving you,' I say, then swallow.

Reuben's eyes flicker, but he doesn't say anything else. And then he speaks. 'My dad died,' he says. 'Not long ago. I've been wondering . . . whether to say. I know you liked him. But it was . . .'

'Oh,' I say.

And then, of course, I can see it on him. The grief. He's slimmer. More lined. Not through age, but through other things; through life and death.

'Anyway,' Reuben says.

'I'm so sorry,' I say.

'Heart attack. I was there.'

'I'm sorry.'

'What do you want to tell me?'

'I don't want to tell you now.'

'Tell me.'

And here it is.

The moment.

We're in our Before. In one sentence, it'll be After.

'Before I tell you,' I say, taking a step towards him, 'will you just . . .'

He stands, motionless, but doesn't move away, so I step closer still. And then his arms are around my body and it is glorious, like all my summers have come at once. I haven't hugged him for so long. The last time was, truly, Before; the night before it happened. But I can't remember. I can't find the distinct points in that otherwise ordinary day, no matter how hard I look for them. They've been buried, like bad news on a good news day, forever obscured by the cloud of what followed.

'I don't know why I'm doing this,' he murmurs.

It's a very un-Reuben sentence, and for just a second I hope something might've happened to open that closed mind I love so much.

I step back from him, and his fingertips stay on my waist just a fraction longer than they would usually. I see a blush creep slowly across his cheeks, stealing across like a rash. I'd forgotten that blush. How much I loved it. The barometer of his emotions.

I take two more deep breaths, and now it's time. I'm ready to move to After.

'I killed somebody,' I say.

And then I tell him everything.

*

He sleeps on it. A very Reuben thing to do. I stayed at the Travelodge, near the Broadway. One last night of freedom, I bargained with myself.

He texts me the next morning, and there he is, waiting in the seventies-style foyer of the Travelodge, less than a mile from where we lived together.

'Do you want to know what happened with Dad?' he says.

He is standing in front of a bowl of apples. Anybody could overhear us, but he doesn't seem to care.

'He reached for me, while Mum was doing the CPR on him. The ambulance was coming. And I was so freaked out by that arm reaching for me – I think he knew he was going to die – that I . . . that I left him and went into the bathroom, and when I came out, he was gone.'

'Oh shit,' I say.

He nods, once. 'I understand avoidance now. You,' he says.

'I don't avoid things any more,' I say.

'Not even HSBC?' he says, with a tiny, tiny smile.

'Nope.' We pause, looking at each other. 'I wish it had never happened,' I say simply. 'I don't know where I'd be if it hadn't, but . . .'

Reuben raises his eyes to mine. 'With me,' he says simply. 'You'd be with me.'

We stare at each other again. Of course. Of course I would. We would never have left each other: never.

He reaches for me wordlessly. Our hands curl around each other in that way they always did, and he enfolds me into him.

'I have to . . .' I say, trying to disentangle myself from

375

him, but I can't; I don't want to. 'I have to tell them. Confess. Go to prison. For life, probably, fifteen years,' I gabble.

But maybe there is an alternative. I can no longer walk without being breathless. I can't have children of my own. I have spent two years, alone, in exile. Perhaps there is an alternative, here, with this man who loves me. I could choose happiness. Accept it when it comes. Rejoin Reuben, and rejoin life.

Reuben places a long, warm finger over my lips. His smell. Oh, that smell. I had almost forgotten it.

He draws me to him again and the tears flow freely from both of us.

'Do you know what I believe in more than anything else?' he murmurs in my ear.

'What?'

'Second chances.'

And I don't know whether he means me and my crime, or us and our life together, but suddenly he is kissing me and I don't care.

'I forgive you. I want to forgive you. So I do,' he says simply.

Two months later

42

Reveal

As I approach the bookshop, I see he's lit up, in the window, wearing a white shirt, sleeves rolled up to his elbows. Oh, how I have missed those elbows, those freckly elbows, those forearms covered in auburn hair. He's standing self-consciously now, and I can tell – only through the decade we spent together – that he's reading something he doesn't like. A Friday night in a bookshop, reading something he doesn't agree with. It is so very *Reuben*.

We've been texting, couldn't seem to help ourselves. It was one text in particular that did it. I had been in the shower when I heard it beep, the special tone I had assigned just for Reuben. I raced to get it, even though I dripped water everywhere.

I have been an utter shit, it said. *I always think I know best but I don't. I ruined your life for my principles. The second I did it, they seemed to disappear. They mean nothing compared to losing you. People matter. Not stances. I was so judgemental. So horribly judgemental. I'm sorry I seemed distant. I'm sorry I seemed embarrassed. I was ill equipped to deal with it. Unlike you. I bow down to you, Jo.*

And then we decided to meet.

I pause, a hand on the round, cool metal door handle. Can I do this? Go in, sit down opposite my husband, shoot the breeze? My hand lingers on the doorknob momentarily.

43

Conceal

I'm expecting to see him, but I nevertheless stop suddenly, stock-still on the street. He's in the café area of a bookshop, reading, and, only two months since our reconciliation, I still find the sight of him so arresting.

He's waiting for me. We're going to read books and drink coffee on this Friday night, together.

There is something about his body language that makes me linger. He's smiling. A small, knowing smile. That smile he reserves only for me.

I hover, the doorknob cool and wet against my palm.

44

Reveal

I take a deep breath, my hand still on the doorknob. He hasn't noticed me. I could walk away. We wouldn't be ready. It's not the right time. Nothing's changed, I tell myself. He hates me. He handed me in, handed me over.

And yet.

It looks to me as though something has changed. I'm not sure what, but perhaps something has.

The reality of us. Would it work? Perhaps . . . perhaps it just takes time to come back to each other, after a two-year break. Because it *was* a break: no intimacy happens in prison. Physical. Emotional. None. Maybe it takes time. To come back to each other. Maybe Reuben needs to know I'm still the same Jo. The Jo who can't concentrate on the top one hundred movies. The Jo who buys Swedish planters on whims and tries to grow Japanese blossoms on the steps of a basement flat in Hammersmith. The Jo who loves sudokus and her husband. Maybe I can tell him all that. That, even though I am changed, more confident, have become a Proper Person, I am still me. More so: I am more me, because I have permission to be. No guilt. I look back at Reuben.

And it's not the portrait of him in the window that does it.

It's not that he's reading, though I love that.

It's not his freckled forearms, though I love those, too.

It's his smile. Nobody else would spot it. The very, very edges of his lips are just slightly lifted. He is smiling. And only I know it. That special smile. The one only I could tease out of him, like that night we met and sat on the stairs and I taught him to chat. Anyone else would think him dour, grumpy, stoic. But I know that smile. It is for me. He has seen me.

And it's as simple as this, really. I prefer my life with him. No doubt he will keep me good. On the straight and narrow. But, more than that: I understand him. He let the Council know he thought the Council Tax was in too low a band. He does twenty-nine miles per hour in a thirty zone. My Reuben. Of course he would tell a barrister the truth. The problem wasn't his truthfulness: it was my lies.

Perhaps another man, another husband, might've lied for me. But the truth is this. I forgive him. I want to forgive him. And so I do.

45

Conceal and Reveal

It's time. I push open the door and go inside, where Reuben is waiting for me. Whatever happens.

'Number three thousand. As good a place to start as any,' he says with a smile as I approach. 'How late you always are.'

'Three thousand and one. How you're so early you think others are late,' I say back.

Epilogue

The Beginning

The street lights are too bright, refracted a hundred times in each drop of misty rain. I can see moisture on the concrete steps like thousands of beads of sweat. The only things I can focus on in the drizzle are the bright blue bridges of deserted Little Venice.

And him.

I look down at the man, twisted strangely at the bottom of the steps. He hasn't moved at all.

I could go to help him. Call an ambulance. Confess. Reveal myself.

Or I could run away. Hide. Protect and conceal myself.

I am paralysed with indecision. What will happen if I leave? What will happen if I stay? I cannot picture where either path would take me.

A strange calm descends upon me as I stand and assess him.

The rain gets heavier, wetting my forehead and slicking my hair to the side of my face.

Stay or go. Fight or flight. Truth or dare.

Which is it to be?

Acknowledgements

My hair started to go grey while writing this novel. So first thanks are for anyone on the receiving end of a text message sent last summer, during which time I was (could it be true?) under contract with Penguin and had chosen to write two books in one for my second novel with them. Ambition might be good for you, but it also turns your hair grey.

Firstly, as always, thanks go to my agent, Clare, who has made all of this happen. She read this novel while on maternity leave, in two days, and gave me notes at 11.30 p.m. one night. She is one of the hardest-working women I know. Thanks, too, to Darley Anderson himself, who sent me a very special email one spring morning, and to the whole rights team who continue to sprinkle my inbox with amazing foreign rights news.

Secondly, to my brilliant editor, Max: you have done so very much for me. Thank you for adopting me and *Everything but the Truth*, and for making it a bestseller. Your notes on this novel made it so much clearer and much shinier, but you never once asked me to change the essence of it, its scale or its message.

To Jenny Platt, my publicist, and Katie Bowden, my marketer. You are tireless and fearless, and I'm astonished by all that you have done for me.

To the enthusiastic, absolutely lovely team at Michael

Joseph: Sophie Elletson, and my brilliant copy editor, Shân Morley Jones. I can't thank you enough.

This book was very research-heavy, and could not have been completed without the kind help of various people I knew and got to know during the course of writing it.

To my sister, Suzanne, who fielded multiple queries about hypoxic brain injuries over many takeaways. And to my father, without whom none of my books could be written: your imagination, characterization and natural flair for realistic plots are of huge value to me, but that you choose to spend your free time helping me is priceless.

To my mum, for helping me with your always perfect grammar, not to mention buying me a Penguin Classics mug with my own book on it.

To Alison Hardy, one of my favourite colleagues, who got me a tour of the Old Bailey for research, and to Charles Henty, who conducted that.

To Liz and Mark Powell, who fielded my queries from the moment I met them at a party and discovered they are police officers, culminating in a tour of police custody by Mark, which, as you'll have read, was fundamental to this novel.

To Ameera from a mosque I visited: thank you for giving me a tour, explaining about Islamic graveyards, and answering my clumsy questions sensitively and accurately.

To Phil and Marie Evison, for reading an early draft and pointing out my many policing errors ('They no longer wear huge boots, Gillian . . .'). To Sami Davies, again, for your medical input, for reading an early version and for introducing me to the mammalian diving reflex. Your answers are always immediate, and they never question my sanity.

To Darin Millar, who read this book alongside my agent and fed back such helpful advice on criminal defence. And to Neil White, who answered many bonkers queries over Twitter DM. I couldn't have written a novel like this without both of you. And Roxie Cooper, who helped me on the law of self-defence and mistake. Thank goodness for lawyers!

To Tom Davis, my English tutor at university, who, one day in 2004, emailed me and said: *I read your blog. Hey, you can do dialogue.* There began a thirteen-year mentoring relationship. I still send him early chapters, about which he is brutal and kind.

And finally, as always, to David. Life coach, therapist, cook, cleaner, muse, sounding board, best friend and lover. I couldn't do anything without you, least of all write novels.

He just wanted a decent book to read ...

Not too much to ask, is it? It was in 1935 when Allen Lane, Managing Director of Bodley Head Publishers, stood on a platform at Exeter railway station looking for something good to read on his journey back to London. His choice was limited to popular magazines and poor-quality paperbacks – the same choice faced every day by the vast majority of readers, few of whom could afford hardbacks. Lane's disappointment and subsequent anger at the range of books generally available led him to found a company – and change the world.

'We believed in the existence in this country of a vast reading public for intelligent books at a low price, and staked everything on it'
Sir Allen Lane, 1902–1970, founder of Penguin Books

The quality paperback had arrived – and not just in bookshops. Lane was adamant that his Penguins should appear in chain stores and tobacconists, and should cost no more than a packet of cigarettes.

Reading habits (and cigarette prices) have changed since 1935, but Penguin still believes in publishing the best books for everybody to enjoy. We still believe that good design costs no more than bad design, and we still believe that quality books published passionately and responsibly make the world a better place.

So wherever you see the little bird – whether it's on a piece of prize-winning literary fiction or a celebrity autobiography, political tour de force or historical masterpiece, a serial-killer thriller, reference book, world classic or a piece of pure escapism – you can bet that it represents the very best that the genre has to offer.

Whatever you like to read – trust Penguin.